PUCK AROUND *and* FIND OUT

SARAH BLUE

SPOTIFY PLAYLIST

Just A Girl - No Doubt
Good Looking - Suki Waterhouse
My Love Mine All Mine - Mitski
Make You Mine - Madison Beer
Out of My League - Fitz and The Tantrums
I Want You - Kings of Leon
Good For You - Selena Gomez, A$AP Rocky
1 Step Forward, 3 Steps Back - Olivia Rodrigo
Paper Rings - Taylor Swift
Skin - Rihanna
Mr Loverman - Ricky Montgomery
The Fox - Yivis
Down Bad - Taylor Swift
Love On The Brain - Rihanna
Sweet Disposition - The Temper Trap
Often - The Weeknd

Something Just Like This - The Chainsmokers, Coldplay
Favorite - Isabel LaRosa

FOREWORD

This is the third book in the Pucked Up Omegaverse, however this can be read as a standalone.

Please note that this book has pregnancy, foster experience, traumatic childhood memories, and discussions of death. For a full list of all the content in this book, please visit my website.

Content Page

QR code to content page

To never settling.

CHAPTER 1

Breakfast is tense as ever at my parents' house. I know why, but I refuse to acknowledge it.

It's a new season for the Foxes, and my Alpha father, head coach, Kristoff Applegate, does not want me coming back to work for his team.

Too fucking bad because I'm coming back, for reasons he would probably hate. I'm willing to negotiate to keep my job, but I'm not going to be the one who cracks first. If he doesn't want me coming back to help manage the social media for the team, he's going to have to fire me, and I know he doesn't have the guts to do it.

It's probably terrible that I know I can manipulate my own dad, but it's entirely too easy. His guilt over feeling like an absent parent when I was younger is just too palpable. I don't blame him, nor do I feel abandoned by him, but it's still how he feels. It's the whole reason he let me work for the Foxes last season. He wanted more time with me, and he wanted to ease some of his guilt.

Well, if I have to use this guilt to keep my job, I will.

It's not even that I especially like doing the team's social media. It's that I have a plan in place, and I will not let him ruin this for me. He'd be so pissed if he knew my ulterior motives, and maybe he has an inkling of what I'm up to, but I'm ready to deal with the fallout when it happens.

My mother Rosemary is the one to cut the silence. It's not a surprise; she's a no bullshit lawyer who has no problem pushing around her Alpha designation when she needs to.

"So are we just going to be silent all breakfast, or is someone going to speak first?" she asks.

"Breakfast is delicious, honey," my Beta dad, Henderson, says to my mom, Willow.

"Thanks, baby," she says to him, and he grins at her.

Our family dynamic is basically stamped in concrete. It hasn't changed much since my childhood. My Alpha parents are the more strict and serious ones while my Beta dad and Omega mom tend to be more relaxed about things. It can be chaotic sometimes. But I can't deny that I love it—it's exactly what I want for myself. I want a pack where everyone loves everyone and it's just one giant love fest like I grew up with.

Working for the Foxes is part of that.

"Sloane, sweetie—" my father starts, and I cut him off.

"No, I'm coming back to work for the Foxes. Liz is expecting me to help. I don't want to be cooped up in my apartment all day, and I love working with the team…and you," I say quickly.

My exhausted father rubs his massive palm against his face. He's the biggest person in my parental pack but also the biggest softie.

"Listen, I love having you around, believe me. But I think…" he trails off.

"Kristoff Applegate, if you call our Omega daughter a distraction, I will poison your food next time," my mom steps up for me.

Willow Applegate is a formidable force, and I learned how to be an Omega from her.

Take no bullshit or prisoners is her Omega motto. It's how you get what you want. She taught me to love my designation and how to use it to my advantage, something I'm sure my father is loathing right about now.

"Not a distraction, it's just some of the guys seem to have a hard time focusing when you're around. We won the cup last year, and we have a lot of new members on the team. There's a lot of pressure on my shoulders, and I don't want to have to worry about looking over my shoulder. Especially now that not one, but two Omegas have been drugged in my fucking stadium," he says.

Okay, I'm going to have to do more negotiating than I thought.

"I'll go on suppressants and use deodorizers," I spit out. My mom gasps and clutches her chest like I said I'm going to commit murder.

"You should not have to conform or put chemicals in your body to make others around you comfortable," she gasps.

"If that's what it takes to be on the Foxes, I'll do it. At least let me stay till my birthday," I plead with him.

I can get what I need by February 14th. It's cliché, being a Valentine's baby with red hair and an absolutely, hopelessly romantic heart, but I can't help it. It's who I am.

"Have you put more consideration into seeing the matchmaker?" my mother Rosemary asks.

None of my parents are stupid enough to mention a dating site or the desire to push me into pack life in front of Mom. She's a firm believer that Omegas can happily have their heat serviced by friendly Alphas and that no Omega should be forced to bond and pack up early, least of all before they truly know themselves. She even wrote a book on it.

I might be the most well-adjusted Omega I know, and she's the reason why.

"I've considered it," I lie.

I've actually been plotting out my dream pack for months now, just waiting for the season to start, but I keep that slightly psychotic behavior to myself. There's nothing wrong with knowing what you want and pursuing it. If anything, it's my family's fault for giving me the best home life ever and wanting to emulate it for myself.

"Suppressants, deodorizers, and you agree to meet the matchmaker? Then fine, you can keep your job," my dad says, knowing if he doesn't agree, he's going to be metaphorically in the doghouse and physically on the couch.

"Thanks, Dad," I say, wrapping my arms around the larger-than-life man.

"I mean it. You don't hold up the end of your deal, I don't hold up mine."

"Yes, Coach," I say mockingly as I go around the table and hug each of my parents before I head to my apartment to get ready.

I round the corner of the kitchen and listen to their conversation before I leave, force of habit, I suppose. I was fascinated with pack life growing up and found myself wanting to know what my parents were up to.

"She flirts with all the players. I won't fucking survive this season. I'm already going fucking gray, Rosemary," my dad complains, and I cover my mouth with my hand to cover a laugh.

"Well, she's our daughter," my mother replies.

"Plus, she can flirt with whomever she wants. I'm sure the boys eat it up. If anything, Sloane could motivate them to play better. Who wouldn't want to impress the coach's Omega daughter?" my mom chips in, and I shake my head.

God, I love that woman.

"You only have yourself to blame for giving her the job in the first place," my dad says, calling him out on his shit.

"Henderson, you're lucky I need to head off to work or else I'd..."

Yup, that's my cue to get the hell out of here. I round the corner and leave the back door. My "apartment" is above the detached garage that my family doesn't use, but I'm thankful for my own space. As soon as I turned eighteen, I needed some separation from my family. Not that I don't love them dearly, but I've seen and heard too much, plus I needed my own private space.

Everything in my apartment is neatly put together and clean. I'm a little particular when it comes to my private space. That's a lie. I'm pretty particular about almost everything in my life. I like things organized and looking a certain way, I don't like a mess, and I like having control to a certain extent.

I think it's why I lean into my Omega nature so much. I control what I can, and I let go of what I can't. I know I need a pack, and I'm getting organized and working on that. I know I'll go into heat within the year, and I also have multiple scenarios on how to handle that situation when it comes along.

I have needs, and I have a plan on getting them met as soon as possible. One of them is a very moody defenseman I haven't stopped thinking about for months. I wonder what it's going to be like when I finally get to scent him again, probably amazing. There might also be a Beta flying under the radar who has caught my attention.

The exhale that leaves me is draining as I pick out my outfit for the day. All of my clothes except my underwear and socks are hung up because I can't stand wrinkles or the smell of clothes after they've been sitting in a drawer.

I don't have to dress exceptionally nice for my job, but I always put in some effort, mostly because I have a defenseman to impress. My favorite color is green, and I grab the emerald green midi dress. It's modest, the neckline covering my collarbone and the sleeves hitting my elbows. I pair it with a pair of knee-high boots and top it with a black blazer and gold accessories.

Maybe I should have worn Foxes' colors?

No, green is absolutely my color, and I stick with it as I gather up my briefcase. I already have my laptop ready to go and charged and multiple laminated files at the ready. I've memorized all the new players, their numbers, and their appearance so I can be professional.

Liz, the marketing manager for the team, will be impressed. She's great at what she does, but she doesn't truly understand a lot of the social media trends, and with each new app that pops up, I help her navigate that.

I also get a lot of face-to-face time with the team. It's hard to deny that I undoubtedly have a thing for hockey players. I've grown up around hockey. When my dad played, I had small crushes on his teammates, and then when he started coaching, I grew crushes on his players. It's hard not to; they're just so big and violent but also total softies.

My father knows the monster he's created, and it's another reason he wants me to find a different job. Actually, I think if he had a choice, he would choose for me to not work at all. Honestly, I think I'd rather not work at all either. But this job puts me in close proximity to the most eligible pack members I can find, and I'm not letting that opportunity go.

Fuck the matchmaker. I'm making my own fate.

The team just finished their workouts and have moved to the conference room. It smells like the most delicious man-brothel I could imagine, but I school my face and don't let the Alpha pheromones distract me. Well, I mean as much as I can. I did wear deodorizers like I promised, and my panties are ultra absorbent in case I get a little too turned on. The suppressants… not so much.

As much as I may have ulterior motives for wanting this position, I still need to do a good job.

"Welcome, team. We're coming off a cup win, which means everyone is going to have a microscope on us this year. I want to keep this momentum going. I know we have some major changes in our lineup, but we're lucky to have Connery and Bandnin join us as coaching staff. They will be here for home games and practices," my dad says.

The Alpha and Omega duo give a nod of agreement, and I can't help but to smile at them. I've gotten closer to Piper in recent months, and I know they're just the happiest little family. I want that for myself. If Owen could do it while winning a Stanley cup, I can certainly do it from the sidelines.

"There are other faces that are back with us this season." My father goes down the line with the owners, coaching staff, training staff, equipment manager, marketing, and then finally gets to me.

"Many of you know my daughter, Sloane," he says, pointing at me. "I won't tolerate any disrespect or ungentlemanly behavior. Treat her like she's your daughter too. There is an absolute no tolerance policy to violence or abuse of Omegas in this stadium, do you understand?"

My cheeks heat, and my nose scrunches. I definitely don't want to be treated like anyone else's daughter but his own. But I leave it for now and look around to my left where a man raises his hand to get my father's attention. He always gets lost in the crowd, despite being handsome and lean with dark, shaggy hair, soft green eyes, and a five o'clock shadow.

I may or may not frequent the diner he works at on occasion to get a glimpse of him. He keeps to himself, and I wonder why he doesn't put himself out there more. But there's definitely something special about the attractive Beta. He makes me want to find out what's going on under the mask.

"And that's the mascot, Finnegan," my father says.

"Ethan, sir," the Beta replies.

"Right. Get suited up, and let's get on the fucking ice," my father says, dismissing Ethan completely.

He doesn't look put out, just like he's used to it. He lags behind as the team and staff pile out of the room. It was so full I didn't even see Bram. I sigh out of frustration.

Ethan is grabbing a bottle of water and looking a little sad and left out, so I can't help myself when I find myself approaching him. I've been wanting to get to know him better for awhile now, I just didn't know if he was someone who would be more of a friend or potentially more. There are Betas who want nothing to do with pack life, which wouldn't work for me. Pack life means everything to me.

"Sorry if my dad was an ass," I say.

"I'm used to it," he says, and then his cheeks heat adorably.

"Not saying your dad's an ass. Just saying no one really gives a shit about the mascot."

"You know, I handle a lot of the team's social media," I say.

"Yeah, of course I know," he says, a small little dimple appearing at the corner of his mouth; it's precious. More than precious as he leans against the wall and crosses his arms. He isn't big like the hockey players, but he has clear defined muscle and black and gray tattoos lacing up his arms.

He's hot, and I'm not sure if he truly knows how gorgeous he is.

"Maybe I could help you get noticed more," I say with a flirty smile.

"Why would you do that?" he asks.

I shrug and hold my clipboard close to my chest. "Everybody loves an underdog."

I leave the meeting room with those words hanging, and something deep inside of me wants to see this Beta succeed.

And quite possibly, something even more.

BRAM

CHAPTER 2

She didn't look at me the entire meeting, and I might be pouting about it while I'm on the ice.

"What's your problem, Nilsen?" Mikael Martel asks as he skates past me.

The two of us together are our strongest line of defense, and I know we're going to need it this year with the subpar Connery taking over the goal. I understand why Alexi's Omega can't play professionally anymore, but did they really have to replace him with his dickhead brother?

"Fuck off," I growl at Martel.

"God, I forgot what a ray of sunshine you are," he says.

"Like you're any better."

The new offensive line coach, and our ex-captain, skates by. "He did get better once he bonded Charlotte and started popping babies out left and right," Alexi says, pushing Martel on the ice.

"We really couldn't get fucking rid of you? We're not even on your line. Go bother someone else," Martel complains, skating away.

"Cheer up, Nilsen. Now that I'm not on the team, you can be the most handsome," Alexi says, and it nearly makes me crack a smile.

No man should be as charming as he is. The large Russian grins at me as he starts barking orders at his new offensive line. Eli Beckford is going to be the staple of the line and the team, and I just hope the rookies can keep up with our new captain.

I don't see her beautiful, long, red hair or the stunning green dress she was wearing anywhere in the practice stands, and it makes my mood sour even more. I, of course, saw her over the various summer parties and team parties I forced myself to go to just to see her, but it's been nearly two months.

Two months with no sunshine.

I shouldn't be pining after the coach's daughter, she shouldn't be the main motivator as to why I re-signed with the Foxes, truly, it's pathetic. But I don't care. I want the little Omega to be mine.

I have a five year contract that prevents her father from killing me; I'd be an expensive motherfucker to murder as one of his most senior players.

Even as badly as I want her, she has to make the first move. Sure, we flirt, so there's a clear attraction there. Not to mention her fucking scent—I may be eating peach ring candies because they remind me of her. In general, Sloane is a very bubbly, outgoing person, and I don't want to misconstrue her friendly nature as anything other than that.

I refuse to be a bastard, especially to an Omega so lovely.

A shoulder bumps into mine, and I scoff, my daydreams of Sloane ripped away from me as the lesser Connery heads to the goal.

Our feud started my rookie year in the NHL, and I hate the overconfident playboy dickhead who thinks he's above everyone else. His pretty face has been plastered all over league pages and online. I think his face could use a good bruising, if I'm being honest. His pretty face should be rearranged to match his rotten insides.

He doesn't speak as he goes to the goal. Does he think for a second he's just going to bump into me and there isn't going to be any repercussions? He needs to learn whose team this is. His contract is only for this season, so he's fucking replaceable.

I skate over to where he's cutting the crease.

"We gonna have a fucking problem, Connery?" I ask.

His helmet is off, his pretty boy face on full display as he cocks a grin at me.

"I don't know. Do you plan on being a shitty teammate again?" he asks, and I narrow my eyes at him.

"I wasn't the problem when we were in Washington, and you know it," I grate back.

"Do I? Because I remember you getting traded for… what was it? Irreconcilable differences? Or because no one on the team could deal with your shitty attitude."

"At least I'm not coming on this team as a hand-me-down to your more talented brother."

Max Connery looks around, grins, and shucks off his gloves. I do the same, and before I can even take the left one off, his fist is colliding with my face.

"Motherfucker," I hiss, grabbing his jersey and swinging back.

We've completely disrupted the goal, unhitching it from its placement as we bang against the wall holding each other's jerseys. It takes Beckford, Martel, Coach Applegate, and Max's brother, Owen, to pull us off one another.

"You've got to be fucking kidding me. It's the first day of practice," Coach yells, tugging Connery by his jersey.

"He started it," I say.

Coach rolls his eyes. "Grow the fuck up. Go get your nose cleaned up. You with me," he barks, dragging Connery off to the side to talk with him.

I grumble under my breath, and Alexi Bandnin laughs next to me. "I also wanted to fuck the goalie last year. I get it."

"The hell are you talking about?"

"You can't tell me that wasn't sexually charged."

I blink at my previous team captain in horror. "I think you took one too many hits to the head."

He shrugs and whistles. "If you say so, Nilsen." He skates away, heading back to the front line, and I shake my head and skate off the ice.

My nose isn't broken, but it is bleeding. I'll get that asshole back the next time. The idea of him being the goalie, the person I'm supposed to protect and work with on the ice, is disgusting.

Come hell or high water, I'm going to make it my mission to find a better first string for the Foxes. I'd try to convince his brother to come out of retirement, but that would be selfish and harmful. Owen Connery all but ripped his body to shreds playing in the NHL as an Omega. It's time for him to step away along with Alexi.

I can't blame them for leaving this behind when they've built their perfect pack. I'm not ready to leave hockey anytime soon, but that doesn't mean I don't want an Omega or a pack. I understand that things would be difficult with my schedule, but that's why you create a pack. When I'm not around, other members of the pack would be there for her.

I grimace as I think about sharing, which is not one of my strengths. Especially when it comes to the Omega I have in mind.

It's like my conscience makes her appear as she turns the corner and gasps when she sees me.

"Oh my God, what happened? Practice just started," she says.

Her pretty lips part as she approaches me. She's already a tiny little thing, but when I'm wearing my skates, I tower over her.

"The new goalie and I got into it," I tell her.

"Come on, I'll clean you up."

I decide then that I will milk this injury for all that it's worth. She leads me down the hall, her boots clicking against the floor as we get to the locker room. She grabs the first aid kit and points for me to sit on the bench.

When I sit, she's eye to eye with me.

Her dark green eyes remind me of a dewy forest as she looks back at me. Her scent isn't as thick as it usually is, and she must notice that I'm trying to scent her.

"I'm wearing deodorizers," she blurts out as she grabs some gauze and starts blotting my nose.

"I wasn't—"

"You weren't what? Trying to scent me, Bram?"

She smirks at me, knowing that I'm completely caught.

"You didn't wear them last year," I mention, realizing after the fact I probably sound like a creep who was constantly trying to get a whiff of her—which I was—but she doesn't need to know that.

"It was part of the deal, my father allowing me to come back and work this year. I think after last year with Owen getting drugged and a few years prior to that with Charlotte, he's worried about my safety."

"You have the whole team looking out for you," I tell her, meaning it truly.

Not only do the new guys fear Coach Applegate, but the more tenured players respect him and have a soft spot for Sloane.

"It doesn't matter. In the end, I got my way," she says with a shrug, still cleaning my nose.

"I imagine that happens a lot."

"What makes you say that?" She smirks, knowing she already has me hook, line, and sinker.

"Because if you'd ask me to jump right now, I'd ask how high."

"Because I'm the coach's daughter?" she asks.

"No, because you're you," I reply easily, and she pulls her hand away from my face to search my eyes, before going back to her work and grabbing Neosporin and a Band-Aid.

We've flirted every time we're in the same room, but this feels significant, different in a way I'm not sure how to explain. Could she actually want to take this beyond simple workplace flirting to something more? It's something I've fantasized about but didn't know it was actually possible.

"I'm a very modern Omega, but there are some things I just can't bring myself to do, one of which is making the first move.

So if you've been looking for the right opportunity, now's the time."

I blink at her as she finishes up with my nose and looks at me.

"Go on a date with me."

"Is that a demand or a question?"

I smile. She's going to be the death of me, and I'll happily walk myself into my grave. "Sloane, I'd love to take you on a date if you'd be interested."

She smiles. "I'd love to."

"Sunday?"

"I'm free Sunday. Do you also want to ask for my number?" she suggests, and I nod my head.

Months of teasing me last season and months apart from the off season and she's finally giving me an in? I'll take whatever I can get.

Sloane grabs a Post-it and writes her number down and hands it to me.

"I think it's best we keep this between us?"

I nod, feeling completely dumbfounded as I look down at her number.

Did I really think I had a chance? No, not really. Sloane can have any Alpha she wants wrapped around her finger within minutes, and somehow she's choosing me to have at her beck and call.

I stand up from the bench, bending my neck to look down at her. I'm not going to fuck this up.

"How's your nose now?" she asks in a soft voice.

"Never better."

"So Sunday?"

"Sunday," I reply, placing the note safely in my locker. "I've got to get back to practice."

"Of course. Oh, and Bram?"

"Yeah?" I turn around to face her.

"My favorite flowers are peonies, I don't eat red meat, and I get car sick with long car rides." She says the last bit shyly.

I tap my head with my finger like I'm locking all that knowledge in. "Noted. I'll text you about Sunday."

"Okay," she says, some of the overconfident facade falling away as her genuine excitement takes over.

The smile on her face? I put that there, and I plan on doing a hell of a lot more than making that woman smile. I plan on making her mine.

CHAPTER 3

"It's the first fucking day, and you're already getting into it with Nilsen?" my brother complains.

Coach Applegate already tore me a new one, and now I've gotta take it from my little brother who, despite his designation and age, has everything I've ever wanted. He's a champion, he has a pack, and he's fucking happy in a way I didn't think possible.

He's always been jealous of me, but it was always him who had everything. Yet I'm the one biting my tongue and wearing deodorizers to make him more comfortable. My scent has always been a point of contention with me and Owen. I know the hatchet has mostly been buried, but I'd rather just avoid that issue all together.

Plus, with my scent tamed, it should help with my little PR problem.

It doesn't matter how I feel. I'm known as some playboy, asshole, bachelor. But willing Betas are the only thing that has kept me company for the last few years. With my schedule, nothing has stuck, but at least for a night or a few weeks, I don't feel so hopeless.

I've been so alone for so long. I'd hoped that coming and playing for the Foxes was going to be the thing to help fix our relationship and possibly help with this unending loneliness that's been following me around for years.

"Max, are you listening to me?" Owen asks, shoving my shoulder.

"Nilsen and I go way back. I don't know what his problem is," I tell my brother honestly.

I truly don't know why Bram Nilsen hates my guts, but on the other hand, he doesn't seem to like a lot of people in general.

"Nilsen is loyal as hell. Whatever you did, you need to make it right. This is going to be a rebuilding year. If we want to make the playoffs, you've got to be in sync with the rest of the defense."

I hate being chastised and consoled by my younger brother, but I just nod my head, not wanting to pick a fight. I also just wish he would pick my side. Why does he automatically think the issue between me and Nilsen is my fault?

"I'll work on it," I tell him.

"You better. I pulled strings to get you here," he says.

Like I needed the fucking reminder. I grab my helmet and skate back to the goal, wondering if this is all worth it. When my contract with the Sharks ended, I was a free agent, and no other team wanted to pick me up based on my overabundant presence in the press. But the Foxes were desperate for a goalie with playoff experience, and my baby brother vouched for me.

The brother who has always hated me for being an Alpha and playing in the NHL is the reason why I'm here.

Isn't that some shit?

That whole time, he'd been jealous of me, pushing me away because I was a reminder of the things he wasn't so easily given. I worked hard to get where I am, and more often than not, I find myself wanting exactly what Owen has.

I'd say the tables have turned, but there was never a time that I didn't want to be a part of Owen's life or have some jealousy over the close relationship he has with our mother.

I groan, hating that I feel like a depressive sack of shit.

Despite my inner turmoil, I get through practice without another altercation, but I do have to deal with my brother critiquing every single fucking move I make.

This is going to be a long season.

Going back to my undecorated, overly gray, lonely apartment just didn't feel right. With the need to improve my image, I don't go to a bar. Instead, I find myself at a mom-and-pop diner that blessedly sells alcohol.

The combination of omelet and a Jack and Coke is a depressing one, but it's better than going to a bar, drinking too much, taking home the first person who touches my arm, and then waking up the next morning to see my face plastered on the internet.

It's not that I don't want anything deeper with anyone, it just seems like no one is truly interested in getting to know me. I'm a good lay, but I'm not sure if I'm worth much else.

I look around for my waitress to get a refill, and when she doesn't come by, I wave a hand at the man working on the nearby tables.

"Hey, can I get another?" I ask him as he turns around. He looks strangely familiar, but I can't put my finger on it.

"Max? What are you doing here?" he asks, looking down at my pathetic excuse for a meal. "Ethan," he says, and I furrow my brow, trying to place him. "The mascot," he sighs out.

"Right," I say, snapping my fingers. "You work here?"

"Believe it or not, mascots aren't rolling in money," he replies.

"But here?" I ask, and he nods.

"It's my dad's place. I've worked here for as long as I can remember. The tips are nice and help me pay my bills while still being able to work for the Foxes."

I blink at him, and he stares at me a moment before taking my glass and getting me a refill. I suppose I never really considered what a mascot makes. Really, I never considered the mascot at all.

Ethan replaces my drink and sits it on the table. I sigh, and the man just plops into the booth across from me. I look around the half-full diner, wondering what the fuck is happening right now, but he just gives me a soft smile.

He's handsome. It's like he's a combination of the burnout kid all grown up mixed with the boy-next-door look. I'm not sure how to explain it, but there's something alluring about him.

No, I'm not fucking the mascot.

"Do you want some advice?" he asks. My immediate response is to tell him to fuck off. But I'm aiming to become a better person —it's fucking awful.

"I assume you're planning on giving it anyway?"

"No one notices when I'm around, and therefore I've learned quite a bit of knowledge about the Foxes' players and staff. But if you don't want some friendly tips from Finnegan the Fox, I can just take my sweet ass elsewhere," he says, using his fingertips to balance himself on the old worn diner table, and I grab his wrist.

"Wait. I'm listening."

"Alright, there's a few things you need to understand," he says, lacing his fingers together, his forearms covered in black and gray tattoos as his tendons flex. "Owen fucking hated you last year, and a lot of that spilled throughout the team. While you two might be good or working on things now, there's still a lot of residual resentment. The team loves Owen. I mean, a goalie starting later in the season from a feeder team and helping lead the team to a cup? He's beloved."

"I'm well aware of how loved my brother is."

"Sheesh, no shit. Sounds like there's some resentment on your end too," he says, and I glare at him. "I have other shit to do if you don't want to listen."

"I'm listening," I reply, toning down my irritation.

"I know all the teams care about family life and all that shit, but the Foxes? It's to the extreme. Not only did the team have the first contracted pack, but have since done more to allow players to bond and have packs and lives off of the ice. Coach Applegate himself is a big family man, so this slutty little image you have has got to stop, or you can consider yourself canned for next season."

"I've already met with PR."

"And I'm sure they gave you the typical rundown to lay low and not get tangled in the press. What I'm telling you is you need to not just have no bad press, you need to make yourself some good press."

"What? Like find a pack?"

Ethan breathes through his nose heavily and sighs like I'm stupid.

"No, man, do some charitable shit. You need to shed away this playboy image; you need people to forget about it all together. Do something good."

"They never notice the good shit. It's not like I've been just some sex-crazed asshole running around. I donate money and time, but that's not the story they want."

"Then find a way to create your own story," he says simply.

"How would I even do that?"

He rubs his chin; he has a soft scattering of stubble that I bet feels great against his fingertips.

"Sloane offered to help me improve my image as the mascot. Maybe she can help you too. She's great with all the apps and shit. She made people obsessed with Alexi last year. Literally, there are so many memes of that man circulating the internet."

"You really think she'd be willing to help?"

"She loves an underdog. Plus, it doesn't hurt to ask. We're meeting at the arena before practice tomorrow. You should join us."

I take a sip of my refilled drink and look over this Beta who is too attractive and kind for his own good.

"Why do you want to help me?"

"I don't know, maybe Sloane helping me made me feel like I need to pay it forward or some shit. Or maybe I know what it feels like to be a part of something but also disconnected at the same time."

I nod my head, wondering if I ever truly had a conversation with any of the mascots of my previous teams. The answer is a simple no, and guilt looms around me for a moment before I outstretch my hand.

"You help me with my image, but what do you get?"

He looks down at my hand and then up at my face.

"You invite me to a team event and include me in other team shit."

His response makes me feel like a dick, but I hold my hand closer to him.

"It's a deal."

"So it is," he replies, smacking his hand into mine as we shake on our agreed upon terms.

Ethan stands up and is about to head away from my table, but he stops.

"There's one other thing you should know," he says.

"What's that?"

"Bram Nilsen is never going to come around to being friends. That motherfucker holds a grudge like no other."

"Why? Do you have personal experience?" I ask.

Ethan laughs and shakes his head. "Me? No. He doesn't even know I exist. But I've heard his pregame meetings with other teammates. When he doesn't like someone, he holds a grudge, and he never lets it go."

"How reassuring," I say, digging my fork into my eggs.

"Just don't waste your energy. He'll reach a point where he's not actively trying to punch you in the face, but it's best to just avoid him until then."

"Thanks?" I reply, and the mascot smiles.

"Right. Well, see you tomorrow morning."

"Yeah, see you tomorrow," I reply.

I don't know what I've done to receive this gift of having some connection to the Foxes, but I'll take whatever I can get. I can't let this be my last season, and I surely can't fuck up my chance with this team while my brother watches from the sidelines.

ETHAN

CHAPTER 4

It's early, but I'm ready on the ice with everything but the fox head on. Unfortunately, it's a liability to have me wear ice skates, but I have on the special shoes they gave me for when I am on the ice. I'm in the stands most of the time for games anyway.

Sloane is lacing up her ice skates on the side, while Max skates around in circles before coming to join me in the center.

"She seems surprised that I'm here," he whisper hisses.

"Because she is surprised. I don't have her number. She just told me to meet her here yesterday. We'll explain it when she gets on the ice."

Her pretty, red hair trails behind her as she skates on the ice looking like a fucking angel. She's dressed like she's going right to work after this with high-waisted black pants and a tight white blouse tucked in.

She tilts her head at Max. "Max?"

"Ethan said I could join you," he says almost shyly.

Sloane gives him a bright smile and nods her head. "And what is it you need help with?"

Max looks over at me, and I sigh. "We're trying to overcompensate for his playboy image."

"I see," Sloane says, looking Max up and down. "But are you going to stop being a playboy, or are you wanting me to help you lie?" she asks boldly.

Max's Adam's apple bobs as he stares down at the very direct Omega.

"No, I don't want to be like that anymore."

"Why?" she questions.

"Because it only ever made me feel good for the moment. I want to feel good all the time," he replies.

Sloane's gaze doesn't leave his, and even I look at the lonely Alpha in a new light.

"Okay. Then I'll help you."

"You will?"

"There are rules, of course," Sloane says, her hands firmly on her hips. I gotta say, her standing on ice skates so effortlessly is a turn on I wasn't expecting. "If I find out you're lying to me, you're done."

Max raises his hands in mock surrender. "Is there anything else?"

"Yeah, I'll do my best, but I can't make any promises."

"And what's in it for you?" Max asks her.

"What do you mean?" she replies.

"Why bother helping us? I'm sure you're busy enough doing other stuff for the team," Max says. I stay quiet, but I'm just as eager to know the answer.

She pauses and thinks for a moment before speaking. "If my dad ever asks if I'm here early, you'll tell him no."

I whistle and adjust the fox's head under my arm. "Lying to the coach?" I say. Her defiance of her father makes her even more charming.

"Part of me keeping my job this year was going to a match-maker, and I don't plan on doing that. So if I'm here early to help you guys out and it just so happens my parents think I'm at the matchmaker instead, then so be it."

Max and I just stare at her for a moment, and she huffs out a breath.

"So do we have a deal?"

"I'm in," I reply immediately.

"I'm in, but if you get caught by your dad, we had no idea about your little matchmaker problem," Max says, clearly way smarter with terms and conditions than I am.

"Yeah, what he said."

"Fine," Sloane says, giving us a once over, and I swear something flashes behind her pretty, green eyes. "I already have a plan for you, Ethan. I'll have to think about what I'm going to do with you," Sloane says, looking Max up and down like he's a problem she has to solve.

"What do you need from me?" I ask her, and she sighs.

"Finnegan the Fox is getting a makeover first and foremost."

"Don't we need approval?"

"Already in the works," she says simply. "I watched you last season, and I went online to see what other mascots are doing. I don't think you're fully embracing your personality. You need to be uniquely you while also taking a page from other mascots' playbooks."

"What does that mean?" I ask, and Max scoffs next to me.

"Do you know how many people love that fucking freak, Gritty, but hate the Flyers? You gotta be more than just part of the team. You've got to be someone everyone can root for," Max says simply.

Sloane nods her head. "He's right. While you're a part of the Foxes, your mascot persona can be something that makes you famous and hard to emulate. Plus, the more popular you get, the more money you can ask for. Make yourself irreplaceable. Show me some moves," Sloane says.

"Yeah, show us some moves," Max says, skating over next to Sloane as I put the mascot head on, facing it so it won't fall off.

It's dangerous, but I've been doing this shit my whole life as I do a couple of flips and land on a split on the ice. I take off the head and look over at Sloane and Max who are both tilting their heads.

"Doesn't that hurt your dick?" Max asks, and Sloane smacks him on the chest, wincing when her hand hits his padding. "Sorry," he mumbles to her.

"Where did you learn how to do all that?" she asks.

"Male cheerleader," I reply sheepishly.

"Huh," Sloane says, tapping her chin. "I definitely think we can use that, especially when we're at events, but it's too dangerous on the ice, and you spend a lot of time in the stands anyway. Finnegan needs a personality."

"You seem pretty sly in real life," Max suggests, and I scoff at him.

"He's not wrong. What if being a prankster and sneaky like a real fox is the angle to go? Maybe we can do a post where it's like you're sneaking up on Max. That way, you both can get some publicity. Introducing Finnegan's personality and making Max more likable?"

"I'm down for anything," I tell her honestly.

One, I don't want to lose this side job. It kind of reminds me of being a part of a team, and a few times a week, I get to hide and be this stupid big fox. It also wouldn't hurt if I could cut back my shifts at the diner either.

"Tell me where you want me." I tell her, and she smiles, grabbing her phone and placing us on different parts of the ice and telling us what we need to lip-sync and what to do.

She smiles behind the camera, skating backwards at some points and pointing and directing us where we need to go. I actually have a good time, and now and then I glance over at Max and realize he's having a good time himself.

I just wonder if it's because we're doing something productive or because Sloane is making everything so fun and easy.

"Okay, I think we got it," she says while looking at her phone, her thumbs moving at a rapid speed. "Here, you guys can come watch," she says.

I walk over cautiously and stand behind her shoulder while Max does the same thing. It's fucked up, but being this close to them, I should be able to scent them. Obviously, I don't have an Alpha's sense of smell, but even with both of them this close, I don't scent anything, and I wonder if that's normal.

Definitely not for Sloane, the woman was all but flaunting it all last season. I'm guessing her father had more stipulations than the matchmaker for her to keep her job.

Sloane holds the phone, smiling as I watch the little skit she put together of me sneaking up on Max along with the stupid sound she picked. It's cute and cheesy, but that's what people want.

"Are you sure I don't look like a stupid asshole?" Max asks her, making her replay it again.

"No, you look cute, less threatening."

"I'm not threatening," he says affronted.

"I didn't mean it like that. You seem more approachable, easygoing, and it shows that you're a part of this team."

"If you're sure."

"You said you would trust me. What about you, Ethan?" she asks, and I immediately perk up. I like that she remembers my name and calls me by it. She treats the mascot like it's a different part of me, and it's refreshing.

"I trust you completely," I tell her honestly.

She gives me a smile and looks down at her phone for the time. "We actually got that done a lot quicker than I realized. Do you mind if I skate for a bit?" she asks.

"Knock yourself out," I tell her, and Max shifts on his skates.

"Mind if I skate with you?" he asks.

"Only if you can keep up," she says, putting her phone in her pocket and skating off like a bat out of hell.

She doesn't stand a chance as Max, even as a goalie, is swifter on his skates and has over a foot over her in height. They laugh as they skate together, and there's a pang in my chest as I watch them.

When was the last time I connected to someone new? I've been in my own little bubble for so long. Outside of my foster dad and other foster siblings, I don't branch out much. Becoming the mascot was supposed to be the outlet and that team comradery I've been missing since I left high school years ago, but it isn't what I thought it would be.

That is, until now.

Even though I'm on the sidelines watching them skate, I finally feel a part of something. And for the first time in a long time, I truly start to believe in myself.

Sloane is laughing viciously as Max chases her on the ice, and I just smile at the headstrong red-headed Omega who has faith in me.

"Grab his arm," she says, and I blink as Max grabs my one arm and Sloane grabs another. It takes me a moment to collect my balance, but as long as I keep my legs locked, I glide over the ice as the two of them push me around.

The cold air smacks my face, and I smile, feeling a part of something, even if it's small. It's not the validation of the whole team, and Max is probably even on the outs, but it's something.

And this something somehow feels like everything. I just don't know how to explain it.

SLOANE

CHAPTER 5

I leave the ice with a huge smile on my face, putting my skates away and trading them for a pair of comfortable heels.

I watch the video a few more times before a notification shows up on my phone.

UNKNOWN

Would you feel comfortable coming to my place on Sunday? Or I can make a reservation. I know you want to keep this between us for now.

I smile at his message before frowning. I'd never want Bram to feel like I don't want to be seen in public with him. I just need to make sure that he's the right Alpha for me before I make the situation awkward with my dad. I change his contact information on my phone and reply.

Bram Nilsen knows how to cook?

BRAM

Bram Nilsen knows a lot of things.

Consider me curious. What time should I be there?

BRAM

6?

It's a date.

I walk through the back halls like I'm on cloud nine. Not only do I have a date with the hockey player I've had a crush on for months, but I also felt something when I was with Max and Ethan.

Ethan is a no brainer; he's charming and funny. I knew we would get along well. But Max was a wildcard. I knew about his reputation, of course, but the man who would do my stupid video ideas seems nothing like the media has made him out to be.

What I know about Max is mostly second hand from his brother and his Alphas, Alexi and Piper. Plus, I saw what happened on the ice last season when Max and Owen got into it. But the guy who skated around the rink with me with a wide grin and not a care in the world? He seems like someone I might want to get to know.

I'm walking down the hallway with a clipboard pressed against my chest as someone calls my name. I turn and see Liz giving me a worried smile.

"Hey, Liz, is everything alright?"

She takes a deep breath and then suddenly starts sobbing. I rub her back and direct her into the office. I grab a fistful of tissues and hand them to her as she sits down.

Liz is in her late thirties, a pretty brunette Beta with a ton of drive. Helping market the Foxes from the ground up was her biggest dream and accomplishment.

"What's wrong?" I ask her, and she sniffles before blowing her nose.

"Phillip's cancer is back," she says, and I rub her back and wrap my arms around her as she sobs against my shirt.

Liz's husband has been in remission for two years. I can't imagine how devastating this must be for the both of them.

"I don't know how we're going to make it through this again," she says between sobs.

"Whatever you need, Liz, I'm here for you."

"Thank you, Sloane."

"Seriously. Anything you need," I reassure her.

"Can you handle the Humane Society ribbon cutting next week? I just can't," she says, and I squeeze her tighter.

"Of course. Why don't you go home for the rest of the day?"

She sniffles. "I'm not ready to talk about it with anyone else yet."

"Do you want me to tell my dad?"

"You wouldn't mind?"

"No, go home. Take care of yourself and Phillip, that's the priority."

She nods, blotting away her smeared mascara as she puts on sunglasses and grabs her purse, hightailing it out of the office. I take a few deep breaths, trying to put myself in her shoes, and I just can't imagine.

Liz and Phillip are high school sweethearts. They've been each other's everything for the longest time. I can't imagine what it's like watching someone you love suffer and trying to be strong for the both of you.

I head directly to my father's office so that Liz doesn't get in trouble for leaving without telling anyone.

I knock on his door.

"What?" he barks, not looking up, and I smile to myself.

"Have a second, Dad?" I say, and he immediately looks up and smiles.

"Yeah, honey, what's up?"

"Liz had to leave early," I say, shutting the door behind me.

"Okay? She could have emailed."

"Phillip's cancer is back."

"Fuck," my dad hisses out, leaning back in his chair.

"She was crying, so I told her to head home for the day and that I'd help pick up any slack."

"It looks like we're lucky to have you on the team, then," he says, and I roll my eyes and plop down in the chair in front of him.

"Listen, old man, if you have something to say, say it," I tell him.

He only has himself to blame for my direct attitude. He grabs his mug and takes a sip of his coffee, his eyes not leaving mine as he sips.

"It's already been said. You're keeping up your end of the bargain?"

"I am."

"How was the matchmaker?"

"Not as bad as I thought," I tell him, not a complete lie. Only, I'm talking about Max, not about the cracked-out matchmaker I don't trust as far as I can throw her.

"What do you and Liz have planned for the preseason?" he asks, crossing his arms.

The thing about my dad is he's the biggest hard-ass I know, but he's also a complete sucker when it comes to me. I know he's busy and stressed, but yet here he is, taking time out of his day to talk to me and make sure it isn't rushed.

"I'm rebranding the mascot."

"What's wrong with Finnegan?"

"He's boring. He's almost as ugly as Harvey the Hound, and Ethan is great. He just needs a chance to let his personality shine through."

"Who's Ethan?"

"Jesus Christ, Dad, he's been the mascot for two seasons now."

He waves me off.

"My job isn't to worry about the mascot."

"Then let my job be to worry about the mascot. I guarantee you I can make a video that gets over a million likes and it's solely mascot content."

"That confident?"

I arch an eyebrow at him. "Want to make it interesting?"

"You get people to like that glorified rodent, and I'll give you five grand. You don't get the likes and you have to go on a blind date with the pack of my choosing," he says.

I grimace at the thought. He would probably set me up with the most boring finance guys he could find in all of Connecticut.

The thought alone gives me shivers.

"You have a deal," I say, reaching out my hand and giving him a firm shake like he taught me.

"Oh, don't forget about your mom's birthday next week," he says as I stand, and I scoff.

"Like anyone can forget that woman's birthday," I reply, and he just laughs it off. I learned from the best Omega, and there would be hell to pay if anyone forgot a major holiday, which includes her birthday.

"Fair enough. I'll see you at dinner. And if there is anything you can think of to support Liz and her husband, just let me know."

I give him a nod and think I have just the person in mind to spearhead a fundraiser. It will look great for Max while helping out Liz and Phillip. I can manage that while also making Finnegan the Fox the hottest new mascot in the NHL.

I go through eight outfits before landing on a simple black dress, heels, and a leather jacket to go on top. Nerves are rippling through me, and the only thing keeping me sane is that I know Bram is likely just as nervous as I am. We've been dancing around this attraction since last season.

At first, I thought he was handsome, and I liked how grumpy and aloof he was, but it was just a pheromone-driven attraction. But as time went on, more shameless flirting, and scenting, I kinda realized that it was more than attraction, that I wanted to really get to know who Bram really is, because there's no doubt in my mind that there's a soft, gooey man underneath that gruff exterior. Which happens to be this Omega's favorite type of kryptonite.

I go sans deodorizers because I'm only wearing that shit to appease my dad. In all reality, I hate hiding anything about myself. I love being an Omega, and hindering my scent at all is honestly quite upsetting. Maybe once I solidify things with Bram and help Max and Ethan, I'll quit. The whole reason I wanted the job so badly was to get closer to Bram in the first place.

Though some of my motives seem to be shifting lately.

I have my car keys in hand and I'm walking to my car when I hear a loud whistle and whip around.

"Going somewhere nice?" my Beta father, Henderson, says as he sneaks a cigarette. He better brush his teeth multiple times and take a shower, or both of my moms will give him hell.

"Smoking again?"

He shrugs his shoulders, snuffing it out and putting it in a ziplock bag. I smirk to myself, loving how the ire of his Alpha and Omega is driving him to hide his dirty secret, but I also wonder what has him smoking again.

"Seems like we both have secrets, then," he says, arching a brow at me.

"I don't know what you're talking about," I say, and he laughs.

"I know damn well you're not going to that fucking matchmaker." I purse my lips and say nothing. "You're our kid. To expect you to not be the strong woman we raised you to be is just Kristoff pretending to be blind. Which one of his players are you seeing?" he asks.

Out of all my parents, he's always been the one to truly call me out on my shit. It's exactly why I want a Beta in my pack. They're always the most observant and levelheaded.

I still don't respond, and he laughs.

"Let me guess, then?" I roll my eyes, and he squints at me. "Definitely one of the big ones."

"Ew. They're all big."

"You know what I mean."

"No, I don't think I do. I better get going."

He snaps his fingers. "Shit, what's his name? The one that got the four-game suspension last season."

Of course, that's the thing he remembers about Bram.

"The less you know, the better. You know, plausible deniability and all that."

"He's worth pissing your dad off?" he asks, and I smirk.

"I don't know, is smoking worth pissing off your Omega and Alpha?" I retort.

He groans and shoves his hands in his pockets. "Your Mormor is coming to town," he whispers, and I hiss.

Mormor Applegate may be Satan reincarnated. I know she's my grandmother, but the issues she's caused for my parents' pack are unreal.

"That explains a lot," I say, and then I wince. "She'll be here for Mom's birthday?"

"Unfortunately."

"The smoking makes more sense now," I reply, and he groans.

"I promise to stop. It just seems to be stressing everyone out."

"When does she fly in?"

"Three days from now," he says and takes a deep breath.

It's not a surprise my parents didn't tell me. The last time she was here, she made me cry, and I hid in my apartment the rest of the week because the old bitch can't climb the stairs.

"You got another one of those?" I joke, handing out my hand, and he grimaces at me.

"Don't even joke, Sloane Loraine."

"Well, I'll make sure that my date has normal or dead relatives."

My dad laughs, shaking his head. He hasn't aged much. You'd never guess he has a kid that is in her twenties.

"Just make sure he's worth it. You deserve the best. And do me a favor and let me know before you plan on telling Dad. Maybe I'll plan a work trip that week."

I shake my head and laugh.

"Deal."

"Have a good time, kid," he says as he slides through the back door and goes through the house to hide the evidence of his naughty behavior.

It's nice knowing I'll have one parent on my side if things with Bram, and possibly other players, work out. That's a lie. I know my Omega mother will be happy with whomever I choose; she doesn't care if they're on my dad's team or their jobs as long as they're perfect for me.

My two Alpha parents are the ones I'm going to have to work the hardest on accepting this.

I shake my head, hating how ahead of myself I'm getting. But that's typical of me, planning ahead, daydreaming about the future. And I got to say, the one I've been imagining lately seems pretty fantastic.

BRAM

CHAPTER 6

I'm more nervous about this date than I was last year during the Cup finals as I make sure I don't burn our fucking dinner.

I thought *pannenkoeken* would be safe. It's one of the few things I know I won't mess up since my mother made it often, and it doesn't include any red meat. I did a savory one with salmon and avocado and a sweet one with apples and raisins.

Shit, I should have asked if there were any foods she didn't like beyond red meat before I started cooking. I thought it would be best that the food was ready as soon as she got here, so if it was awkward and she hated it, she could leave.

I'm not sure why I feel as though Sloane won't enjoy our date. Perhaps it's because we've been teetering on this edge of flirtation for so long I worry that once she gets to know me, she won't like what she sees.

It's also been an incredibly long time since I've dated someone. Let alone courted them.

Because the fact is, Sloane is the courting type.

She's an Omega, one who is nearly at the age to go into heat. There's no way she's looking for casual, she's looking for her pack.

I'm not sure if the thought scares me or not. For sure, the idea of sharing isn't appealing. It's not something I grew up with. I had Beta parents and was an only child.

Sharing was not something I held in high regard, it never has been.

The toppings melt into the top of the sweet *pannenkoeken* as a knock hits my door. I regret not offering to pick her up, but I couldn't simply just pull up in front of my coach's house.

My coach who inexplicably has said multiple times for us to keep our paws off of his Omega daughter.

As much as I respect the man, this is a rule worth breaking.

I plate the food, turn off the burner, and wipe my hands before taking a deep breath and answering the front door. As soon as I open it, I look down to see a smiling Sloane looking like an absolute vision in a simple black dress and a leather jacket.

"Come in," I tell her, opening the door wider and stepping to the side.

"Smells amazing," she says as she begins to take off her jacket, and I help her by grabbing the back as she slides her arms out. I hang it up on the rack as Sloane glances around my home.

It's not overly large, but it's a great neighborhood, and I knew it would make a great investment property if I ever got traded to another team. It's minimalistic but still warm and inviting at the same time.

"Your home is lovely," she says, glancing around to the kitchen, and I place a hand on her back and lead her to the island to sit on a barstool.

Her scent wafts after her, and I have to keep myself in check. It's been so long since I've scented her in full force. The woman drives me fucking crazy. But I'm not going to ruin this. I'm serious about this girl, and I need to prove my intentions and make sure we're on the same page.

"I figured you might be hungry already, so I thought it would be best to eat first," I say, and she gives me a warm smile.

It's hard not to stare at her. It's not just that she's beautiful with her unique red hair, freckled skin, and piercing green eyes. Sloane is like a magnet I can't pull away from. Something about her presence soothes a part of me I didn't know I ever needed.

She calms me in a way I haven't felt in a very long time. It's consuming, and I wonder if having her in my home for our first date was the best idea.

Sloane is too tempting for her own good.

"It looks amazing. Pancakes?" she asks as I slide one of the savory and sweet dishes in front of her.

"*Pannenkoeken.* It's a bit in between a crepe and a pancake. You typically roll it and eat it. My mother made them all the time," I tell her, and she smiles.

"Are you still close with your mother?" she asks, and I shake my head.

"Unfortunately, she is no longer with us."

"I'm sorry to hear that," she says like she truly means it, and I'm grateful she doesn't ask me more details about her. "Any other family?"

"I have a few cousins, and my father still lives in the Netherlands, but none of us are close. In fact, you probably know one of my cousins."

"Oh yes, Kristiansen, he's on the Canes, right?"

I nod my head, my lips thinning into a frown when I hear her say his name. But I swallow down the irritation at the mention of the other Alpha I can hardly tolerate. Instead, I just move on, not wanting to discuss the self-entitled asshole. He broke my nose when we were seven, and I haven't forgiven him for it.

I place a fork and knife next to her plate as I stand while I eat, rolling and cutting a bite of my dish. Not half bad. Sloane does the same.

"This is delicious," she says, taking a bite of both options.

"Thank you. What about you? You have quite a large family, yes?"

"My parents are in a pack of four, but besides that, I don't have any siblings or a ton of other relatives."

"What was it like growing up with your parents being in a pack?" I ask her, and a wide grin takes over her face.

"Amazing. There was always someone around, you know? I always felt cared for and loved. And I grew up seeing what true love really looks like. I know a lot of people don't get that. Plus, having Omega, Alpha, and Beta parents prepared me for what my future could possibly look like. You just had two parents?"

"My mother and father were Betas, yes. They were never married and in the end turned out to be better friends than lovers."

She chews on her food, thinking over my words for a moment. "Are packs common where you grew up?"

"Yes and no. Back home, it is more common for an Omega to have multiple Alphas, but bonding isn't necessarily as frequent as it is here. Especially bonding with Betas or having Betas in a pack."

"Oh," she says, looking down at her food with crinkled brows.

Great, I'm already fucking this up.

"But that is back home. Connecticut is where I live now," I reply, hoping to salvage this.

"Really started this date off with a bang, didn't we?" she says. I feel it too. All this time with platonic flirting with no expectations of it going anywhere. But now that she's in my home, things are real, and neither of us really know how to act.

I let out a small laugh and shake my head. "I know this isn't casual for you, Sloane. It makes no sense to pretend otherwise."

She places her elbow on the granite, her fist under her chin. "You know, your no nonsense bullshit is one of the things I like most about you?"

"Are you sure it isn't my dazzling looks?"

"Do you want me to tell you how handsome you are, Bram?" she teases, and I thank the stars I didn't fuck this date up before we've had our meal.

"It wouldn't hurt."

She leans forward, staying in the same position. "I think you're one of the most handsome Alphas I've ever met. Not to mention your scent," she says.

"What about my scent?" I ask, leaning forward, getting a hit of hers. I've never been one for compliments, but I may become addicted to the soft affirmations leaving Sloane's lips.

"It's rich and masculine. Your house smells like you," she says in a whisper.

I lean over the countertop, getting into her space, analyzing all the brown and yellow speckles in her green eyes.

"And what of your home? Does it smell like peaches and sunshine?"

"Is that what my scent smells like to you?"

I circle the counter, and she swivels her chair to face me as I cup the back of her head, finally feeling the soft strands of her hair on my fingertips as I lean in, my nose touching the soft skin of her neck as I inhale her scent deeply.

She perfumes at the motion, her scent only getting thicker as I hear a soft gasp leave her lips.

"You smell sweet. Like a peach soaking up the sun on a warm, sunny day. The sunshine loves you, I bet."

Her hand wraps around my wrist as I inhale her scent even further and do my best to not let the sweet little Omega in front of me know that I'm getting hard. But there's no way she doesn't scent my arousal.

I want her. More than I've ever wanted anyone. With our scents so heavy, I'd have known by now if she was my scent match. A pipedream for most Alphas and Omegas, but fuck, this has to be close.

I'm going to do whatever it takes to make sure I get a hit of her peachy scent for the rest of my fucking life.

"You smell earthy. Like spicy citrus," she whispers out. Her small hand grips my wrist as I pull back and look at her.

The air around us feels palpable, but this wasn't my plan. My plan was to take things slowly. To really get to know Sloane before we took anything further, and while that's still my intention, I can't deny how badly I want her right now.

"Bram?"

"Hmm?" I mumble, glancing down at her soft pink lips.

"Are you going to kiss me?"

I glance back up at her eyes, my hand sliding from the back of her head to cup her jaw. She's so much smaller than me that it feels like my hand could span her whole face.

She's delicate, and I find myself wanting to take care of her and give her whatever she wants.

"My intention was to take things slow with you," I say, my hold on her face gentle.

Her soft skin is a complete juxtaposition to my large calloused hand.

She licks her lips, and now all I want is a taste.

"I'm looking for my pack, Bram. I'm not looking for casual."

I can't help but to smile at her honesty. It's one of the reasons I like her so much. She's direct and says what she means. There's no deciphering her words. She's an Omega who knows what she wants, and I can't fault her for that.

"I'm not looking for casual, but I'm also not very fond of sharing," I tell her honestly, wanting to give her the same respect that she's given me.

"You'd have to learn. I know what I want, Bram. I like you. I want to know you better in so many ways. But if you can't handle pack life, I should leave now before we take this any further."

My gaze searches hers and then back down to her lips.

Can I do this?

I know I have what it takes to care for an Omega; I have no doubt in my mind I could be a loving, supportive, and caring Alpha. But can I share? Can I give up control and work with others?

I'm a team player, but at times it could be hard. It's something I had to work long and hard to overcome. But the NHL was important, hockey was important, so I overcame and continue to try and be a better teammate.

It seems like zero to one hundred as a first date, but I knew this about her before she came over. Sloane is a pack Omega through and through. And the most precious things are the ones you have to work hard for.

Just like I did with hockey, I'll have to find patience and understanding. Because I've never felt like this before, never this early and never this strong.

Sloane is worth it.

I prove this to her by leaning forward and placing my lips against hers in the softest show of affection. Caving to her wants feels as easy as breathing.

She sighs against my lips, her body relaxing as I do my best to assure her through the kiss.

Our scents intermingle, and I shift my body closer to hers. One of her small hands fists my shirt, and I have to hold back a moan that wants to slip out of my mouth.

Has a kiss ever felt like this for me?

No. Not even close.

I don't know if it's because Sloane is an Omega and my Alpha nature calls to her, or if it's just the strong, lovely woman herself. But I want more. I want everything.

It makes me lose control, placing my body closer to hers and parting my lips to kiss her deeper. The small Omega moans into my mouth, and my chest rumbles with a satisfied purr.

Her nails are digging into my shirt, and she shifts her body to the edge of the seat, her thighs touching my own legs. What I wouldn't do to pick her up and toss her on the counter and devour her whole.

"Alpha," she whispers against my lips, causing me to snap back to reality.

I pull away from the kiss, which is the biggest test of self control I've ever had in my life.

"This won't be easy for me, but I will try. For you, Sloane, I will try."

She opens her eyes like she was in a slight haze, my shirt still fisted in her hand.

"Wait. You were serious about taking it slow?" she says, blinking at me, and I shake my head and laugh, my hand sliding from her jaw to press against her delicate collarbone.

"Very serious. I want to court you. I want to make sure this is truly something I can do."

She licks her lips, tasting me, and I nearly lose it. Instead, I change the structure of the evening.

"We should go for a walk. Unless you want more to eat?" I ask her.

"Are you trying to kick me out of your house?" she asks with narrowed eyes.

"If we stay in my house, I worry I will do very un-gentlemanly things to you."

"What if I want you to? What if there's something even better on the menu?" she whispers.

She was sent to test me, I realize. Sloane is a lesson in restraint and patience sent by the universe.

"You're a very dangerous Omega," I tell her, which makes her laugh.

"Alright, fine, Mr. Take It Slow. Let's go for a walk. We can talk more and get to know each other."

I let out a sigh of relief and remove my hand from her skin.

"I'll grab your jacket."

"It's not that cold outside."

"I'll grab your jacket," I repeat, and I swear she pushes her thighs together.

This Omega is the ultimate test indeed.

SLOANE

CHAPTER 7

Bram holds my hand as we walk around his development for what feels like hours, both of us talking about our childhoods, what we do and don't like.

He's exactly what I thought, rough exterior but gooey on the inside.

The fact that he isn't a sharer but wants to try for me already has my little Omega heart squealing. Yes, I indeed can change his mind.

It's honestly a little pathetic on my end. But what started as infatuation before the night began is now a full-blown crush. I'll probably be doodling Bram Nilsen designs or the number forty three and then laminating them for preservation purposes.

Being "all in" kind of people seems to be a common thread that both Bram and I have. But there's still a big fat elephant following us as we walk through the pretty tree-lined streets of his neighborhood.

Sharing.

We've brought up the fact that I'm looking for a pack, but there's so much that goes into that, like dating other people while still getting to know Bram.

I know one Alpha will not be enough for me during my first

heat, and I also can't conceptualize the idea of going into heat without feelings. I need that connection almost as much as I want to bond and build this dream life for myself.

"Should we talk about the pack stuff?" I ask him, squeezing his massive hand.

He looks out over the lake, and some weird growling noise emanates from his chest. I definitely didn't forget how he purred earlier when we kissed. Part of me wants to climb him right now and make him do it again while we make out.

But as much as I want to change his mind on his sharing stance, I don't want to fundamentally change him. He wants to take it slow, it's something that's important to him, and as badly as I'd like to just test drive his knot, I'm going to have to be patient.

"I think it would be best that I don't know until you've decided someone is worth your time," he says, and I click my tongue, wondering if that's the best way to go about this.

I try to think back to my mother Willow's stories of how they became a pack; it wasn't all smooth sailing, and I don't expect building my own pack to be any different.

Bram is adjusting for me, so I'll do the same for him.

"Okay, deal, we won't talk about it until I think it's worth bringing up. But should I tell them about you?"

"Yes," he says quickly, and I bite my lip.

I'm not sure how well this possessive Alpha will do in a pack setting, but I already like how intense he seems about me. Now I'd like to double it by two more men who will be equally as obsessed with me.

Maybe it's weird that the two other people currently invading my thoughts are two people Bram knows.

But he just clearly said he didn't want to know until it was serious. I only have a friendship with Max and Ethan, no matter how cute or intriguing I find them. Again, counting my chickens before they hatch.

The sun has long set as Bram walks me over to my car. The

large Alpha seems a little lost for words and how to act when I unlock the vehicle and stand there.

"Bram?"

"Hmm."

"Kiss me good night, and tell me what a lovely time we had."

He gives me a rare smile, one that tells me that I was right about him. That this pull toward him wasn't just because of his scent or looks. There's something more here, and we'd be fools not to explore it.

His large hand cradles the back of my head, and I quickly realize I'm addicted to the sheer size of him. Maybe it's because I know he'd be a great protector or I like feeling small. Either way, I want his hands to explore more than just my face.

Feeling bold, I place my palms against his muscular chest that's tragically covered by a tight gray T-shirt.

"I had a lovely evening. Can we do this again when I have another free day?" he asks, and I nod.

I'm more than familiar with a professional hockey player's schedule. I knew exactly what I was getting into when I approached him and laid all my cards out on the table.

He has to lean down significantly to kiss me, and I take that moment to really explore his chest.

Good lord, I might just faint when I see him shirtless.

His lips are soft and sweet, completely different to the way he usually carries himself. I can tell he's using all of his self control, which makes me want to break it even further.

I've never been much of a rule follower, and when I want something, I want it. But I'm also trying to respect his wishes.

We'll take it as slow as I can possibly tolerate.

When he pulls back, I groan in frustration.

"Patience," he tells me, rubbing his thumb along the back of my neck.

"I'm not the most patient."

"I know you aren't," he says with a smile. "Text me as soon as you get home?"

That sends a flutter in my belly as I nod my head and begrudgingly get into my car and drive home from what might have been the sweetest date I could have ever asked for.

I don't live far, and as soon as I park and walk up to my apartment, I send him a message.

Home safe.

BRAM

Think of me. Good night, Sloane.

I melt into my mattress and dip into my toy drawer to take care of this built up sexual frustration and do exactly as he says. I come alone, but the idea of his scent and body are in the forefront of my mind while I do.

※ ※ ※ ※

Changing a mascot's uniform is a lot harder than I thought it would be, but the owner, my dad, and the marketing team have all agreed to my changes. It took a lot of big Omega doe eyes and comparing us to the other conference team mascots, but they crumbled under my persuasion.

I collected the pantone colors, created a sketch with extremely detailed instructions, and sent it off to a local woman who seemed to do work for the furry community. I just so happened to leave that aspect out of my presentation.

I also don't let it get to my head when she tells me it's the most detailed instructions she's ever seen for a costume, and she's fortunately agreed to move us up in her schedule.

Finnegan the Fox should have a brand new look right before the Humane Society ribbon cutting and the first game of the season.

I already exchanged numbers with Max and Ethan so that we can plan our meetings. I could have taken it from the employee registrar, but I'm attempting to not break any more rules than necessary.

> Me: Check out the new Finnegan the Fox costume.

ETHAN

Holy shit, Sloane. You're a genius.

MAX

Less Rabid, more like that animated Fox with charisma.

I cover my mouth in laughter, realizing the cartoon Max is bringing up. Now that I look at it, he isn't completely wrong. Though Finnegan is wearing a home jersey and not a slouchy button-up shirt.

ETHAN

Way to make it fucking weird, man.

MAX

Am I wrong?

> No, you're not wrong.

ETHAN

I feel sexualized.

> Anyway. It will be here before the Humane Society event, so we can unveil it then. Max, I need you to think of some item you can bring for the kids to sign and prepare for a hefty donation.

MAX

You got it, boss.

My stomach does a little flip, and I feel a little of a fuck it moment coming on.

> Do you two want to meet to discuss the event?

ETHAN

I have a shift at the diner, but we could meet
after. I'll treat you two to some pie.

MAX

Sly fox with his sly pie. I'll be there at eight.

ETHAN

Sloane, I don't feel safe. I need hot fox
insurance.

I'll see you two weirdos there.

I smile to myself, setting the phone to the side, and try to focus on the rest of my day. I schedule a few posts and plan out a thorough schedule for the team and my side project for Max and Ethan.

There may be some intervals of daydreaming, but I'm thoroughly knocked back into reality when my dad knocks on the side of my cubicle.

"Sloane, hun," he says. I have a smile, which quickly fades as I see my pinched face grandmother beside him.

Her back is arched straight, her blonde and gray hair in a tight chignon as she eyes my cubicle with disdain.

"Kristoff, why is she working? Is your pack on hard times?" she says.

My father takes a deep inhale through his nose and shakes his head. "No, Sloane wanted to work."

"You are pretty and young. You should have a pack by now," she says, not pulling any punches and hitting me right in the gut.

"Oh, didn't you hear? I'm going to go to one of those facilities where you have your heat serviced."

Her mouth parts in shock, and my father sighs.

"She is not. She's currently working with a matchmaker."

"You're here early, Mormor."

"Yes, well, I seem to have confused my dates," she says tersely. "It would be such a shame if this was the last time I could visit the states with no great-grandchildren in sight," she says, and my mouth drops.

"Right. Let's get to lunch. Sloane, we'll see you at home."

"I have a thing this evening. I won't be there for dinner."

"Sloane," he says more sternly.

"Sorry, I can't change my plans. I wasn't expecting her till tomorrow."

My father huffs out a breath. I can feel the tension radiating out of him. It's the effect she has every time she visits.

"This is much smaller than the other team's facility," she says as my father gives me one last pleading look. I shrink away, turning back to my computer.

I decide in that moment, I'll just go to the diner early cause there's no way in hell I'm coming home to that disaster.

There's another knock at my cubicle, and I brace myself for another god-awful conversation. But I'm greeted by a delivery man holding a vase full of peonies instead.

"Sloane Applegate?" he asks, and I nod my head as he has me sign for the flowers.

When I open the card, my heart flutters.

Sloane,
Pretty flowers for a pretty Omega.
Missing you,
Bram

It's short and sweet, just like him. I put them on display on my desk but pocket the card so no one sees. If my dad asks, I'll tell him it's one of the matchmaker suitors. I inhale the floral scent and swoon.

Bram fucking Nilsen is courting me.

Maybe I can pull this all off after all.

MAX

CHAPTER 8

It's probably pathetic that I'm at the diner so early, but I had nothing else to do. I considered going to Owen's house, I even put on more deodorizers, but when I got the text from Sloane and Ethan, I felt relieved that I didn't have to invite myself over to his pack's home.

Our relationship has come a long way, but we're definitely nowhere near sitting around a campfire and talking about our childhood trauma and all of our deep-seated feelings of resentment.

Hard fucking pass.

So instead of sitting in my stale apartment by myself, I'm going to pathetically sit at this diner for an hour and wait for Ethan to finish his shift and for Sloane to get here.

I smirk at myself, thinking about the Omega.

What in the hell is her dad thinking about, letting her work for the team? Don't get me wrong, she's clearly amazing at what she does. But good lord, it's hard not to stare at the sweet, confident redhead.

The diner is a bit of a shithole, but the food is good, so at least that's a plus. The bell overhead dings at my arrival, and Ethan is holding a tray of drinks and waving at me with a tattooed arm.

"Sloane's at the last booth in the back," he says, not able to stay and chat as he goes about his primary day job, which for some reason makes me feel guilty.

It's clear Ethan is an athlete and cares about being the mascot for the Foxes, he shouldn't have to work in a place like this too.

I head down the row of booths to the left and see the back of her head. A large man is leaning forward in the booth, invading her space, and I find I don't like that one fucking bit.

"Aw, come on, sweetheart, you're here all alone. Let me treat you to dinner," the man says, and as I approach, it's clear as day he's an Alpha.

"No thank you," Sloane responds, not even looking at the man, just browsing the menu.

"I can tell you're unbonded. What's a sweet thing like you doing here all by yourself?" he asks.

I'm finally close enough to the booth, my shoulder pushing the man in question to drop an unexpected kiss on the top of Sloane's head. I swear I get a hint of her scent in her hair, but I'm pulling back too fast to deal with this asshole to confirm.

"There you are. Sorry for making you wait, baby."

Her smile widens as she looks up at me. "It's no problem," she says in her soft voice.

I look over at my shoulder, the gruff Alpha looking irritated.

"Can I help you, pal?" I ask in a condescending tone.

"You shouldn't leave your Omega unattended like that. People might get the wrong idea."

I stand to my full height, having a few inches and way more muscle on this guy. I cross my arms over my chest and make sure Sloane is blocked from his view.

"And what idea would that be?" I ask, making it as uncomfortable as possible.

The man stumbles and waves me off before pouting and stomping his way out of the diner.

"Thanks for the save," Sloane says as I take the seat across from her.

"Does that shit happen often?" I ask, and she furrows her brow before nodding.

"You haven't spent time around many Omegas?" she asks, and I shake my head.

"I mean Owen, but when he designated, I was out of the house, and he was always doing everything he could to hide it anyway. Our mom and stepdad are Betas. Speaking of which, how the hell did he know you were an Omega?"

"I've been here before. I only started wearing deodorizers," she says with irritation.

"You don't hide your scent on purpose?" I ask.

"No. It's a stipulation for working for the team this year."

I smirk, and it makes sense. She's already a slight distraction with her beauty. I'm sure if she was perfuming all over the place, we'd all be tripping on the ice and unable to focus.

"It seems like you're one of the few Omegas out there who isn't trying to hide your designation."

She rips off a straw wrapper, folding it into a perfect square, before placing the straw into her water and taking a sip. Her deep green gaze searches my face.

"You just sound inexperienced. None of your conquests have been Omegas?"

I roll my eyes. "They weren't conquests. And there weren't as many as you think, and no, I've only ever been with Betas and Alphas."

That has her stopping her drink, popping her lips off of the straw.

"Men or women?" she asks, her hand twirling her straw.

I rest my arms on the table and smirk at her. "You tell me a secret, and I'll tell you a secret."

She squints at me and parts her lips for a moment, then closes them like she's trying to think about what to say before a smirk takes over her pretty face.

"It needs to be a comparable secret," I say, noting that I'm being a complete jackass. Flirting not only with the woman who is trying to help me with my reputation, but the coach's off-limits daughter isn't my smartest move.

"I was with a female Alpha once," she says, shrugging her shoulders.

"You didn't like it?"

"It made me realize my preferences lean more toward men. I think if the right female Alpha came along, it could change things, but our chemistry wasn't there."

"The answer is yes, both," I reply to her earlier question.

"Interesting," she says as Ethan comes over to our table.

"You guys are unfashionably early. Is there anything I can get for you while you wait?" he asks, taking out his little pad and pen. He's quite handsome, even with his faded gray T-shirt and questionable apron wrapped around his waist.

"I'll have the southwest omelet, please," Sloane says.

"Same," I reply, and Ethan nods his head as he writes it down.

"Ethan, order's up," a female voice says, and Ethan acknowledges them with a wave.

"Sorry, I'll get that right out, and as soon as my shift is over, I'll come hang out," he says, and Sloane gently grabs his wrist.

"Take your time, Ethan. We're early and in no rush."

Relief flushes the Beta's face as he heads back into the busy diner.

"What does interesting mean?" I ask Sloane, going back to our original conversation.

"Huh?" she replies.

"Why is it interesting that I've been with both men and women?"

"Oh, just that you were only ever pictured with women in the tabloids. So your interest in men comes as a surprise," she says matter of fact, and my guard drops suddenly, realizing there isn't judgment, just surprise.

"How many of these tabloids have you sifted through?" I ask, feeling some shame wash back. I don't want Sloane to think I'm this untrustworthy man whore. I don't know why I care so much about what she thinks, but I do.

"Which one are you most worried about, Mr. Connery?" she asks, and I can tell she's teasing me. Whatever she sees on my face has her hand reaching out and grabbing mine over the table. "I don't judge you, Max, if that's what you're worried about. There's nothing wrong with exploring your sexuality. I'm sure that it's hard being in the public eye."

I lick my lips and don't pull away my hand. Hers feels so small and smooth against my own.

"It was mostly to curb the loneliness," I say, and as soon as it leaves my mouth, I regret it. How entirely fucking pathetic of me, spilling my guts to this Omega. I go to pull my hand away, but the fierce woman grabs my hand even harder, not letting me.

"Hey," she snaps, forcing me to look at her. I don't see pity there, just passionate honesty. "Thank you for being honest. Being lonely sucks. But you have friends now."

"You and mascot?" I say.

"Don't call him that. You know his name," she says in a no bullshit tone. It does something to me. God, I'm going to get kicked off this team quicker than I'm on it if I keep flirting with her. But she said we're friends. I can be friends with a pretty, straight forward Omega, right?

"You and Ethan," I repeat, feeling guilty for referring to him as just mascot. It was rude.

"Yes, Ethan and I are your friends. We're both here to help your image and be your friends."

"Don't you have a ton of other people you'd rather be hanging out with?" I ask her, and she sighs.

"We've only lived here for two seasons. It's hard to make friends when everyone your age is finishing college or starting their lives. I've become friends with Piper, Charlotte, and a few other WAGs, but they're both super busy. Piper is working on her fellowship, and Charlotte has her hands full with the kids. So we're not all that different, Max."

"So you're lonely too?" I ask her.

She looks down at our joint hands and then back up at me. "Yeah, I suppose I am."

For the first time, I look at her beyond her designation or beauty, and I think I found a kindred spirit in the most unlikely of places.

We joke while we eat, and it comes so naturally, just eating dinner together and talking. I learn that Sloane likes organization, fashion, her favorite flowers are peonies, and she doesn't eat red meat. I tell her about my rookie season, some of my childhood, and what it was like living in California.

We've eaten and drank as much as we can stomach, and the diner finally slows down.

A disheveled Ethan unties his apron, bundling it in his fist. Sloane scoots over, and the Beta smiles before sitting next to her, an exhausted huff leaving him as he gets comfortable.

"Thanks for waiting," he says, and Sloane leans in.

"You smell like waffles," she says.

His dark brows furrow. "I'm a Beta. What do you mean?"

She smiles and shakes her head. "Doesn't mean you don't have a scent, maybe not one that perfumes. You must smell like waffles from working in the kitchen. I like it," she says, and I note she gets even closer to the Beta.

Why do I feel slightly jealous? And why am I not sure who I'm jealous of? Because to be quite frank, I'd like to sit between both of them.

Christ, maybe I need to go home and jerk off to get some of this tension out.

They are my friends, not my conquests like Sloane so casually put it.

"Oh." Ethan's cheeks heat, and Sloane touches his arm.

I've hardly spent time with Sloane, but it's clear physical touch is casual and yet needed for her.

"How was your shift?" she asks.

"Same shit, different day. My foster dad owns the place. All of my foster siblings and I work here. Well, minus a few," he says with a shrug.

"That's sweet. I'd love to meet him sometime," Sloane says.

"Yeah, sure. So the Humane Society event?" Ethan says, changing the subject.

"Right, well, you already saw the costume, but I was thinking maybe you need a signature song and dance."

"A dance?" I say, covering my mouth with laughter.

"Oh, you won't be laughing when Finnegan the Fox is trending and you're not, Mr. Connery," Sloane says.

Why does she have to be refreshing and call me out on my shit?

"I can definitely do that. I'm off tomorrow, if you want to help. If not, I can totally send you clips or something," Ethan says.

"I wish I could, but the antichrist is in town," Sloane replies.

"The antichrist?" I question.

"Yeah, my grandmother."

Ethan and I both laugh, and Sloane takes a sip of her drink.

"She's that bad?" I ask.

"Yeah, she's that bad. She came to town early, and I only saw her for all of about five minutes when I was asked why I don't have a pack or why I'm not pregnant yet."

It's one of those times I should bite my tongue, but per usual, I don't, the words spilling off my stupid tongue.

"Well, why don't you?"

Sloane and Ethan both cut me a glare so severe that if looks could kill, I'd be dead on the spot.

"I didn't mean that to be rude. I'm just genuinely so confused as to why you're single. Are you hoping to find your scent match or something?"

Ethan still looks like he wants to punch me in the arm, but Sloane softens and sighs.

"I may be a hopeless romantic, and despite what's happened on the team for Charlotte and Owen, I know how rare scent matches are. I'm not going to put my life on pause for a three percent chance in finding that perfect pheromone match. But I am looking for the perfect pack *for me*, and I have a lot of stipulations. One being I don't want to join a pre-established pack."

Ethan and I look at each other, clearly the both of us clueless as hell when it comes to packs.

"What's wrong with a pre-established pack?" I ask.

She rests her chin against the palm of her hand.

"Nothing. There's just something romantic about the idea of me being the reason my packmates love each other. I'm not really sure how to explain it."

Ethan tosses his arm behind her in the booth as he smiles down at her.

"It makes sense to me. You're the Omega, so the pack centers on you," he says.

"Does that make me sound like a spoiled brat?"

"No, it sounds like you know your worth," Ethan says.

It's at that moment I realize I'm not worthy of either of them, not their friendship or this attraction I'm trying to shove down. But I'm going to try not only to become a valued team member, but a true friend to the two kind-hearted people across from me.

❄ ❄ ❄ ❄

Your younger brother being your coach is honestly the worst experience of my life, and that's saying something.

"Your left side is weak. You've gotta practice more," he says, and I think about taking off my skate and slitting my own throat.

It's very melodramatic, but I remember I have two friends to live for now. Not to mention I'm fueled by competitiveness and to prove to my little brother that I'm just as good as he is.

So instead of talking back, I'm silent, going through drills and doing what I've been doing for the last five years.

Coach Applegate blows the whistle, announcing we're going to run a scrimmage. The backup goalie, Gagnon, is on the other side, and I'm stuck with Nilsen, Boucher, and Ahonen on defense.

"Try not to fuck this up and make us all look like shit," Nilsen says in a sharp tone, and I take a deep breath.

I honestly have no fucking clue what his issue is with me. It's like he decided he hated me our rookie year and just never let it go. Whatever his deal is, I wish he would move the fuck on and stop being such a monumental prick.

"Nilsen, let it go man," Boucher says, being the sweet Canadian prince he is.

The dickhead defenseman doesn't give him any shit as he just skates away, and I try to refocus on the scrimmage at hand.

I don't let any goals in, and my team scores two, which has me feeling a little better about my position on the team.

"Still need to work on that left side," my brother says as I skate off the ice.

Again, I just nod and hold my tongue as we funnel into the locker room, despite how much I want to tell him to leave me the fuck alone and to please get another job. When I was traded, I didn't know my baby brother was going to be coaching the goalies. At least I'll get a break from him on away games.

I just need to lie low, do a good job, and get a more permanent contract. Or get traded to another fucking team.

But even the thought of going somewhere else sours my stomach. I don't want to start over. I like the weather and getting closer to Owen, even if he is a dick right now. But most of all, there's something more with Sloane and Ethan. They might be the people I've gotten closest to since I joined the NHL, which is so pathetic. But last night meant something to me.

It might have been a meeting over basic diner food for Ethan and Sloane, but for me, it's the first time in a long time I've felt like me again. I smile to myself as I think about the three of us laughing and talking over pie last night.

The Foxes are going to be my team, and if dealing with Nilsen's surly attitude is part of that, then so be it.

CHAPTER 9

Hell exists, and it's currently nestled in the quaint town of New Haven inside of my family's home.

My dad, Henderson, looks like he wants to smoke a cigarette. My mom, Willow, looks like she wants to cry. My other mother, Rosemary, looks ready to kill someone. Then my big former hockey player father looks like he wants to crawl in a hole and die.

"Willow is still in her forties. She could easily have another child," my Mormor says, and I watch as my mother Rosemary grips her fork hard enough to bend the damn thing.

"Sloane's birth was incredibly hard on Willow, so we decided to not have any more children," she replies.

"You certainly could have bore children if you weren't so busy with your career," Mormor replies.

Both of my dads blow out air at the same time.

My mother licks her lips, grabbing a glass of wine and taking a deep, heavy swig, and mumbles something under her breath.

"Something to say?" Mormor asks, and my mother goes to open her mouth.

"Oh, that's right. Dessert. Rosemary, sweetheart, can you come help me?" my mom intervenes, saving us all from another battle of wills.

"Of course," she replies, taking a deep breath and following her Omega into the kitchen.

My Mormor wipes her mouth. She's a wasp of an old woman, frail almost as her hand clutches her water and she takes a sip. As ancient as she may seem, there's a spry nature to her clear blue eyes. She knows that she gets under people's skin, and she thoroughly enjoys it.

"Tell me more about this matchmaker. I assume they are connecting you with Alphas who are well established and financially competent." she says.

"Yes, well, her services are not cheap for Alphas. Being an Omega client is free."

"Yes, well, Omegas get their fair share handed to them, don't they?"

Great, now I fear my inherited temper is rising.

"Please, Mormor, tell me what's been handed to me?"

"Don't act stupid, it's unbecoming. Omegas are revered and treated like spun glass. While I believe a woman's place is in the home, Omegas take it too far. I had hoped you'd be a Beta," she says.

"Mother, that's enough," my dad steps in. I can tell he's about done too. She hasn't even been here for two days.

"What, am I not allowed to have an opinion?" she responds.

"There's an opinion, and there's being hurtful. You're being callous for no reason," he replies.

"I'm sorry I'm such a horrible mother and Mormor. It must be so difficult."

"Jesus fuck. I'm going to go help with dessert," my Beta father says, excusing himself, leaving me with my dad and this mean old bitch at the table by ourselves.

My dad rubs his temples, trying to keep his cool and keep the peace. She visits once a year, if that, so we always try to make it work. But I almost wonder if it would be better if we severed ties completely.

"I shouldn't have come, it seems," she says, laying the narcissistic, passive aggressive bullshit even thicker.

"You know what, Mom? Maybe you shouldn't have," my dad says. My mouth gapes open as he pushes back from his chair and heads to the kitchen.

She dabs her mouth, her lips pinched. Her face looks harsh when she makes that face, and I wonder what exactly happened to her to make her like this.

"Hopefully you don't treat your parents this poorly when they're my age," she says, and I let out a sigh. "Well, dear, by all means, if you have something to say, you may as well speak your mind."

"Every time you come here, you cause a rift. You're mean for no reason and constantly pick at everyone's flaws. It's hard to have you here."

She smiles, and it almost feels wicked as she taps her water glass.

"Great, now that we're being honest. You should be ashamed that you're still living here, poaching off the generosity of your parents. You should have long had a pack and be well on your way to starting your own family instead of impeding on the life of your parents. Kristoff has spoiled you and made you too soft. You're embarrassing the Applegate name."

My breath hitches, and my eyes sting as I soak in her words.

As much as I try to be strong and confident, deep down in my soul, I'm a sensitive bitch who can't handle criticism.

I can feel the tears hitting the back of my eyes, and I just can't give her the satisfaction. Instead, I pull back my chair and storm out of the dining room to the backyard and head to my apartment.

She could have said something, but I don't hear it as I leave. I'm not sure why I let her get to me; I know my parents love having me here and would never push me out of the nest. But there's still some insecurity there, too, that I've held off on truly starting a pack till now, that I'm not where I should be in life.

I swipe at my warm cheeks as my phone buzzes in my pocket.

BRAM

I know it's late, but I am craving ice cream.
Would you be interested?

I'd love to. I'll meet you two blocks over.

BRAM

I'll be there in five.

You live fifteen minutes away.

BRAM

I was kind of counting on you saying yes.

I smile and wipe more of my tears away and grab a jacket from my apartment before heading down our driveway and making the walk down the neighborhood.

I wrap my arms around myself, fresh emotion hitting me now and then. I refuse to let her words get to me, for her to make me feel like shit. She hates everyone, her own son, her own granddaughter.

Someone so miserable shouldn't be the one to tell me how I live my life.

The sun has long set, and the cold air permeates around me as I wait for Bram to get here. Truly, it's not a great night for ice cream, but I needed to get out of that situation, and it's almost like Bram could tell I needed him.

I smile at that as his white SUV parks in front of me.

I open the door and slide into the passenger's seat, and as soon as I do, Bram is grabbing my face with his massive hand.

"What's wrong?" he says, and I shake my head. "Sloane," he says in a deep tone, not an Alpha voice, but still deep enough to do something for me.

"My grandma is in town, and she's mean as hell. She said some things at dinner that upset me."

"She made you cry?" he asks, his fingers lightly digging into the soft flesh of my jaw.

I don't know why, but him asking about it brings even more fresh tears. Bram curses under his breath, removing his hand from my face, which only makes things worse.

But then I realize the only reason he stopped touching me was to move his seat back as far as it can go.

"Come here," he says, and I don't know why, but I don't hesitate as I climb over the center console and fall right into his arms, which he firmly wraps around me.

His hand nearly spans my back as he moves it up and down. I'm not sobbing, but I'm also trying to keep my shit together.

My ear is pressed against Bram's heart as I grip his shirt like a lifeline. A rumble starts in his chest as he begins purring.

Interesting, so he uses it as a soothing technique and when he's turned on. Either way, I like it. No, I more than like it. The deep rumble and his thick, earthy scent wrap around me.

I feel safe.

My body relaxes, my eyes aren't burning anymore, but I soak up all his Alpha goodness. I'm not about to turn down this epic cuddle. He's so big, warm, and cozy.

"Better?" he asks.

I rub my face against his chest, absently scent marking him.

"Yeah, it's better."

He clears his throat and stills for a moment; I realize then I may have been inadvertently grinding on him, and the cab of the car smells more like peaches than masculine citrus.

I pull up to where I'm sitting in his lap, the steering wheel pressed against my ass. His hands are on my waist, and I like that he doesn't pull back.

"I didn't mean to cry all over your shirt," I say, looking at the small tear stain.

The purr of his chest has slowed, almost nearly nonexistent now, and I kinda want it to come back.

His one hand comes up, and the pads of his fingers wipe away my tears.

"You can come and stay at my place if your grandmother is a problem," he says.

I smile, a typical man trying to solve shit and not talk about it.

"I have my own apartment over the garage. Not that I wouldn't mind staying over at your place sometime."

"Other than your grandma, you've been okay?" he asks, and I nod my head.

"Been busy getting things together for an event. Helping some guys with their social media presence."

"Who?" he asks.

"Ethan and Connery."

He scoffs at Connery's name; I don't miss that for a second.

"Who the fuck is Ethan?" he asks.

"Oh my God, you're just as bad as my dad. Ethan is Finnegan the Fox. The mascot," I reiterate.

"Why the mascot?" he questions.

"I'm going to make him an internet sensation," I reply with a smile.

He squeezes my hips, pushing me down on his lap. This certainly isn't the same Alpha who said he wanted to take things slow, but I'm definitely not mad at it. My Mormor's words ring in my ears, and I wonder if I even have time to take things slow.

Maybe it's because I'm hot boxing his car or that I'm pressed against his dick, but I'm definitely not complaining about the way he's looking at me right now. Bram always has an intensity about him, but it's different from the man I've witnessed on the ice many times.

"I don't like Connery," he says, still looking at me intensely and holding me close.

"Why not?" I ask, and he shrugs his shoulders like I should know the answer. "He's my friend."

"Just your friend?" he asks, his body tensing in a not fun way beneath me.

"Yes," I reply, not lying. Max is only my friend, but I do find him handsome and charming. But if Bram really doesn't like him, he will need to stay a friend.

His grip loosens, and I don't like that one bit.

I drag my nails over his beard, glancing down at the soft lips I haven't stopped thinking about for days.

"There's only one Alpha's lap that I'm sitting on right now. Only one who wiped away my tears and who sent me my favorite flowers," I say.

He licks his lips, and his brown gaze meets mine.

"I'm glad you liked them."

"Do you know what I'd like even more?" I ask.

"What's that?"

He shifts me on his lap, and I'm not sure how I'm supposed to act like a decent woman when he's so hard and muscular underneath of me.

"If we could speed things up, just a little."

"What does speeding things up look like for you, Sloane?" he asks, his scent nearly causing me to malfunction.

"Touch me," I whisper.

"I am touching you."

I grab his hand off of my hip and place it above my pussy. The back of his head falls back against his headrest, and he lets out an agonized groan. But thankfully for my ego and my wanton body, he doesn't pull his hand away.

"You were just crying," he argues. Still not moving his hand, though.

"I'm not anymore. But if we don't get a little more skin on skin action, I just might cry all over again," I reply as a joke, but I might be serious.

It's been so long since I've had someone touch me intimately. Not only do I miss it, I want it from Bram. Our constant flirting has felt like the longest edging of my life.

"Please, Bram."

His eyes search mine, and something in my face must break him down because he slides his hand into my yoga pants, shifting them down my hips. Bram looks down at my panty-covered pussy before toying with the edges.

I can't take it anymore and grab his chin, leaning over for a kiss. His lips meet mine in an almost growl as he kisses me back, his fingers sliding over my wet clit and entrance.

His other hand fists my hair, controlling the kiss.

I feel consumed by his scent and his presence, not even caring that we're two blocks from my house or parked on the side of the street right now. I need this.

I need to feel alive.

I gasp when Bram pushes two fingers inside of me, our lips parting as I let the much-needed sensation roll through me.

"You're drenching my hand, Omega," he says in a gruff, deep tone. His chest is rumbling with a purr.

God, I'll never get enough of the fact that I do that to him.

"What are you going to do with it after?" I ask in quick pants.

The large Alpha smiles at me, his hand tightening in my hair.

"What would you like me to do? Lick it clean? Stroke my cock with it?" he asks, and I can tell he's absolutely serious.

"I want the first time you taste me to be with your lips on my pussy," I whisper, making him groan and shift my body harder against his cock.

"You're such a tease with this sweet wet pussy and that dirty mouth, little Omega."

"How am I a tease when your fingers are dee—"

He cuts my words off, curling his fingers inside of me while his palm rubs my clit. The moan that rips through me ricochets throughout his car as I place a hand on the ceiling while I ride out my orgasm on his hand.

I can feel how wet his hand is, and it only makes me come harder.

"Fuck," I hiss out. My body is shaking as my cunt grips his

fingers, wishing it was a knot. God, I bet Bram has a thick knot that would stretch me so good.

He slows down his pace, his fingers leisurely rubbing against my walls, and I come down from my orgasm.

I lick my lips and meet his eyes before smiling and kissing him again. This time it's slower, more sensual, as our lips explore.

Suddenly, my phone blares from the passenger seat, and I jolt on Bram's lap as I lean over and dig out my phone from my purse. His hand slides out of my pants, and they're still halfway down my thighs as I see my dad's name and picture on the phone.

I sit back down on Bram's lap, and he adjusts my panties and slides my pants back up, making for a very wet and uncomfortable moment for me.

"Hey, Dad."

"Sloane, where did you go? We dropped Mormor off at the hotel," he says.

"I just went for a walk," I say, looking over at Bram who rolls his eyes.

"Honey, it's dark. What do you mean you went for a walk? Where are you? I can come pick you up."

"That's okay, Dad. I'll be home soon."

"What did she say? I knew it must have been bad. Your mom lost it and told her she had to stay in a hotel until she apologizes."

"I don't want to talk about it," I tell him, and he sighs.

"If you're not home in twenty minutes, I'm going to come out looking for you."

"I'll be home soon."

I hang up the phone, and Bram looks at me expectantly. "Coach?" he asks.

"Yeah, he's just overprotective. I should be getting home," I tell him, though there's really no other place I'd rather be than here on Bram's lap. I don't get up to move, and he squeezes my hips.

"Do you want to talk about it?"

"No, you did everything I needed to feel better," I say, leaning down and kissing him softly again.

"We have our first string of away games next week," he says against my lips.

"I know," I reply.

"I'd like to talk on the phone or at least text every day to make sure you're alright," he says.

My Omega heart does a little flip in my chest as I lean forward and kiss him again. He's turning out to be the exact Alpha I thought he was.

"Yeah, I can definitely do that." I kiss him again, wishing I could spend all night with his lips pressed against mine. "Night, Bram."

"Text me the minute you get home," he tells me.

I nod and crawl back over to the passenger seat before getting out and heading home. I can sense a white SUV following me the entire walk back, but I do my best to ignore him and cherish the fact that he cares enough to watch me get home. As soon as I walk up the driveway, I send him a text.

> Home safe. Thank you for tonight.

BRAM

> I'm here for whatever you need. Good night, Sloane.

I smile down at my phone. I left the house this evening in shambles, but I'm returning feeling refreshed and cared for. That's exactly how your Alpha should make you feel.

CHAPTER 10

I have the bottom half of the Finnegan costume on as Sloane meticulously lint brushes some of the orange hair and makes sure everything with the jersey is in place.

She has a lint roller, brush, tape, scissors, and a needle and thread.

"Sloane, sweetheart, I think it's perfect."

She pauses for a moment, probably pondering the pet name, before taking her small scissors to the patch on the new jersey and cutting off the tiniest thread.

"It is now," she says, brushing down the orange fur. "You're going to crush it. I can picture it now: Finnegan the Fox holding a bunch of kittens for adoption. It'll blow up online, and everyone will be obsessed with you."

"I wouldn't go that far," I reply.

"Why not?" she asks, putting away her little kit.

"I mean, no matter what, it will be Finnegan getting big, not me. I'm just the Beta under the mask."

She tilts her head at me and gives me a shake of disapproval.

"Ethan. I'm going to hold your hand when I say this," she says, grabbing my hand. "You're fucking hot and talented. Acting like you're not isn't cute."

She drops my hand, and I blink at the woman before me.

"You think I'm hot?" I ask, clearly my brain only picking up that part.

"Come on, Ethan. You have the tattoos, the dark hair, you're super sweet and athletic. Yes, I think you're hot."

The fact is, I didn't think I had a shot in hell with Sloane. She deserves a pack who can buy her things and take care of her. I work at a diner, and I'm a fucking mascot part-time.

Sloane sighs.

"I'm really getting tired of asking people to ask me on dates, you know," she says, and I swear I'm having an out-of-body experience.

"Do you want to do something together after the event?" I ask, having no clue why she would even want to go out with me. Sure, she's stated she's my friend and that she's helping me, but a date... with me, a Beta by all means who doesn't have his shit together?

"I thought you'd never ask. That sounds great," she says with a smile, handing me the fox's head and helping me secure it to the body.

She messes around with the head a few times until she's satisfied. I'm still mystified and wondering how the fuck I'm supposed to get through this event knowing tonight is my shot at making a move on the girl who is well out of my league.

"Alright, let's go unveil Finnegan the Fox," she says, taking out her phone as "What Does The Fox Say" plays on the radio and we head outside to the ribbon cutting.

Kids are cheering and people are laughing as I bust out my best moves, doing a few flips and cartwheels before getting to the ribbon itself.

Sloane takes the mic and smiles at the crowd.

"Hello and welcome to the grand opening of the New Haven Humane Society. I'm Sloane Applegate, daughter of the head coach of the New Haven Foxes. I brought Finnegan the Fox here to celebrate as well as some of our amazing players. Please give a warm welcome to Nix Ahonen, Max Connery, and your fearless captain, Eli Beckford."

The crowd cheers as the three players come stand next to me.

Sloane hands me the scissors as the director of the new building comes up and gives a speech before thanking us, and I cut the ribbon. Sloane films everything between me and Max, making sure that we're together and separate, taking pictures with kids and animals alike.

I'm super dramatic with the kids playing games, and I even hold a few babies. I'm proud to say, not a single one of them cries in my orange furry arms.

It's announced over the speaker that Max Connery has paid the fees for the first one hundred animals to be adopted, and the crowd goes wild, more and more people coming up to him to take pictures.

It's no easy feat to make a brand new traded player with a past likable, but somehow they are pulling it off.

"Okay, I need to get a shot of you holding some kittens, and do some more backflips. Oh, and do that cute little thing with your hips again," Sloane tells me.

Thank fuck she can't see how red and sweaty I am under this suit.

I do the dance and some flips, kids are cheering, and I feel like I'm almost back in high school again. It's not that I miss high school itself, but cheerleading was something that always made me happy.

This version of Finnegan fills that void. No, this version of *me* fills that void.

When we get into the kitten room, Sloane thinks it's hilarious to grab two orange kittens and make someone take our picture.

"We're all orange, get it?" she says, and I laugh at her holding my arms out for the cats.

One is sleepy and lazy in my arms as the other one uses the fur of my suit for purchase and climbs up on top of the mascot head. Sloane gets every moment of it on camera, and I can tell she's pleased with the amount of footage and content she got tonight.

I hand her the one kitten, and I have to get down on my knees so she can pry the other one off my head.

"Mr. Finnegan," a small voice says, approaching us, and I stay on my knees.

I tilt my head to let the small child know that I'm listening. Rule number one of being a mascot is you don't speak and ruin the illusion.

"My daddy loves the Foxes, but I love you. Can you sign my jersey?" he asks with his little lisp. He can't be older than four, he's wearing a Foxes shirt, and he hands me a Sharpie with the cap on.

Sloane sniffles, leaning over and unclasping the Sharpie, helping put it securely in my hand as I sign his shirt. Sloane pulls out her phone, taking a few videos and pictures, and hands the mother her card.

"Send me an email and I'll make sure you and your family get seats to a home game this year," she says.

"That is so kind, thank you so much. I also think it's amazing you're working as an Omega. I saw the article on *Hockey Fanatics* about you and your father working together," the mother says, seeming in awe of Sloane.

It must be universal, then.

I can tell Sloane is holding in a grimace over the mention of the article. I also read it, and it did not shed a good light on Sloane. It read as an opinion piece on nepotism and Omegas in the workplace. But Sloane takes it in stride, smiling at the woman and the little boy.

"My daddy said Omegas shouldn't work. But you work with Finnegan the Fox. That's the best job ever," the little boy says.

Sloane bites her lip before nodding her head and smiling. "It is the best job ever. And Omegas can do whatever they put their mind to."

"I'm so sorry," the mother whispers to Sloane who waves her off.

"Make sure you send me an email, and we will make it happen," she reiterates.

I'm about ready to shed the mascot suit as Max and Eli come strolling in. They look friendly with each other, which isn't surprising. Eli Beckford is kind to everyone.

I rip the head off, taking a breath of fresh air. Sloane glances at me, and I wonder if I look like a sweaty mess. But that can't be cause I swear I can smell the faintest hint of peaches. There's no way I have this Omega perfuming. No way. Besides, I haven't really been able to smell her since the start of this new season.

"Wow, Sloane. You did an amazing job," Eli tells her. Both of the men halt; can they smell her scent too? Or am I delusional? I can't smell anything now, so I must have imagined it.

Pure masculine pride rips through me as I give a shit-eating grin at Max.

"Thanks. Honestly, Liz did a lot of work. I just took over for her."

"Don't sell yourself short. You crushed it," Max says, slinging an arm over her shoulder casually. Is this motherfucker trying to put some claim on Sloane?

Eli notes the motion but doesn't comment.

"I'll see you tonight for our flight to Dallas. Gotta spend some time with the wife and kids before we head out," Eli says, waving us all off.

"Getting casual with the captain, are we?" Sloane says, bumping her hip against Max's leg.

"He's actually pretty fucking nice."

"Speaking of nice, your donation was great, and the rally towels were a good call."

"Thank you," Max says, his cheeks heating. "I appreciate you for thinking of me to join the event and show people I'm not a complete dick."

"Key word being *complete,*" I toss in, and the large Alpha narrows his eyes at me.

Sloane sighs. "I got a lot of great videos. I'll be posting throughout the week. I was thinking about another way you could help and also improve your image," she says.

"What's that?"

"I'd like to hold a fundraiser for Liz's husband. See if we can't offset some of their costs."

"I'm there," he says. He leans down and kisses the top of Sloane's head almost absent-mindedly, taking them both by surprise. "Uh, yeah. Well… I got to go get ready for the game. It was good seeing you both," he says, clearly feeling awkward.

I'm glad I'm not the only one.

"Did he just kiss your head?" I ask her.

"Yeah, for the second time," she says a little wistfully as we watch his large ass retreat out of the building.

"The second time?"

Sloane waves me off. "Some Alpha at the diner was being aggressive with me."

I hold the head of the fox against my hip.

"Who was it? I'll make sure they don't come back again."

"It's not a big deal. I can handle myself. Plus, Max was there anyway."

I nod my head, still not liking it one bit. "Let me go change, and we can head out."

"Sounds good. I'll meet you out front."

As soon as I get to the back, I immediately regret not bringing better clothes to wear, but how was I supposed to know that Sloane fucking Applegate was actually going to give me the time of day?

I slide up my khakis and toss on the gray hoodie I've had for years, making sure I properly store the mascot costume, before going outside and looking for Sloane.

She's sitting next to the same boy who had me sign his shirt. I look around for his mother and see her animatedly speaking on the phone.

"My daddy doesn't like cats," the boy says sadly.

Sloane looks frustrated but is able to keep her thoughts about this kid's shithead father to herself. The man is clearly a huge selfish prick.

"That has to be hard when you like cats," she says.

"The hardest. I just want one so bad."

I come over and step behind the bench; the kid looks me up and down, completely unimpressed. Apparently, Finnegan is hot shit. Meanwhile, I'm just some asshole standing behind a park bench.

"This is my friend Ethan," Sloane tells him. "This is Harrison. His mom is trying to convince his dad to let him get a kitten," Sloane says.

I look around, wondering why she just left her kid with Sloane, even if she is only a shouting distance away.

"I wasn't allowed to get a pet either," I tell him, and he finally takes an interest in me.

"Was your dad mean too?" he asks, and I watch as Sloane attempts to stifle her emotions down.

"I had a foster dad. He was allergic, and we didn't have enough space. Maybe there's a reason."

"Maybe," he sighs.

"That's a pretty sick Finnegan the Fox signature you got there," I tell him, and he smiles.

"Miss Sloane and Finnegan invited us to come see a game," he says enthusiastically.

"You know, Miss Sloane is great at her job. I bet we can get you your own stuffed Finnegan the Fox to take home."

"You mean it?"

"Totally, little man," I reply, and he looks proud of himself as his mother comes back to the bench.

"I'm sorry about that. Harrison, sweetie, let's head home. I'll make sure to email Miss Applegate as soon as I get a moment.

Thank you again," she says, grabbing her son's hand as they head to their car.

"You were sweet with him," Sloane says.

I shrug my shoulders. "I had a lot of younger foster siblings," I say, waving her off. "Do you have a car here?" I ask, and she points at a small little red car. "Do you mind if we pick it up later?"

"Not at all," she says as we head over to my ancient truck.

I open the passenger door, putting the suit in the backseat, before helping Sloane get in the car. When I get in the driver's seat, she looks over at me.

"So what should we do?"

I turn to her, realizing I can't take her anywhere fancy. But I think back to Harrison. He wasn't looking for anything fancy. He just wanted to be seen.

I'm going to show Sloane I see her.

"How are you on roller skates?" I ask her, and a wide grin takes over her face as I hightail it out of the parking lot.

SLOANE

CHAPTER 11

Ethan is on his knee, lacing up my rental skate, which I'm still not sure is completely sanitary. I had them show me four pairs in my size till I decided this pair met my standards.

"Tighter," I tell him as he tugs on the laces.

"That's what she said," he whispers under his breath, and I shake my head.

We're very clearly the oldest people at the skating rink at this moment and time. In fact, it must be some fundraiser tonight because all the kids are wearing some shade of neon as they skate around the rink.

"Alright, Canterbury Elementary. It's girls vs. boys. When the music stops, you need to stop skating. If you move, you're out."

"Oh, the girls are totally going to win," I tell Ethan.

"You wanna bet on it?"

"If the girls win, I pick what we do after skating. If you win, you get to pick."

"Deal," he says, holding out his hand. Up to his wrist is covered in tattoos, and I find myself wanting to get very acquainted with every piece of art on Ethan's body.

I tug on his hand, bringing him closer to my face.

"Something you should know, Ethan… I don't play fair," I say, shoving him away from me as I hightail it onto the rink and start zooming in circles as the music plays.

His eyes widen as he tracks me and tries to catch up to me on his skates.

He's got a lot more height on me, so it doesn't take him long until he's wrapping a long, tattooed arm around my waist, slightly lifting me off the ground.

"That was sneaky, Applegate."

"Who, me? I'm not sneaky," I protest as his fingers dig into that spot right underneath my ribs, making me laugh. "Put me down," I wheeze out.

Two kids skate by, giving us dirty looks. "Who let those freaks in here?"

Ethan puts me down as we both laugh. The music stops, and we both don't stop in time and have to skate to the center of the rink.

"Does our bet still count even if we're not a part of the winning party?" he asks.

"Oh, definitely. Girls are still going to win."

"Confident and cute?" he says, and I grab a fistful of his shirt.

"Ethan, baby. You have no idea."

The girls next to us are whispering. "He's a hot Beta, maybe that's why she's into him," one of them says, sending a ping of frustration throughout me.

I don't know if it's because I need to prove it to these little brats or if I need to let Ethan know his designation doesn't mean shit to me. But I tug on his shirt, making him bend down as I lean forward on the stoppers of my skates and give him a kiss.

"You being hot is very low on the list of why I'm here with you," I whisper against his lips before going back down on four wheels and glancing up at him.

He licks his lips, and I track the motion.

"It won't just be adolescent judgmental girls who think things like that," he says, glancing at the girls who got too uncomfortable and decided to move.

"I don't give a fuck about what other people think. You know one of my dads is a Beta, right?"

He shakes his head, and I grin, thinking about my dad. "My dad Henderson is one of the best people I know. He evens out my parents' pack, and he is seriously the funniest. I know Betas in a pack is considered unconventional, but those closed-minded assholes can go fuck themselves."

Ethan looks at me like I hung the moon.

"And there we have it, girls win!" the announcer says over the speaker.

Ethan seems lost for words as I grab his hand, the lights dimming as disco lights fill the space. "Come skate with me while I figure out what we're going to do with the rest of our evening," I tell him.

His hand feels right in mine. We continue to get a few odd looks as we skate, but I couldn't give a single shit.

I feel like I'm floating on air as we skate, joke, and the world seems effortlessly simple.

❄ ❄ ❄ ❄

"Sloane, this is a bad fucking idea," Ethan says.

"Don't worry, my dad isn't home. Plus, we parked down the street. They won't even know I'm home."

He's still reluctant but follows me in the dark as I lead us to the side entrance of the garage, and we climb up the stairs to my apartment.

Ethan looks around, taking in my space, and clicks his tongue.

"It's very clean," he says, and I shrug.

"Do you want a drink?" I ask as I open up my cabinet.

Ethan comes to stand behind me and glances at my options, which are organized by type of liquor and alphabetically.

"Might as well go with tequila because if your dad knows I'm here, he might fucking kill me."

I laugh and grab two glasses, pouring us both a hefty glass.

"My death's funny to you, Applegate?" he says, sitting on the couch as I hand him the drink.

"It's just so funny. Everyone fears the man who would read me *Franklin the Turtle* books in different voices."

"Well, we can't all be precious little Omegas, now can we?"

"Hmm. Precious, you say?" I joke, tucking my legs under me as I rest my head against the back of the couch.

"I don't need to have a knot or go fucking feral over your scent to realize you're special," he says.

I tip back some more tequila, hissing at the taste, before putting a coaster down and then my glass on the coffee table.

"Tell me more," I say, leaning more into his space and putting a coaster down for him as well, which he quickly utilizes for his own drink.

"You're kind, compassionate, patient, and you're the first person in a really long time who's believed in me," he says.

My heart breaks immediately, and I do my best to hide how much it hurts. But I'm terrible at hiding my emotions as Ethan cups my face.

"I didn't say that to make you feel bad."

"It just makes me sad you felt overlooked."

He laughs, resting his arm against the back of the couch. "Betas might take up most of the world population wise, but it's an Alpha and Omega-run world, and we all know it."

My heart fractures a little more as I grab his chin. He doesn't have a lot of facial hair, not like Bram. It's more scruffy like a soft five o'clock shadow around his jaw and chin.

"I think you might be pretty precious too," I tell him.

He surprises me by taking control after the soft words leave my lips. His hand cups the base of my throat as he kisses me passionately. I do my best not to compare him and Bram, but I notice instantly how fervently they both kiss.

But whereas Bram has a lot of self control, thankfully Ethan does not. He pushes me down, a whoosh of air escaping me as I fall onto my back, and Ethan crawls on top of me. His knee presses against my core as his elbows rest against the sides of my face.

His fingers tangle into my hair as his kisses become more exploratory, kissing my jaw, neck, and collarbone.

I'm not sure how to explain it, but his touch feels like worship. His knee shifts against my core, and I moan, wanting more than just friction.

His dark hair is soft in my fingers as I try to direct his head further south.

The Beta doesn't need the push as he lifts my shirt up and starts placing soft kisses against my torso before tugging down the cups of my bra, folding the material under my small breasts.

"Fuck," Ethan hisses before sucking a nipple into his mouth, making me arch my back and dig my nails into his scalp.

His tongue is deliciously indecent as he tastes, nips, and sucks on my skin.

He circles back to my mouth, my bare breasts rubbing against the soft fabric of his hoodie, which I grab at the hem and tug over his head along with his shirt. I pull away from his mouth to get a view of the body he hides away under an apron or his costume.

"God, you're beautiful," I tell him as I glance down at his lean torso that's decorated with black and gray tattoos.

"You're gonna give me a fucking complex," he says, grabbing my chin and kissing me hard, his tongue swiping in my mouth, the sweet and earthy taste of tequila thick in my mouth as he does.

He goes back to kissing my face and neck, stopping right behind my ear. "You're going to make me fucking addicted to you, aren't you? As soon as I get a taste of your peachy cunt, I'm going to be hooked for life, aren't I?" he asks.

My perfume goes absolutely feral as I grind my pussy harder against his thigh.

I can't deny that his words strike a chord with my desires. It's what I've been searching for, what I've always wanted. He doesn't need to be a scent match or a fucking Alpha; he just needs to be obsessed with me. And the way Ethan is touching and speaking to me right now, I think he's already halfway mine.

He doesn't ask permission or wait for my go ahead as he pulls up and unbuttons my jeans before leaning farther back to tug them off my legs. He grabs my foot, shucking off both of my socks, before kissing my instep and working his way up my leg.

Ethan's pretty amber eyes don't leave mine as he torturously kisses his way to exactly where I want him. He licks the outside of my panties, making them wetter than they already were. A deep hum of pleasure rumbles from his chest when he does, and it only makes me even more turned on.

There are no pheromones, no outside factors. I just want this man in the most carnal of ways.

He sucks my clit through the cotton of my panties, and my fingers tangle in his hair. Ethan holds my hips, his fingers dancing around the hem of my underwear as he eats me out with my panties on.

It's the best kind of torture.

He shows mercy on me, finally sliding the crotch to the side, and his lips press a delicate kiss against my clit before he starts ravishing me.

Ethan Heart eats my pussy like it's his last meal.

He sucks, slurps, and moans around my wet and needy cunt. All I can do is hold his head and let desperate whimpers fall out of my mouth.

His fingers are just as deft as his tongue as he pushes two inside of me. His half-lidded eyes glance up at me, and I fall apart as he sucks on my clit, curling his fingers inside of me.

As badly as I want to keep eye contact, my head falls back as a wanton moan escapes me.

I don't untangle my hands from his hair, and he still lazily explores me with his tongue before sliding his fingers out of me and putting my panties back into place.

He kisses my thighs as he moves to sit back on the couch.

"Can't say I wasn't warned," he says.

"What?" I ask. Clearly I don't have post-orgasm clarity just yet.

"Definitely addicted," he says, and I laugh.

I lean forward and press a gentle kiss against his lips, tasting my release and liking the way I taste on him.

When I pull back, Ethan is looking at me in a way that I always imagined my future packmate would. It's then I realize I haven't been completely honest, and a pang of guilt shoots through me.

"Ethan, there's probably something I should have told you before you did that."

BRAM

CHAPTER 12

I sit at the table, feeling more anxious than I have in a long time. I rub my temples and remind myself that this is what I signed up for.

It was Sloane's suggestion that we all meet outside of town, and I wonder if she specifically chose a public place so I wouldn't cause a scene.

A few deep breaths help curb my frustration over the situation as the reality sets it.

I want Sloane. Even with the small time we've had with each other, I know that Sloane is the Omega for me. I guess I had just hoped or imagined that this wouldn't happen.

She flat out told me she was looking for a pack. It wasn't ever going to just be me. But I can't deny it hurt all the same when she called me the third night I was away to let me know she had feelings for the *fucking mascot.*

I've tried to recall what he looks like, but I can't. I remember that his name is Ethan and that he's a Beta. Because Sloane all but bit my head off when I called him mascot. Which is what he fucking is.

Him being a Beta is probably the only reason I'm semi-holding on to my shit right now. If she wanted me to be introduced to another Alpha, I'm not sure how I would stomach it. I suppose this is a scenario I'm going to have to come to terms with sooner than later.

There's still a part of me that wants to court and do things right when it comes to Sloane. It's important that our foundation is strong. Then there's this feral, possessive side of me that wants my mark on Sloane immediately so every motherfucker knows that she's *mine*.

But she won't ever truly just be mine.

Even though I've known this from the moment Sloane told me to ask her on a date, it's still not an easy pill to swallow.

"Sir, would you like a drink?" the server asks me while I wait for the two to arrive.

"Water is fine, thank you."

He nods his head and leaves. As soon as he does, I see Sloane in a deep green dress walk in. The Beta holding her hand is tall with dark, shaggy hair. The longer I look at him, I realize I've seen him before but must have never paid close enough attention to who was beyond the mask of Finnegan the Fox.

I stand from the table as Sloane drops Ethan's hand and gives me a hug. Her body feels perfect against mine as I wrap her in my arms and get a hit of her sweet, peachy scent.

Even though we talked every night while I was gone, I still missed her. It didn't help that this has been hanging over my head this whole time.

"I know you two mostly know each other. Bram, this is Ethan. Ethan, this is Bram."

The Beta holds out his hand, and I shake it. His jacket rises up his arm, showing me the faintest peak of tattoos. His grip is firm, and he doesn't shy away from my stare, so I give him points for that at least.

Ethan looks around at the restaurant, almost like he's uncomfortable with the opulence.

"Thank you for having me," Ethan says kindly as we take our seats.

I'm not sure what to say, so the only thing that comes out of my mouth is a stupid, "of course."

Sloane takes a sip of her water and glances at both of us from the top of her glass.

"I made this really awkward, huh? Maybe we should have just met at your place, Bram. I just… I don't know. I didn't want either of you to feel you're being lied to or that there wasn't complete transparency. Building a pack from the ground up is no easy feat, but I really like the both of you, and I was just hoping that maybe you'd hit it off or at least become friends. I'm rambling," she says with a sigh.

"Dinner was a good choice. You've been clear with me from the beginning about your looking for a pack. So it's something we can all work through," I say, even if I'm faking being laid back.

Part of me wants to strangle the Beta sitting at the table. The other part of me is slightly intrigued and wonders what exactly Sloane sees in him.

"Well, you two already know each other from the team," Sloane says awkwardly.

"Not really," the Beta whispers.

I'm back to wanting to punch him.

It's been nearly a week, and I haven't had a moment alone with Sloane. Meeting this asshole is cutting into my time.

"Right, I'm the mascot, and I work at a diner on my time off. When I'm not at my one-bedroom apartment I'm usually at my foster dad's place," Ethan says, and I nod my head.

He's the mascot and works at a diner. What the fuck, Sloane?

"I play hockey, and then I go home," I say, and Sloane rubs her forehead.

Her phone vibrates on the table, and she mutes it, forcing a smile between us.

"So we all like hockey, that's something," she says, and I let out a sigh.

Maybe it doesn't matter how deep my connection with Sloane is, maybe I'm just not cut out for pack life. A feeling of loss and rejection fills me until Sloane grabs my hand and squeezes.

"Hey. You're here, you're trying. That's all I can ask," she says, and I search her face.

Her phone goes off again, and her brows furrow, but she mutes it again.

"Man, I don't know what the fuck I'm doing either," Ethan says, and my perception of him shifts ever so slightly.

Sloane's phone goes off again, and she turns the screen.

"I'm sorry, guys, I'm going to take this really quick," she says, and we both nod.

Ethan breaks the silence first.

"Listen, if you're wondering what the fuck Sloane is doing with me, I've already asked myself the same question a million times. The fact is, she's the girl of my dreams, and if you think you're going to go all macho Alpha on my ass, you can try. But I'm not going any-fucking-where, so bring it, motherfucker."

His speech makes a smile take over my face against my will. But the Beta has balls, and I like that.

I rest my chin on my palm.

"Do you think you could kick my ass, mascot?"

He looks me up and down and clicks his cheek. "No, but I'm pretty fast. I could tire your big ass out and then use my wiles to take you down. Some David and Goliath shit."

My smile widens.

"You aren't so bad," I reply, and his eyes widen.

"Is this some reverse psychology bullshit where you make me feel comfortable and then slit my throat in my sleep?"

I look him up and down and sigh.

"No, Sloane likes you, and I'm trying."

Ethan looks like he's seen a ghost as I say that. "You know, you have a bit of a reputation for not liking people."

"Well, I like Sloane the most. And what did you say? She's your dream girl? Same. Being a dick to you doesn't fit my agenda."

"Your agenda?"

"Making Sloane mine."

Ethan shrugs like he gets it. "Have you figured out the whole bit where her dad is terrifying and also the coach of the team we work for?"

"I have a five-year contract. I'm not going anywhere. What about you? How long do cute little mascot contracts last for?"

"Cute I'll accept. I'm not little," he says.

"Smaller than me," I reply.

"Isn't most of the population?" he says, and the smallest laugh escapes me.

Okay, Sloane. I get it.

"Sloane is helping me gain more popularity so that I can become irreplaceable."

"How does one even become a mascot? Is this one of those furry or *My Little Pony* things?"

Ethan laughs out loud and shakes his head.

"I was a cheerleader before. Didn't go to college and was looking for something outside of my foster dad's diner. There was an open casting after the first mascot threw up in his mask after a night of hard partying, and I got the job."

"Americans do love their cheerleaders. I'm assuming you were quite popular?" I ask.

He smirks. He's a bit of a cocky little shit, this one.

"Mmm. Very popular. With most of the cheerleading squad and the football team," he says confidentially. "What about you, Bram? You seem more like the scary kid who never spoke and everyone wondered if they were a psychopath."

"Never hurt my chances with the cheerleading or football team. The real football team, not this soccer shit you all have here."

Ethan tilts his head at this new piece of information.

"Does Sloane know that?"

"Know what?"

"That you play for both teams."

"Right now, I'm only on team Sloane," I reply to him. "So I don't see why that matters."

He takes a sip of his water. "I didn't think you'd surprise me, but here you are," he says, waving his hand at me.

I'm about to come up with a comeback when Sloane is clutching her phone against her chest with wide, vacant eyes.

"Sloane?" I ask.

She sits in her seat and grabs her water and takes a heavy sip. Ethan seems worried but lost on what to do.

I scoot my chair closer to Sloane's.

"Can I get you started with some appetizers this evening?" the server says. My focus is completely on Sloane.

"If you can come back in a little while," Ethan tells them.

I grab Sloane's chin and force her to look at me. Her eyes are unfocused.

"She's dead," she whispers.

"Who?"

"My Mormor. She was staying at a hotel. My dad went to check in on her now that you're back from your away games. She had a stroke," she says almost robotically.

"What do you need?"

"My last words to her were 'It's hard to have you here,'" she says as her eyes fill with tears as she tries to tug away.

I grip her face with both hands, not being delicate with her at all.

"You are a good person, Sloane. I'm so sorry this happened. But you are not to blame. This is not your fault. Tell me what you need, and I will take care of it all. We can leave now, I can take you home, we can go to my house. Whatever you need, let me take care of you."

She takes a deep breath, not crying but on the cusp.

"Can we go to your house? I'll tell my dad I'm staying with Piper," she says, and I nod my head.

I look over at Ethan. "Did you drive here?"

"We got a ride share," he says, looking at Sloane like he's trying to figure out what he can do.

I tug out my keys and hand them to Ethan.

"You drive. I'll sit with Sloane in the back. I live in East Rock," I tell him as he grabs the keys.

I take out forty dollars and leave it on the table for the server's time as I wrap my arm around Sloane and shield her through the restaurant before sliding into the backseat of my SUV.

I buckle her in and rub her thigh as she leans against my shoulder. She doesn't cry, but she doesn't speak either. Ethan doesn't turn on music, and we make the drive back to New Haven in relative silence.

I kiss the top of Sloane's head, and she melts a little more into me.

"Are you hungry?" I ask her, and she nods. "Grilled cheese back at my place okay?" And she nods again.

I give Ethan directions to my place, and he pulls into the driveway. I unbuckle Sloane and open my door, getting out and grabbing her hand to bring her inside.

She almost seems like she's completely disassociated as I set her up on my couch and wrap her up in a blanket. She sniffs the material and melts into the sectional as I head into the kitchen with Ethan.

I'm busy getting the frying pan, bread, cheese, and mayo out.

"You're good with her," he says, resting his hip against the counter. "Have you been around other Omegas before?" he asks.

"No. I don't know how to explain it. Everything with her is so instinctual."

"You know what, Nilsen? I think this might just work after all," the Beta says, slapping my ass where I stand at the oven, shocking me before walking back to the couch to look after Sloane.

Tonight is one hundred percent not how I expected things to go.

SLOANE

CHAPTER 13

I wake up on a bed that is somehow softer than my own and also smells like Bram.

I turn my head on the soft pillow that smells just like his rich bergamot scent and blink my eyes to see Bram sleeping right next to me. I'm not sure when I ended up in his bed or when I even fell asleep.

But everything from last night floods back to me.

It's weird because I don't feel sad, which only makes me feel even more guilty, which was my original feeling.

Bram sleeps on his back. One hand under the covers, likely in his boxers, and the other tossed over his head. He looks soft, almost gentle when he sleeps. But then again, that's the Bram I know.

He took charge last night and didn't even have to think twice to know what I needed.

My fingertips graze against his cheekbone, and his one hand quickly snatches mine.

"Good morning," I whisper.

"Morning," he mumbles, grabbing my waist and tugging me against his body. His nose is nestled against the back of my head as he holds me. "How are you?" he asks.

"Is it bad that I'm not upset?" I ask, feeling completely vulnerable.

How fucked is that? She was still my family. I'd known her my whole life. But there isn't this never-ending sadness rippling through me. Just a crippling guilt that my reaction isn't normal.

"I think family is one of the most complicated things in our lives. You do not ask to be related to them, yet you are. From what I can tell, the relationship was a tense one. It's okay for your feelings to be complicated."

I run my fingers along the veins of his massive forearm, lifting his hand and kissing it.

"Thank you for last night."

"You're welcome," he says, and I smile, liking that he didn't say some bullshit like it's no problem or acting like he did nothing.

"Did Ethan go home?"

"Your Beta is on my couch," he replies, and I turn around in the bed and search his face.

"I want this to work, Bram. Tell me we can make it work."

"He isn't so bad," he replies, and I smile and grab his chin and give him a kiss.

"If he wasn't in the other room right now, I think I'd make you consider your whole moving slow stance."

"I might be changing my mind," he replies.

"Is that so?"

"I missed you while I was gone. More than I've ever missed anyone. Not to mention I rubbed your slick on my shirt after I fingered you so I could bring your scent with me," he admits.

Oh, my sweet Bram, ever so honest.

"You rubbed my slick scent onto your shirt and used it to jerk off?" I ask.

He nods his head and cups my jaw with one hand. "Yes."

"That's actually pretty romantic, I'm not going to lie," I reply, and he smiles.

"Me, you, and the Beta. I can make it work."

"Ethan," I remind him.

"Me, you, and Ethan. I can manage that," he replies.

I smile at him and place a delicate kiss against his lips. "You have the day off on Wednesday?" I ask, and he kisses me again before nodding his head.

"Just me and you, we can do whatever you want."

"I'll plan something," he promises.

His bed is soft and warm. It doesn't hurt that it smells just like him either.

"I guess we need to get out of bed, huh? I probably should head home and see how my dad is doing anyway. Don't say anything to him or the team unless it's brought up."

"Practice is in an hour," he grumbles, resting the bridge of his nose against my neck. When I look down at the larger than life man wearing only boxers, I have to lick my lips and mentally do my best to try and calm myself down.

God, he's gorgeous. His chest is broad and muscular with a light dusting of chest hair that trails down to his boxer briefs, which are clearly housing a very hard to ignore cock.

"Ignore that," he mumbles.

"It's hard to ignore," I reply, not ignoring it and staring a bit at the impressive bulge in his black underwear. Fuck, I bet his knot is massive. Just thinking about the stretch has me wanting to climb him and see just how big it actually is.

Bram's hand slides from my jaw and down my body till he grabs a fist full of my ass.

"Little Omega, you better get out of my bed before my knot is deep inside of you and you won't be able to move for hours."

I lick my lips, my hand grazing down the hard muscles of his chest. His stomach flexes against the brush of my fingertips before he grabs my wrist.

"Just a little touch," I tell him.

"Sloane, I'm all over little touches with you, and I need all night to fuck you the way I want to."

I swallow heavily as his bedroom door flings open. Ethan is standing there shirtless with only his boxers on.

Fuck, he has slutty thigh tattoos.

"Oh, are we having some morning delight? I made pancakes. But this is better if you all are down for a third," he says with a wide grin.

Bram moans as he sits up, my hand no longer near his very impressive length. I just wanted to touch it a little.

"Another time," Bram says, grabbing a T-shirt and throwing it over his body. Ethan and I both look at him lasciviously.

Wait... both Ethan and I?

I glance over at him, and the hot Beta, with a stack of pancakes in his hand, leans against the doorframe.

"He's hot," Ethan says plainly, and then I glance over at Bram who's eyeing up "the not so bad Beta."

"He's good looking," Bram says with a wave of a hand before going to the bathroom.

Wait a damn minute.

"Sloane?" Ethan says, breaking me out of my mental calculations.

This is what I had always hoped for. Having a pack who are best friends is amazing. But a pack where everyone is lovers?

That's the fucking ultimate dream.

"Sloane?" Ethan repeats as the spray of the shower from the closed bathroom door breaks me out of my thoughts.

"You both think each other is good looking?" I say lamely.

"He's not really a man of many words, but I guess he doesn't have to be with a body like that," Ethan says with a shrug, and I laugh. He looks me over with a smile and sighs. "How are you feeling, though?"

A deep pang of guilt hits me. Not only did I not really feel bad before, but I was totally about to fuck Bram and Ethan if the stars had aligned just a few minutes ago.

"I'm okay," I tell him.

"Let's go feed you pancakes, and then we can have that beast of a man drive us both home," he says.

I want to live in Bram's bed and not face my problems, but I do. The pancakes are almost as delicious as this morning's revelations.

I scrub the hell out of Bram's scent off of my skin before getting dressed, adding my dreaded deodorizers and grabbing my phone, which has a ton of notifications.

When I switch over to the app, I grin, seeing that the press coverage from the Humane Society event is doing exactly what I wanted it to.

The comments on the video of Ethan are amazing, and would you look at that, it looks like I won the bet with my father, not that now is the time to bring it up, but it still fills me with a sense of pride. Ethan is good at what he does. He just needed the right push and media attention to get him there.

My smile quickly falters as I click the link to the article that was posted in *Pack Weekly*.

Lady's Man No More?
By Serenity Jade

It's been quiet in the world of New Haven Foxes news as the season kicks off. While it's definitely looking like another Stanley Cup isn't in the cards, it has me wondering if we have a goalie that's actually going to stick around for more than one season.

Most of you know Max Connery as our beloved Owen Connery's (Stanley Cup winner, Alexi Bandnin's Omega, and over all heartthrob) brother. Or maybe you know him from his reputation of being a womanizer who likes to party on the town.

Since joining the New Haven Foxes, it seems like the older Connery brother has kept his nose clean.

Or has he?

We spotted the goalie with his arm flung over none other than Sloane Applegate, the coach's daughter and his pride and joy. It's why she has her job on the team in social media management.

It makes this writer want to know: Is Max Connery's image improving? Or is he going steady with the forbidden fruit?

I roll my eyes and click out of the article. Serenity Jade is known for writing articles that are speculative and never fact checked. Case and point here, but the fact is, people read this trash, and no matter what, there will be rumors.

Here's to hoping that no one else on the team bothers reading this shit. The last thing I need is someone getting upset over something that's not true.

Though when I look at the picture of Max's arm slung over mine, I can't deny that there is some longing. I quickly shut that thought down as I put my phone away and head over to my parents' home. There are more important things to worry about than a stupid, inaccurate article.

My dad is in the kitchen, and I wrap my arms around him before he does the same.

"You okay?"

"Yeah, honey. I'm okay. What about you?"

"I just feel kind of guilty, that's all," I reply.

My mother Rosemary walks in, placing a kiss on my head before kissing my dad. "Leave it to Malin Applegate to fucking make people feel guilty from the grave," she says before going to the coffeemaker.

I have to cover my laugh, and my dad shakes his head.

"She was a hard woman to love, but she was my mother. We're

having her cremated. Her sister is going to hold a service back home," he says, and I rub his back.

"Are you going to tell the team?" I ask.

"No, it's none of their fucking business. Today is just an ordinary day. Do you need a ride to work?" he asks me, and I shake my head.

"No, I'm going to drive. Let me just go see Mom before I go."

My dad rubs my shoulder, holding a conversation with my mom as I head upstairs to my mother's nest. There's no doubt that she's there right now. I lightly tap on the door and hear her soft voice from the other side.

I open the door but don't enter.

A nest is a really personal space, and even though I'm her daughter and I can't be scented right now, it could still be upsetting. Honestly, it depends on where she is in her heat cycle.

I make sure to avoid the house completely when that business goes down. It sucked a lot when I was younger because we don't have any close family, so my parents basically rotated out of my mom's heat to watch me or they paid babysitters.

"Hey, sweetie, come take a seat," she says, tapping her massive beanbag chair.

I plop down next to her, and she rests her head on my shoulder. She grabs my hand and laces our fingers together.

"I called the matchmaker," she says.

Shit.

"I know you aren't going to her."

Double shit.

I go to open my mouth, and my mom gives me a look that says to save my lies for someone who will believe him.

"It's one of the players from your father's team, isn't it?"

"Did you talk to Dad?" I ask.

"Henderson might have crumbled under some light questioning," she says. "Plus, I saw some things online," she says, and I groan.

My Beta father and I are going to need to have a little chat. Part of me thinks about throwing him under the bus for smoking. But even if he didn't slip up, she would have seen that stupid article anyway.

"It is," I reply. I've never been great at lying to my mother Willow. I don't know if it's because she's also an Omega or just how incredibly close we've been my whole life.

"Kristoff will hate it, but he'll get over it. But you need to be sure you want to keep him. You know your father is going to put him through hell regardless."

"I really like them," I reply.

"Them?" she says with a laugh. Her long red hair falls behind her. "You're going to give him a fucking heart attack."

"Well, right now it's one player and the mascot."

She shakes her head and laughs. "You are my kid. But, Sloane?"

"Hmm?"

"I can tell your heat's coming around sooner than later. You need to be prepared for when the time comes, no matter what that looks like. Whether you want to wait to bond or bond before, but at least have that talk with them."

"Dad's gonna flip when they have to take off mid season for my heat," I say with a wince.

"At least it isn't during the Cup like that poor sweet goalie last year," she replies.

That makes me think about Max and how some feelings have been lingering with him, but Bram has all but stated he hates the guy. I'm asking Bram to bend so much already; asking him to be packmates with someone he hates is just too much.

"When did you know?"

"Hmm?" she hums.

"That you were going to go into heat?" I ask.

She's already given me the best education I could have asked for on being an Omega. Hell, on being a person.

"It's like an itch you can't scratch. Sometimes it sneaks up on you, and other times it's a gradual ache. Obviously feeling aroused is a part of that, but there are other signs too. Like needing comforting scents, only wanting very particular scents. If you need more touch than usual is another indicator. The pain usually only hits right before your heat is about to start, but if you're preemptive and sated, the pain shouldn't last long at all," she says calmly.

"I had hoped I'd be bonded before my heat," I say, feeling a little dreary about it all.

"You have time. Plus, a bond isn't required, just trust and proper planning. We both know you're great at planning."

I smirk. She doesn't even know the half of it. But her guidance has me thinking a little differently. If my heat comes sooner than expected, I need to be prepared and truly be in tune with my body.

We both relax into the soft beanbag.

"I was on a date with them when I got the call about Mormor."

"Leave that woman to ruin a date even from the depths of Hell," she says, and I shake my head as she laughs. "She was a mean fucking woman who never liked me. Your dad should have cut her out of his life years ago, but he's too forgiving and kind. You don't have to be sad, Sloane. If anything, just make peace with however you're feeling because it's valid."

"Thanks, Mom," I reply.

"Also, I'd appreciate a heads up before you tell your dad about..." She glances over at me, and I sigh.

"Bram," I whisper.

"I knew it. The alternate jersey you bought last year was his. But what about the new guy Connery?"

"We're just friends," I say with a hint of sadness.

"As long as you're happy, Sloane we'll be happy. Follow your heart and your instincts. Your body and your mind know what's best for you. You just have to listen."

"Thanks, Mom."

"I'm always here for my girl," she says as she kisses my head.

I think that despite my parents' upbringings, I've been gifted the best parents in the universe.

CHAPTER 14

It's post practice when my brother's mate Alexi Bandnin approaches me.

"Come to dinner at our place," he says. It doesn't seem like a question, more like a command.

I'm slowly thinking of an excuse as Ethan comes by and bumps me on the shoulder. "You still able to help me with that video tonight?" he asks.

Bless this fucking Beta.

Having friends isn't so bad.

"That's right. Shit, sorry, Alexi, another time?" I say.

"Hmm," the big Russian mumbles. "What videos does Finnegan the Fox need the goalie's help with?"

Couldn't just leave it alone? Could we?

"You're avoiding your brother," the over-perceptive Alpha says.

"Isn't it enough that he bosses me around all day at work? I'm not sure I can sit at your dinner table again while you and Piper try to make small talk between the two of us. The only things we have in common are hockey and our overbearing mother."

"Lori is the best," Alexi says lovingly.

I'm sure he would think so, considering the woman coddles my brother like he won't survive without her. At least she will be staying at their house when she comes to visit.

"Max said he would help me shoot some stunt videos," Ethan lies.

Alexi clicks his tongue before wagging his finger at Ethan before tapping the Beta's forehead. "Bad lying fox," he says before walking away and thankfully dropping the invitation.

"I just lied to Alexi-fucking-Bandnin for you, so you owe me," he says.

"I sure do," I sigh.

"Your brother doesn't seem that bad." Ethan responds.

"It's not that he's bad, it's just... I go over to his house, see his amazing pack, their fucking pictures winning the Stanley Cup, and how much better my brother is doing than me. It's pathetic."

"Nah, I think that's just what having a sibling is like," Ethan says, and I thankfully feel like less of an asshole.

"Really?"

"My foster siblings and I could get really competitive, and that was over dumb shit. I can't imagine what this feels like. I'm not judging you."

I sigh and rub my hand through my hair.

"Do you have any plans tonight?" I ask, not wanting to go home alone.

"Sloane's busy," he says.

"Didn't ask about Sloane, mascot. Asked about you."

He clicks his tongue, and a wide smile takes over his face.

"Let's go, goalie," he says, and I wonder what the fuck I just set myself up for.

"You've gotta be fucking kidding me," I say as Ethan takes one side of the couch and I take the other.

"You're the one who needed an alibi to get away from your brother-in-law," he says as we both take a breath and lift the heavy beige loveseat that's kind of a piece of shit.

"First off. It's my brother that I'm avoiding. Second off, where in the fuck are we taking this?" I ask as I go up the first set of stairs and he carries the bottom.

"My dad—foster dad—he doesn't really leave his place anymore. His current couch should be condemned. This one was on Marketplace for eighty bucks. So I figured I'd grab it for him and get that other piece of shit out of his place."

"No other foster siblings to help out?"

"No massive Alpha ones. Most of them are younger. Only Kimmy and Marisol still live in town."

"How many foster siblings do you have?" I ask as I heft the motherfucker around the bend to go up the second section of stairs.

"Who knows? Dave took in so many kids back in the day. Some stayed a few days, weeks, or months. Then there's kids like me who never left."

"You like your old man?"

"Yeah," Ethan says simply. "What about you?"

"My stepdad is cool. Mom's overbearing. Brother hated me until recently," I say with a shrug.

"Family shit is always complicated."

"I know that's fucking right. Christ, what floor does he live on?"

"Third," he huffs out as I continue up the stairs, both of us exerting our strength to get this piece of shit up the stairs.

Ethan takes out a key and unlocks the door.

"Hey, Dad," Ethan says as an old man with an oxygen tank turns off the TV and glances at the two of us.

"The fuck you got there?" his dad asks.

"You can't sleep on that shitty couch anymore. I got you a new one," Ethan says as we put the couch down.

The older man grabs his walker and takes a moment to stand, his oxygen tank trailing behind him.

"Looks nice, thanks, kid. Who's this?" he asks, tilting his head to observe me. His eyes are milky, and most of his hair is gone. He's clearly not doing so great.

"Max. He's the goalie for the Foxes."

A smile takes over the old man's face.

"See. What did I tell you? As soon as they got to know you, they'd love you."

"Dad," Ethan hisses.

"What? Bunch of stuck-up Alpha assholes. No offense," he says, glancing back at me.

"None taken," I reply. The old man isn't too far off. Until he introduced himself and there was a reason for me to know Ethan, I basically ignored him.

I feel guilty thinking about it. Ethan isn't someone who should ever be ignored. He's probably one of the most genuine people I've ever met.

"He's a great fucking mascot and a good man. That team is lucky to have him," he scolds, and I hold up my hands in compliance.

"I'm with ya, man."

"Sorry. It's just, he's my boy."

Ethan looks proud and embarrassed at the same time.

"Move that piece of shit out of here. I'll make you boys lobster rolls," he says, waving a hand and shifting his feet to make his way to the kitchen.

"At least this couch seems smaller," I say as Ethan and I carry the couch down the stairs. It's basically wood and upholstery with hardly any fill left in the cushions.

We place the couch by the community dumpster, and Ethan lets out a breath.

"If you don't want to stay for dinner, it's cool," he says.

"And miss lobster rolls? Free lobster rolls? Good try, mascot," I say, shoving his shoulder, and he smiles at me. "Your dad seems like a good guy."

"Pretty sure I would have ended up dead without him," Ethan says, and I glance over at him.

"How old were you when you came to live with Dave?"

"Fourteen, and the shit I was doing before I came to live with him was fucking reckless. He owned the diner, and his friend Craig owned the old gymnasium. When I wasn't in school, I was either at Craig's gym or working at Dave's. It kept me out of trouble. I owe him everything for it."

I wrap my arm around his shoulder and tug him close. He doesn't shove me off, and I find I like being near him like this.

He's your friend, Max.

You're not looking for anything besides friendship, remember?

I drop my arm and pat his back.

"Let's go get some lobster rolls, huh?" I ask, and he nods his head as we take the three stories back to his foster dad's apartment.

I've been nervous about this game since the start of the season. Playing against my former team isn't ideal. Not that I harbor any ill will. To be honest, I miss a lot of guys on the Sharks. But it's just this weird place of having a connection with your old team and your new team.

I can't let the Foxes down. I can't let myself down.

Lingering feelings of not being good enough plague me, and I'm trying to shove them down.

I'm mostly dressed as my attention is averted, Sloane standing in front of me. She's wearing high-waisted, plaid pants with a black shirt and a belt. It makes her look taller than she actually is. She gives me a warm smile.

"Hey, Max."

"Hey, Sloane," I say, feeling a little out of it. My mental space is just clogged with all these feelings I can't really talk to anybody about.

"It's a big game for you. I thought maybe I could post some clips highlighting you tonight, if that's okay."

"Whatever you think is best," I say, and her brows furrow, and she takes a step closer to me.

Still no scent.

"Is everything okay? Are you nervous for tonight?" she asks.

"Yeah, just pregame jitters. It'll all be fine."

She taps the top of my head three times like I'm a good dog.

"You're going to crush it. I'll be watching and recording all your cute little goalie stretches and saves. You got this."

She lightly punches my shoulder, shaking out her hand afterwards. I grab her hand and inspect it.

"No more doing that shit," I say, making sure she didn't hurt her knuckles.

She clears her throat. "Okay. Have a great game," she says, walking away.

As she leaves, she records a few of the guys and says hello. Everyone seems extremely cautious of Sloane, making sure to be respectful and not cross any lines. That is, everyone minus Nilsen.

Who is currently staring at her like a hawk. The moment she leaves the room, his gaze snaps to me.

Just what I need, this asshole starting some shit right before the game.

He makes his way over to me in a few strides and grabs a fistful of my jersey.

"You don't fucking touch Sloane."

"I only touched her because she smacked my pads. She's my friend. What's your fucking problem with me, Nilsen?"

He laughs sardonically. "You really don't remember? Figures." He drops my jersey with disgust. "You stay the fuck away from her," he says, pointing down at me.

Mikael Martel strolls along with a sigh, clearly used to dealing with Nilsen.

"Who are we staying away from?" Martel asks.

"Sloane," Nilsen says, staring daggers at me.

"Oh yeah, Nilsen all but pissed a big mean circle around the coach's daughter last year, Connery," Martel says.

"I didn't piss on anything," Nilsen counters.

"It's a figure of speech. Literally everyone on the team watches this big asshole pine after her. Not that he'd ever do anything about it. Right, Nilsen?"

The large defensemen shrugs, not confirming or denying.

"God, this season is going to be something, isn't it?" Martel says.

"Just tell this asshole to cool it. He's gone out of his way to start some shit with me. I'm supposed to be his goalie. We're supposed to be a team. Sloane is my friend, and I don't know why he hates me, but it has to stop."

"Gotta say, I kind of agree with him," Martel says, taking my side.

Nilsen finally breaks his glare to grimace at Martel. "He won't last past the season anyway," Nilsen says, waving me off like I'm trash.

Martel whistles as Nilsen walks away before glancing back at me.

"Christ, Connery, what the fuck did you do to him? I mean, don't get me wrong, Bram's an asshole on a good day. But the only person I've ever seen him hate this much is his cousin." Martel taps on his chin. "You know what? I don't think any of us know that story either."

"I've tried to make peace with him. I don't even know what I did."

"Well, I'd tell you to stay away from Sloane, but if she's set on being your friend, you're kind of fucked in that department."

I glance up at him, and he shrugs his shoulders.

"She hangs out with my Omega, Charlotte, sometimes. I

thought Charlotte was an intense Omega, but she doesn't have shit on Sloane. I don't think I've ever met an Omega so assured or okay with her designation. Coach has his hands fucking full."

"We're just friends," I reply, and Martel laughs.

"Yeah, and I never wanted an Omega," he says, walking away. I have no clue what the significance is, but I let it roll off my back as I hit the ice and pray I don't fuck this game up.

SLOANE

CHAPTER 15

Part of my employment deal with my father is that I watch all games from the box. I'm only allowed to leave the box if I have an escort. It's honestly a very micromanaging move on my dad's part.

But at least Charlotte and Piper are both here for the game. That hardly ever happens.

Charlotte is sipping on a fancy cocktail and hums as she swallows.

"Fuck, that's good."

"Aren't you breastfeeding?" Piper says.

"We're going to pump and dump tonight. It's my first night without a twin attached to my tit. I'm going to enjoy my night," Charlotte says, and I smile.

"That's oversharing, *Kulta*," her Alpha Anders says.

He's a little distance away from us but clearly eavesdropping.

"Oversharing would be telling them we have a room rented for the night and all the deplorable things we're going to do without interruption with your parents in town watching our children."

Anders clicks his tongue.

"She's got you there," Piper says.

"Tell me more," I say, resting my elbow on the table and my jaw on my chin.

Charlotte laughs and shakes her head. "My life is amazing but relatively boring these days. You should be the one telling us your salacious stories about finding a pack."

I lick my lips and lean in closer, causing both of the women to do the same.

"Three words. Finnegan the Fox."

Piper tilts her head. "In or out of the uniform."

"Out, you fucking weirdo," I reply, and she shrugs her shoulders.

"Ethan, right?" Charlotte asks, and I nod with a smile.

It makes me happy when people can see him as the guy under the mask.

"I saw the kitten video. Well, I think everyone with a phone saw the kitten video," Piper says, and I grin.

Five million views for the Humane Society video with Ethan holding the kittens. I got a pat on the back from my dad and kudos from upper management on the decision to give him a makeover.

"He deserves the recognition. He's crushing it," I say, and Piper whistles.

"Oh, she's got it bad."

"Damn. I miss those early days," Charlotte says with a wistful smile.

I look around the box and lower my voice. "I know they are your scent matches, but how did you know that they were the ones?"

"There's no denying a scent match. But with Anders and Eli, it was nearly instant. Mikael took a little more time, but it was a bit of a whirlwind. I fell in love with them over my college summer break," she says lovingly.

"And you?" I ask Piper.

Charlotte snorts, and Piper lightly pushes her friend.

"It took me a lot longer to realize I wanted Alexi and Owen in that way, but once I did, there was no stopping that train."

The word "train" has Charlotte laughing, clearly the one cocktail hitting her already.

"Oh my God, Charles, grow up."

"Well, we're all adults who've been through a heat before," she says.

That has me leaning down and taking a sip of my own drink.

"Wait, really?" Charlotte asks, and I shake my head.

"Not yet. But I know it's going to be sooner than later."

"I told you to come by the clinic," Piper scolds.

"I know, I've been meaning to. I just… I'm not sure how to go about this whole thing."

"You have Alphas in mind?" Piper says with a raise of a dark brow.

I nod my head. Well, Bram. I know I want Bram for my heat. There's this nagging in the back of my head about Max, but we're just friends. It's what Max needs, and Bram has already told me he doesn't like him.

I've already asked so much of Bram, I can't ask to have Max too.

"Write up a heat contract. Have them sign it for your peace of mind. They also need to be aware of everything beforehand, Sloane," Piper says in her no bullshit Alpha voice.

"What am I missing?" Charlotte asks, holding up her drink for her Alpha to fetch her another.

"Well, I have a lot of particular rules I'd like followed," I say, and Piper gives me a look that reads I'm full of shit. "And I'm not on birth control."

"We could do the implant next week," Piper says, and I shake my head.

"I've tried going on all the forms. It makes me depressed. I gain weight. I don't feel like myself."

"Get a diaphragm," Charlotte says.

"What? Are those still a thing?" I ask in shock.

"Yes, they're still a thing. Anders and Eli got the snip snip. Mikael, well, we haven't decided yet. So we live life on the edge, but I wear one of those during my heat since that's when I'm most likely to get pregnant anyway," Charlotte says as Anders drops off her drink. "Thanks, honey," she singsongs.

"Diaphragms are like eighty percent effective," Piper says. "The Beta should wear condoms too."

"Why not the Alphas?" I ask, and Charlotte laughs.

"Because their big fat knots rip those little bitches anyway," Charlotte says.

"Christ," Anders hisses from the corner, and Charlotte laughs.

"She's knot wrong," Piper says, and we all begin laughing like a bunch of idiots as we take our seats as the game starts.

Piper leans down to whisper to me. "Seriously, if you need any preheat planning, you'll come and see me. You can't put this off any longer, Sloane."

I nod my head, knowing that time is really running out.

"I will. I promise."

"The more you have in place, the better things will be. We can get you sized for your diaphragm and get some condoms and spermicidal lube."

My nose scrunches when I think about it.

"If you don't make an appointment in the next week, I'll bring the appointment to you, Sloane."

I flutter my lashes at her. "Okay, Alpha."

She lets out a breath and shakes her head. "What am I going to do with the two of you?"

"Share some of those chips," Charlotte says, taking a handful as we watch the start of the game. I get my phone out, and I can't help myself as I gather clips of Max and Bram. When the jumbotron flashes to Ethan, I get clips of him too.

I'll figure it out. I totally have enough time.

* * * *

It's my date with Bram, and to say he better fuck my brains out or I might lose my mind is an understatement. Though I guess if he did fuck my brains out, technically, I would lose my mind anyway.

I'm really pulling out the punches with this tight navy blue dress, no deodorizers, and making sure my eyeliner is sharp enough to kill.

There's no way Bram Nilsen stands a fucking chance.

I'm putting on my lipstick when there's a light tap at my door.

"Come in."

My mother Rosemary steps in, her heels clicking against the hardwood. She whistles, and I glance at her in the mirror. She looks spectacular, and I can't deny every bit of fashion I got from her.

"Date night?" she asks.

She makes sure to not go through my things or invade my space.

"Yes," I reply quickly.

"With a pack or with an Alpha?" she asks.

"An Alpha," I reply, trying to keep it short.

I can lie rather easily with the big picture. That I stayed on with the Foxes because I wanted Bram and how I can't seem to quit, even though I have him, is another story.

"What's he do?" she asks.

"He's, uh…"

"Oh, save it, Sloane. I already cracked Henderson like an egg," she says, and I groan.

God, my moms have their Beta wrapped around their fucking finger.

"Oh yeah, well, he was smoking a cigarette," I snap back.

"I'm sure he wished he could've smoked something a lot stronger that week," she says and then covers her mouth. "That was rude."

I shrug my shoulders and go back to doing my makeup.

"Are you going to tell Dad?" I ask.

"No," she replies easily, and I glance back at her.

"So let me get this straight. The three of you are okay with keeping a pack secret from him?"

My mother steps forward and brushes a piece of hair off my face.

"When you're ready for this relationship to be out in the open, it will be. Kristoff is stressed, and as much as he hides it, he's dealing with his mother's death in his own way. I trust you, we trust you."

Great, well, now my eyes are welling up with tears, and I just put on the most symmetrical eye liner of my life.

"You do?"

"We raised you. If we didn't trust you, it would be our own doing. You've always been someone who goes for what they want. Your dad will adjust. But I think it's best you give him a little more time," she says.

I blink a few times. "Did I mess up my makeup?"

"No, honey, you're perfect," she says, wrapping her arms around me. "Just keep us in the loop, okay? As much as we trust you, we want you to be safe. You sneaking around and not telling us where you are is unacceptable. You need to turn your location back on for me," she says.

My cheeks heat as I pull back, and I nod.

"Okay, yeah. I can do that," I agree. Especially because I know she's right. I know I've been trying to keep this all a secret, but safety comes first.

"Have a good date. Let me know if you won't be home," she says, squeezing my shoulder before leaving.

I swallow thickly and grab my phone.

You little traitor.

DAD H

I'm a weak man. They cornered me!

Likely story. You owe me, Dad.

DAD H

Well, we're all keeping your dirty secret from
Kristoff.

Ugh, having four parents is too much.

DAD H

Love you too. Have fun on your date.

Jesus, a girl really can't keep a secret when she has this many prying parental figures around. I fix my makeup and drive two blocks in the neighborhood where Bram's white SUV is waiting for me.

He gets out of the car and opens my door. As soon as he's in my space, his massive hands are wrapped in my hair.

His kiss is nearly feral as he pushes my back against the car, and he kisses me like he's taking his last breath between my lips.

It's a cold ass night, and I can feel goosebumps on my legs, but all I really want to do is ride my skirt up and have him fuck me on the side of my car.

He suddenly pulls away and looks me up and down.

"You're gonna kill me, you know that?" he asks, and I roll my eyes and grab his hand.

"So are we going out, or are we going right to your house?"

"Seems wrong to not take you out when you got so dressed up," he says.

"This," I say, waving my hand at myself, "was all in an effort to get knotted tonight. Please, for the love of God, take me back to your house."

He scoops me up, his forearm under my ass as he carries me over to his passenger door, holding me with one hand and opening the other. He moves me gently into the seat, adjusting my dress and putting my seatbelt on before kissing the side of my head and pointing at me.

"You sit here, don't talk, and let me focus on the road. If you're good, I'll give you what you want," he says sternly.

Oh God. It makes me perfume, and he huffs out a breath.

"Fuck's sake," he says, shutting my door and rounding the front of the vehicle.

I think I may have broken Bram Nilsen, and I don't think I ever want him to be put back together.

BRAM

CHAPTER 16

It smells like peaches and sunshine and the hot little redhead wants my knot.

My knuckles grip the wheel with such a vise I'm worried I'm going to crack the fucking thing.

So much for slow and for courting.

But at the end of the day, I'm just a man, and my need to claim Sloane has been weighing heavily on me. I'm not sure if it was the introduction of Ethan or something else. All I know is it's taking every single ounce of effort to not pick her up and sit her on my cock right now.

I don't glance over at her, because I know if I do, I'll just give in. What the fuck has she done to me? I consider myself rather controlled, but Sloane makes me want to throw everything I know out the window.

Sharing? A pack? Those things weren't ever things I considered. But for Sloane? I'm willing to abandon everything.

Maybe I need this sexual connection to prove what I already know, that she's mine.

One day I'm going to sink my teeth into her and mark her as mine. Hell, I'll mark up the Beta too, if that's what they both want. Not that it would be a hardship on my end. I can easily understand her affections toward him, and maybe one day I could see myself feeling the same.

Friendship is fine for now. Sloane is my main priority. If the Beta sticks, then we can go from there.

"Bra—"

"No," I reply sharply, keeping my gaze on the road. "No talking. No fucking anything until I get you to my house," I reply.

It makes her perfume even more, and I scrub a hand down my face.

"Fuck me," I mumble.

"That's the plan," Sloane whispers under her breath, and I have to bite my tongue to not laugh or chastise her for not listening.

I push the button, my garage door raises, and I pull inside. The moment the ignition is off, Sloane is climbing over the console and propping herself on my lap.

My hand wraps around her delicate throat, enough to let her know I'm in charge. As much as Sloane may run most of my life, right now she needs to be the one who listens.

"Do you like breaking rules?" I ask her, and she licks her lips.

Her scent is thick and tempting. But I refuse to give in to her whims completely.

My thumb trails down the tendon of her neck, right where I plan on marking her one day.

"Do you like consequences, Sloane?" I ask, and her breath hitches.

"What kinds of consequences?"

"I told you to sit there and no talking till we got home."

"But we are home," she says.

My thumb drags down her throat, and I grab a fistful of her ass, making her squirm on my lap.

"You're used to getting your way, aren't you?" I ask her.

She bites her lips and nods as I drag her face closer to mine. Our lips are so close, just a few millimeters and we'd be kissing.

"You're not in charge tonight, little Omega," I whisper against her face, and she shivers. "Out. On my bed," I demand.

Her scent is driving me near feral as she searches my eyes before turning and opening my door. Her body shamelessly glides against mine as she gets out of the car, and I follow her.

She opens the door and walks through the mudroom into the kitchen.

"I forget, where's the bedroom?" she says quietly, and I know she's fucking with me, but I don't care.

"Upstairs," I tell her, and she turns to the left and heads up the stairs.

I watch her ass swish in her tight little dress the whole way, wondering how someone so small can be such a fucking handful. A handful I undoubtedly want to be mine.

I wonder if Sloane indeed likes consequences or if no one has ever given her any.

"Third door on the left," I whisper, and she jumps ever so slightly before going to my bedroom door and grabbing the handle and entering my room.

She looks around, taking in the minimalist decor, before turning to face me.

"Sit on the bed," I tell her, and she does so agreeably.

I get down on one knee and unzip her boot, taking it off along with her sock, before moving on to the other.

"This doesn't seem like a consequence," she says.

I look up at her, arching a brow.

"Do you want me to edge you for hours on end, or should I spank that sweet ass for not following directions?" I ask plainly, rubbing her exposed calf.

Her eyes widen as she blinks down at me.

"Which… which one would you like?" she asks.

I grab her heel, massaging her foot as she rests her weight on my bed. I think about my hard aching cock, and I don't think I'm patient enough to edge her, not that I'd say it out loud. My hand wraps around her ankle, tugging her so slightly.

"We don't have to do either if you're uncomfortable," I tell her honestly.

This could be too much too fast.

Fuck, I went from wanting to take things slow to wanting to spank her ass. How did we even get here?

"I'd like to try," she says shyly.

"Which one, *liefje*?"

She bites her lip and doesn't even ask about my slip of Dutch.

"Spanking. I think. I mean, you wouldn't do it too hard?"

"I'd never hurt you, Sloane. Never."

"You'd get enjoyment out of it?" she questions.

I kiss her calf as I stand to my full height, and her head tilts to continue making eye contact. I bend over, my palms pressed against the mattress as I lean over her.

"Marking you up is going to be my new favorite thing," I tell her, and her lips part in a gasp as her sweet sticky scent fills my bedroom.

I may never wash these sheets.

Fuck, I may have to bring one of my pillows or blankets with me for the next away game if they smell like her. My cock twitches in my pants as Sloan's delicate hands drag down my chest.

She looks nervous but eager. It's clear to me she's used to giving orders and getting what she wants.

I think my little Omega might find she enjoys letting go and letting me take control.

"Where do you want me?"

I pull up from where I was towering over her space and sit at the edge of the bed.

"Take your jacket off, and come here," I say, patting my lap.

She sucks her bottom lip between her teeth and nods her head, removing her jacket and crawling over the top of my lap. I push her long wavy hair off to the side as she looks up at me.

I'm not sure anyone has ever looked at me the way Sloane is right now. Like she fully trusts me and knows I'll take care of her. It's as heady as it is erotic.

I pat her ass lightly, and she wiggles with a smile on her face.

"If at any point you aren't into it or it's too much, you will tell me to stop," I tell her.

"Yes," she replies.

I smack her ass a little harder this time, and she moans.

"Yes, Alpha," she says, making the sentence oh so much fucking sweeter.

"Such a good girl. Except when you don't listen. I needed to drive us here safely. I had plans for you, but you wanted to be in control. I'll do pretty much whatever you ask of me, Sloane. I only ask when it comes to your safety, you listen to me."

"I can do that," she says.

I pull the hem of her dress up, exposing her perky ass. There's a spotting of freckles along her thighs and cheeks that I find myself wanting to get very acquainted with.

"Five, I think. Does that sound fair?" I ask, and she smiles as we negotiate her spankings.

"After five, do I get your knot?" she asks sassily, and I pull my hand back and smack her ass for real this time.

She hisses and moans at the same time, and I can feel my cock getting harder against her stomach.

"Okay?" I confirm, and she lets out a breath.

"Yes, I like it," she replies, and some of the tension that was building up in me falls away. There was a part of me that thought she wouldn't enjoy this. It wouldn't be a deal breaker, but I like the idea of dominating this sweet Omega more than I can even articulate.

"Good girl."

Her body becomes pliant against mine as I spank her ass again. Her scent washes over me, and I can feel the pooling of slick against my thigh.

Fuck.

I pull my hand back and smack the same spot two more times as Sloane moans and adjusts herself on my lap.

"Last one," I remind her.

The last one is the hardest, and her left cheek is a beautiful shade of pink once I'm done. I grab her thong and push it to the side, needing to see how wet this encounter made her.

I'm not disappointed in the slightest when my fingers are greeted with nothing but salacious wetness as I slide them into her cunt.

"You're so fucking wet," I tell her as I slide my fingers in and out of her, admiring her pink ass and the way her pussy is wrapped around my fingers.

"Knot. Now," she says, and I grin to myself as she climbs off my lap and quickly rips her dress off, leaving her in her white bra and panties. I tug at the side of her underwear, sending it to the floor. I use my foot to push them under the bed so I can keep them for later.

She approaches me and unfastens my belt.

"Condom?" she questions, and I clear my throat and nod to my nightstand. She quickly heads over to the nightstand and pulls out an Alpha Max condom and comes back to stand between my legs.

"Are you going to take my cock out and ride it?" I ask her, and she lets out a little whimper as I help her undo my zipper and pull my cock out of my boxers and pants.

She gasps as she looks down at where I'm stroking my shaft.

"A-fucking-men," she says, climbing on top of me and straddling my thighs. She has to nearly be on her toes to notch the head of my cock in her entrance.

Her dainty hands grab on to my neck as she slowly slides down my length. Both of us moan with pleasure as her warm, wet pussy takes me deep inside of her. She doesn't take my knot, but just the prospect of her taking me that way has it swelling in anticipation.

"That's it. You feel so good," I tell her, and her nails dig into the back of my skull.

"God. You do too. Fuck. I needed this," she whispers against my face as I grip her ass and shift her up and down my cock.

She winces slightly as I grab her tender flesh, and I can't help it as I lift her up, my hands gripping her ass as I switch positions and lay her on her back so I can fuck her.

Our height difference makes it hard to kiss her, and I grunt, pulling out nearly all the way so I can lean down and crash her lips to mine.

She's just as ravenous as me, kissing me like both our lives depend on it. Her scent is consuming, and her body is wrapped around me in some delicious sense of ownership I can't handle.

Her heels are pressed against my ass, her cunt gripping me tightly while her fingers dig into my shoulders like I'm not close enough.

As I push deep inside of her, our gaze meeting and our lips parting, I realize she owns me wholly.

This isn't a courtship. It's a matter of when.

I glance down at her throat, wishing my mark was already on her, that we were bonded and I could feel how much she's loving this moment.

But I settle for the second best thing, shoving my cock and knot deep inside of her, stretching her to fit around me. The only thing that would make this better is if there was no condom between us.

Her nails are sharp against my back, and I groan in pleasure from the seducing pain.

"Are you going to come around my knot, little Omega? God, I want to fill you up."

Her head falls back as a needy moan slips through her lips. My knot swells to its full size as her walls wrap around me with her orgasm.

I watch her face the whole time. The way her brows furrow and her lips part. The imagery makes my cock twitch as I rut into her relentlessly, wanting her orgasm to last and needing to finish myself.

With a few more thrusts, I place more of my weight on her as I fuck her as deep as physically possible.

I come with a moan, my chest purring with my satisfaction as the Omega below me sighs and lets the softest whimpers of release fall out of her.

I'm catching my breath as Sloane rubs my beard and head softly. It's an affection I've been withdrawn from for quite some time.

Knowing we're going to be here a while, I do the same thing, stroking her hair and placing gentle touches against her face.

"Better?" I ask her with a cocky smile.

"So much better," she says, grabbing me around the shoulders and pressing more of my weight on her than I'm comfortable with.

"I'll crush you."

"No, you won't. I like it. Just keep purring," she says.

So I do, my chest rumbling against hers with my knot deep inside of her.

I don't think I've ever been this content in my life.

CHAPTER 17

I t's been a terrible fucking shift at the diner. Things have been bad for the last couple of years with my foster dad not being able to work any more.

As much as I love Dave and owe him my life. I just don't see this being where I end up. I want more. And part of me hopes that as soon as I'm on my feet, he'll be ready to sell this place and keep the money for the remainder of his retirement.

Being a mascot may sound stupid, and maybe it's not the complete end goal, but I love it. I love being with the kids, bringing them joy and being able to do something that is both physically and mentally simulating.

It's getting late, and the last people here are mostly truckers.

That is until Sloane and Bram come strolling into the diner. I'm not even an Alpha, and I can tell that their scents are intertwined. I wonder what they got up to, and a very perverted part of me wishes I was there to watch.

"Where's your section?" Sloane says sweetly as she gives me a hug.

"This booth is good. I'll get you some menus. Things are slowing down here, so I should be able to hang out soon," I tell her.

She smiles, taking Bram's hand as they sit on opposite sides of the booth, which the big Alpha doesn't look pleased about.

"I could have made you something," Bram says in a hushed tone, and Sloane shushes him.

"What'll it be, the usual?" I ask, looking at Sloane.

"Please, and a side of maple bacon."

"You got it. And for you, big guy?" I ask Bram who arches a dark eyebrow at me.

"The same."

I grin and drop off their waters. I wonder how Bram Nilsen would feel knowing that Max Connery also ordered the same thing as the sweet little Omega not that long ago. I also wonder how he would feel knowing I ate Sloane out not so long ago.

Speaking of which, I definitely need to find some more alone time with the Omega. Or hell, I'd like them to invite me to join because I definitely need another hit.

I put in three orders of southwest omelets so I can join them. I let Cassidy know I'm going on break when the order is up.

Sloane looks more than pleased when I have a meal for each of us. She leans into me ever so slightly, and I try not to let it go to my ego.

"Is this a setup?" Bram asks.

"I feel like I already did that. This is me being hungry and us going out to eat where Ethan works because we miss him," Sloane says, and I throw one arm over the booth while I eat with one hand.

"You haven't been missing me, Nilsen? I've been missing you," I say with a beaming smile.

Sloane acts like it's the most precious thing, but Bram doesn't seem so amused.

"Come on. Lighten up, man. You've got an omelet, and you're here with us. Based on the scents you two are rocking, I'm pretty sure you all had a good night. You can't be a grouch when you've been inside Sloane."

Bram laughs a genuine laugh, which makes Sloane follow suit.

"I'll give you that one," Bram says, pointing his fork at me.

"Look, sweetheart, he's half in love with me already," I say to Sloane.

Bram blushes. The big giant beast of a man blushes and goes back to digging into his food as I turn to Sloane.

"What are you two up to tonight?"

"Just wanted to stop by and get some food before bed," Sloane says easily, and I nod, not wanting to ruin their date together. "But there is something I wanted to talk to you two about."

She's pushing her food around, dividing everything up and making sure it doesn't touch.

Both of us give her time to speak, though I notice both of us stopped eating to hear what she has to say.

"Okay, so there's no easy way to go about this, but it's kind of the big, fat elephant that follows every Omega around." She lets out a sigh and takes a breath before continuing. "My birthday is in February. The fourteenth so you can mark your calendars, by the way."

"Sloane," Bram says sternly, and she nods her head.

"There's no true science to when an Omega starts her heat, and lately it's felt like it's coming on sooner than later. I know things are still relatively new and that this is a big ask, especially with the season picking up. But if I were to go into heat—"

"We'll be there," Bram cuts in, answering for both of us.

I can't even be mad at it cause it was hot as shit.

"He's right, we'll be there," I say.

Sloane's eyes water, and she leans into me. "Thank you. It could be months or even a year from now. But I just needed to know. It was weighing on me."

"You feel like that again, you come to one of us right away," Bram says, and Sloane and I both nod our heads.

Bram looks between us, not saying anything about my agreement, just grunting his satisfaction.

"Is there anything you need from us beforehand?" I ask Sloane.

"Not right now. I promise if anything changes, I'll let you know. But for now, I think I'm all set."

"Would it be at your apartment?" Bram asks, which is honestly a great question.

"Yeah, are we going to show up to your house to take care of you and your dad is sitting on your porch with a rifle? I really do like being a mascot and not riddled with buckshot."

"First off, you already snuck in and saw that it was detached. I'd also say if you're willing to be there for my heat, you're also willing to be officially mine in front of my dad," Sloane says.

"We can tell him tomorrow if you want," Bram says.

I glance over at Sloane who is blushing.

"Ordinarily, I'd say yes, but he's still going through it after his mom passing. I think I'd like to wait until he's in a better headspace."

Bram and I just both nod in agreement.

"Okay, well, I feel so much better," Sloane says happily.

Her shoulders relax, and it's almost like she was physically caring this burden around.

"Can I get up to go to the bathroom?" she asks, and I nod, getting up and giving her space so she can walk to the restroom.

"We need a plan," Bram says.

"Like what?"

"Like if we're going to be helping her with her heat, we should probably get to know each other better and know everything she needs," he says plainly.

I rub the back of my neck. "I never really thought I'd wind up helping an Omega in heat."

Bram shrugs like it's no big deal. "Well, now you are. If I'm the only Alpha, we're going to need to get creative."

"What, like fisting?" I say, shocked.

His face is deadpan. "Whatever gets the job done."

"I'll do some research online."

"Good boy," he replies with a smirk, and I feel like I melt into the booth.

"Sleeping with Sloane really did a number on you. I don't think I've ever seen you this happy."

"Me either. She wants you there. This is the real deal, so I'm in. We're both hers, but if we're a pack, it makes you mine too, in whatever way you want," he says it so casually I wish I could rewind and listen to it again.

"You'd want to date the mascot."

"No, I'd like to date you, Ethan," he says, and before I have a moment to process his words, there's a commotion over by the bathroom.

"Get your fucking hands off me," Sloane says sternly.

Bram and I are up quicker than I've ever moved in my life as we storm into the direction of the altercation.

The man I recognize as a regular. Is this the fucker who accosted her previously?

"Come on, your man's not even here," he says.

Sloane glances our way, and when I see the man's hand gripped around her wrist, all I see is red as I pull back my fist and punch him in the face. He's bigger than me, clearly an Alpha. But I don't give a shit as I pull back and hit again and again. My knuckles ache, and besides the pain in my fist, all I can see is this weak motherfucker beneath me.

"Hey! Hey!" is shouted. I don't know where from until two big arms wrap around me. I try to pull back from their hold.

The man on the ground is spitting blood and groaning as the arms tighten further.

"Enough," he grumbles, and I realize it's Bram.

He squeezes me tightly like he's trying to calm me down, and I suppose he is.

"He's done. Sloane's fine. He's done."

He lets go of me, and I shake my hands out, and there's this incessant need to hit the man on the ground again. Flashbacks from a time I never want to remember whirl in the back of my head.

Suddenly, Bram is grabbing my face roughly.

"Look at me," he nearly growls.

I take a deep breath and look at him.

"Good. I need you to breathe. To calm down. Can you do that for me?"

"Yeah, I'm good," I reply.

I'm not fucking good. None of this is okay. I blink out some of the haziness, and reality slaps me in the face. What the fuck did I just do? Is Sloane afraid?

I glance over Bram's shoulder.

"No," he says deeply, his fingers digging into my cheeks. "Don't talk to her until you know you're really okay."

"I'm not okay," I admit, and he nods his head.

"Sit at that booth. Let me make sure Sloane gets home okay. We'll take care of this."

I don't know why Bram is helping me, but I know I can't refuse it. I might have just ruined my life by assaulting that man.

Fuck.

I'm going to ruin everything. Sloane is probably scared shitless. Cassidy is likely already on the phone with the cops or Dave.

Instead of looking up to see the regret or fear in Sloane's eyes, I sit in the booth as I'm told. My hands shake with anger, disgust, and frustration as I steeple my fingers and rest my head against them.

All this work. All this effort to work on my anger and here I am. I'm near tears but hold it in. What the fuck was I thinking?

I saw someone hurting Sloane, and it's like every life lesson, every tender moment, had been erased and I'm back to being ten years old again.

Sloane asked me to be in her heat. She was helping me hard launch Finnegan the Fox, and now I'm no better than the man I've spent my entire life hating.

I'm not sure how long I sit in the booth, my hands shaking and my eyes closed. My stomach aches, the omelet I was eating earlier threatening to come up.

It feels like it's been an eternity as a strong hand touches my shoulder. It's probably the fucking cops. Great, I'll be a goddamn felon just like him.

"Help me carry him out of here," Bram says.

I swallow and look up. "What?" I ask.

"No one else saw what happened. Cassidy told everyone there was a fire in the kitchen and to evacuate. He threatened your Omega. You have every right to act the way you did. So we're handling this ourselves."

"What?" I blink at him.

He grabs my chin roughly and leans down to get in my face. It isn't menacing, it's almost tender in a somewhat terrifying way.

"Grab his legs, and I'll grab under his armpits."

I stand and do as he says as we take him out to the back of the restaurant.

"Is Sloane okay?" I ask him, feeling like a fucking asshole.

"Yes. Piper picked her up," he says easily.

"Is she scared?"

"No. She's worried about you. She didn't want to go."

"Thank you for that. I don't want her to see me like this," I reply.

This man is heavy as hell as I push the bar on the door, the stench of the dumpster filling my nose as my shoes hit the wet pavement.

"If you wouldn't have done it, I would have. You would have done the same for me."

He says it so assuredly, and it's the truth. I would have.

"We might not be bonded to her yet. But we're gonna be a pack. This is what a pack does. As long as you promise me that you would only raise your hand to someone who is a threat."

"I'd never ever raise my hand to her. Ever. Or to my pack. Just seeing him touching her and threatening her like that—it fucked me up."

"Here, put him against the dumpster," Bram says.

I swallow, wondering why he didn't make any more comments about my outburst. Or ask me further questions.

"What's the game plan?" I ask him.

"Grab his wallet," Bram says, and I do, handing it over to him.

Bram empties the contents on the concrete as the man groans and spits. Bram gets down to his haunches and looks the man over.

"Shame you were mugged. If I see you here again or anywhere around my Omega or Beta, we'll ruin your fucking life. You'll have a lot more to worry about than a broken nose, Justin Lann of 568 Witt Ave," he says, looking at the man's license before pocketing it.

"I won't," the man rasps out.

Bram is clicking through his phone. "You certainly wouldn't want to break probation. I'd bet you want to get your face fixed and forget this ever happened."

Bram stands up, slightly kicking the man's leg.

"Come on, grab your shit, and let's go," Bram says.

"What?"

"You're coming back to my place," he says as we walk back through the diner, and I grab my stuff and just blindly follow Bram to his SUV.

He's quiet and contemplative the whole drive to his house.

As soon as we get there, he leads me into the kitchen and tells me to put my hands under running water. I wince as I scrub up the dried blood but eventually have my hands clean.

Bram is delicate with my hands as he cleans the wounds and bandages them up.

"Piper is dropping Sloane off," Bram says easily.

"I'm sorry for fucking up your date," I tell him.

For what feels like the millionth time tonight, he grabs my face, and the kiss is so chaste and quick I almost think it isn't real.

"You didn't. Now go make sure you're ready for Sloane to come home and dote on you."

I blink at him as he turns away, putting his first aid kit away.

What in the fuck happened tonight?

SLOANE

CHAPTER 18

"Sloane, are you going to tell me what happened?" Piper asks in the car ride to Bram's house.

I'm in the backseat with her while Owen and Alexi are upfront.

"Also, why am I driving to Nilsen's house?" Alexi asks playfully.

"Alexi, what would you do if someone pinned Owen to a wall and was trying to grope him?" I ask.

An angry noise leaves him, and Piper smirks.

"Probably kick their fucking ass."

"I can handle myself," Owen says.

"Okay, well, basically, that's what happened," I say easily.

"Nilsen beat someone up? He can't get in trouble mid season," Owen says, turning around to look at us in the backseat.

"It wasn't Bram. It was Ethan."

"Who's Ethan?" Owen asks.

"Jesus fucking Christ. The mascot," I grate out.

Alexi whistles. "Finnegan the Fox can fight, huh?"

I rub my forehead, and Piper pats my thigh. "I'm sure every-thing's fine. Bram said that both he and Ethan are back at the house, right?"

"Right," I remind myself.

"Listen, I know you have no control over this. I know I didn't. But if you could go into heat during an easy string of games, that would be ideal," Owen says.

"Owen," Piper hisses, and he shrugs his shoulders.

"Like I said, I know she has no control over it. But maybe she could manifest when we're playing the Jets or the Bruins or something."

"Don't listen to him. He's one to talk," she says, giving her Omega a look.

Alexi pulls up to Bram's house.

"Do you need an escort? I'm always happy to take an opportunity to piss Nilsen off," Alexi says.

"No. This is fine. Thank you again for coming to get me."

Piper grabs my hand and squeezes. "We're friends. Whenever you need us, we'll be here."

"Thanks, Piper," I say before getting out of the car.

Before I even have the door shut, Bram is standing outside of his front door with his arms crossed, waiting for me. Alexi and Owen both wave at him, and he gives a nod of respect as I approach.

"Is everything okay? Is he okay? Did they call the police? This is all my fault. I should have been paying better attention. I should've—"

"He's fine. None of this is your fault. He's lying down in my bed. There were no cops, and there won't be," he promises.

He pets my hair in a ridiculously soothing way.

"How do you know?"

"Because the dick was on probation. No one else in the diner saw, and we cleared everyone out. If anything, Ethan is just worried you hate him now."

"How could I hate him? He was protecting me. I mean, albeit a little over the top, but it still came from a protective place."

"You helped him?" I ask, and Bram shrugs his shoulders. "He was a mess, Bram. You fixed all of this."

"He's future pack," he says easily, and I grab on to Bram's shirt, looking up into his brown eyes.

My sweet, gentle, maybe sometimes grumpy giant.

"You like him?"

"Yes. I like the Beta. Now go make sure he's okay," he says, acting like he isn't an outstanding human being.

I tug on his shirt, and he leans down to kiss me. His earthy scent surrounds me and reminds me of everything we did earlier today.

"You're a good man, Bram Nilsen. I chose right," I tell him against his lips before pulling away, leaving him dumbfounded as I head up the stairs to check on Ethan.

I'm not sure what I expected, but him snuggled up on the left-hand side of the bed wasn't it. The lights are still on, and I proceed with caution.

"Ethan?" I whisper.

"I'm up," he says, not turning around.

I take off my dress and bra. My panties were lost and not returned after my and Bram's sexy moment earlier. Instead, I rifle through his drawers. I grab a T-shirt and a pair of boxers that are all too big before crawling into bed.

Once I do, Ethan turns around.

"I'm sorry, Sloane. I promise that won't happen again. I'm not a violent person."

"I know you're not," I say, brushing some hair out of his face. "You're mine, and I'm yours. You were protecting me."

"When I saw his hands on you, I lost it."

"Is there a reason why?"

"Yes."

I can tell he's uncomfortable.

"It's okay, we can talk about it some other time." I wrap an arm around him, and he takes the deepest sigh of relief.

It doesn't take me long to fall asleep, and when I wake up in the morning, I'm not just snuggled up with Ethan, but between both him and Bram.

I feel nearly whole.

✻ ✻ ✻ ✻

I feel like poor Max has taken a back burner with helping his image out. Though his press has been good lately, I still have alerts on my phone when any of my guys are mentioned. Even if Serenity Jade wants to write speculative articles, there's been nothing more on me and Max. If anything, most of what I've seen out there is people hoping he stays on the team.

Maybe I've been avoiding him, which makes me feel even more guilty. Especially because I can't help but to miss him.

He and Bram don't get along, and I'm with Bram, so being around Max almost feels like a betrayal in a way.

It's silly, but it's also not because when I'm around Max, I have an amazing time. He's easy to talk to, handsome, funny, and there's a connection there I can't deny.

But there's only so much I can ask of Bram, and this would be taking it too far. I know I can be selfish sometimes; it's part of the territory of being a single child and an Omega. But doing this feels hurtful, which I just can't swallow.

Yet I have to do my job.

So here I am, waiting for Max to meet me in my cubicle so we can talk about the fundraiser for Phillip, Liz's husband.

There's a tap against my cubicle wall before he takes a seat in the vacant chair next to me.

"Hey there, stranger," he says, and I give him a watery smile.

"Hey. Been busy. How about you?"

"Actually, getting along with the team. Well, most of the team minus Nilsen, fucking dick."

"He's not so bad," I say, wanting to defend him in earnest, but we aren't public knowledge yet.

"He hates me, and I don't even know what I fucking did. But that's besides the point. Everything is going pretty well, if my brother would let off my ass a little bit. My PR lady seems super happy with all the footage lately. Thanks for that," he says with a smile.

"You're welcome."

"Sloane, are you okay?"

I rub the back of my neck and nod. It's just the end of the day, and everything is wearing off. I need to go home and relax, maybe take a nice bath or do some of the things on my checklist.

"Yeah, sorry. Just tired," I reply, and he furrows his brows and nods.

"We can work on this later. You should go home and take care of yourself."

"I promise I'm fine. I have everything planned anyway. It's pretty straightforward. We have the home game against Vancouver. And right after, we'll hold the fundraiser in person and online for Phillip with you handling the social media aspect."

"Perfect, I can do that. Are you sure that you're okay?"

"Yeah, I'm good. Just a lot of balls in the air right now. I know we have a few weeks, but I'll get everything organized. You're doing a great job with your image all on your own," I tell him, hating the last sentence.

I feel like such a horrible friend.

He seems dejected but just nods his head. Dammit, I know I'm being so weird; I want to talk to him like I used to, but I pull myself back.

"Alright, well, I'll see you around."

I give him a soft smile, hating that I know I'm making him feel awkward.

"Yeah, see ya," I say, packing up my bags and getting up to go home for the night.

I have planning to do, and it doesn't involve former playboy goalies.

Definitely not.

❄ ❄ ❄ ❄

I sneak Ethan into my apartment, though I don't think my dad would really care if we were dating. It's just truly none of his business. It's been a few weeks since the diner incident, and he's been odd. Almost like he's afraid if he touches me wrong or says the wrong thing, I'll go running for the hills.

I meant what I said in Bram's bed, and of course I want to know about his past but only when he's ready.

Bram and my father have been super busy with the hockey season picking up. I see him when I can, but he still calls me or texts me every night. How he's able to make me feel special no matter where work takes him is exactly why I know he's the right Alpha for me.

Even if there is another Alpha on my mind, one that absolutely shouldn't be.

"Sloane, sweetheart, I don't think this is all necessary."

"It is, keep chopping," I tell him.

"We can feed you just fine. You don't have to do all this work."

"They're my favorite comfort foods, just the way I like. If we have them frozen and you can put them in a crockpot, it will be great for heat meals. The less that has to be done during my heat, the better."

"Whatever makes you happy."

"Good, this makes me happy."

"Are you alright?" he asks me, and I huff out a breath.

"Why does everyone keep asking me that?" I snap, and I swallow back the attitude. "I'm sorry. I didn't sleep well, and I feel bad about Max."

"You feel like you can't be his friend because of Bram?"

"Not necessarily that."

"You're attracted to Max and can't be around him because of Bram?" he asks while he chops carrots.

"Bingo."

"I might also be in this very specific and ridiculously loyal club as well."

"I feel bad," I say as I run my skincare routine sheet through the laminator and add glue dots to the back so I can post it on the mirror.

"Do we know why he hates him anyway?"

"I haven't been brave enough to ask," I admit, and Ethan nods his agreement.

"Me either."

"We're a little pathetic," I admit, and Ethan laughs.

"I'd say Bram has been there for both of us when we really need it. Not to mention we're both really into him. Max is a friend, nothing more. We'll figure it out."

"Hmm," I say, not completely agreeing or disagreeing.

I get up and glue my skincare routine to the mirror before going back to my binder and seeing what else I may need to add.

"Sloane, I don't think you need a manual."

"Oh, yes. I definitely need a manual. It's all of my favorite things, things that soothe me. Not to mention how to use my washer and dryer and how much detergent."

"That seems very specific," he replies.

He's throwing the sliced vegetables into the freezer bag, and I sigh.

"If you put too much, they don't smell right, too little and they don't get clean. It's a fine balance. I don't know what I'll be like in heat, but I can guess that I might be a little particular."

"Nothing wrong with knowing what you want."

I hum at his words and go back to printing out and putting a video link on how to use and remove a diaphragm. You can truly never be thorough enough. While I know Bram and Ethan are more than happy to be in my heat, I can't seem to give up complete control. I need to know everything will be perfect, and even if I can't communicate, they'll know what I need.

My phone buzzes with an incoming call, and I pick it up.

"Hello?"

"What are you up to tonight?" Bram says in a sleepy voice.

The Foxes somehow beat the Lightning tonight, and I know he took a few hard hits.

"Ethan is over, and we're working on heat stuff," I reply.

Ethan arches a brow as I place the phone on the desk and hit the speaker button.

"You're on speaker," I tell him.

"She's making me make Crock-Pot freezer meals for her heat," Ethan says, throwing me under the bus.

"Sloane, you don't have to worry about any of that shit. We're more than capable."

"It has nothing to do with you being capable," I tell them both.

Ethan looks confused, and Bram sighs over the phone.

"Whatever gives you peace of mind," Bram concedes, even though he can't see my smug smile over the phone.

"Are you sore? I saw you take that hit tonight," I say, trying to keep the worry out of my voice.

Ever since the night of the diner, it seems like we're all relatively unified as a pack, but nothing has moved forward. I can tell Ethan and Bram have a connection besides me being the tether between them.

But it seems like Ethan might be keeping Bram at a distance as well.

Knowing that they're both going to be there for me during my heat is the only thing settling my nerves and not making me spiral. We don't have to be bonded for my heat, or maybe I have more time than I think and things will speed up.

"I'm fine. Icing my shoulder," Bram responds and yawns over the phone. "When I get back, the three of us should do something."

"I'd love that," I agree easily. "I wish you were here."

"Me too. Don't go crazy with the planning. We've got you. Have a good night, you too, Ethan," Bram says.

"Night," both Ethan and I chime at the same time.

I hang up the phone, and exhaustion whirls through me.

"Is that your last bag?" I ask as Ethan makes sure it's airtight and labels the bag with a Sharpie before tossing it into the freezer.

"Last one."

"Let me wash my face and get my pajamas on. Stay the night?"

He swallows thickly but nods his head as I get ready for the night.

By the time I finish everything I need to do, Ethan is waiting shirtless in my bed, looking uncomfortable as ever.

I climb under the sheets and rest my head on his chest. While I'm all about respecting boundaries, the wall Ethan has put up is bullshit.

"I'm not going anywhere, Ethan," I promise him, my eyes getting heavy.

He squeezes my shoulder, but I swear before I fall asleep, I hear him whisper, "That's what they all say."

MAX

CHAPTER 19

We won the game, thank fuck.

I showered after and put my suit back on and ditched the deodorizers. Owen wasn't going to be at the event and, to be completely honest, I'm getting tired of wearing them. I have to deal with him being my coach. He can deal with me being myself. I'm not even sure why I've been such a stickler about wearing them. I guess I thought I was being considerate to Owen disliking my scent. We're slowly getting closer, maybe I can really be myself from here on out. Not to mention we've been on a winning streak.

Nothing would have been worse to have lost and then have to moderate this fundraising event for Phillip.

He's a good guy and apparently doing better according to his wife and the head of marketing, Liz.

"This was seriously so kind," Phillip says as I shake his hand.

"It was Sloane's idea, but I'm happy to help in any way that I can."

"We appreciate it. Things are looking better; it's just the bills have been a lot," Liz says shyly.

Sloane is panning around the room. We're on a live feed where fans can donate through a link, not to mention the in-person donors at the event who are donating, myself included.

Most of the team is here, including Bram who follows Sloane with his eyes like some sort of predator.

Ethan is dressed up as Finnegan the Fox as he takes pictures with fans and does some general goofing around.

I'm not sure if I fucked up with him the night we moved his dad's couch, or maybe something is just wrong with me? Maybe I'm the reason why I can't hold friendships down because it feels like Ethan and Sloane have been slowly keeping their distance.

I suppose I can't blame them.

But no matter the internal pity party I'm having, I'm not going to slip up. Not even as a very tall, pretty brunette approaches me with a smile.

"Max Connery, right? You played amazing tonight," she says, a champagne flute perched between her manicured fingernails.

She's a Beta as far as I can tell, and a year ago I'd be putting the moves on her like no other in an effort to bring her back to my place.

Even though she's pretty, and seemingly kind, I find it's not what I'm looking for.

"Thank you. And thank you for coming out tonight to support Liz and Phillip," I say.

"It's so great what you're doing here. Caring for employees outside the team. I really respect what the Foxes have built in New Haven."

Suddenly, a small redhead with a phone in her hand is in front of me, giving what seems to be a forced smile to the brunette next to me.

"Mind if I steal Max for a minute? We have some fan questions," Sloane asks, and the woman nods her agreement as Sloane grabs my wrist and drags me to a quieter corner.

"Who was that?" she asks.

I point down at her phone, and she shrugs.

"It's on mute for a moment. Sorry. We should answer some of these questions. Are you ready?"

"Did I do something to piss you off?" I ask her, and her cheeks redden.

I'm not sure why she's feeling embarrassed at the simple question.

"It's a little complicated," she says. "You didn't do anything wrong, Max."

"It feels like I did," I reply, hating the vulnerability slipping off my tongue.

She takes a step closer to me, and she stills, her eyes going wide as she looks up at me in shock. It looks like she's about to cry as she rubs the side of her throat but says nothing.

I touch her shoulder. "Sloane, are you okay?"

She shakes her head, and her hand comes up to her face, covering her nose and throat.

"Excuse me. I'll be right back," she says as she scurries off to the bathroom.

I watch her leave and give her space. What the hell just happened?

Ethan is in his mascot costume, and I can barely hear him mumbling under the head.

"What?" I ask, and he leans in even closer.

"What happened with Sloane?" he asks.

"I don't know. We were talking, I was about to go on her live stream, and then she looked like she was going to be sick."

"I'll go check on her."

"Dressed like that?"

"I'll take the head off," he says, and I shake my head with a light laugh.

"Me, you, and Sloane, we're good, right?"

"Yeah, man. I'll go talk to her," he says.

I wish I could see his face or hear him better because it definitely doesn't feel like the three of us are okay. Instead, I just nod, and the Beta wearing the massive fox head makes his way to the bathroom.

The water in my hands doesn't feel strong enough as I watch Bram Nilsen approach me. Just what I fucking need. More shit from this asshole.

"If you're coming over here to tell me to stay away from Sloane or how much you hate me, I really don't want to hear it."

"Where did she go?" he asks, and I glare at him.

"Probably somewhere to stop you from staring at her all night."

"She wants my advances. She likes me. It might be hard for you to fathom because you don't care about anyone but yourself," Bram says.

I rear back.

"Man, what the fuck are you talking about?"

"It doesn't matter. Where did Sloane go?"

"The bathroom," I tell him, wanting him to get away from me.

As far as encounters go with him, this isn't the worst but probably the most confusing. What does he mean I don't care about anyone but myself?

I'd leave the event if it weren't for needing to know Sloane's okay. Plus, she still may want me to do something on the live stream.

I play it safe by taking a seat next to Ahonen.

"Good game tonight," he says, and I nod in agreement.

"We keep playing like that, I don't see why we wouldn't make the playoffs."

"Would be brutal not to after last year's big win."

"Right," I say, wondering if this is how Owen felt growing up.

I feel like I'm in my brother's shadow, living up to his expectations, which are sky high.

When Coach Applegate takes the seat at our table, both of us straighten up as the man eyes us both.

He's no bullshit, a little grumpy, and relatively intimidating.

"Have you seen my daughter?" he asks both of us.

"Think she was headed to the bathroom the last time I saw her," I say, and Coach grunts.

"You two played well tonight. Keep it up and this season won't be a wash like everyone expected it would be."

"Of course, Coach."

"And, Connery?"

"Yes, sir?" I respond, wanting to sink into the floor right about now.

"Stop letting your brother get in your head. You're here because this team needs a strong goalie, and you're it."

"Sorry?" I say, more confused than apologetic.

"Don't get me wrong, I don't want you talking back to coaching staff or not taking his advice. But grow a fucking backbone," Coach says before tapping on the table twice and standing up. "I'm headed home. If you see Sloane, let her know I left?"

I nod my head, and Ahonen glances over at me.

"Did Coach just tell you to stop being a pussy?" he asks, and I glance over at the overly nice Canadian, wondering if I've ever heard him say that word.

"Did you just say pussy?" I ask him, and he grins.

"I'm kind, but I'm not always a gentleman," he says with a shrug as he leans back in his seat. "How much longer are we supposed to be here?"

"I've got no clue. Where the hell is Sloane?"

SLOANE

CHAPTER 20

I can't run to the bathroom fast enough as I hold my hand over my mouth and nose.

My heart rate is erratic and my hands are shaking as I swing open the bathroom door and head to the mirror. I take a hard look at myself as the reality of what I just learned hits me.

Max Connery is my scent match.

His eucalyptus and pine scent was like getting smacked in the face. As soon as I scented him, I felt it.

A pull so undeniable it felt like my only course of action was to run away and take a moment to breathe. If I hadn't, I'm not sure I'd be able to resist climbing him and begging him to take me right then and there.

Fuck.

The man I've already decided is my Alpha hates my scent match.

I turn the faucet on and splash my face with cold water, not caring about fucking up my makeup. I just need to calm down. I need the remnants of his scent to wash away so I can think rationally.

My fingers are gripping the countertop so hard that my knuckles are white. I scream as I look into the mirror. A giant fucking fox stands behind me in my reflection, nearly giving me a heart attack until my brain catches up with my eyes.

It's just Ethan.

Ethan. I need Ethan. He'll make all of this feel better.

I clutch my chest, and Ethan removes the head of the costume.

"Sorry, didn't mean to scare you. Are you okay?" he asks, and I shake my head.

I want to cry, scream, and dance all at the same time.

While I've always believed in true love and romance, I never really believed I'd ever find a scent match. It's a miracle and a huge blessing. Not to mention, it doesn't hurt that I already like Max as a person and find him attractive.

But then there's also Ethan and Bram, the two men I've chosen. One of which who does not get along with my scent match. I have everything falling right into my lap, but it's also complicated and messy.

There's also the fact that after scenting Max, I'm incredibly turned on. It's a level of horniness that I'm not sure I've ever experienced. It's almost like if someone doesn't touch me soon, I might combust.

This is such a damn mess.

"Sloane, sweetheart, what's wrong?" Ethan asks, gently putting the fox head on the counter as he approaches me.

He places an orange, furry hand on my hip, and it's nearly enough for me to calm down after everything that's happened. It's so stupid and silly, and it makes me realize how much more I need validation from Ethan right now.

He's been so standoffish since the incident. Not only do I need to be touched, I specifically need Ethan's reassurance.

"Kiss me," I tell him.

He swallows but does as I ask, leaning down and kissing me. The tender moment quickly fades as reality hits me. What if someone walks in and sees this man half dressed as a fox with his paws all over me?

Ethan pulls back and searches my face.

"What happened?"

Do I tell him everything?

I hate lying, but I also worry that if Bram finds out now, he'll maybe change his mind. Maybe I'm not giving him enough credit, but the man holds a grudge like no other. He hasn't been jealous of Ethan, but how would he feel about Max being my scent match?

I lick my lips, and it's almost like I can taste Max's clean, sharp scent.

It makes me wet, and I'm thankful that Ethan isn't an Alpha. He might scent or be able to tell that I'm turned on, but he doesn't know the extent.

I'm nearly on the edge of losing it. I need him; I need this spiraling feeling to go away.

"Whatever you need, Sloane. Just tell me, and I'll make it happen."

I glance up at him. Maybe if I come, then I'll be able to think a little more clearly.

"Touch me," I whisper.

I need it not only to dull this ache, but I also miss Ethan. I want him to be sexual with me again. He looks skeptical, and I won't push him on it, but fuck. I need something.

"Please, Ethan."

He holds up his fox paws like he's asking what he's supposed to do with the suit.

"Take it off," I tell him, and he swallows thickly. I'm into a lot of things, but adding furry to the list isn't one of them.

"Here?" he asks, looking around the bathroom, and I nod my head.

I need him right now; I need some clarity and this foreign feeling to go away. Not being in control of my emotions is frustrating. But I'm given some relief as Ethan takes off the costume and puts it on top of the counter.

He's wearing a simple white T-shirt and a pair of salaciously tiny pair of shorts.

I grab a fistful of his shirt.

"Please, Ethan."

He licks his lips and searches my face. "Are you going into heat?"

"No," I reply.

I know I'm not, but it feels like something akin to it. Are mini heats a thing? Or pre-heat. I don't fucking know. All I know is Max set this off, and it could be a lot worse.

"You're sure?" he asks, his hands nearly shaking as he pushes back my hair and cups my face.

"I told you, I'm not going anywhere."

He leans forward and kisses me. It's soft and delicate and absolutely not what I want right now.

I pull down his shorts and fist his hardening cock, making him moan against my lips.

Yes, that's exactly what I need right now.

Touch me, fuck me, claim me.

Ethan grabs me by the hips and lifts me onto the counter where I shimmy out of my panties, fisting them and putting them on my counter before pulling my dress up.

Yes. This is what I need.

"You'll need to pull out," I tell him, wrapping my legs around him and tugging him close to me.

"What?" he asks, his eyes going wide as I grab his length and line it up.

"Pull out," I tell him again, pushing him forward.

One of his hands grips my hip as the other is flat on the counter, supporting his weight as he slides into me.

His cock is perfect and hits that right spot deep inside of me.

"Yes. Harder," I tell him.

His hand pulls away from the counter to cradle the back of my head as he kisses me roughly while he fucks me against the counter. It isn't tender or soft, it's everything I need.

It feels like his fingertips are digging into my skin, and I hope they leave a mark. I need a lingering reminder of just how good Ethan can make me feel.

His ass muscles flex under the press of my heels, and my thighs slap against his with every thrust. I clutch on to Ethan like a lifeline.

He feels safe, even while he fucks me roughly.

Such a good Beta, being there for me when I need him the most. I've made the right choice.

His teeth graze against my bottom lip as I lean back on the counter. I let myself slip into the bliss that is his body against mine. Nothing matters right now, just this.

A clearing of a throat startles both of us, and we pause, embarrassment heating my cheeks as I look over Ethan's shoulder. He doesn't even move, keeping me covered even though his ass is probably on display. I let out a sigh of relief when I realize who was watching our impromptu bathroom fuck.

"Lock the door next time," Bram says, flicking the lock himself. "What do we have here?"

"Fuck," Ethan hisses.

He pulls most of the way out before pushing back into me. Knowing it's Bram lets some of my shame slip away. If anything, it's only made things hotter. Shame disappears completely when Bram approaches us and stands behind Ethan.

He presses his large chest against Ethan's back and shoves him deeper into me.

I absolutely love the look of them together. My pussy is full with Ethan's cock, but my heart swells, seeing them get along. I try to push away all the other feelings because this is always what I wanted, a pack who all love each other.

"You smell so fucking good," Bram says, and both Ethan and I shiver. "Did our Beta get you so hot and bothered you had to fuck him during a charity event?" he asks.

The words are crass and yet somehow sexy at the same time.

Bram's one hand slides into Ethan's messy, dark hair, and I

nearly come on the spot as he tugs on the strands and pulls Ethan's head back, exposing his neck.

"Couldn't control yourself?" he says against Ethan's face. "Can't blame you. Our girl is something, isn't she?"

Ethan hisses, his thrusts increasing in pace as his hips snap against mine.

Bram's other hand lightly collars my throat, and I lick my lips as I look at him. His earthly scent cocoons me, and it's like I can breathe again.

"You look so pretty when you're getting fucked."

If his hand wasn't around my throat, the back of my head would probably fall back and hit the mirror.

Ethan is glancing down at where we're connected, and my gaze rotates between Ethan's and Bram's.

"Are you going to make her come? Or do you need help?" Bram asks Ethan, and I moan.

Bram's hand trails down my body where his fingers strum my clit. His lips descend on Ethan's neck, kissing his dewy skin, and I lose it.

All semblance of rational thought escapes me as I come around Ethan's cock and Bram's fingers. The orgasm is as wicked as it is desperate, and I fall back against the mirror as Ethan's hips snap against mine.

He's shuddering, close to finishing, as he pulls out. I expect him to stroke his cock and cover me with his cum.

But instead, Bram falls to his knees and takes Ethan's cock into his mouth. He fists the base of his shaft while his lips wrap around the head of his cock, sucking out his release. I feel like I could come again, knowing that Ethan is spilling down his throat and that his cock tastes like me.

Ethan's one hand is gripping my thigh for dear life while the other holds his shirt up as Bram sucks him off.

Bram groans and glances up at the Beta as he swallows every drop. Ethan and I are panting, and I suppose I expected Bram to immediately stand up, but he doesn't. He grabs my hips and drags me to the edge of the counter where his tongue descends on my messy, wet pussy.

I moan as he licks me up. He isn't going down on me; instead, he uses his tongue to clean me. It feels like a form of worship I've never had before.

It's a level of care I never could have anticipated, and it hits me like a ton of bricks.

I'm in love with Bram.

Him cleaning my pussy in a public bathroom shouldn't be the moment I realize that, but here we are.

It sinks like a rock in my chest.

There's no way I can deny Max as my scent match. Physically and mentally, it's impossible for me.

But I also can't let Bram go either.

The large Alpha stands to his feet and grabs the back of my neck, forcing my face near his. He kisses me, spearing his tongue into my mouth so I can taste both Ethan and myself. I hum against his tongue, feeling so cared for and so confused at the same time.

What do I do?

Do I tell Bram right now? Do I tell Max?

Bram pulls back from the kiss, and the way he looks at me like I'm his entire world has me swallowing back any words that threaten to fall out. He's falling for me too, and this may just break his heart.

I glance over at Ethan who is slightly dumbfounded like he doesn't know how this all spiraled out of control either.

"Are you okay, *liefje*?"

"What does that mean?"

Bram clears his throat and rubs his mouth with the back of his hand.

"The Dutch aren't the fondest of pet names, but it roughly means darling, someone you care for."

I swallow heavily.

"I like it."

He pushes my hair back as Ethan washes his hands and starts putting the mascot costume back on.

"You went down on Ethan," I say lamely, and Bram shrugs his shoulders.

"He seemed to like it."

"I did like it, but I'm still very confused how the fuck all of this even happened," Ethan says with furrowed brows as he slides his arms into his uniform.

"How did this happen?" Bram asks.

I shrug. "I was just feeling needy," I say, wondering if he can tell I'm holding back the whole truth.

The Alpha puts his hand on my forehead and seems pleased that I don't have a fever.

"No running into bathrooms by yourself anymore, okay? If you're not feeling great, you come get one of us. I don't like the idea of your scent attracting other Alphas."

I sniff my shirt. "I have deodorizers on when I work."

"Well, whatever was going on, your scent's strong as fuck right now. They aren't working."

My cheeks heat, and Ethan has Finnegan's head under his arm.

"I've gotta get back out there and take some more pictures with the kids. We can... uh... talk about this later?"

I nod, and he leans down and kisses me softly. He glances at Bram, and I smile as the two of them briefly kiss.

Ethan unlocks the door and leaves me and Bram here on the counter.

"What happened?" he asks, brushing my hair off my shoulders.

I don't know why, but the question makes me cry.

Fuck.

Bram grabs the back of my head and rests it on his chest. Surely, whatever happened between him and Max isn't completely irreparable. I need them both, so I'll just have to figure out a way to make this work.

He rubs my back soothingly, and I start to calm down.

Bram uses his thumbs to wipe from under my eyes.

"Let's get you home."

"But I was supposed to be handling the live for the event."

"They've already met the funding goal. I'm not going to have you out there smelling like this. Also, your makeup is a bit—"

I turn around in the mirror, and I look like an absolute disaster. I can't believe Ethan wanted me, runny mascara and all.

"Why didn't anyone tell me I looked like an emotional raccoon?" I ask, sliding off the counter and grabbing a paper towel before wetting it and cleaning off my face.

"Does this mean I can take you home?"

"Yes," I say as I roughly swipe at my face.

Bram grabs my wrist and takes the paper towel. He's gentle and sweet as he cleans my face.

I can't lose him, but I can't deny Max either.

I'm an excellent schemer, and I'll figure out a way to make this work. Because there's no way I'm letting the men of my dreams slip through my fingers. I'll make this work—somehow.

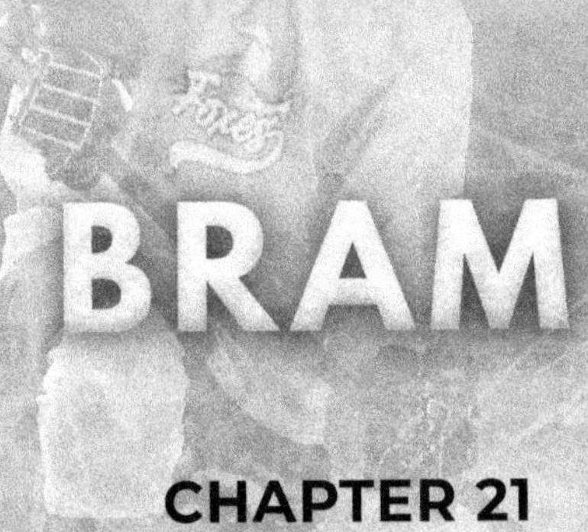

BRAM

CHAPTER 21

I drive Sloane home, and the whole ride home, she's fidgeting.

Reaching across the console, I grab her hand and put it on my thigh. It doesn't seem to help anything.

"What's wrong?"

"Oh, what? Nothing. Nothing's wrong," she says.

"Not that I'm complaining about what happened in the bathroom, it just seemed to come out of nowhere. Are you having pre-heat symptoms?"

"That might be it," she says, biting on her nail.

"You'd tell me if something was bothering you?"

Her green eyes glance over at me before quickly looking down at where our hands are interlaced.

"Can I ask you something?"

"Anything," I tell her.

"Why do you hate Max Connery so much?"

I grunt and let go of her hand to hold the steering wheel with both hands. She then wraps her arms around herself, and I immediately feel guilt over the action.

"It was a long time ago, my rookie year. It's not worth bringing up."

"But it's a big enough deal that you still don't like him."

"He's a selfish asshole, and he hasn't changed in the last handful of years. The team will be better off when he eventually gets traded. Why are you asking?"

She swallows and looks out the window. "I was just asking."

"You should stay far away from him, Sloane. All he does is use people and think about himself. He's not a friend worth having."

"Right," she whispers, looking out the window.

I feel like whatever I'm saying is fucking this all up, or whatever she isn't telling me is weighing too heavily on her.

I grab her hand and kiss her knuckles before putting it on my lap.

"Sloane, I want to be in this with you. But you've got to tell me what's going on."

"It's just stress, I think. Not knowing when my heat is coming and I think I'm worried about you and Ethan being able to handle it on your own. I don't mean that I don't trust you or that you won't take care of me. I just don't know what to expect. What if I need another Alpha?"

I grunt, hating the idea.

Ethan, I like; that was an easier adjustment than I had imagined. But Ethan is also a Beta, an attractive one who I wouldn't mind also being involved with. But an Alpha? I'd long ago given up the idea of ever being involved with an Alpha.

Fuck, that's a selfish thought, isn't it? I only care if it's someone I could see myself with.

"Is there someone else?" I ask as calmly as possible.

"No," she whispers, and I feel like it's a lie.

I hadn't thought Sloane had lied to me ever since we've been together, so why is she starting now?

"If there's another Alpha, I suppose we would do what you did with Ethan. Getting to know each other and going from there. I won't lie and say it will be easy for me."

"You get along with Ethan. I mean, more than get along with Ethan after tonight," she says softly.

"If you could find an Alpha like him, it would be appreciated," I joke with a smile.

She doesn't return the smile and just nods her head.

"It's too cold, so I'm dropping you off in front of your house."

"Okay."

I want to push more and figure out exactly what's bothering her.

"We have a string of away games coming up soon. You'll call me right away if you think you're going into heat? I'll drop everything," I promise her as I park in front of her house.

She turns her head on the headrest to stare at me. She looks tired and sad, and I hate it.

What am I doing wrong?

"You're a good man, Bram," she says, and I lean over to kiss her.

She accepts my kiss, and it's tender and sweet, nothing like the frantic encounter in the bathroom.

"Let me know when you get inside," I tell her.

"I will."

She kisses me one more time before getting out of the car and walking to her apartment. A few moments later, she texts me.

SLOANE

I'm home. Good night, Bram.

Good night

I drive home with a sinking feeling in my stomach, and I'm not sure how to make it right.

Ball Arena is a shitty name and an even shittier stadium. The ice is slushy, and I feel like the whole place might collapse if someone blinks the wrong way.

We're playing like shit, it's the second away game in a row, and everyone is exhausted, and it shows.

It's not even midway in the season. We can't be falling apart now.

I have the left forward against the boards as I shove my shoulder against his back, using my stick to try and control the puck. His helmet keeps banging against the glass, and I smile to myself.

It's like a rhythmic clinking of his head and the crowded banging against the glass.

There's a simmering anger resting under the surface for me lately. I don't know if it's because things with Sloane feel like the other shoe is going to drop or if it's something deeper.

All I know is I have enough frustration to get me through this string of games so I can get back and figure out whatever the fuck is going on with my Omega.

The Avalanche player is trying to get out of the corner I've put him in as one of his teammates attempts to help him, causing Martel to come to my defense.

"Give it up, you fuck," he growls at the player at my back.

My thighs are burning as I keep digging, refusing to let up. We're down by one, and there's only four minutes left in the third.

We can't afford to give them any advantages. We need to get more shots on goal, and there's little time to be fucking around.

My skates are slipping on the slush as the fucker elbows me in the nose.

A whistle is called immediately as I put my gloved hand up to my bleeding face.

"Fucking *klootzak*," I hiss under my breath.

"What does that one mean?" Martel says, skating to our bench as we wait for the double-minor penalty to be called.

"Scrotum," I say as the medic holds the bridge of my nose.

Martel laughs and rests against the bench. "That's cute."

I narrow my eyes at him, and he smiles as the penalty is called.

The crowd boos, as we have the rest of the game to play with a man down against Colorado.

The line shift changes, focusing heavily on the offense, and I know I likely won't be called in for the remainder of the period. Our hope is either to score during the power play or force overtime.

I hold the gauze against my nose, willing the bleeding to stop as I watch the rest of the game with bated breath.

The Foxes have the advantage and are gathered on the offensive side, taking shots and keeping control of the puck.

Until they're not.

One of the Avalanche gets a break away, skating faster than the rest of our team, even as they use their sticks to try and stop him. But he's too fast. It's one on one with Connery.

The motherfucker scores albeit a good shot, despite the Foxes' power play.

I curse, forgetting about the gauze as the blood pours out of my nose. I hiss and hold it back against my face.

"This is fucking bullshit," Martel grumbles next to me, and I grunt in agreement. "We're fucking blowing it right now."

"It's the fucking goalie."

"I tried to get Anders out of retirement, and I thought Charlotte was going to stab me in my sleep. So we're stuck with him. And honestly, he's just as good as Owen. What's your deal with him anyway?"

"We played together our rookie year. What they say in the tabloids has all been true. I don't want someone with that character on our team."

"Yeah, because you're so charming," he retorts, and I glare at him, which must not be threatening with a bloody nose. "Learn to deal with him. Save all your hate for the games, please."

I narrow my eyes at him, wondering how a fellow hater can be so level headed.

He shrugs. "We're not going to win if you two don't get along."

"Whatever," I groan back as the whistle blows and the Avalanche celebrate their win.

Coach Applegate has his arms crossed, his face stoic, and I know he's pissed as the team skates off the ice and we head to the visitors' locker room.

I just want to go to my room and call Sloane. Instead, I sit my ass on this bench as her father chews us all out.

"What the fuck was that? A goal on a double-minor in our favor? We're the reigning Stanley Cup champions. This is not how we should be playing nearly halfway into the season. We have our game in Edmonton in two days. We fly out tomorrow. I swear to fucking God, if we don't step it up, there will be some major changes. This is not the same team that won the championship last year. I know we lost Connery and Bandnin as players, but that's no excuse. Watch tonight's game over and over, and see where you fucked up. Go to sleep," he says waving off his hand.

Yeah, definitely not worried about telling that man that I'm fucking his daughter and plan on bonding her anytime soon.

I scrub my face.

"I'm sorry, guys," Max Connery says, and I glare over at him.

"It's not your fault, man. There's no reason he should have had that break away when we were a player up. It was a fuckup," our captain, Eli Beckford, says.

Deep down, I know it was a good shot, that it's not Connery's fault. But my stupid ego and grudge just won't give it up. Maybe it's because Sloane brought him up or because my nose aches. But I lose it.

"Really? We just get our asses chewed out, come off another loss, and you're just patting him on the back and telling him it's all good?" I say, and Eli sighs.

"Yeah, Nilsen. That's what I'm doing."

"We've been playing like shit lately, and our goalie not stepping it up is only making things worse."

Max steps up, his goalie gear still on except his helmet.

I can't believe I found him attractive once.

"You want me to fuck up your nose again?" Max says, shoving at my chest, which I quickly shove back.

"Yeah, I just might. Let's fucking go."

He rears back and punches me in the face, which I quickly reciprocate.

Now my nose and lip aches, and I'm about to hit him again when Martel grabs me and Beckford grabs Connery.

"Stop it," Martel says, gripping me tightly.

"I'm good. Let go of me."

He tightens his arms around me before letting go, and Beckford does the same with Connery.

"It doesn't matter anyway. We're still deep in the season. You don't have a contract with the team, and you won't," I sneer.

"Go to the fucking hotel. Now," Beckford demands.

I shuck off my gear as quickly as possible and shove all my shit in my bag before getting dressed.

As soon as I'm back at the hotel, I video call Sloane, needing to calm myself down.

Once her pretty face is on my screen, it's like I can think straight again. What the fuck is happening to me? I know I can be petty and spiteful, but things with Connery are out of hand, and I don't know why.

Sloane gasps. "I didn't realize he hit your lip too," she says, concerned, and I shake my head.

"I'm fine. How are you feeling?"

"I feel better. I'm more worried about you. Did my dad chew you guys out after the game?" she asks with a wince.

"Yeah, it wasn't great."

There's a long pause as she pans the screen over to Ethan. I'm actually glad he stays local and can be there when I'm not.

"Rough game. Hopefully, more luck in Edmonton."

"Yeah, I sure as fuck hope so," I say, lying back in the bed, exhaustion deep in my bones.

"Bram, baby, are you okay?" Sloane says, and I nod.

"Yeah, I just miss you two."

"We miss you too," she says softly.

Everything still feels a little stilted between us, and I just want answers.

"When I get home, we'll spend some time together."

"I'd really like that," Sloane says.

"Me too. Good night."

"Good night."

SLOANE

CHAPTER 22

"What aren't you telling us?" Ethan asks from where he's perched on my bed.

Tears well in my eyes, and I just sob. It's all been weighing on me so heavily, and I feel like I'm about to burst.

His eyes go wide, and he gently grabs my face.

"Shit, Sloane. I didn't mean to upset you. What's wrong?"

"I'm about to have everything, but I feel like I'm going to lose it all at the same time. I don't know what to do."

"You can tell me. We can work through this together."

I try to catch my breath, and Ethan pets my hair and wipes my tears away.

"Fuck, I hate crying like this," I say as I lick my lips and try to compose myself. "The night of the charity event, something happened."

"Yeah, I very much remember our time in the bathroom."

"Before that. I found out something. Something big."

His brows furrow as he strokes the side of my face in a soothing way. It helps knowing I won't lose Ethan.

"How would you handle it if I wanted someone else in the pack?" I ask him.

"Sweetheart, you're an Omega. I might have never planned on

being in a pack, but I went into this knowing you would need multiple partners. I'm just glad to be one of them. Fuck, you could have fifteen dudes, and I'd be grateful for any sliver of attention you gave me."

I give him a watery smile and wrap my arms around him, holding him tight.

"Max is my scent match," I whisper so softly I know he can't hear me mumbling against his chest.

"What?"

"Max is my scent match," I reply, saying it louder and wait for his reaction.

"Shit."

"I scented him for the first time at the charity event."

"Does he know?" he asks, petting my hair and holding me close. The pressure of his arms wrapped around me feels nice and is stopping me from spiraling completely.

"No… I mean, I don't think so. I always wear deodorizers at work. I'm guessing he usually does too. I'm not sure why, but it probably has something to do with his brother. He must not have reapplied after the game and gone to the event."

"That's why you were so desperate in the bathroom."

I make a groaning noise, and he squeezes me tightly.

"I didn't mean it like that. You know I didn't. I could sense something was different but didn't know what it was. Not going to lie, I was glad for it. You made me put my bullshit to the side, and it felt so good to finally have you. But it makes sense why you needed me so badly then."

I nod against his chest, and I wish Bram was here. His rumbling chest against my face as Ethan stroked my hair, that would be the dream.

But now, Max is a part of the mix. Where does he fit in this fantasy?

"Bram doesn't know?" Ethan asks, even though he knows the answer. I shake my head against his shirt, not worried about my tear stains.

"I tried to ask what the issue is between them, and he only doubled down on me staying away from him. I'm worried that when he finds out, he won't be able to handle it. I can't lose him, but I can't let this thing with Max go either. I need them both, and they hate each other."

He strokes my hair. "If it helps, I do think the hate is one sided. Max doesn't even seem to really know why Bram hates him."

"He told you that?"

"Yeah. You really think Max has no idea?" he asks.

"He's never said anything or acted like I was his scent match. So I don't think so. I just can't figure out how to tell Bram. There are times on the phone where I'm about to say something, and then I just can't. I don't want to mess up his mindset before his games, and I think I'm just so scared."

"Do you want to tell Bram before you talk with Max?"

"I think I have to. Bram is big on trust, and as much as I know Max deserves to know I'm his scent match, I can't start anything without Bram knowing. But the idea of telling him has been making me sick to my stomach."

He kisses the top of my head. "You've been keeping this all bottled up for too long. I've got your back; we'll figure this out."

"How do I tell him, Ethan? I'm in love with him, and I'm probably about to break his heart when that's the last thing I ever wanted to do."

"If he feels anything like I do, he'll get over it. They'll have to figure their shit out. You're worth the minefield, Sloane."

Well, that just makes me cry more.

"Can you tell him?"

"I can, but I think this needs to come from you. Do you think writing a letter would help?" he asks, and I breathe through my nose and nod.

"That's actually a pretty good idea. Let me go get a pen and paper."

Ethan strokes a hand down my back as I go to my desk and

open the top drawer, grabbing one of my favorite pens before grabbing my notebook, and I spill all my feelings on paper.

It feels cathartic and freeing, and I'm able to process everything without being interrupted or sobbing.

I hand it over to Ethan to read, which he does twice.

"This is perfect. When are you going to give it to him?"

"Does it make me a coward to put it in his locker so he reads it when they get home in a few days?"

"No, I think that's a good idea. He'll have time to process before he reaches out."

I fling my arms around his neck and squeeze him close.

"Thank you, Ethan. I don't know what I'd do without you."

"Here's to never finding out," he says, squeezing me close.

For the first time in the last couple of days, it doesn't feel like my world is going to come crashing down.

❄ ❄ ❄ ❄

I don't sleep, and I feel like I've been hit by a bus. But I've got to swing by the stadium and drop off my letter.

I thought about dropping it off at his house, but what if he doesn't check his mailbox for days? If I tape it to his locker, he won't be able to miss it when they get back from their game.

There's a few hours before they get home, and considering that no one else should be there, I don't put much effort into my appearance.

I'm too fucking stressed to look cute.

Instead, I'm wearing sweatpants, a crewneck that has so much piling it should be tossed out, and my favorite pair of sneakers.

When I have to defrost my windshield, I contemplate every moment of my life, but somehow my anxiety lets me persevere.

It's like I'm on autopilot the entire drive. But my shaky legs make me walk the distance to the locker room as I place the white envelope with his name on the front where he can't miss it.

I stare at his name in my script, wondering if this really is a good idea or if I'm making something worse.

But before I can snatch it back, I hear male voices coming down the tunnel to the locker room.

Fuck.

I thought they were supposed to get back at three?

No way I can confront him now, and Max will be with them. I don't have any deodorizers on.

Fuck. Fuck. Fuck.

I glance around and open the door to where the ice baths are and shut it behind me.

I take a seat in one of the swivel chairs and lean against the wall by the door. If anyone looked through the glass, they wouldn't be able to see me.

I bite my nail, hating the way my stomach feels like it's going to fall out of my ass. The need to throw up is just on the brink as I lean forward and rest my head on my knees.

This feeling of not knowing what's going to happen and if I'm going to hurt someone I care about makes me want to disappear.

Why can't they just get along? Why did my scent match have to be the person Bram dislikes the most?

Not that I'm upset about it being Max, which only makes me feel even more guilty.

I like Max; I think he's handsome and kind. He's been a great friend while I haven't. He might not really be experienced with Omegas or understanding pack life. But deep down, I know that he would try, and he's a good man.

How can two things be so true at once?

I want Max but also wish things weren't so complicated.

The door creaks open, and when I glance over, it's a wide-eyed Max Connery staring down at me.

He shuts the door behind him and looks at me like it's the first time he's actually ever seen me.

"Your scent. You're…"

He doesn't finish his sentence. He comes over and grabs me under his arms and clutches me to his chest.

"No fucking way," he mumbles against my hair.

He isn't masking his scent either. The fresh crispness floods my nose, and it's like all the anxiety and fear from earlier disappears.

My scent match wants me.

Max is holding me like I'm some precious miracle, and my body can't help but respond to how he makes me feel. I wrap my legs around his waist, and he shifts his hands so that he's gripping me by my thighs.

He pulls back ever so slightly, his pretty blue eyes meeting mine.

It's like something snaps between the both of us, and his mouth is on mine in an instant.

His lips are soft but demanding against mine as he takes a few steps and pushes my back against the wall.

I moan, and his fingers dig into my thighs.

My scent match wants me, and I feel drunk with the feeling.

Max's lips leave mine only so that he can kiss and nip my throat. A deep rumble leaves his throat every time he scents me. If that wasn't enough to let me know how he's feeling, his long, hard length between my legs does.

There's an overwhelming feeling of need rippling through me. While my scent match clearly accepts me, I need him to claim me.

Make me his so that I don't have this empty feeling anymore. My Alpha will make things better.

He was made for me, after all.

I use the heels of my feet to tug down his waistband, and he sets me on my feet. His lips never leave my skin as he tugs down my sweatpants and panties. I step out of them, and he has me back in his arms again.

His cock glides between my pussy lips as I cover him in my slick.

"Just like that, baby. Fuck. I want to be covered in your scent and slick."

Oh. I like that.

Max sucks on the side of my neck, and I almost feel like I could come from that alone. He'd just need to sink his teeth into me, and things would be perfect.

That sounds amazing actually.

I grab the back of his head and hold him against my throat as his hips shift, grinding against my body.

The head of his cock rubs against my clit and while it feels fantastic, I need my Alpha's knot.

Nothing else will take away this ache.

"Need you. Please," I tell him, and his hands slide more to my ass, spreading me apart.

He stops kissing my neck and looks down at me. Both of us still have our tops on.

Max licks his lips and swallows.

"Sloane, baby. What does this mean?" he asks.

"Alpha, please," I reply.

This isn't the time for talking. This is the time for fucking. His job is to make me feel better. I need him.

He swallows again like the reality of the situation is hitting him in the face.

"You're really mine?" he asks.

There are no thoughts in my head right now besides the Alpha holding me. My scent match needs to stop talking and start thrusting.

"Yes. It hurts. Make it better," I ask him, not caring how pathetic I sound.

"Okay, baby," he says.

He holds me against the wall with one hand as the other fists his cock before pushing it deep inside of me.

"Fuck," he shudders as he fills me completely.

His forehead presses against mine as he fucks me against the wall. The stretch is everything I wanted. In fact, I want more.

"I knew you were special," he whispers before his mouth is back on mine.

He tastes perfect; everything about him is perfect. My scent match thinks I'm special and perfect. Is there a better feeling?

Apparently, there is as he pushes his knot deep inside of me.

A loud moan attempts to escape me, but he uses his hand to cover my mouth.

"Those sweet sounds are only for me now, baby. God, look at you. Fucking perfect. This pussy was made for me. You smell so goddamn good."

My eyes roll back ever so slightly with the praise and the sensation. My thighs are shaking, and my nails are digging into his shoulders as I try to keep myself wrapped around his cock.

"Come on, baby, I want that slick dripping against the floor," he says.

His knot swells, and I fall apart, my body pulsating against his length as my body shakes and my vision goes hazy.

He feels so good.

Everything feels so right as he spills inside of me.

I grab his neck, and he pants as he rests his face against mine, rocking his hips with what little he can, like he can't get enough of me.

His forehead is against mine, and he pulls back, his brows furrowed. Max uses the wall to balance me as he rests the back of his hand against my forehead.

"Sloane? Are you sick?"

The back of my head thuds against the wall as I try to organize my thoughts. His scent is so consuming, and really, the only sensation that's filling me is the stretch of his cock.

Definitely not sick, just very happy.

"No," I whisper. "Good."

He looks like he doesn't believe me, and I'm about to convince him to let me rub my clit against his pelvis while we're knotted when the door swings open.

A furious Bram glances over in our direction.

It's like cold water is being splashed on me, but at the same time, I'm drowning in feelings I can't decipher.

Bram just stands there for a moment in shock.

"Get the fuck out," Max says, and I shake my head.

"No. Alpha. Stay," I tell Bram, and he looks like he's about to lose it.

His hands are balled into fists. He doesn't speak, just breathes through his nose and walks and turns away.

The previously euphoric sensation fades away. I can't run after him. I'm knotted to Max.

I rub my forehead.

Think rationally, Sloane.

"Sloane, what the fuck was that?" Max asks, glancing over at the door where Bram just left.

Tears fill my eyes as the reality sets in of what just happened and what's about to happen.

Fuck.

"Call Ethan," I manage to whisper, and Max looks at me, confused. But calls him anyway.

Thank God.

I clutch on to Max, holding him tightly, letting his scent calm this raging feeling of rejection and hurt.

This wasn't how it was supposed to go, and now, I don't know what's about to happen.

My heat is here, and everything is fucked.

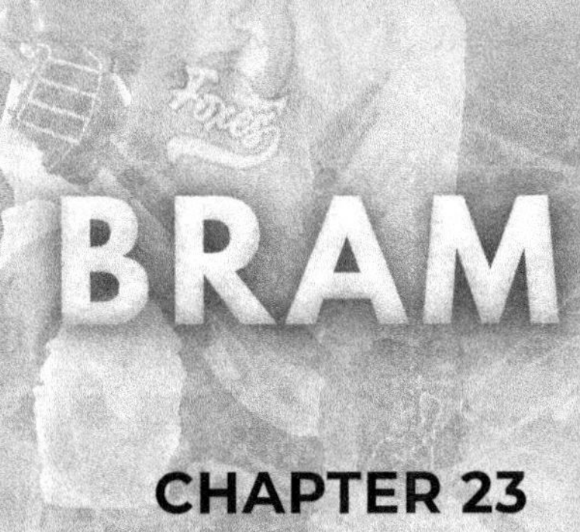

BRAM

CHAPTER 23

The drive to my house is like I'm on autopilot. As soon as I walked in on them, I just tossed everything into my bag and ran out of there.

The only reason I went in the room in the first place was because I could scent Sloane and was wondering if she was waiting for me to get back from my game to surprise me.

Well, I was surprised but definitely not in a good way.

I didn't know I could feel hurt the way I'm experiencing right now. There's an ache in my chest that feels like it might swallow me whole.

How could I be the only one in this relationship feeling this way? How could she do this?

She promised that she would tell me if she was interested in someone else. Why would she fuck Max? Let alone at the goddamn stadium?

Is this what she was hiding from me since the charity gala? I saw her talking to him, but it didn't seem like they were anything beyond friends. Is that why she was asking me why I hated Max? Because she's been sleeping with him too?

There's such a deep feeling of betrayal that I'm not sure if I can work past this.

Even if she had told me she was interested in Max, I'm not sure if it would work out. At least not in any conventional sense.

I need to breathe and have space to process everything.

I'm in love with her, and the idea that she was with him hurts more than anything I've ever felt before.

My phone is vibrating in my pocket. Ethan has called four times, probably trying to rationalize this bullshit. Fuck, did he know too?

I toss my bag on the floor as I sit on my couch and stare at the blank glaring screen of my TV.

How did I get here?

I thought I was being an attentive, good Alpha for Sloane. She told me I was a good man and that she missed me.

But then I found her knotted with a man who's also left me with this similar gaping feeling in my chest.

What's wrong with me that no one wants to stay?

Why am I not enough?

My phone continues buzzing, and I put it on silent, Just sitting and stewing, trying to make some sense out of it all.

I'm not sure how long I sit here, not even changing out of my clothes from the plane ride, when there's a loud banging at my door.

I look through the glass pane and see Ethan standing on my front step. I sigh and consider telling him to fuck off, but some soft part of me opens the door.

Ethan presses the door, pushing it open and entering my space.

"Why aren't you answering the fucking phone?" he questions.

"You know why."

Ethan scrubs his face. "Did you get Sloane's letter?"

My face scrunches. What the hell is he talking about?

"The letter. She left it in your locker," he reiterates.

"It doesn't matter. Did you know?"

He tenses and sighs.

"This wasn't how this was all supposed to happen. Where's the fucking letter?" he asks.

I'm shoving his shoulder to get him to leave my house as he barrels past me and opens my bag, digging out a white envelope with my name scrawled on the front.

"This letter, read it, then we'll talk."

I snatch the letter out of his hand, a deep sense of regret still filling me. As much as I'd like to just figure out a way to work through my feelings, I can't do that with him here. And as frustrated as I am, I can't stomach the thought of manhandling him out of my home either.

I pry the letter open and unfold the paper written in Sloane's neat handwriting.

Bram,

I'm writing you this letter so that I can get everything off my chest without stumbling, crying, or making a complete fool of myself.

I think it's pretty obvious by now that my feelings for you are real and deep. You're the first Alpha I truly saw a future with. You're honestly the entire reason I wanted to work for the Foxes this year. I needed a reason to be around you, and things progressed so beautifully and quickly between us.

None of that has changed. I still see you as my Alpha and the man I want in my pack.

But there's something I've been hiding, and I didn't know how to tell you.

The night of the charity gala, I realized that Max Connery is my scent match. It's why I acted the way I did in the bathroom and why I haven't been myself lately.

Max doesn't know, and I haven't told him. I couldn't in good conscience act on this until I told you what was going on.

I know you don't like him, and you've warned me multiple times to stay away, and out of respect for you, I have.

But I can't walk away from a scent match.

The idea of hurting you has caused me to be physically sick. I haven't been eating or sleeping much out of fear of how you may react.

I know this isn't ideal, and the thought of being in a pack was already hard for you, let alone with someone you aren't fond of.

I'd never want to change you. I love you how you are. I hope that you feel just as strongly as I do so that we can work past this.

It's a lot to take in, and I understand if you need time to process how you feel. That's why I dropped this letter off so you could read it as soon as you got back from your games.

I want you as my Alpha in my pack. But I need my scent match just as much. Please tell me we can make this work.

Yours,
Sloane.

I read it two more times before glancing up at Ethan.

"But she didn't wait."

Ethan rubs the back of his neck. "I think that was out of their hands."

"What do you mean? I walked in with him knotted inside of her. I didn't even get a chance to read this letter."

"Listen. I don't know shit about scent matches. All I know is Sloane went to the stadium to drop your letter off, not expecting you all to arrive for a few hours."

"We left ahead of schedule," I reply, and Ethan nods.

"Right, and she went and hid in the side room. She wasn't wearing any deodorizers because she wasn't expecting to run into anyone. I guess Max wasn't covering his scent either. So when he scented her and found her in the room, they both went a little feral."

"Why is Sloane not here telling me this?"

"Well, because she's in heat, and she's locked herself in the bathroom, crying over you and the fact that her dad is threatening to kill Max and myself."

"She's in heat?" I say with shock.

She's in heat, and she's crying and upset.

I glance back down at the letter. She didn't mean for this to happen. Fate took her life into its hands and caused this mess.

But the idea of watching Max with *my* woman makes my chest ache.

"She really didn't mean to?" I ask, the letter tight in my hands.

"I was there when she wrote the letter. She's been sick over the thought of losing you."

"And Connery?"

"She didn't seem worried about how he would react, mostly worried about upsetting or losing you. You and I both know there is no one better than Sloane. This is a once in a lifetime opportunity. So are you going to be a petty bitch about it, or are you gonna pack your shit and get in my shitty truck and drive over to her place and take care of her when she needs us most?"

It's like the Beta has slapped me across the face with the cold-hearted truth.

No one will ever live up to Sloane. I'm obsessed with her. I'm in love with her.

"How am I supposed to be around him for days on end?" I ask Ethan.

"I'll be your glorified Beta buffer. Let's get her through her heat, and then we can worry about the other shit later."

I nod and sigh.

"Coach knows?"

"Oh yeah. Coach knows."

"Fuck," I hiss as I turn around and grab a few things out of my bag. "Give me five minutes, and we'll head over there."

Ethan sighs with relief, but all I'm filled with is tension.

This is not going to be the vision of what I thought Sloane's heat was going to look like.

❄ ❄ ❄ ❄

When we pull up to Sloane's driveway, parking over by her apartment, Coach Applegate is pacing, kicking clunks of snow while he mutters under his breath. His Omega, who I've met at a few team events, is trying to console him.

"There you motherfuckers are," he says, and I can see his breath from the bitter cold. "What fucking part of treat her like your own daughter didn't you get, Nilsen?"

"Kristoff, enough. The one upstairs is her scent match, and she chose these two."

Coach Applegate rolls his eyes. "Some fucking choices. She's in there crying over your ass," he says, pointing a finger against my chest.

"You know it's more complicated than that," his Omega says.

"Willow, for the love of God, please stop being rational right now. I just found out my goalie, my most tenured defensemen, and the fucking mascot are here to be in our daughter's heat. I think I have the right to be a little pissed."

His Omega sighs, rolling her eyes. "Why did you think she wanted to work there so badly? The apple doesn't fall far from the tree."

He gapes at his woman while Ethan and I just keep our mouths shut.

"You knew?" he asks her.

"Oh, right. I forgot about the muffins in the oven. So nice meeting you boys," she says with a wave, leaving Coach Applegate there gaping at her.

The apple doesn't fall far at all because that's definitely some shit Sloane would pull.

"So I need a goalie, a new defensive line, and a goddamn mascot for our next game?" Coach says, resolved but still pissed off.

"It appears so, sir," I say.

The Alpha coach approaches me, pointing a finger against my chest. "If she wasn't in that state right now, we'd be having a way deeper conversation. But as pissed as I am right now, I can't let her suffer. Go take care of my daughter. I swear to fucking God, if you or that idiot upstairs bonds her when she can't consent fully, then you'll be looking for a gravesite instead of a new team," he says.

He glares at both of us before stomping back to their main property. His pack Beta, who I can't remember his name, strolls up, and I wonder if we're going to get another lashing.

Instead, he whistles. "That was extremely dramatic. I apologize on Kristoff's behalf. Let me give one of you boys my number in case you need anything during Sloane's heat."

Both Ethan and I blink at the man, and he holds out his hand, waiting for a phone.

I'm about to dig out mine, and the man shakes his head.

"I'd rather the sanest one have my number on their phone," he says to Ethan, who pulls out his phone and hands it to the man, who quickly enters his details.

I glance over, and then his name clicks. Henderson Applegate.

"Sloane can be impulsive. But not with something like this. Kristoff will come around, and I'm sure Sloane will come to all your defenses once she's coherent. Take care of our girl," he says, smacking my shoulder before following Coach back into their house.

"What the fuck just happened?" Ethan whispers behind me.

That is a great question because it feels like I'm in the twilight zone.

Ethan leads me up the side stairs, and Sloane's peachy scent is permeating through the hallways. It nearly knocks me off my ass.

She's absolutely in heat.

When he opens the door, I'm greeted with Connery sitting on the ground with his head in his hands.

"Thank fuck you're here," he says, and I glare at him and then glance at the shut bathroom door.

I don't speak to Max because the last thing I need to do is get into it with him right now.

I tap my knuckles against the door.

"Sloane, it's Bram, open up."

She opens the door and grabs my wrist, tugging me into the bathroom with her before slamming the door.

Her small arms immediately wrap around my waist.

"Sorry. Sorry. Sorry," she chants over and over.

"I read the letter. I'm sorry I ran out earlier. I didn't know what was happening and assumed the worst."

Her hands are clutching my shirt like a lifeline, and it seems like she's trying to hold on and not go into a complete heat-induced state.

"Don't leave me," she says in a cry, and my hands tighten around her.

"I'm not going anywhere. You're still mine."

She cries against my chest, squeezing me tightly, before her hold loosens and she begins to rub the bridge of her nose against my chest, scenting me or marking me with her scent, I can't tell.

"Come on, let's go get you into bed."

She takes a deep breath, and it sounds almost exhausted as she nods her head and turns the knob to her bedroom.

The apartment is small, and my and Max's scent are competing against each other, mingling with Sloane's.

I don't know how many days I'll be trapped in here with him. Not even just trapped, the things Sloane needs right now, I groan just thinking about it.

This moment I thought was going to be so perfect between Sloane, Ethan, and myself now has a six-foot-three dickhead elephant in the room.

SLOANE

CHAPTER 24

Keep it together, woman.

All I want to do is climb my Alpha and kiss his face and tell him how relieved I am to have him here. That he cares about me enough to look past all this.

Then I glance over at my scent match and whine. I would also like to climb him.

"Sweetheart, you okay?" my Beta asks.

Oh, how I adore him.

He's so handsome, sexy, and he's going to take care of every-thing during my heat. He also very much deserves to be climbed.

I shake my head to rid the naughty thoughts.

What was it I wanted to do?

Right, the contract and the manual.

I go to my desk, pulling out the binder and the three contracts for each of the men along with three pens that they better return and hand them those.

"What's this?" my scent match asks.

"Her heat contract and her manual," my Beta says.

He is so helpful and deserves all the love. So I remove my sweatpants and sweater to give him all that love. Plus, it's scorching hot in here.

Is the air unit on?

I go to click the buttons and hear the AC activate. All the men look around confused.

Aren't they also burning up?

They're all glancing through the contract. My Beta signs first and approaches me. I bite my lip.

Yes, touch me, fuck me, make it all go away.

"Where's your diaphragm?" he asks.

Boo.

Get me pregnant. What do you mean a diaphragm?

I shrug, acting like I don't know where it is.

"Sloane, you made me promise," Ethan says.

Promises were meant to be broken.

My strong, grumpy Alpha approaches and grabs my cheeks. I moan at the way his fingers dig into my skin.

"Diaphragm and condoms, *liefje*. Where are they?"

I sigh, pointing at my nightstand drawer as he goes and places condoms on top of the nightstand.

Absolutely not.

I come right behind him and grab a crystal jewelry holder and place the condoms neatly into the container.

He unclicks the plastic of the torture device, aka, the diaphragm that is going to stop their cum from completely filling me, and I shake my head.

Nope. I don't want it.

"Do we need to direct you to section 1A of the Sloane heat manual where you distinctly say you're not on birth control and these are the methods you chose?" my Beta asks.

My scent match has his brows furrowed, watching the conversation and reading that stupid fucking binder full of bullshit I clearly didn't mean.

I want them each to fuck me one by one and fill me with their cum and give me a baby.

"I think we have some things to work through before we start discussing babies," my Alpha says, and I pout.

Didn't realize I said that out loud.

"None of that. Let me put this in, and I'll fuck you so good. I'll make it all go away," he promises.

That does sound nice.

Actually, it sounds really, really nice.

"You're hurting, aren't you, sweet Omega? Let me take it away. Take those panties off, and lie back. Let your Alpha take care of you."

His words are sweet, and considering how I thought he wasn't going to be here for me but is, I concede.

I'll just take it out when they aren't looking.

"Good girl," he says as I lean back and spread my legs for him.

He places two fingers inside of me, curling them deep, making me moan. He's fully dressed as he leans forward and puts his lips against my pussy and licking my clit.

I rake my nails against his scalp, and his chest purrs.

The smile that takes over my face is probably ridiculous as he glances up at me while eating me out.

He's here, he's mine, he loves me.

Or at least I thought he did before he pushes the soft silicone— no fun—device inside of me.

He reaches over to grab a condom, and I shake my head.

"Sloane," he sighs my name.

"She's okay with just one or the other," my Beta says.

He's sitting on the couch with my scent match. Which is irritating. Why are they not all ravishing me at the same time?

This is bullshit, and I'm about to pout about it when my Alpha pushes his cock deep inside of me.

Yes. This is what I needed.

Just as a cramp is rolling through me, he fucks me harder. His large cock thrusts in and out of me, making me forget about everything.

My pack is here. They're perfect. I'm going to be okay.

So I let go completely and enjoy the feeling of his body over mine.

CHAPTER 25

I'm completely reeling.

Honestly, close to having a fucking panic attack over the whole situation. I was just coming home from our away games to find out that I have a scent match.

Sloane Applegate is my scent match, and she's in heat. And the man who hates me for no reason is currently fucking her a few feet away from me.

I'm flipping through her manual.

"How long did it take her to make this?" I ask Ethan who is sitting next to me.

"A few weeks. She's a bit particular."

"So you, her, and Nilsen?"

"Yeah," he sighs, and I nod.

"At least it makes sense now why you two started separating yourselves from me. I thought I had done something wrong."

Ethan places a hand on my shoulder and squeezes.

"I'm sorry about that."

"Makes sense why he stormed off. I'm sure he's only going to hate me even more now."

"All that matters right now is Sloane, okay?" Ethan says. "All the other shit like what being a pack looks like and how we're going to do this, that can wait. Right now, we just need to make sure she's taken care of."

I swallow and nod. Her scent is so thick and only getting thicker while she's getting knotted on her bed. I blink a few times, trying to conceptualize it all and work through this jealousy that I feel.

It's something I'm going to have to get used to, I guess.

An Omega wasn't really on the radar for me, especially not one like Sloane.

How does someone's life change so dramatically in just a few hours?

"I have no clue what I'm doing," I whisper to Ethan.

"I don't think any of us do. Just read the manual, follow your instincts. She's your scent match, Max," he says with a soft smile, and I let myself relax a little.

"Are you okay if I make a quick call?" I ask, and he nods.

"She's busy anyway. I'll just sit back and watch the show," he says, spreading his stance wide as he watches Bram rut the fuck out of Sloane.

What in the hell is happening?

I step outside and walk downstairs to the main garage area. As soon as I do, I feel unsettled like I need to go right back upstairs. But I refrain and pull out my phone and call the person I never thought I would for advice. I shiver. It's colder in here than it is in Sloane's room. It doesn't help that there's snow outside either.

He answers after a few rings.

"Hello?" Owen says.

"Owen, I need your help."

"Are you okay? What's wrong?" he says in a panic.

I suppose he has every right to be. I've never called him asking for help once in my life.

"Sloane is my scent match, and she just went into heat."

"Holy shit," he whispers. "Are Bram and Ethan there?" he asks, and my brows furrow in confusion.

"How do you know about them and Sloane?"

"Piper and Sloane are friends, and Piper is my scent match and therefore the person she tells secrets to. Also, we dropped her off at his house once, and they were both there. But I didn't think he was her scent match."

"He's not."

"And he hates you," Owen says, and I groan on the phone, wondering if this was a bad idea. "Sorry, that's not helpful. What can I do?"

"I don't know what I'm doing," I say, hating the vulnerability.

"Mom did give us the sex talk about a decade ago."

"Forget I asked," I say, about to hang up.

"Sorry, I'm being an asshole. What do you need help with?"

I clear my throat, feeling awkward as fuck. "It happened really fast, like really fast. I don't know anything about heats or what I should be doing. Sloane and I haven't been able to talk, and I've never shared with anyone else. I'm probably going to fuck this up."

"You like her?"

"I liked her before I found out she was my scent match. Now it's like I'm not even sure how to explain it. She's everything to me."

"Maybe I should get Piper on the phone to talk through it?"

"You're an Omega. I want to know what I should be doing for her."

"It's not all that complicated, Max. Just give her what she wants, and if she begs for a bond, suck on her neck and tell her how good and amazing she is."

"What about Nilsen?" I ask.

"That is a tougher question. Alexi and Piper liked each other before I was involved. But if he cares about her, which it seems like he really does, he'll come around. Maybe just try not to engage with him or step on his toes too much so you can get through the heat."

"What if I can't share with him?"

"Jesus Christ, Max, it's Sloane, not sharing your favorite toy truck. She's your scent match, I get it, I do. But to me, I love Piper and Alexi the same. There's just some differences in how my body reacts to her. You might be her literal pheromone wet dream, but you have to remember she chose him too."

Owen is making too much sense.

"If you have any problems, call me or Piper." He pauses for a long second. "Wait, does Coach know?"

"Oh, yeah. Expect a foul mood at practice."

"Fuck, Gagnon is going to have to start."

"Hey, at least it's not in the middle of playoffs," I say, and he laughs.

"You know what's funny, I specifically asked Sloane not to do that. Listen, I know things have been weird. But I'm happy for you. Call us if you need anything."

"Thanks, Owen."

"Oh, and you better tell Mom before she calls me," he says before hanging up, and I curse under my breath.

I take two stairs at a time, and when I enter the room, it's like I'm walking through a row of peach trees with how strong her scent is.

It's overwhelming, and it's like my feet have a mind of their own as I approach her and Bram on the bed.

He's deeply knotted inside of her and growls as I lean over.

Ethan claps his hands and sits between the two of us, pinching Sloane's chin.

"You've got these Alphas all growly and shit over you. Do you like that?" he asks her, and she smiles with a nod. "Little trouble-maker. How's that knot treating you?"

She grabs the back of Bram's head, making him contort his body so that his lips are against her neck.

"Such a good Omega. Suck her neck," he tells Bram, pushing his head even further down.

"How'd you know how to do that?" I whisper, and Ethan rolls his eyes.

"You won't get very far in life without a library card or the internet, Max."

"Excuse me for just learning about my scent match a few hours ago."

"Fair. I'll give you a pass," he says, petting Sloane's hair. "Also, for my sanity, you and Bram are on different Sloane rotations. When he's inside of her, stay away from the bed. That goes for you too, big guy," he says, patting and rubbing Bram's back.

I watch the three of them together, feeling like an outsider. It's not a new feeling; I've felt it most of my life.

"You're with Bram too?" I ask, getting off the bed and standing there as he pets and touches Sloane and Bram.

Part of me wants to rip Bram off of her and wrap my hands around his neck, but then the other part realizes that if I did that, I would be hurting her, and that would make me a horrible scent match.

"Uh. That's a little more complicated. He's like half sucked my dick, and we kissed a few times," Ethan says with complete honesty.

"How do you half suck a dick?"

"I'll show you sometime," Ethan jokes, and Bram makes a guttural sound again.

"Why don't you work on closing all the blinds and put something together to eat?" Ethan says.

Loving that I have direction, I do just that, and for the first time since I brought Sloane home, I feel semi useful.

* * * *

Bram is hoarding my scent match, and I've had just enough of that shit.

I've tried to be reasonable, not that he's given me a reason to. He's been a dick to me since I joined the Foxes, and now he's keeping my scent match away from me.

Why am I the one who's supposed to be understanding and not step on toes?

In our work life and now in our personal life, all he's done is walk all over me, and I'm fucking sick of it.

Sloane stirs on the bed, and immediately, I walk over and scoop her up into my arms.

Bram grabs her hand to tug her back to his chest, and Ethan wraps his hand around Bram's wrist.

"He's her scent match. He won't hurt her. You need rest. Knock it off."

He grumbles but listens to Ethan. I whisper a thank you to the Beta as I clutch Sloane to my chest and carry her to the bathroom.

As soon as we're in there, she's tugging off my shirt. Her skin is splattered with freckles, and I trace the ones on her shoulder before placing a tender kiss there.

"Not sure how the fuck we got here," I tell her, and she hums, her fingers exploring the expanse of my chest. "When you're not in heat, I'll do things right. I can be a good man for you, Sloane. I promise."

She leans forward, licking from right above my nipple to behind my ear, making me shiver.

"Do you want to take a shower?"

She shakes her head.

"Knots," she whispers.

"I promise to fuck you in a bed at some point," I tell her as I sit her down on the countertop and brush her wild hair away from her face. "Fuck, I don't know how I got so lucky."

She grabs my waistband, not giving a shit about my revelations, as she tugs them down, springing my cock free.

Her pulse quickens, and as I look at her neck, all I can think about is bonding her and making her mine. But I know if I do, her dad will very likely kill me. I just found my scent match. I can't afford to die.

"Look at me," I tell her, taking in her pretty green gaze.

I figure if I stare at her face, it might help with some of this incessant feeling of bonding with her.

"Good girl. You want your Alpha's knot? You like the way I stretch that sweet little pussy of yours?"

"Mmm," she says, her eyes half lidded as she spreads her legs wide, showing me her cute little cunt.

"Look at you dripping slick all over the counter," I tell her.

I want to taste, but the idea of Bram's cum still inside of her makes my need to fill her with my own even more intense.

I hold her ass with one hand and my cock with another as I slide deep inside of her. I grab the back of her neck gently, making her look at where we're connected.

"We look perfect together," I tell her.

She must agree because she doesn't stop looking at where I'm fucking her, not even for a second. I love that she likes to watch, that she's so into me. It makes me fuck her harder.

Sloane holds on to my shoulders, and I make sure I don't fuck her too hard on the counter.

Her peachy summer scent wraps around me, and my cock is covered in her slick and scent.

God, I want her so fucking bad. I bite my bottom lip to just still myself, but all it does is catch her attention.

Her hands slide from my shoulders, her nails raking down my chest, which tingles down my spine.

I thrust hard and push my knot inside of her, and she moans so loud it ricochets on the bathroom walls.

Good, I hope it ruined Bram's sleep.

She pushes my head against her neck, and I open my mouth. I want to do it so badly. But instead, I suck on her skin, hard enough I know there'll be a bruise.

She hums in approval.

Thank fuck I took that phone call earlier.

"Such a good Omega for me," I say, kissing the side of her throat, and I rut into her pussy as my knot swells to its largest size and I spill inside of her.

It calms the feral Alpha part of me that hated seeing her with Bram, and I sigh in relief.

My balls and thighs are covered in her release, and I want to rub it into my skin.

I cup the back of her head, peppering her face with kisses as she sighs contentedly.

When I pull back, she points to a paper attached to the mirror labeled "Sloane's Skin Care Routine."

"You want me to wash your face?" I ask her, and she points to step one of the routine like I'm an idiot.

I glance to the left, and there are four bottles, each of them with a number on it. She was thorough.

I go through the steps, and Sloane is half asleep throughout all of it, my knot still deep inside of her. I think that's it for the night when she grabs a different washcloth and uses the same routine on me.

My skin has never felt so good, and she smiles with hazy eyes as my knot deflates and a ridiculous amount of cum spills out of her.

"Do I take the diaphragm out now?" I ask her, and the smile that takes over her face is nearly wicked. "Never mind. I'll consult the manual."

She pouts but enjoys the warm washcloth as I clean her up.

"You're taking a shower tomorrow, baby."

She gives me a dirty look but holds out her hands as I pick her up. Not wanting to be anywhere near Bram, I lie on my back on the couch with her splayed against my chest.

Maybe I can do this after all.

ETHAN

CHAPTER 26

I scrub a hand down my face.

These last twenty-four hours have been a whirlwind. Fuck, the last few weeks have been.

I knew being with Sloane would be complicated. Being with Bram would be complicated.

But now Max is her scent match and in the mix.

Is it wrong that I'm not upset about it? I've missed being close with him. There were so many times I thought about asking him out for a beer and just talking through what was going on, but I couldn't.

It wasn't just some loyalty to Bram, which I undoubtedly have. No one besides my foster dad has ever looked out for me in that same way. Not only did he make the situation at the diner go away, but he's never judged me for it.

Neither has Sloane.

Even when I tried to pull away and create some distance, Sloane wouldn't let me, and I'm so thankful for it.

It's not that I think I would ever hurt her. I know I wouldn't. But that side of me coming out honestly scared the fuck out of me. My goal in life has always been to be nothing like *him*.

I don't want to open my eyes because truth be told, I'm tired. But then there's an undeniable bickering that I can't ignore.

"Give me her," Bram demands.

"No, she's comfortable where she is. Fuck off," Max snaps back.

"Just because you're her scent match doesn't make you any more important than me or Ethan."

"Doesn't it?" Max says, and I wince, blinking away sleep and rolling out of bed.

Sloane shifts off of Max's chest and stands there, completely naked with her hands crossed over her chest.

Frankly, she looks both precious and pissed at the same time.

"The fuck did you say to me?" Bram says, taking a step forward, and Max stands to his full height. They're both large, but Bram is the bigger one of the two in height and bulk.

He is also completely naked, and I do my best to not glance down at his swinging cock. I fail miserably.

"You know how to pick 'em, sweetheart," I mumble under my breath, and she glances back at me before staring daggers at Max and Bram.

"I said that I am her scent match, and that makes a difference. I don't see your bond mark on her, Nilsen," Max says, going right for the jugular.

I wince, but I also understand that Bram has been digging the knife deeper and deeper into Max's side. He's bound to fight back eventually.

"*Yet.* My bond mark isn't on her *yet.* Because she chose me. She wanted me for me. Maybe you should reflect on why she wants you," Bram says, and I can't help but to grimace.

I don't know if it's the lack of sleep or insecurity, but it makes Max snap as he pushes Bram's shoulders.

Fuck.

These guys fight all the time for a living, and it shows as Bram pulls back and punches Max in the face. The two Alphas are a swarm of limbs and grunts. I'm not even going to mention how ridiculously hot it also is because it's so fucked. But Bram is in tight black boxers, and Max's giant cock is just flapping in the wind while they fight. I'm only a red-blooded male; I can't control the striking visuals.

When I turn to Sloane, tears are running down her face as she watches the two men she cares for fight over her.

It honestly brings back memories of when I was fighting over her, but this is completely different.

I cup her face as the two men wrestle on the floor. It's truly pathetic.

"Do you want me to try and stop them? Or do you want me to take you away so you don't have to see it?" I ask her.

She glances down at the Alphas and back up at me. It doesn't hurt my ego when she sighs, knowing that both of the men are much larger than me.

"I'll break up this little fight, and then we'll take a bath together, alright?"

Tears are staining her cheeks as she nods her head and walks into a corner where she sits on the floor and wraps her arms around her legs. She rocks back and forth and eventually uses her hands to cover her ears to distract from the two Alphas fighting.

With her ears covered, I put two fingers in my mouth and whistle as loudly as I possibly can, getting both of their attention.

They're both breathing heavily, and it's clear they will both be walking away from this fight with bruises.

"Look at what you two are doing," I say, directing my hand over to Sloane. "She's crying and scared. One of you needs to get dressed and take a walk. If you can't figure out how to be in here together, we will have to do a rotation where one of you leaves."

They both grumble, and I cut that shit out immediately.

"You're both her Alphas. She cares for both of you. Grow the fuck up. Look at her," I say with emphasis again.

Both of their faces fall when they see what their little outburst is doing to her.

"Sloane, baby," Max says.

"Little Omega, come here," Bram says.

"No. No little Omega for either of you. She's mine until you two figure out your shit. We're not doing this again. So either one of you cools off and leaves, or you figure out your differences so we can get through Sloane's heat semi peacefully."

I turn away from their dumbstruck faces and hunch down to where Sloane is in the corner. I pull her hands away from her ears and gently tip her chin so that she's looking at me.

"Hey, sweetheart. They aren't going to fight anymore."

She glances behind me and glares at the Alphas; I hope they both feel shame with the way she's glaring at them.

"Come take a bath with me?"

She scrunches her nose at the idea, and I trail my hands down her arms.

"Warm water would feel so good on your muscles. I'll take care of you. Your Alphas are going to work on their behavior problems," I promise, and she eventually concedes, letting me carry her bridal style over to the bathroom.

"Oh, and one of you put the stew in the crockpot," I say, not even glancing at the two men before shutting and locking the door.

I set her down on the counter before turning on the faucet of the tub and closing the drain.

"We're going to need a bigger place for your next heat. This small apartment can't hold both of their egos," I tell her, dropping some bubbles and shit into the tub.

"It's been a few hours. Let's take that diaphragm out," I tell her as I turn around, and it's the first smile I get out of her since the two Alphas got into it. "You know, you're kind of a menace not in heat, but you're down right devious during your heat."

She just grins as she parts her legs, and I slide two fingers inside of her and grab the edge to pop it out of her. I wash it off in the sink before putting the purified water in the sterilizer and turning it on to clean off the device.

"You know, the chances of me getting you pregnant are like slim to none," I tell her, and she shakes her head in disagreement.

Her hands are gripping my waist as I step between her legs. There's some commotion in the bedroom, and I sigh and grab her face.

"They are big boys. They'll figure it out. It's just you and me right now. That's all that matters."

She smiles as I lean in and kiss her swollen lips. Even as a Beta, I can appreciate her sweet scent, but I'm thankful I can still keep a clear head about things.

"I'm always on your side, Sloane. No matter what, I'm always in your corner, okay?"

She bites her lip and nods her head, spreading her legs even further. Her slick pools against the counter.

"Alright, none of that, it is indeed tub time."

She makes a noise of protest as I pick her up and bring her into the bath with me but slowly starts to melt against the warm water. I sit behind her, cradling her body as I use the pink loofah—per the manual—to use her unscented body wash—also per the manual.

"Not trying to brag, but I do think reading your little binder before your heat put me at an advantage here," I tell her, scrubbing her smooth freckled skin.

She melts into me like butter, and I can tell her muscles are tense from sleeping on Max's chest like that.

I kiss her shoulder, and she sighs. I wonder what's going on in her head right now and how much she's going to truly retain.

It's a chicken shit move. But I've had this weighing on me too long.

"That night at the diner, I didn't mean to push you away after. I was just scared," I tell her. She hums but doesn't speak. Not that I thought she would.

She isn't facing me, and she likely won't remember the conversation. But that's okay, I really just need to get it off my chest.

"Growing up, things were terrible in my house. My father beat my mother near daily. I wasn't excused from his fists either, but she primarily took it all. My mom was sweet. I remember all the small moments where she tried to make things special for me. We didn't have a lot of money, but she would make me a cake on my birthday and take me to the park. I don't know how she got my gifts for Christmas, but she made it happen."

I scrub her skin gently, and slowly, the fear of telling Sloane the truth fades away the more I share.

"I don't know why she didn't leave. I can only assume she had nowhere to go, no money to get us out of that situation. Until, one day, my dad hit me so hard he fractured my jaw. I cried throughout the night. When my dad went to work the next day, she took me to the hospital and admitted abuse was happening in the house and requested I'd be removed from their custody.

"I remember being so upset and wondering why my mom didn't want me home with her. But on my second night in a new foster home, my social worker came to visit me and told me that my mother had passed away and that my father was in jail. I found out later that he had beaten her to death."

Sloane's body stills against mine, and I wonder how much she is understanding and retaining right now.

"So when I tell you I'm not a violent man, I mean it. I'd never, fucking ever, raise my hand to you. Who I was that night scared me, but I know I'm not like him, and I'm sorry for pushing you away, and I'm sorry for word vomiting this all to you now when you likely won't remember it when you're done with your heat. I just needed you to know that you're my priority, and I'll always keep you safe, sweetheart."

The water sloshes over the lip of the tub as she perches on my lap. When I look at her face, I swear it's like she's fighting with her rational mind. She sighs in frustration as she cups my face and furrows her eyebrows.

"Special," she says simply, lightly tapping my cheek, making me smile.

"Fuck, you're cute."

That makes her smile as her fingers explore my face. It's sensual and far more intimate than I expected her heat to be. She leans down and kisses me before wrapping her arms around my shoulders and squeezing me tight.

"Being with you is the most special I've felt in a long time, sweetheart," I whisper, and I swear the Omega holds me even tighter than she did before.

SLOANE

CHAPTER 27

I hold my Beta tightly.

I love him. He takes such good care of me.

It means even more now that he's told me more about his childhood and why he was so afraid. It's hard to keep my mind focused on the way he spilled his heart out to me. But damn, am I trying.

His strong tattooed arms are wrapped around me, and the warm water has done wonders for my muscles.

I try not to think about the Alphas fighting in the other room. It will just make me sad.

Right now, I have my Beta, and he's perfect and loving. Despite everything he's been through, the fact he is capable of such tenderness soothes me.

Until a cramp rolls through me so fiercely I nearly double over. I can't help it when my nails dig into my Beta's back as the pain ripples through me.

I need a knot, but the sweet Beta holding me right now can't give me that. Fuck.

I wince, the pain hurts. Everything hurts. This stupid water sucks, and I just want to get out and make the pain go away.

My eyes are welling with moisture as my Beta slides a hand

between us. His fingertips dance around my pussy as he slides three of his fingers inside of me.

"It hurts?" he asks, and I nod my head.

In reality, I want to scream. Duh, it fucking hurts. Do your job, and make it stop. Instead, I cry.

My Beta shakes his head before placing delicate kisses against my skin.

"Can't have my girl hurting. How many fingers do you need?"

All ten, obviously.

He adds another finger, just his thumb strumming my clit. I glance down, and I realize what will make me feel better. I grab his thumb and push it against my entrance.

I need his whole fist, at least every knuckle deep inside of me.

"Okay. God, you're dripping all over my hand," he says, which makes me preen but also has me questioning why he is taking so long in giving me what I want.

He follows directions, pushing all five fingers inside of me but doesn't go past the knuckles.

I grab his forearm and shift my body down on his fist, pushing him inside of me up to his wrist.

Yes. Yes. Yes.

This feels so good, so much of the ache is starting to go away.

My Beta stares at me with a gaping mouth, and part of me wants to close it with a kiss, the other half of me wants to fill his mouth with his fingers he's had deep into my cunt.

"Holy shit," he mumbles as I use his hand to fuck myself on.

It's good, filling even.

But I need more stretch,

I reach over and grab his other hand and direct him to have it join the one that's already inside of me. He looks leary but focused enough to make this good for me.

"Sloane, sweetheart. Maybe the Alphas figured out their shit and one of them can give you what you need."

"You give," I tell him, and he sighs.

But I can tell whatever I said has inflated my Beta's ego as he uses both of his hands to stretch my pussy. He steeples his fingers like he's praying as he pushes in and out of me.

He winces a few times. I'm sure his hands are uncomfortable.

But that's the price you pay to please your Omega.

The stretch around his hands is bringing me comfort as I hold on to his shoulders and let everything else fade away. This moment is bliss.

"Come all over my fists, sweet girl," he says, and I bite my lip.

I am pretty fucking sweet, aren't I?

I nod my head that I'm close, but then he shocks me by placing his cock inside of me while keeping one hand inside of me as the other toys with my clit.

Fuck yes.

I rise on my knees and slide down his slick-covered fingers and cock. He moans and whimpers as I slide down.

The noises are a direct hit to my clit as he stretches me so perfectly.

"Yes," I whisper.

"You like how your Beta can stretch your sweet little cunt so nice?" he says, and I shiver.

Who knew I'd hit the jackpot with a Beta who's not only hot, but also freaky and sweet?

I dig my nails into his back and press his lips against my throat.

It's not a bond, not even close.

But I just need his claim on me. I need everything.

When he makes his fist larger inside of me and whispers my name. I fall apart. My pussy contracts around his hand as I reach my release. It hits deep in my lower belly, numbing some of the pain.

He gently pulls his abused hand out of me, and before he can do anything, I slide his cock back into me and wrap my arms and legs around him.

This feels so nice.

Different from being stuck when knotted.

But I like this just as much.

My warm pussy clenches around his cock, keeping him nice and warm inside of me.

I don't shift my hips or move. I just hold him, and he holds me, his hard, patient cock deep within me.

Neither of us moves besides our hands soothing skin. My Beta makes a few pained noises when I move a certain way. I like that he's wrapped around my pussy and eventually also wrapped around my finger.

He absolutely should be.

BRAM

CHAPTER 28

I'm holding a rag to my nose. More specifically, a rag that can be used for this because Sloane has labeled which rags serve which purpose.

Max holds an ice pack to his cheek as we both glance at one another.

"This can't happen again," he says.

"No, it can't," I agree

The thought of Sloane crying and cowering in a corner is not the vision I had of her during her heat. She should be blissed out and boneless right now. But we've hurt her, and I can't do that.

I can't change that Max is her scent match. I don't know how, but I'm going to have to change my opinions on the man. At the very least, we've got to learn how to coexist.

The past has to fuck off, and we've got to figure out a way to make this dysfunctional pack dynamic work.

I personally don't feel like bringing up what happened all those years ago, probably because of my ego, and the fact that he keeps playing dumb just makes it worse.

But can I really be in a pack with him?

Live with him?

Share Sloane and Ethan with him?

I'm going to have to or else I risk losing everything.

"Truce," I say, holding out my hand.

Max looks at my palm like it's toxic but shakes it regardless.

"Truce."

"No more fighting in front of Sloane," I say, and he nods his head in agreement.

"I'm not saying you're the one who started it, but you kind of are. You're the one with the bigger problem than me," he says.

I inhale deeply, too embarrassed to bring up what happened over five years ago.

"I'll work on it. But you also need to work with me. I've been with Sloane for months now, slowly getting to know her and dating her. You just swooped in out of nowhere. It's been more than an adjustment."

"You know, this was all out of my hands. I'm happy about it, and I feel blessed. But I didn't ask to come in here and upend anyone's life."

Deep down, I know that. I know that Max didn't maliciously try to ruin everything I've worked for, but I can't help that I still feel that way. I've just got to push it down. Not just for Sloane, but for me too. I don't want to be an angry asshole all the time, especially not around my pack. That's the one time I should be able to be myself.

I don't forgive Max, simply because I'm a petty asshole, but I can try to forget. If only for my own selfish reasons.

"Should we talk about why you hate me so much?"

"No," I snap back quickly, and the other Alpha sighs. "Past is in the past. We're moving forward to be what Sloane needs."

"And what does that look like for the rest of her heat? You can't just rip her out of my arms."

"Is that not what you did to me last fucking night?" I snap back and take a deep breath and rub the bridge of my nose. "Fighting over her is only going to upset her more. It's my job—"

"Our job," he interrupts.

I kinda want to hit him in his pretty-boy face again.

"Our job," I drone, "to make sure she's taken care of and happy. So no more ripping her out of each other's arms, and we'll have to take turns. After this heat, we'll have to deal with the rest of this, but I'm not going anywhere. I don't care if you're her fucking scent match. I'm not leaving her, and I'll do whatever it takes to make her mine, even if that means having to deal with you for the rest of my life."

"You know, if my face wasn't half numb, I'd probably smile and say that's kind of romantic."

"Fuck off."

"I thought we were in a truce," Max says.

"Truce doesn't mean I can't tell you when you're being a fucking moron."

"I think I'm growing on you already, Nilsen."

"You're not," I deadpan, and the man smiles and winces.

"I think you're gonna be my friend before you know it, and you're going to be so mad at yourself for not being able to hold a grudge for the rest of your life."

"Don't count on it."

"I'm very charming," Max says.

"You're not."

"I definitely am. Ethan and Sloane think so anyway."

Great, he's coming for my Beta too. I thought I was going to come home, see my girl, get her to tell me what was going on and take the steps forward to solidify our pack. But then Max came crashing in and took us two steps back.

I still can't wrap my mind around being around him forever, especially if he's this fucking annoying.

"Just stay out of my way, and I'll stay out of yours. After the heat, we'll figure out how to make this work."

Cause he sure as shit isn't moving into my house. The house I wanted to ask Sloane and Ethan to move into but haven't been bold enough to ask yet.

But after these early days of Sloane's heat, there's no fucking way I can have her still living here. I know I travel a lot for work, but I need her close. It's nice that Ethan always stays local, and I can trust him with her.

Now I just have to deal with this dirty blond motherfucker.

"I'm going to go check on them."

"They locked the door."

I wave Max off and knock on the bathroom door with no response, which immediately has my hackles rising. Taking a chance, I graze my fingers along the top edge of the doorframe, pleased when I find the small mechanism to unlock the door.

As soon as I unlock it, I wasn't sure what I'd walk into, but Sloane riding Ethan's fist wasn't it.

Ethan glances over at me, a nearly pained expression on his face.

"Thank fuck. Did you two make up?"

"Somewhat." He narrows his eyes at me. "We won't be having anymore altercations," I promise him.

"My fist isn't enough," Ethan says as Sloane whimpers and rides his hand.

I pull down my underwear and sit my bare ass on the cold hard tile.

"Come here, Omega," I tell her, and she immediately glances my way and stands up.

Ethan shakes out his newly freed hand as he makes sure she safely gets out of the tub. She drips water everywhere, and she notices, whining about the mess.

"I'll take care of it, sweetheart," Ethan says, draining the tub and grabbing one of the gray towels.

The purple towels are decoration, the gray towels are miscellaneous, and the white towels are for actually drying off.

He tosses me a white one, and I use it to dry off Sloane slightly as she straddles my lap. She's ravenous, kissing my chest and grabbing my cock, no preamble, and shoving it inside of her wet and ready pussy.

"Mmm. You need a knot? This sweet Omega pussy needs to be stretched, doesn't it?" I ask her.

She whimpers as she bounces on my cock. Ethan has cleaned up the mess and has his towel wrapped around his waist.

"You want your mouth full too, don't you, *liefje*?"

She licks her lips, her hips shifting against me as I hold her soft ass in my hands. I let go of one cheek and fist Ethan's towel, bringing him closer to us.

"He's been such a good Beta, hasn't he?" I ask Sloane, and she nods her head, tugging down his towel, his cock springing free. "He's so good for us, so pretty. You chose so well," I tell her, which makes her preen. "Now put his cock in your mouth, and show him how good he is."

She does just that, fisting him at the base and licking the tip of his head. I bend my legs for more leverage so I can fuck Sloane from below. She hums and drools around his length. My gaze shifts from watching the way I fuck her pussy to her tits bouncing, her lips around Ethan's cock, and his lean but seductive build.

"That's it. Can you take all of him?" I ask her.

She bobs her head and uses my shoulders for purchase as she takes a breath and works on swallowing Ethan down the back of her throat. She gags and pulls back, a line of spit collecting on her bottom lip connecting her to Ethan's cock.

I find myself wanting to taste it, so I do.

I wrap a hand around Ethan's thigh and tug him toward me before wrapping my lips around his length.

His hand tangles in my hair, and Sloane moans loudly before moving faster on my lap. She leans forward, her face pressing against mine as her tongue slips out, licking Ethan's cock and my lips.

My hand grips her ass harder, making her move along my shaft while also taking Ethan's cock.

I love the way he feels in my throat, but I love the way he looks down at me even more. Like he's shocked I would want to perform such an act on him.

Oh, sweet Beta, there's so much more I want to do with you. My cock is just a bit busy right now.

Sloane's pussy flutters as she sits down flush against my knot, her mouth latching onto the base of my throat where she sucks and licks.

I pull back from Ethan's length for a moment to whisper two words. "Bite me," I tell her.

She moans as her teeth sink into my skin and my knot swells. I work Ethan with my fist as his hand reaches out and slaps the wall for stability as he shudders, and his cum coats my chest.

"Fuck, sorry," he hisses.

I'm about to reply when Sloane moves her mouth over my chest and licks up the Beta's cum.

It sends me over the edge, my knot swelling to its full size, filling her tightly. Her pussy grips my knot like a vise as I spill into her, and the Omega shakes and moans on my lap.

Her cunt flutters around me as I throw my head back in ecstasy. I breathe through my nose as I let the euphoric sensation roll through me.

This is what it's all about.

Heats are magical.

Jesus fucking Christ.

I come to, blinking away the best orgasm of my life, to a very irritated Omega on my lap.

I sigh and rub her thighs.

"Your little scent match and I made up," I promise her.

She arches an eyebrow at me and grabs Ethan's hand, forcing him to sit on the tile with us.

"What exactly does that mean?" Ethan says, stroking Sloane's back.

Her body leans into his, and I wince as she jostles against my knot.

"No more fighting. We're working on sharing."

Ethan hums in disbelief, and I rest my head against the wall, kneading Sloane's flesh.

"Also, are we going to talk about how you keep sucking my dick by surprise?" he says, which makes me laugh.

It makes Sloane clench against me, but I can't stop laughing. I'm oversensitive, but fuck does it feel good to laugh.

This has all been so hard, and it's nice to just have a normal quiet moment, just the three of us.

"Are you complaining, mascot?" I say, arching a brow at him.

"Not in the slightest. I guess I just feel like I owe you one or something."

I laugh again and shake my head. "You can surprise suck my dick anytime."

This has Sloane smiling and petting my face. I guess I'm out of the dog house for the time being. Her fingers trail the spot where she bit me.

"You like that?" I ask her, and she digs her finger harder into the wound, making me wince.

"I'll take that as a yes," I say.

There's a tap on the door frame. Max looks down at where we're all sitting on the floor, and it doesn't seem like malice in his eyes, just acceptance.

"Your dad called Ethan's phone. He wanted to know if you wanted McDonald's," he says, speaking to Sloane.

She claps her hands and smiles, which is as good as a yes that we're going to get.

"Good, cause I forgot to put the food in the crockpot," Max says, rubbing his neck.

"Oh, Sloane, sweetheart, what are we going to do with these Alphas?" Ethan asks, and she smiles and kisses the Beta, which spurs her grinding down on my knot and my fingers rubbing against her clit.

Maybe we can survive this, after all.

CHAPTER 29

I f this big dickhead isn't going to share, I'm about to completely go back on my word with this truce.

He's feeding Sloane cut-up grapes so she doesn't choke. Why didn't I think of that?

Fuck, I'm terrible at being an Alpha and shit. What if Sloane realizes it and decides I'm not a worthy scent match after all?

"I feel like I deserve compensation for making sure everyone stays sane during this heat," Ethan says, cracking open a beer for himself and handing me the other one. "Bram's a caregiver. Genuinely, I think he gets hard feeding her the grapes. You don't have to be like him."

"But she chose him. She didn't choose me."

"For the love of God. Shut the fuck up," Ethan says, grabbing my chin and planting a rough kiss against my lips.

He pulls back, and I blink at him, dumbfounded.

"Yeah, wanted to do that for a while. You're not a burden, Max. Sloane liked you before she found out you were her scent match. She was excited, but she was also afraid. Stop worrying so much, and just act how you want to," he says.

So I do, grabbing his face and kissing him back.

Being with Ethan is easy, comfortable, and simple. I'm

attracted to him, and he is to me. Bram isn't as big of a complication with me and Ethan, and there's no pheromones, just feelings.

He grabs my cock and starts to jerk me off.

"I want to fuck you," I whisper in his ear, feeling bold.

I feel like solidifying this thing between me and Ethan will help make this all real and help me feel like a part of this pack. I also want him—*desperately*.

"Where's the lube?" I ask.

Before I can even answer, it's like Sloane transported in front of me with the lube. Bram stands behind her, awkward as ever as she hands it to me, and just blinks.

I clear my throat. "Is this okay with you, baby?" I ask her.

She nods enthusiastically as she shoves a naked Ethan on to his back.

"Stronger than she looks," he laughs. "Do you want to ride my face while your scent match fucks me?" Ethan asks boldly.

Sloane hasn't been dressed her entire heat, a mix of being too hot and ready to be fucked at a moment's notice.

Bram stands there, also completely naked.

The only reason it's not completely jarring is the amount of time I've spent in a men's locker room.

"You could suck your broody Alpha's cock too. You're so good at that," Ethan says, and Sloane preens at his praise.

Ethan lies on his back, and Sloane immediately straddles his face. Not a care in the world.

I'd like to get on their level when it comes to comfortableness. The two of them seem like a mixture of best friends and lovers. While what's happening with Bram seems more intense, and I'm really still trying to figure out where I fit in all of this.

Bram seems irritated, which is his factory setting, I'm pretty sure. But he doesn't storm off, push me, or say anything. He just grabs Sloane's face and kisses her while she's riding Ethan's tongue.

I can't look away when Bram slides his dick between Sloane's lips. But when he catches me and glares, I immediately look away and focus on Ethan's tight little ass.

He's covered in tattoos on his thighs, arms, chest, and shins. But his perfect, tight, pale ass is just there for the taking.

I lube up my fingers and rim his asshole with the sticky liquid before sliding a finger inside of him. He moans against Sloane's pussy, which makes her garble around Bram's cock.

"Just like that, *liefje*,"

I try to tune him out, but I enjoy his deep voice.

No, wait. I don't enjoy anything about Bram. Well, except maybe how he treats Sloane and Ethan. Or possibly how good he is at hockey.

Ethan interrupts my thoughts, grabbing my wrist, indicating he needs more, and I oblige, sticking two more fingers inside of him.

His cock is hard and leaking against his stomach as I stroke my dick, lubing it up and pushing it against his entrance.

Unlike how I can with Sloane, I make sure to keep my knot out of the mix.

He's tight and warm, and the sound of pleasure he makes when I slide all the way inside him, everyone moans. It's like a ricochet of pleasure.

I smile to myself as I fuck Ethan, thinking about how in some fucked-up roundabout way, I'm fucking Bram.

I shake the thought away and stroke Ethan's cock while I fuck him.

"How's your Beta's tongue, baby?" I ask Sloane.

I want to touch her but refrain. Bram and I have a truce, and touching her while his cock is in her mouth seems like crossing a boundary.

She hums around Bram's length, and Ethan's ass clenches around my dick. I continue stroking him as I push back his thigh roughly, giving me a better angle of his tight ass.

Should I feel proud when Bram is the first one to come? Probably not. Should it be so hot that some of him slipped out of her mouth and landed on Ethan? No.

But when Bram helps Sloane turn around, Ethan's lips still sucking on her clit, and she leans forward and smacks my hand away from stroking Ethan, I lose it.

Her tongue licks the head, and I can watch the way I thrust in and out of him while she lavishes his cock.

"Fuck."

She smiles, her tongue sliding against his slit, and I can't help but to fuck him harder.

Ethan is whimpering and moaning, his thighs trembling from the pleasure, but neither Sloane nor I stop.

"Such a good Omega. I'm going to come," I say, my knot hitting his tight entrance with each thrust. "God, Ethan. This fucking ass."

That does it.

My cum fills Ethan as he comes down Sloane's throat.

I pant and slowly pull out of Ethan who winces as Sloane sits up on the couch, spreading her legs wide as she plays with her pussy.

"That was awfully selfish of us," I say, and she nods her head in agreement, making me laugh. "You got any toys, baby?"

"The second drawer on the left," Ethan says, his arm strung over his eyes. Slick is glistening on his chin, and he looks completely worn out. When I look around the room, I finally notice that Bram must be in the bathroom.

Well, more Omega and Beta time for me.

I go to the drawer and pull out a big, fat, pink dildo with a massive knot on the bottom.

"Baby, you're going to give me a complex," I say as I sit it on the table.

I take a risk, hoping that Bram is in the shower, and I'm lucky that he is and didn't lock the door. I sanitize my hands and dick and grab her diaphragm while I'm in here.

We did take it out last night, and no one fucked her since then, right? I shake out the thought and come back to the living room.

"They'll be right back." Ethan is consoling her and rubbing her pussy.

"I'm here. Let's fill this sweet girl up," I say.

Her cheeks are red, and her hair is sweaty. It's evident she's worn out. It's her first heat plus all the issues along the way. She has to be mentally and physically exhausted. I can't even deny that I'm so ready to get out of this apartment and just go for a walk. It smells like debauchery and all of our scents mixed together, and I'd like to be able to think straight.

But right now, Sloane needs relief.

I get down on my knees, dragging the toy along her clit and seam before pushing it inside of her.

I lick and suck her clit while I fuck her with the toy. Her nails dig into my hair as she moans and pants, needing more. Her poor pussy is so overused and sensitive she's having a hard time coming, and that's what she needs to feel better.

"I think there's a small vibrating bullet in there too. Should I get it?" Ethan asks in a worried tone.

"Yeah, go grab it," I say, and Sloane immediately pushes my face back to her clit.

I smile as I eat her out, and Ethan returns with the small vibrator. I turn it on its highest setting and push the knot of the toy into her, moving it around inside of her.

Her back bows, and I don't know what takes over me, but I lean forward and suck the meat of her thigh hard.

It sends her completely over the edge. Her grip on my hair tightens as I watch her pussy clench around the toy, and she moans in pleasure. Her orgasm lasts a while, and as soon as she passes the crest, she's begging for the vibrator and toy to be moved.

I'm gentle as I turn the device off and slide the toy out of her. The amount of slick that pools onto the couch is obscene. But

Sloane, ever the planner, had already put waterproof protection on just about everything.

She's shuddering as she holds her hands out. I pick her up and carry her over to the bed.

I cradle her against my chest, and Ethan lies in front of her, petting her messy, sweaty hair off of her face.

"You both did so well," I tell them.

"Not going to lie, you fucking me was not on my heat bingo card, but I'm not mad about it."

"Is Bram mad?" I ask. Not that I care or anything.

"I think maybe he just needed a moment to himself. Just enjoy this, it's about to be over," Ethan says as Sloane passes out in my arms.

Fuck, once her heat is over, what does that mean for the four of us?

SLOANE

CHAPTER 30

There's an overwhelming sadness that hits me once I'm out of my heat. I can't tell what time it is, but I just know everyone is sleeping.

I'm between Max and Ethan while Bram sleeps on the couch.

It's not easy, but thankfully, everyone is too exhausted to notice as I slink out of the bed and make my way to the bathroom. I turn the shower to hotter than hell and sit on the shower floor and let the spray hit me.

The tears flow out of me so violently I can't make myself stop crying. My stomach lurches, but there's nothing. My stomach is too empty.

I'm not even sure exactly what is upsetting me the most. It's just too much. Everything is so overwhelming. My body aches, I'm exhausted, and my heart hurts.

I remember Bram's hurt face when he walked in on me and Max. I never even got Max's true consent to be in my heat. I'm sure he signed the form, but it was probably out of obligation. Then there's Ethan. I remember bits and pieces of his background, but it's so jumbled up. All I can really recall is that he came from an abusive household.

Maybe the more time that passes, the more will come to me.

I feel lost, so fucking lost.

Where do we go from here? Did Bram just join my heat because he knew I couldn't do it without him? Is he going to stay with me? How is Max handling having a scent match?

The only person I don't have to worry about is Ethan, and that's where I find some comfort. He's not going anywhere, he told me in those literal terms.

I'm trying to breathe and calm myself when I hear the door open. Immediately from his scent, I know it's Bram.

Fear laces through me, and I start sobbing again. My stomach muscles are cramping so badly, but I can't calm down.

He turns the water to a more tolerable temperature and steps behind me, cradling me from behind.

For the first time since my heat started, or at least that I can recall, his chest rumbles with a purr, which doesn't help my crying situation one bit.

"Don't cry, little Omega. Tell me what's wrong."

I'm trying to talk, but it's too fucking hard. Instead, I turn around and wrap my arms around his massive form.

"I—I love you. Please don't leave me," I cry out, and his arms tighten around me so fiercely I feel like he may break me in half.

"I love you too, Sloane. I'm not going anywhere."

"I'm so sorry. I didn't mean for any of it to happen this way. Oh, god. How many games have you missed? Is my dad upset? Are you okay? I know you and Max don't get along. I know you two fought. I'm so sorry."

"Shhh. You already apologized, and you have nothing to be sorry for. We're working on things. Our relationship with one another isn't your responsibility. We missed two games. The Foxes still won, and right now there's a whole subreddit about where the fuck Finnegan the Fox is. Apparently, someone noticed the lack of social media posts and Gagnon playing as well."

"Oh, well, that will be good for social media," I sniff, and Bram laughs.

Between his purring and his laughter, I'm jostled ever so slightly. I never want to leave his arms. I feel safe and whole.

Staying in this shower forever seems like an awesome idea. Because reality is going to be difficult.

"While you're crying probably isn't the best time to ask this," he says, and I pull back and look at him.

His beard is growing long, and I can't help but to drag my fingers through it.

"What?"

"I'd like for you and Ethan to move in with me," he says.

I swallow thickly. Max's name was clearly not mentioned, and honestly, this is a loaded question when I'm trying to pull myself together.

"Don't answer. Just think about it. I know you like planning. Make a pros and cons list, and let me know what concerns you."

Instead of listing off the tons of things that concern me, mainly how comfortable my scent match would be coming over to Bram's home, instead, I just rest my face against his rumbling chest.

The gentle hum of his purr is the only thing keeping me grounded at this moment.

I take a deep breath and relax my muscles. Okay, this is all okay. I don't have to worry about Ethan or Bram. I just need to worry about Max and how the hell I'm going to make this pack work because come hell or high water, I'm going to make these two like each other.

"How do you think my heat went?" I ask, my hands playing with his wet hair.

"That's a loaded question. All I know is you need a better nest next heat. This is tight fucking quarters. We need more space and options."

"A designated nest sounds nice," I reply.

"My house has a basement. I want to give you your dream nest."

I pull back and search his face. He means it, he's truly all in, and it's the greatest relief of my life. I kiss him gently, and his purr intensifies.

"I want to bond. As soon as we have a better grip on what's happening with the four of us, I want to bond you."

"Truly?" he asks.

"Truly. I also want a wedding someday, but we can talk about that later."

I yawn and rest on his chest again.

"Should we get out and sleep?" he asks, and I shake my head.

"No, I'm quite happy right now in your arms."

✻ ✻ ✻ ✻

When I wake up, I'm snuggled in clean sheets and more revelations of doom because Max is nowhere to be found. In fact, neither is Bram.

My heart is racing, and it quickly goes away as Ethan hurries over to the bed with a chocolate croissant and a pumpkin spiced latte.

"Hey. It's okay. They had to go to practice."

"But they're probably so tired."

"Sweetheart, you've been asleep for nearly a whole day."

My eyes widen. "A whole day?"

I grab the croissant and moan as the flakey pastry melts on my tongue.

"Your dad Henderson dropped off breakfast for us. He's a whole lot less intimidating than Coach. But I think your mom Rosemary might take the cake for the scariest Applegate."

I snort and grab the coffee.

Sweet caffeine.

"What did she say?"

"She didn't say anything. That was the scary part. It's like she could read my mind by just staring at me."

"They've always been protective of me, only child syndrome and all of that."

I take another sip of coffee before inhaling the rest of the pastry.

"How did they seem before they left?" I ask.

He moves up the bed, tossing his arm around my shoulder, and I lean against him with ease. I sigh with contentment. Things with Ethan have always been easy, and I'm so grateful for that.

"They didn't talk to each other. Neither of them wanted to leave you, but they did miss six days already."

I jolt up and blink at him. "Six days?"

He scrubs a hand down his face. He's rocking more facial hair than usual too.

"Yeah, six days. Your mom said that was normal for a first heat."

"You texted my mom?"

His cheeks heat, and he nods. "I mean, she did write *The Art of Nesting*."

I groan and put the coffee on the nightstand and slink back into bed. "My head hurts."

"You're probably dehydrated. Let me get you some water," he says. I grab his wrist and tug him down.

"Wait."

"What? What's wrong? Does something else hurt? Do you need an ice pack or a heating blanket?"

"No. Well, maybe an ice pack. My clit feels like it's swollen to the size of a strawberry. But no. I... um. I remember bits of our conversation from my heat. If you don't want to talk about it, we don't have to. More of it is coming back to me now that I'm fully awake."

He clears his throat and feels tense beside me.

"It doesn't scare you?"

I lace my fingers with his and squeeze. "Why on earth would the circumstances of your childhood scare me? You had nothing to do with what happened. I'm just so sorry you had to go through that."

"How do you keep impressing me?"

"Well, mister. You should probably stop doubting me."

"You're right, never again. It was probably a cop out. It just felt easier to tell you then when you couldn't reply. I had an ex who wasn't comfortable with my father being a convicted murderer."

I wrap my arms around him and squeeze.

"Then they're fucking stupid."

He laughs and holds me back. "So as amazing as all that was, it was kind of a shit show."

"I think we only got through it because of you. You did a great job mediating."

"It might take some time, but I don't think they're a lost cause."

I pull back to search his face, knowing that he was lucid and present my whole heat.

"So you think you can sign up for four of those a year or what?" I joke.

"I think I'm signing up for a lifetime of them, sweetheart."

Yeah, I fucking cry again.

I'm just an Omega, and this has been exhausting me.

"Hey. Hey. I didn't mean to make you cry."

"These are happy tears. I just don't know how I got so lucky."

"It seems like manifestation, if I'm being honest," he says, and I snort.

"I'm not looking forward to seeing my dad."

Ethan blows air out of his mouth and sighs. "Yeah, me either. At least he seems way more frustrated at Max and Bram than at me."

"Hopefully he isn't being too hard on them at practice."

"Even if he is, it would be worth it."

I know I've been sleeping for what feels forever, but a little cat nap won't hurt. So I do just that, passing out cuddled next to Ethan and trying to let all the anxious thoughts evade me while I rest.

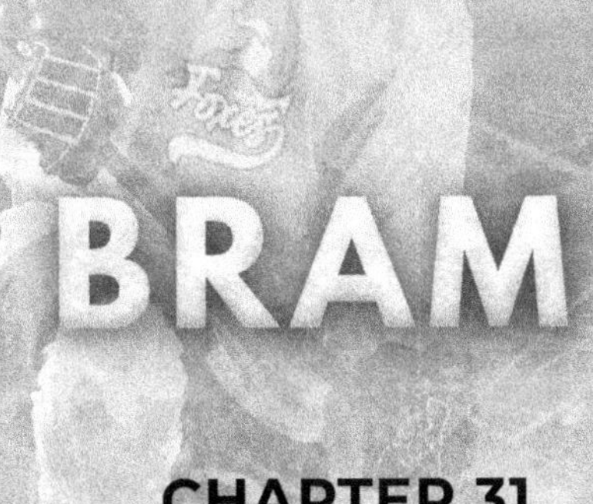

BRAM

CHAPTER 31

"Skate faster," Coach yells from where he's idling on the ice.

Yeah, he's fucking pissed.

I was already sore from fucking his daughter straight for a week, so this takes the cake.

Either way, it's worth it.

He can make me do as many drills as he wants. I'm not going anywhere.

She said she loved me.

I smile to myself as I skate over the goal line and catch my breath.

"Are you fucking smiling during suicides?" Martel pants next to me.

"You'd be smiling too," I tell him.

He rolls his eyes at me as we skate to the bench to grab water.

"Well, I'm not smiling because we all know that drill was punishment for you touching… no… defiling the coach's daughter."

"Fuck off."

"What I want to know is how the fuck did that go with Connery there? Don't you hate his guts?"

"Yes," I reply sharply.

"Yes, you hate him? Yes, what?"

"I'm working on my hatred of him."

Martel smacks my shoulder. "I think this is what they call maturing or personal growth."

"I didn't say I liked him."

"Right. Is this one of those enemies to lovers things?"

I bump him hard with my hip, and he laughs, spitting his water out of his mouth.

"What's so funny?" Coach Applegate asks, standing before us.

"Nothing, sir," I reply.

"Are you su—" I slap Martel in the stomach before he can finish his sentence.

"I'd like to see you and Connery in my office after practice," Coach says before skating off.

Martel makes a hissing noise next to me.

"Oh shit. Do you think he's going to clean his shotgun at his desk while he tells you how disappointed he is? Or maybe he'll just stare at you and Connery, letting his disappointment leak through the silence."

"Don't you have a whole family to bother? Stop being annoying."

Martel grins as Eli Beckford skates up and tosses his arm around his packmate. Must be nice to get along and have already been best friends before they found the Omega of their dreams.

"How's Sloane?" Eli asks.

"Good," I lie because I don't know how she's doing. She was sleeping for fucking ever, and we were basically told by Coach that if we didn't show up to practice, we would be benched for the foreseeable future.

"Glad to hear it, and glad to have you back. You'll need to download a tracker on your phone so you can predict her next heat."

"Not that it's ever truly accurate," Mikael mumbles.

Eli winces and holds up a few fingers and winces. "That will probably put her next heat in late March, early April."

It could be worse, but around that time is when teams are playing extra hard to clinch a playoff spot.

"That's a good tip, thank you."

"Oh, *he* gets a thank you?" Mikael complains.

"He was helpful. You've been a pain in my ass."

"Well, have fun explaining to Coach just how long you've been chasing his Omega daughter around," he says before skating off.

Eli sighs at his packmate and smacks my shoulder.

"He won't want to hurt Sloane. You'll be fine," he says, and it feels like a lie.

Either way, I'm headed to the locker room and changing. Connery and I are the last ones left and give each other a glance.

We haven't spoken since our little truce moment.

And to be quite honest, the jealousy filling me over thinking about him with my Omega and Beta is making this truce feel more than far-fetched.

We don't speak as we both make the tormented walk to Coach's office.

His door is open, and we both walk in and take our respective seats across from his desk. His hands are steepled with his fingertips pressed against his lips.

It's a terse silence before Coach breathes through his nose and rests back into his chair.

"You two have put me in a really shitty fucking position," he says.

Neither of us speaks. I think talking right now would piss him off more.

"I'm not deluded enough to think my daughter isn't the main instigator of all of this—"

"I'm her scent match," Connery interrupts.

I think at that moment both the coach and I want to punch him in the throat.

"Did I ask you to speak? No. I don't think I did," Coach says, not giving a shit about Connery being his daughter's scent match. I can't help it when my lips tilt. "The fuck are you smiling about, Nilsen?"

"Nothing, sir."

Coach scrubs his hands down his face and taps on his desk.

"You'll need to get your current contracts amended and file for a pack contract," he says.

"Sir, we're not bonded," Connery says.

Why does he keep talking and making this worse?

Coach arches an eyebrow at him, and anger is written all over his face.

"Is your intent to just miss games, be her scent match, and not bond her? Because if that's the case, we have a bigger fucking problem."

I'm more than used to Coach cursing, but even for him, this conversation has had a lot of fucks.

"I fully intend on bonding with Sloane," I interrupt and glare at Connery.

Yeah, fuck you, buddy, we've already talked about it.

"It's not that I don't want to bond with her, it's just there hasn't been any time to discuss it on my end," Max snaps back.

"Right, because she didn't choose you, did she?" I reply.

"For the love of God. You two need to figure your shit out on the ice and back at home. Sloane is my daughter, and I love her more than anything, but I won't risk the team's chances of going to the playoffs because you two are in a pissing contest. And when it comes to my daughter, I'm not going to stand by and watch you two rip her spirit apart. Sloane has a big heart and will put her feelings aside to make you two happy. If you truly care about her, you won't put her in that position."

He's right; I know he's right.

I glance over at Connery, and he does the same to me.

"We'll talk to Sloane."

"And your agents," Coach snaps.

"Yes, sir," we reply in unison.

Coach nods his head, a clear dismissal as we both stand up and make our way to leave his office. He clears his throat.

"And, gentlemen? You hurt my daughter and I'll ensure you never play professional hockey again," he says, spinning his chair and likely plotting the different ways he could kill the both of us.

"Pack contract?" Connery asks.

I sigh and try to not get irritated with him.

"It's what Martel and Beckford have. It would tie our incomes and our trading possibilities together. Wherever you go, I go," I say, the idea churning in my stomach.

"So if the Foxes dropped us?" he asks.

"We'd have to be picked up as a duo by another team."

I hate the idea of tying myself to Connery, not only for Sloane, but also my career. I'm sure I can work on not holding this grudge, but I don't know if I'll ever truly like the man. But the fact is, there aren't a lot of goalie slots, and my career would be completely correlated to his.

"I mean, Coach wouldn't drop us over this?" he says, the same thoughts catching up with him.

"We can only hope his love for Sloane and wanting to keep her close outweighs his anger with us," I say.

My own words hit me hard in the chest.

Because my love for Sloane outweighs the stupid, bitter anger I've held against Max all these years. I'm letting my feud with him go, but sharing my Omega with another Alpha is a completely different story.

I guess it's time to start maturing.

"Should we head back to Sloane's?" Max asks.

I roll my eyes and walk away.

How did I ever have a crush on this fucking moron?

❄ ❄ ❄ ❄

I don't go to Sloane's right away. Instead, I work out to relieve some more tension before going home and packing a small bag in hopes that she asks me to stay the night.

I have even higher hopes that she agrees to come and move in with me. Her apartment is way too small, and if we finish the basement of this house, I'd be able to build her the nest she deserves and two more bedrooms. That would give the three of us our own rooms, a pack bedroom, plus a guest room.

The fact that Max is not in my building plans is not lost on me, and I sigh, knowing it's inevitable.

Maybe I'm bitter that I'm not Sloane's scent match.

If anyone should be her scent match, it should fucking be me. Max has no clue what he's doing, and Sloane deserves Alphas who know how to take care of her.

Hell, in my eyes, Ethan is more capable than Max will ever be.

Another pang of jealousy fills me.

Max fucked Ethan.

Max fucked Ethan before I could fuck Ethan.

I groan and sit on my couch, wondering if I'm even capable of taking the high road. How do I keep Sloane happy? How do I keep myself happy?

Maybe I need therapy, or maybe we need pack therapy.

Because I can't keep Sloane happy if I'm constantly riddled with jealousy, bitterness, and resentment.

But the idea of saying what started this resentment is embarrassing. Almost as embarrassing as needing therapy before we're even bonded.

I'm about to text Sloane to see if she needs anything before I head over when there's a knock on my door. I heft myself up off the couch and open the door to find a watery-eyed Sloane and Ethan's very full truck in my driveway.

"So is that offer to move in still good?" she asks, and I blink at her with surprise.

"Of course it is. What happened?"

She sucks her teeth and sighs. "My dad might have fired me," she says as I grab the tote bag off of her shoulder.

"He what?"

"To be fair, I did break all of my promises I made to him when starting the job. But also, I was great at what I did. He's handling this whole thing poorly, and I'm an adult who can make my own choices. So I'm choosing not to live there anymore as long as the offer is still on the table."

"Yes, come in," I tell her as I look her over.

She looks exhausted. I cup my hands on her face and stroke her cheekbones with my thumbs.

"What do you need?" I ask her.

She just wraps her arms around my waist and smothers me in a tight hug.

"I just need my pack," she says.

"Tell Max he is invited over, then."

Sloane pulls back, and the tears in her eyes really well. "Really?"

"I mean an extra hand to move all your shit into your new house wouldn't hurt."

She wraps her arms around me and squeezes tightly.

"Thank you for trying. It means everything to me," she says.

My chest rumbles from her words, and she doesn't let me go. I missed her today so much. And now she's moving into my home.

I can do this. We can do this. We'll get through these growing pains.

Our hug is interrupted as Ethan walks in with a plastic tub and sets it on the floor.

"So are you going to use those big Alpha muscles to help carry in our girl's stuff? Or am I the only one getting left out of the hugs right now?"

I pull one arm from Sloane, and Ethan smirks as he joins this ridiculously sappy hug.

"I'm actually a few weeks behind on rent if the offer to move in also extends to me," Ethan says.

"Tough call. What do you think, Sloane?"

"Definitely. I guess it's only fair I help you pack since you helped me," she says with a smile.

"More so followed your very specific and detailed orders on how you wanted things packed."

"I do have more stuff, but I only brought the essentials for now. I also guess that I don't have a job, so I can't exactly pay rent either," Sloane says with a wince.

"You won't be paying rent," I tell her.

"Okay," she says easily and hugs me again.

"Just like that?" I say.

"I'm an Omega. My mom never had a standard job, she wrote, but it was something she loved. If you wanted me to contribute, I'd find something I can do from home, but if you're happy taking care of me, I'm going to let you."

"I would also like to be taken care of," Ethan says, and we all laugh.

"You can't stop being the mascot, but you could probably quit the diner. I mean, as long as your dad can hire someone to fill in your spot," Sloane says.

I'm not even mad because I was going to suggest the same. I need Ethan home with her when I'm away for games.

"Really?" he asks, looking at me.

"Yes, really. The diner has you working too late. If there's something from home you want to do, fine. But I think it's best if you're here with Sloane when I'm traveling for work."

"I'm finally going to be living my dream of being a kept Beta," Ethan jokes.

"Let's get your stuff settled into my bedroom, and we can order Chinese."

"That sounds perfect. I'll invite Max," Sloane says easily before heading outside.

"Light lifting only," I shout behind her, and she waves her hand.

Ethan glances up at me and pokes my side. "This is all very mature, Mr. Nilsen."

"I'm fucking trying," I mumble.

He fists my shirt and tugs me down for a gentle kiss.

"I know you are. She knows you are. Give him a chance. I promise he's not the man you knew all those years ago," Ethan says before going outside to help Sloane.

Max might not be the same man five years ago, but I am. I need to make sure he doesn't go back to his old ways and hurt Sloane in the process.

CHAPTER 32

I'm sitting in my bland apartment when I get a text from Sloane.

SLOANE

Hey, I'm at Bram's. Well, I guess I kind of live here now. My dad fired me. Long story. But we're ordering Chinese and unpacking my stuff. I'd love it if you came by. I know we have a lot to talk about, and doing it over text seems pretty ridiculous.

Nilsen is okay with me being at his house?

SLOANE

Yes, and it's my house now too, and I want you here.

Me: You do?

SLOANE

Yes, Max. We all want you here.

Me: I'll be there in twenty minutes.

I highly doubt Nilsen wants me in his home. But I don't doubt his feelings for Sloane. How could I after everything I've seen? But it's clear he doubts my feelings for the little Omega, and I'm just going to have to prove that I'm here to stay.

The whole way there, I just think about what I'm going to say. I haven't been able to talk to Sloane after her heat. Not to mention her father fucking fired her and all, but claimed he would do the same to me if I hurt her, which I have no intention of doing.

When I pull up front, they're moving boxes and containers from Ethan's truck into the beautiful house.

I feel like a failure compared to Bram.

Sloane chose him. They were dating before her heat. He knows her better than I do. Not to mention his contract with the Foxes is a great one, and the roots he's been able to put down here?

It makes me feel inferior. It makes me wonder if I even deserve to be Sloane's scent match.

I sigh to myself. It's not about deserving anything, it's about fate, something I have no control over. But what I can control is becoming the kind of man and Alpha I think Sloane and Ethan deserve.

I get out of my car and head to the back of the truck and grab a box.

"Hey there, stranger. Well, not so strange considering how much we saw each other naked last week and the fact that we've had sex and that was unplanned and we haven't been able to talk about it since you had to leave after Sloane's heat," Ethan says with a grin.

"How is she?" I ask, and Ethan shakes his head.

"She's okay. Didn't seem surprised about being fired. I think she's taking a stand and letting her family realize she's an adult and starting her own family, which Coach isn't taking well."

"Did he threaten to fire you too?"

Ethan swallows and tucks a box under his arm. "Uh, no. Oh, fuck. Is he going to pull me into his office next?"

"Maybe you'll be safe from his wrath."

"Being a Beta has its perks."

"You seem relatively happy with your designation," I comment, and as I speak, I can see my cold breath in the air.

"More than happy, especially now."

"Should we talk about it?"

"What, how you fucked me while Sloane rode my face?" Ethan says. I can feel my cheeks getting even pinker, and he smiles. "I know shit's complicated for you right now, and Sloane is everyone's priority, as she should be. But just know, I'm not going anywhere either."

"I needed to hear that," I tell him honestly.

Ethan bumps into my side. "If it's ever too much coming to Bram's, just let us know, or you can just let me know, not Sloane. But I'm really hoping we can make this all work out."

"Yeah, me too," I sigh as we walk through the door and add Sloane's box of stuff to the pile.

Let's just hope the night doesn't end with Bram and me at each other's throats. Because first and foremost, I need to talk to my scent match. Who comes happily walking down the stairs with a huge smile on her face when she sees me.

Well, that's a relief.

"Max, thanks for coming. Food should be here soon."

I can't sit through Chinese and act like nothing is on my mind for the next few hours.

"Can we talk for a sec?"

"Sure," she says with a smile, grabbing my hand and tugging me to what appears to be a mudroom before shutting the door.

I'm even more shocked when she wraps her arms around me and squeezes tightly before taking a deep inhale of my scent. I do the same with her, and it calms me down easily.

"Should I start?" she says.

I'm a chickenshit because I nod my head.

"I liked you before I found out you were my scent match. I'm sorry for not telling you when I found out. In retrospect, maybe things wouldn't have turned out so complicated."

"Hey, I don't blame you for that," I tell her, and she smiles.

"But like I was saying, there were already feelings there, complicated ones, but I always liked you, Max. I'm not upset in the slightest you're my scent match. I know you and Bram have a confusing history, but I am really hoping that everyone can learn to get along and we can be a pack. You and Bram don't need to be romantically involved in any way, but I'm hoping that you two can learn to be friends."

"I'm hoping for the same thing. Finding out you are my scent match is one of the best things that has ever happened to me. I want to spend more time with you and get to know you better. I want to be in your pack no matter what it takes."

"You did a good job taking care of me during my heat."

"I did?"

She laughs and nods her head. "It was literally sprung on you that day. Yes, Max. You're a good Alpha; you're an Alpha I want. I know things won't be smooth sailing, but all I ask is that everyone tries."

"I can do that."

"Good, we're all just figuring this out as we go."

I kiss the top of her head, and she melts into me. Being hers is worth whatever hell Bram, her father, or the world wants to throw at me.

This is my chance to be important to somebody. Well, somebody outside of my mother, which makes me wince and pull back.

"My mom wants to meet you. Well, officially. She remembers you from the games last year."

She grins. "Your mom is awesome. I can't wait to meet her as your Omega."

As my Omega.

I kiss the top of her head and hold her tightly, knowing I probably won't get her to myself like this again this evening. I try to fight down the festering jealousy that she lives in Bram's house. Even though I was invited over, I'm not sure how welcome I'll feel.

"Let's go eat and spend time with each other when we're not

all naked and barely functioning," she says, and I follow her out to the living room.

Because the truth is, I'd follow Sloane anywhere.

The night was going fine.

Well, as fine as things can go when the house smells like another Alpha and I'm trying to keep the peace.

Yet I find myself getting more irritated as the evening goes on.

It's not that Bram is hostile, it's almost that he's smug.

Sloane chose him. Sloane is living in his house. Sloane knows him better.

I'm simply here because of some cosmic fate, and it brings up so many of my insecurities.

It doesn't help that he's been so difficult to get along with, even if he's being moderately pleasant right now. We still haven't discussed why he doesn't like me or why he has such negative feelings about me in general.

So we're all just going to ignore this underlying tension as we eat our fried rice and noodles.

Sloane wants us all to get along, so we'll fake it till we make it. Or at least, that was my intention. Until the permeating stench of Bram makes me open my stupid mouth.

"So how are we going to do this? Are you going to stay at my house sometimes?" I ask.

"No," Bram replies sharply, and I glare in his direction.

"You're being unreasonable. Do you really expect me to only come here when I want to see my scent match?" I'm a dick for throwing out the scent match card, but I really don't give a shit.

"It's her house now too. You can get over it," Bram says.

"Like you've gotten over whatever issue it is you have of me. An issue I don't even fucking remember, and you won't even talk about it."

"It's in the past."

"It's clearly not. God, I can't even think in this fucking house. It smells like you."

Sloane bites her lip.

"Do you need to get some fresh air?"

"I'm sorry. I just… How? Sloane. How do we work when he's hoarding you like he's the only one to have a claim on you? I want to get to know you better, but how do I do that when this house smells like him and I don't feel welcomed? We're both on the same travel schedule, so it's not even like dividing time is easy either."

I'm shocked when Bram opens his mouth.

"We can go to pack therapy?"

"What?" Ethan says before anyone else has a moment to.

"Pack therapy," Bram says simply like we're the idiots here.

"You'd do that for me?" Sloane asks.

All three of us give resounding yeses.

"I'll look for a therapist with openings around your schedule. I'm also going to do my best to make sure everyone feels like they have even time. I don't ever want any of you to feel you're getting less attention. We can make this work."

We eat the rest of our food in silence, and I wonder if therapy can really fix this fucked-up pack.

CHAPTER 33

Learning to live with people is much harder than I thought it would be. It's even more difficult when two of my boyfriends can't seem to get along.

Don't get me wrong, they aren't fighting, which is progress, but there's still this constant tension between the two of them.

I've been researching therapists when I get a little curious and start looking at the Finnegan the Fox subreddit—which is a serious mistake.

r/hockeysluths

Foxy Lady

What the hell is going on in New Haven?

Am I the only one who is following what's been going on with the Foxes? Does anyone else think it's weird that Finnegan the Fox, Nilsen, and Connery were all missing during the same games with no word from the higher ups?

I thought maybe it was a cover-up, or maybe they were quietly being put on probation. It's no secret that Nilsen and Connery haven't gotten along this season.

And no matter how much the press tries to make Connery palatable for the fans, I just don't buy it.

DotheGritty – 1 day ago

I have a friend who does catering at the stadium. Word on the street is the coach's daughter just got fired. She handled a lot of their social media. If you look back to last week, all the posts were repeats or clearly canned posts. If you go a step further, Nilsen, Connery, and the coach's daughter (Sloane Applegate) did not post on social media. I tried to find out who the mascot is, but no luck.

HockeyStan22 – 1 day ago

Great, just what this team needs, another fucking pack contract. If they keep doing this shit, all we're going to have on teams is packs that no one can trade. Shit like this is ruining the sport.

I take a deep breath and keep scrolling. There are far more comments than I realized, most of which aren't that great.

UConnPrincess – 1 day ago

I took this picture a while ago. Back then I didn't think much of it. Could the tattooed guy be the mascot with Nilsen and the coach's slutty daughter?

I blink rapidly as I look at the image of the three of us; it was the night my grandma died and I introduced him. The rest of the comments are harsh, mostly speculating, slut shaming, and hating on pack contracts.

I'm not sure why reading all this makes me feel guilty and has a gross feeling in my stomach. It's not like I really care what strangers think about me or my pack, but it still doesn't help this feeling.

Not wanting to let this get to me, I close the laptop and head upstairs.

I should know better. Knocking is essential when you live in a home with four parents.

But then again, walking in on Ethan on his knees for Bram isn't a bad sight at all. Neither of them stops, and Bram just looks at me while Ethan sucks his dick.

I lean against the doorframe, just enjoying the show.

The large Alpha has his hand tangled in Ethan's hair as the Beta savors him.

They look good together, and I smile, happy that they're forging their own relationship outside of me being involved.

"Fuck, mascot, just like that," Bram tells him.

My mouth is open, ready to scold him, when Ethan moans around Bram's length.

Huh. Maybe Ethan is a little into degradation.

Well, he's going to have to get that from Bram because he's a sweet angel to me.

"You like our Omega watching while you suck my dick?" Bram asks.

Ethan turns ever so slightly, glancing in my direction before getting back to pleasuring Bram.

"Take it all the way," Bram tells him. "That's it, choke on it. Fuck."

Well, now I'm exceedingly horny.

But I don't move, not wanting to interrupt their moment. As much as it feels like everything is about me, this is not.

"Swallow it all down like a good boy."

I rub my thighs together, trying to take away some of the ache.

Ethan gags, but Bram holds his head in place as he fucks his throat before swallowing him down.

"I think our Omega needs you next," Bram says, helping Ethan off the floor and giving him a kiss before heading to the shower.

"Wow," I rasp out.

Ethan laughs and picks me up by my hips and tosses me on

the bed before tickling my sides and putting a huge smile on my face.

"I heard you might be needing my mouth too," Ethan jokes, crawling down my body. "So lucky to be the pack fellatio and cunnilingus master," he says, and I laugh even more as he kisses up my leg.

All the posts and comments I was reading earlier completely slip away.

❄ ❄ ❄ ❄

Much to Bram's chagrin, I'm spending the night at Max's tonight. His apartment is bare and bland, but it smells like him at least.

I thought it would be better to stay over here for a change. It's clear he feels some type away being at Bram's. I'm not sure if it's because it's his house and he feels like an unwelcome guest or because Bram's scent is so embedded in the home that it brings out a deep Alpha side of him.

But Max and I were thrust into each other's arms, and it feels unfair that he constantly feels uncomfortable.

We're lying on his couch, his arm around me as I snuggle into his side. I love his size and scent so much, but even in his own home, he doesn't seem to be able to truly relax.

"Max, what's wrong?" I say, sitting on my knees to face him.

"Nothing's wrong," he says as his phone vibrates repeatedly on the arm of the couch.

"Your phone has been going crazy, and you've seemed on edge all night."

He scrubs a hand down his face. "I just wanted tonight to be relaxing with you and me."

I'm about to ask him why it can't be when he hands me the phone.

It seems the speculation about our pack has left Reddit and moved over to national news.

Shit.

The first article is the worst. The title is "The Coach's Daughter and the Rake." It's a picture of me and Max smiling at the Humane Society event weeks ago. The article is rife with misinformation that basically calls Max a slut who can't hold down an Omega and wondering if he's the reason my father fired me.

Max looks mortified, but I keep scrolling through the different things he's been sent.

There is one funny one at least.

"A Deep Dive into the Beta Hottie Under the Mask."

I laugh. "Well, Ethan will love this one," I say, and Max gives me a forced laugh.

For whatever reason, the article doesn't mention much about Bram. I suppose I've been in public more with Ethan and Max.

"I'm not sure why people are sensationalizing this. It's not like I'm famous."

Max holds out his arm, and I go back to my previous position. His body seems to relax a little more now that he's shown me what's bothering him.

"There's only been one more pack contract since Eli and Mikael's pack. I think add in the mascot and you being the coach's daughter, it's exciting for people to speculate."

"Don't forget you and Bram being enemies."

He clears his throat, and I pat his chest.

"I'm sorry, I didn't mean to bring him up," I say, even though we need to get over this.

I can't have my Alphas living in separate houses, and I can't help but to think all this media attention might make things even worse with the two of them getting along.

"I just wish we didn't have to travel again tomorrow," he says, kissing the top of my head.

"Me either," I agree.

The only reason I've been able to stay sane is a mixture of Ethan being home with me and the promise that we'll figure out our shit and I'll finally have the bonds I've been pining for.

Part of me kind of wants to rip the bandage off and just bond with them to see if it solves the problem, but I know it could make things worse.

I don't want them to fight, and I hate that I'm part of the reason they don't get along.

Max squeezes me close to his chest like he can sense my train of thought.

"We're going to get this sorted, baby. We have an appointment set, and for the most part, Nilsen and I have been getting along."

"I know, I just feel guilty, I think."

"Don't. You're worth whatever we need to go through to make this work."

I sit up and straddle his lap, trailing the skin of his jaw. He's so handsome and big. The universe knew what it was doing.

"Do you miss me while you're gone?" I ask, grinding on his lap.

"More than anything."

I take off my sweater, leaving me in just a bra as I take his phone and start snapping pictures of the two of us.

"Your shirt needs to go too," I tell him, and he happily agrees, ripping his shirt from the collar and tossing it on the floor.

I take a few pictures of us kissing and him without his shirt on before tossing the phone.

"Maybe those will help," I say, smiling while I kiss him.

"I think it will just make me miss you even more," he says.

His scent is a warm comfort, and I'm one hundred percent taking his shirt home with me so I can get a whiff whenever I need one.

He kisses down my neck, paying extra attention to one spot where he sucks and licks my skin.

"One day, I'm going to mark you here, baby."

"But where will I mark you?" I joke.

"Wherever the fuck you want," he mumbles, squeezing my ass, making me grind harder on his lap.

I unbutton my jeans and stand up and slide out of them as he pushes down his shorts.

"There are condoms in the bathroom," he says.

I walk mostly naked to the bathroom, feeling a little pissed he has condoms. I mean, logically, I know we need one, but I also don't like the fact that he probably purchased them before we were together. It's stupid, but I'm just an Omega.

When I come back and slide the condom on his cock, he pulls me on his lap, and I slink down his length. The stretch and feel of him feels like a warm caress, and I let myself and my jealous feelings go.

Unlike all the other times I've been with Max, this is different.

It's sweet and slow.

His strong hands don't leave my body as I ride him, our lips constantly on each other as I just enjoy the scent and feel of him.

"You're so perfect," he says, and I shake my head.

I'm far from perfect. I was just jealous of condoms.

"Heat Sloane would have loved that comment," he jokes, and I laugh before grabbing his jaw and kissing him harder.

"Then you're perfect too," I whisper against his lips.

"I want everything with you," he says as he shifts his hips, fucking me from below.

My hands are clasped behind his head as I search his pretty blue eyes.

"Everything, baby," he repeats.

It has me sliding down, taking his knot and moaning out my orgasm. His release follows as he ruts me from below.

I rest my head against his shoulder, and he pets my hair. A feeling of contentment ripples through me, and I know that I'll do anything to help Max fit into the pack.

"Don't listen to any of those articles," I tell him.

"I was going to say the same to you."

"They don't know us, they don't know you. That's not who you are anymore," I tell him.

He holds me tighter, not saying anything for a long moment before mumbling into my hair.

"Thank you for always believing in me."

I well up with some tears but shove them down.
"That's what a pack does," I say, and I mean it.
Because we will get through this. We will be okay.

ETHAN

CHAPTER 34

It's been a few weeks of living at Bram's house and trying to find an everyday normal. There's finally a lull in the guys' schedule, and we find our asses perched on a soft, cream-colored sofa at a therapist's office.

I sit next to Max while Sloane sits between me and Bram.

Things have been… tense, to say the least.

Bram is trying to control his temper and not be a possessive asshole when it comes to me and Sloane. While Max salivates for time with us while trying to not step on Bram's toes.

Not to mention the amount of press coverage that's been going around. None of us have made a public statement, which may have made things worse. Sloane and Max's character are a constant thing that the press seems to be targeting and neither of them have been taking it well.

It's honestly a hot mess, and it's clear the stress is getting to Sloane.

Nilsen has taken the least amount of heat in the press, but it's clear he wants to strangle every single news report or online thread that calls Sloane a succubus or Yoko Ono. It doesn't help that the Foxes defense has been playing like shit, so everyone is blaming Sloane for making Max and Bram's relationship worse.

She bites her nails, and I tug her hand away and give it a tight squeeze. As strong as she is, there's only so much someone can take. The only good thing is that Max and Bram have been more irritated with the online slander than they have been with each other.

"Welcome, I'm Dr. Mahdoni, I've read each of your questionnaires I had you fill out prior to our session, and if it's okay with you, I'd like to just jump right in."

"Please," Sloane says while Bram and Max both shift in their seats.

The doctor smiles, and something in her expression has me hopeful that she can help us.

"It's not uncommon for Alphas to fight for dominance in packs, especially packs that have been formed around an Omega. When Alphas form a pack and then find their Omega, there's a lot more cohesion and a hierarchy in place. It's evident to me that the hierarchy of this pack has not been set and therefore why you're having issues."

"It could also be that Bram hated me well before Sloane and I realized we were scent matches," Max says, and I want to wince, but I don't. The whole reason we're here is to work through our shit.

"Let's talk about it, Bram," the doctor suggests.

"I'd rather not," Bram says, and Sloane elbows him in the stomach.

"This was your suggestion," she hisses under her breath.

The massive Alpha shifts in his seat, and I can tell he is extremely uncomfortable, which is very uncommon for him. I'm also on the edge of my god damn seat, wanting to know what caused this grudge.

Not to mention hopeful. I hate that we're not all under the same roof, not even just for Sloane's sake, but for mine too. We need to get on the same page so we can work through this as a pack.

The sooner Bram and Max sign a pack contract, the more quickly we can dispel some rumors, and Sloane will be more content.

"It's stupid. It's in the past," he says.

"That's a cop out. If you want to forge some sort of pack mentality with Max, we're going to need to work from the root of the issue," the doctor says.

Sloane is nodding her head in agreement, and I'm giving Bram a glare. We don't have all the time in the world to figure out our shit. It's taken far too long to even get this fucking appointment. If we don't leave here without some sort of direction, I'll take Sloane to spend the night at my dad's and make these petulant Alphas suffer.

"He rejected me," Bram says so quietly I almost don't hear him.

"I what now?" Max says, and Bram sighs audibly.

"See, this is why I don't want to bring it up. He doesn't even remember."

"Feeling rejected can build up a lot of resentment. Why don't you tell us what happened?"

"Yeah, tell us what happened?" I chime in, not even realizing that I'm saying it. I just can't believe Bram would ever be interested in Max?

"You had feelings for Max?" Sloane says softly, and Bram grumbles.

"This is why I didn't want to say anything," Bram complains. Clearly, the big Alpha's ego was scorned by whatever Max did. But the Max I know isn't like that...

"What are you even talking about? You never liked me," Max says in complete disbelief.

"I did. I thought you were attractive, and you weren't as annoying as the other players on the team. I always tried to be on your team during scrimmages and always did my best to protect you in goal," Bram says.

Max furrows his brows, and I'm sure I do too. Because how does that equate to being into someone?

"It was at the away game in Florida. We were celebrating pretty hard. I kissed you, and you laughed in my face," Bram says.

Sloane gasps and holds his hand as she glances over at Max.

It all truly feels like a telenovela at this point.

"I didn't do that," Max denies.

"You did. You laughed and walked away, and I've never felt more rejected or belittled in my life," Bram says, pointing at Max.

"You're full of shit," Max says defensively.

"Why else? Why else would I harbor these feelings against you?"

"Because you're a dick," Max says.

Dr. Mahdoni holds out her hands in a placating gesture.

"This is good. You're both allowed to express yourself. Max, were you drinking that night?"

"Of course I was drinking. Everyone was."

"Excessively?" she asks.

"Bram, is it possible that you approached Max when you had your own liquid courage and he truly doesn't remember this encounter?"

"No," Bram says, and I pinch my nose.

The doctor doesn't get discouraged and decides to turn her direction to Sloane who is looking both shocked and frustrated.

"Sloane, can you tell me what traits you like in Bram, Ethan, and Max?"

"Ethan is kind, protective, and I can tell him anything, and I know he won't judge me. Bram is gentle with me, always there when I need him, and he takes the best care of me. Max is easy to talk to, fun, and watching how much he's grown over the few months I've known him has given me such joy. He'd also give the shirt off his back to anyone who needed it," Sloane says, and I squeeze her hand.

"I need for each of you to see yourself how Sloane sees you and how she sees the other members of the pack. If you care for your Omega, then you'll understand her intentions with every one of you. If it's okay, I'd like to set up individual sessions with both Bram and Max and you two together."

Both of the Alphas grumble but agree.

"I know you all have busy schedules, but I'd like for you to spend more time as a pack, not broken up in trios," she says.

"Thank you, Dr. Mahdoni," both Sloane and I say before getting up and leaving the building.

Sloane's phone chimes as we walk out, and I look over her shoulder. Of course she has alerts on her phone about when any of us are mentioned in the news. This time, it's a picture of her smiling as she's getting smoothies with Piper and Charlotte.

The headline reads, "Unbonded Team Wrecker."

She exits out of the article and puts the phone in her purse, acting like it doesn't bother her. I'll need to have a talk with Max and Bram. She can't keep seeking out this shit; it's only going to drive her crazy.

Bram drove all of us to the appointment, and he holds Sloane's hand to make sure she doesn't slip on any ice. The parking lot is covered in dirty snow as she glances over at me.

"I don't feel so good. Sit in the back with me?" Sloane asks, and I agree, even if it puts Max and Bram together in the front seat. He opens the back seat, and we both climb in before Max and Bram get in the vehicle.

Sloane doesn't look so great next to me, but when I touch her head, she doesn't have a fever.

"You've got to stop getting alerts for that trash," I whisper to her.

She rubs her forehead and nods. "I know," she replies, resting her head on my shoulder.

The rest of the drive is quiet, almost uncomfortably so, until Max cuts through the tension with a metaphorical sharp knife.

"I didn't reject you," Max says, and I sigh.

"What, I'm just making it up?"

"I'm not saying you can't feel that way. But how the fuck can I reject you when I didn't even know you were propositioning me? This could have all been solved years ago if you didn't try to approach me when I was drunk."

"That would have been difficult, considering you were constantly drunk that season," Bram says.

Well, this could either go great or terrible.

"I don't feel so good," Sloane says again.

"Aw shit, are you going to be carsick?" Bram says, the malice slipping from his tone as he looks at us in the rearview mirror.

She covers her mouth and nods.

"Fuck. As soon as I get over the bridge," Bram says, glancing back in the mirror.

"Look—" Max shouts, but it's too late.

The screeching of metal on metal against Bram's SUV is disturbing as another car hits us on Bram's driver's side.

My shoulder twinges instantly, and I'm trying to collect myself as the shriek of metal and another car hitting us from behind makes me realize what's happening.

The car is going directly into the icy depths of Mill River.

I'm sure there's screaming around me as I brace myself for impact. I glance over at Sloane who is thankfully buckled in and has just thrown up on herself. In a blink of an eye, the car smacks against the water, disorienting me for an unknown moment in time.

A sharp smack hits my face.

"Sorry. Sorry," Sloane says as she unbuckles her belt, and I blink myself awake.

My cheek stings, and it's not from Sloane's slap, I must have hit my head on something on the way down.

Sloane has tears streaming down her face as cold water starts to rush my feet.

Both of the front airbags activated, and Bram and Max seem to both be unconscious.

"Wake up. Wake up," Sloane says, shaking Max who is sitting in front of her.

She's sobbing as she tries to wake him up.

The car is sinking, thankfully rather slow, so I don't think the river is too deep. But with the way it's rushing from the latest snow, if we don't get out of here soon, the car could fill up, or we get hypothermia.

"Wake up. Please. Please. Wake up," Sloane is crying, and I shake my head, trying to get my brain fully functioning.

I reach across the seat and feel that Bram still has a pulse before reaching over to Max.

Okay, they're both good.

When I lean toward the trunk, Sloane looks at me like I've gone crazy.

I pull apart Bram's bag until I find what I'm looking for and open the smelling salts.

As soon as I put them under Max's nose, he wakes up with a jolt. Unfortunately, Bram doesn't do the same.

Max makes a startled sound as he realizes what's going on as the cold water laps at our shins. He shoves at Bram's shoulder, but he doesn't wake up. I don't see any blood anywhere, but I don't have the greatest vantage point either.

"Get her out of here," Max says.

"We can't leave Bram," Sloane says with her teeth chattering.

"I'll get him out," Max promises. "Go, get her out and somewhere warm, now," Max says, and I nod my head. I grab a long sleeve workout shirt from Bram's bag and tie one sleeve to Sloane's wrist before tying the other to mine so she doesn't drift away from me.

"We can't leave," she chatters.

"Go to safety now," Max says, using his Alpha voice.

Sloane's eyes go wide as she stares at him and then glances at Bram.

"Baby, I won't leave him. Please go," Max pleads, trying to hold back his own emotion.

I roll down the window and climb out first. I can stand on a rock, but the water is brutally cold, and the current seems to want to drag me along with it. I hold out my hands, and Sloane climbs out, her teeth chattering as I direct her to lie on her back, and we let the current take us down river.

Once we're close enough to the bank, I grip her hand and drag her to shore.

We're both so fucking cold. I don't think I've ever experienced this level of cold, like every inch of me is freezing yet on fire at the same time.

Sloane holds herself and sits in the snowy, muddy bank, just staring at where the car is half above water and half below.

If the car floats away, we're fucked.

But we also need help, immediately.

"Sw-sw-sw. Fu-ck."

I can't even get the words out. I'm shaking so bad.

"St-ay here," I grate out, and she just shivers as she stares at the car.

I climb the bank and wave down a few cars. Four cars pass me until one pulls over and calls the police.

She blessedly has some blankets in her car, and I take them back down to the bank where Sloane is sobbing.

She's staring at the car, and neither of the Alphas have come out of the watery depths.

There's no way I can swim against the current. There's nothing either of us can do except wait for emergency services.

The woman who pulled over is trying to console Sloane while she's on the phone with dispatch.

It's looking hopeless.

Things get worse as we see the car shift, and we both fear the worst.

Suddenly, a lone dirty blond head gasps for air out of the river.

But he's completely alone.

Sloane begins to hyperventilate next to me, and my heart sinks.

No, there's no fucking way.

Bram can't still be in the vehicle. Max promised.

I can't lose Bram. Sloane can't lose Bram before we even get to bond and be a real pack.

There's no way we're coming back from this.

SLOANE

CHAPTER 35

My Alpha is gone.

I can only see Max's light hair above the surface. I didn't get to bond him. I didn't get to live my life with him. He's taken away from me before I'd gotten to experience what true pack happiness is.

I can't breathe. I feel like I'm dying.

"Oh, honey. The police and fire department are on their way," a woman I don't recognize says.

It feels like every inch of me is frozen, and talking is impossible.

The man I love is stuck in that vehicle that's nearly fully submerged. Only about a foot from the top of the SUV is still sticking out.

I need him. This can't be real.

We were just in therapy working on all of this. He was trying. He was trying so fucking hard because he loved me.

Bram chose me; he protected me; he's my Alpha.

I can't lose him, not when I've barely had him.

I shrug off the blanket that was providing me some semblance of warmth and step toward the running river bend. I'm not sure what my plan is, I know I can't out swim the current, but I can't sit here and do nothing.

Arms wrap around me, and I know they're Ethan's.

He supports my weight as we both fall down into the snowy sand and watch Max's head float in our direction.

"No," I call out, and Ethan holds me tightly, his own body shaking with sobs.

The amount of despair I feel in this moment is like my heart is being yanked out of my chest. The promises of everything that we could have been slipping through my fingers like grains of sand.

Bram wasn't even thirty.

He had so much life to live, so much love to give.

I need him. Ethan and I both need him. How in the fuck can I go on without him? Without the Alpha who purrs so loud for me it rattles comfort every time I'm with him. The man who can be closed off to others but opens up to me.

This can't be happening.

It's all my fault for feeling sick. I should have sat in the front seat. I know I get motion sickness.

Bram is gone, and it's all my fucking fault.

My chest convulses, and I feel like I'm going to die. Even if I don't, I can't help but feel like I wish I was dead. How can I live without Bram? How can I live with this being all my fault?

"Lo-ok," Ethan shivers, pointing out to the river.

I use my shaking, nearly purple hands to wipe my eyes.

Max is using one arm to swim, and his other is wrapped around… Bram.

Bram isn't swimming, though. He's just floating next to Max.

I take another step into the river, and Ethan pulls me back. The sound of sirens become piercing as the fire department parks on the bridge and by the shore we're on.

They're speedy as they rapidly go over plans, and the ambulances and EMTs join the fray.

Max still seems so fucking far away, and I can't see how Bram is doing. Why isn't he awake in this freezing cold water?

A silver, crinkly blanket is placed over my shoulders, and I clutch it to my chest.

"Miss, come with us," he says, and I shake my head.

I need to see Bram pulled out of that river—I need to know that he's alright.

"Miss. Your chances of hypothermia are higher the longer you stay out here. We need to take you to the hospital."

I shake my head, tears not even coming out of my eyes anymore because I'm so cold.

Ethan grabs my face, his fingers cold as ice. "We-e have t-o. Bram w-w-ould want y-y-ou to go," he says.

I shake my head even though he's right.

The firefighters are putting on waders and making their way out to Max and Bram. Ethan's hold on my face tightens.

"Pl-ease," he begs me.

When I glance over, I see there are multiple ambulances lined up, and it's the only reason I decide to go.

I'm no good to Max or a recovering Bram if I don't get help myself—I refuse to think otherwise—he has to be okay.

They place Ethan and me in the same ambulance, warming our skin and hooking us up to IVs. The whole ride to the hospital, my mind wanders to how they are doing and the worst possible scenarios.

Ethan and I stay close the entire time. They even give us a room together as they use warmers and continue our warmed saline drips. They take blood, and Ethan turns on the TV to see if there are any updates or coverage.

The hospital staff promised to tell us as soon as they arrive.

Ethan clicks to a local news station, and I watch in horror as they show footage of the wreckage and emergency crew onsite.

"The car belongs to Bram Nilsen, starting defensive lineman for the New Haven Foxes, but that's not the only shocking part. Starting goalie, Max Connery was also in the vehicle along with the head coach's daughter, Sloane Applegate. A fourth party was in the vehicle but has yet to be identified. Our sources show that the unidentified male and Miss Applegate are both in the hospital and should make easy recovery. Status on the two hockey pros has not been released, but we fear the worst," the prim news reporter says.

"It's unclear what caused the accident, but this bridge is notorious for being dangerous after a large snowstorm. We've reached out to the New Haven Foxes for comment but haven't received anything."

Ethan clicks to another channel where they are also reporting on the accident.

"It's been heavily speculated online about the relationship of the two New Haven Foxes players, the mascot and the coach's daughter. This accident seems to confirm that something has been going on, but our sources indicate that none of them are bonded." The news reporter holds the mic as he approaches an older man bundled up in a jacket, scarf, and hat.

"Sir, can you tell us what you saw?"

"I didn't see anything. But I can tell you it was probably Max Connery's fault. The team hasn't been the same since he joined. I wouldn't be surprised if he was the one driving and under the influence."

"That's very speculative. Did you see anything that would give you that impression?" the reporter asks.

"He's just—"

"Turn it off," I croak, and Ethan pushes the power button, shutting the TV off as I try and hold it together.

"Hey, they're going to sensationalize everything. Don't listen to them."

"Then why aren't they here yet?" I ask Ethan.

"Maybe they got taken to a different hospital."

I can't help but to think if I bonded them and we pledged as a pack already, I'd be able to get more information. Not to mention, I'd be able to shut up some of the rumors. But hearing them talk about my scent match like that forms a pit in my stomach.

Max stayed. Max did what he promised. He's a fucking hero,

and he's a good man. I can't help but to feel so endlessly hopeless right now.

I need my Alphas to be okay. There's no other option. I'm not sure how I can go on if they aren't healthy and safe.

Ethan grabs his IV bag as he holds the back of his hospital gown closed and comes to lie in bed with me. He holds me tightly.

"They're so strong, Sloane. They have so much to live for. It's going to be okay."

I want to believe him. God, do I want to believe him. But why haven't we heard anything? I guess it doesn't help that our phones were left in the car and we can't get a hold of anyone.

My parents are probably scared shitless. I imagine they'll be here any moment.

I'm trying to be brave and be strong about all of this when the nurse and doctor walk into our room. If they're upset about us cuddling in bed, they don't say anything.

"Both of your color looks much better. I know it was jarring being brought to the hospital, but the blood work looks great. We just want to bring in an OBGYN to check in on the baby," the doctor says casually.

"The what?" I ask.

The doctor's eyes widen, and she clears her throat.

"I'm sorry, you didn't know?"

I burst into tears, and Ethan holds me closely. I'm sure the doctor is mortified.

This should be the best news. I always knew I wanted to be a mother, and I knew who I wanted to be my pack. We might be dysfunctional, but I love them, and we were going to figure it out.

I'm pregnant, and I don't even know if my Alphas are okay.

"If you can just give us a few minutes," Ethan asks, and I can't hear them leave the room over my sobbing.

All the saline they gave me is now just rushing out of my face.

"Just let it out, sweetheart."

This time, he doesn't tell me it's going to be okay. He doesn't lie to me. Because right now, nothing feels alright.

"Maybe that's why you weren't feeling so great," Ethan says, and I sniffle. I hadn't had any other symptoms. I mean, my heat was about a month, month and a half ago? Right?

"What are we going to do?" I ask Ethan.

"I'm going to be with you no matter what, Sloane. I'm not going anywhere," he says, throwing the same words back at me I did to him. "I'm not going anywhere," he repeats.

I believe him, and I take a few deep breaths. I might not know how to take care of myself right now, but there's something bigger than me that I have to take care of. Even though I want to break down, I can't. I need to make sure my baby is okay.

Right now, I have to be strong, even if all I want to do is fall apart.

There's a knock on the door, and Ethan tells them to come in. A woman in scrubs is pushing a machine and gives me a sympathetic smile.

"I'm assuming as an Omega you've had one of these before," she says, holding up the wand, and I nod my head. "It can be really hard to tell this early, but we should be able to check and make sure everything is okay. Your blood levels are indicative of a viable pregnancy," she says.

Ethan climbs off my bed but holds my hand as she lubes up the wand and places it inside of me. She's searching around, and when she smiles, the smallest bit of relief escapes me.

"There they are. Let's see if we can get a heartbeat. It's still early."

She angles the wand, and it's so nearly faint I think I'm imaging it. But there it is, my baby's heartbeat.

I decide from that moment on, no matter what happened to Bram or Max, I have something to live for.

CHAPTER 36

I blink my eyes open as warmth flows through me. To my right, there's a warmer full of saline, and warming blankets are wrapped around my body.

When I look to my left, I see my crying mother and my extremely worried brother.

"Looks like the tables have turned," I rasp. "Where's everyone? Are they okay? Did I save him?" I ask.

My mom brushes her hand through my hair.

"Sloane and Ethan were taken to a different hospital. They are keeping them overnight."

"Bram?" I ask, emotion clogging in my throat.

I promised Sloane and Ethan; I told her I would get him out, and I did. But he was unconscious the whole time.

"He's in the ICU, but it looks like he's going to be okay. They couldn't tell us much because we aren't family. They told Coach Applegate who updated us."

I sigh and rest my head on the back of the hospital bed, relief filling me. I don't know if I could ever forgive myself if Bram wasn't okay.

The accident wasn't my fault, I'm fully aware of that. But the only reason Ethan got Sloane out was because of my promise.

"You're sure?"

"We'll keep you updated as soon as we know more. Sloane and Ethan are going to come here tomorrow after they get released. You need your sleep," my mom says. "I'd also really fucking appreciate it if you two would stop ending up in the fucking hospital."

I crack a smile. There's the mom that I know.

"I'm glad you're okay. The whole team is worried about all of you," Owen says.

"Gagnon gets to shine once more," I say, my eyes closing.

"Your spot is waiting for you as soon as you're ready to come back. They want to keep you overnight but think you can go home tomorrow. You can stay at our house," he says.

"I'll think about it," I mumble.

Though I know it's a lie.

I want to be with my pack, and if I didn't feel so exhausted, I'd be trying to get hold of them right now.

"Sloane's okay?" I confirm again, wishing we were bonded and I could feel her.

"She's okay, honey. Do you need anything?"

"Sloane," I whisper, but pure exhaustion takes over, and I pass out.

❁ ❁ ❁ ❁

A warm hand is rubbing my knuckles when I wake up, and I know exactly who it is before I open my eyes. Sloane sobs and places her head on my chest as she holds me close. I brush back her hair.

"Shh. It's okay, I'm here."

"You're okay," she says, more like she's consoling herself.

"Moderate hypothermia. I'll be okay."

Ethan runs a hand through my hair and rubs Sloane's back. I grab his wrist and kiss his hand.

"Thank you for getting her out when you did. I know it wasn't easy."

Ethan nods, but it's clear he's trying to hold it together.

"We're a pack, we take care of each other," Ethan says.

I don't know why. Maybe it's the confusion, all the adrenaline wearing off, or the fact that I almost lost everything before I truly had it.

Tears roll down my face.

Sloane doesn't say anything. She just wipes my tears with her thumbs and presses her cheek to mine.

"We're okay. We're okay. We're okay," she chants.

"How's Bram?"

"I think he's leaving the ICU tomorrow, so we can see him," Ethan says.

Sloane pulls back, and I cradle her face.

"You're okay? You both are okay?" I ask, needing confirmation.

The two share a look, and I wonder what that's about, but Sloane just nods. "Mild hypothermia. They just wanted to keep me longer because I'm an Omega."

"That makes sense," I reply, and Sloane nods with relief.

There's a knock on the door. Before my mother comes into the room, she immediately embraces my Omega in a huge hug. They both seem effortlessly comfortable with one another, and I'm grateful.

"I'm so happy you're all okay. Scared the shit out of me," my mom says, and Sloane nods into her shoulder. "How are your parents holding up?"

"They're okay. They visited in the hospital." Sloane glances over at me and winces. "They want me to move back home."

"What did you tell them?"

"No. I live with my pack now."

Most of your pack, I think, keeping it to myself. But Ethan reads me like a book, squeezing my hand.

"Max, you saved his life. I think it's safe to say he'll be more than happy to let you move in," Ethan says like I'm being ridiculous.

"I think Bram may be the one exception when it comes to a life debt," I say, and Ethan shakes his head.

"Max, stop being such a drama queen," my mother says. "He's always been like this, you know? The one time I took his Gameboy away, he packed up his whole room and said he was running away. I said go right on ahead, see how long you last. He snuck back in during the middle of the night. I caught him in the pantry eating stale crackers later that night. Didn't even last a damn day."

"Mom," I complain.

"What? It's the truth. Don't even get me started on the time he had his first crush. Oh my God, he made this—"

"Mom." I raise my voice, and she sighs, waving me off.

"Fine, ruin my fun. I'll give you all some time together. I'm staying with Owen if you all need anything."

My mom pets my cheek before giving both Sloane and Ethan a hug before leaving. Both of them look tired and worn out, but at least they're here. At least they're safe.

"Was there anyone else in the accident?" I ask.

Ethan shakes his head. "No one else was significantly hurt on the bridge."

"Good," I reply. "So I guess our next therapy session is delayed."

Sloane scrubs her face. "Yeah, I'd say that's on the back burner for now."

I slept at Bram's house last night so that all of us could go to the hospital and see Bram today.

I'm a million more times conscious about my driving. It's clear Sloane and Ethan feel the same way. We're all dead silent the entire drive.

Before we even turn the hallway, we can hear Bram complaining.

"When can I leave?" his gruff voice says, and as soon as Sloane hears it, she's racing around the corner into his room. Ethan and I quickly follow her; I don't want her out of my sight, even for a moment.

As soon as we enter, Sloane is clinging to the Alpha as he pets her hair and consoles her.

The side of his face and nose is bruised. He's holding back a wince as Sloane leans against his side.

"I'm okay, *liefje*."

"You're not okay," she says through tears.

Bram turns to his nurse and sighs. "Can you ask the doctor to come by and explain my condition to my pack?" he asks.

The nurse nods and sighs. I imagine Bram hasn't been the best patient.

"When can you leave? What care do you need?" Sloane asks.

"The doctor will tell you everything. I'm okay. I promise."

Sloane is touching all over his face, and he winces when she touches a certain spot on his hairline.

"What's wrong? Does it hurt?"

"It's mild, Sloane. I've had worse on the ice."

"What do you mean? You have a fucking brain injury?" she says, a little louder than her usual voice, and Bram winces. "Sorry," she apologizes quickly.

"It's okay. I'm okay," he says, kissing her wrist and glancing back at Ethan. He holds out an arm and hugs the Beta who doesn't really say much. I wonder if Ethan is shaken up from the accident because he usually has some quip rolling off the tongue.

Sloane tries to help Bram eat his lunch, and he has a fit about it the whole time while we get a run down from his doctor. Sloane does a good job holding back tears until the doctor leaves the room.

Bram pets her hair for what feels like an hour before clearing his throat and glancing over at me. "Can I talk to Max?" he asks, and I swallow thickly.

"We'll be right in the hall," Sloane says, kissing his cheek and eyeing both of us before leaving the hospital room.

I shove my hands in my pockets and look at the floor, not knowing what to say.

"You saved my life," Bram says.

"I wasn't going to leave you there. Even if I didn't promise Ethan and Sloane."

"Getting me out of there couldn't have been easy. You were exposed to the cold water longer in helping me."

I shrug my shoulders, and Bram sighs.

"I'm sorry," he says.

I blink and tilt my head at him. "What?"

"I'm sorry for being such a dick to you this whole season. Sorry for thinking you didn't deserve Sloane. But beyond anything, I'm sorry for thinking you didn't have good character."

"You would have done the same," I say, not knowing how to handle the compliment.

"Is this what being a pack is?" Bram asks with a laugh. "I have to tell you, Connery, apologizing isn't one of my strengths. Just accept it, and we'll move on. Really move on this time."

"You actually mean it this time?"

"How could I not? You saved my life. You protected Ethan and Sloane. If there has to be another Alpha in this pack, I'm honored that it's you."

There's emotion clogged in my throat.

I'm not sure how to handle Bram giving me compliments along with Sloane and Ethan. It's almost too much. I'm not a hero. I could save him, so I did.

"Are you all doing okay at the house? You can have the secondary guest room until we finish the basement," he says.

It's so fucking casual like he has our entire lives planned out. I sit down on the chair next to his bed and put my head in my hands. I've never cared about anyone as much as I care about these people, and it's fucking terrifying. Nothing I've ever had has been more precious than this pack, and I could have lost them. Under different circumstances, I could be dead right now, Bram could be dead right now, and our lives would look a hell-of-lot different.

Bram's big hand pats the top of my head like I'm a dog or he doesn't know how to console me.

"You did good, Max."

"We could have lost them. We could have lost everything."

"But we didn't. You'll be medically cleared to play hockey in a week, me, maybe a month. Ethan and Sloane are completely fine. If anything, this woke me the hell up," he says.

"Is it always going to feel like this, worrying about each other?"

"Probably even worse when we bond with them."

"Fuck," I hiss, and he pats my head one more time.

"As soon as I'm medically cleared, I'm going to bond with Sloane and Ethan," he says, and I pull my head out of my hands and blink at him. He just said it would be worse after we bonded. He shrugs his shoulders and winces. "Not being connected to them, having them be listed as my emergency contacts? I can't wait any longer. It was torture not knowing if everyone was okay."

"I'm fucking terrified."

Bram sighs and shifts back into his bed like he's tired. "Let me be pack Alpha, then," he suggests.

"What do you mean?"

"Let me be in charge. Let me carry the burden."

"You're in a fucking hospital bed."

He glares at me. "Yeah, right now I am. I can kick your ass when I'm not feeling like shit though."

I shake my head and sigh. "It's like the fucking therapist said. We need a hierarchy in the pack. Let me be pack Alpha, make most of the decisions, and take care of the pack."

I bite the inside of my cheek, the deep inner Alpha part of me not knowing if I can submit to another Alpha like that.

"I'm not saying you're not capable, Max."

He says my first name, which garners all my attention as I look at him, bruises and all.

"I'm saying I like it. I like making decisions and feeling that responsibility. So let me have it. They need you as an Alpha just as much as they need me, but I feel like being head of the pack is my place. If we're really doing this, this is how we move forward."

"All I had to do was save your life for this revelation?"

"Apparently," he grumbles. "Think about it. Send Sloane back in. I need to hold her a little longer before I go to sleep."

When Sloane comes back in the room with tears in her eyes, it's clear she's been listening to the whole conversation.

"Jesus Christ, come here," Bram says.

Sloane sobs into his chest—the side that wasn't bruised in the accident.

"Well, hypothermia may have been worth this extremely precious Hallmark moment," Ethan whispers into my ear.

For the first time since the accident, I laugh. Maybe we'll survive this after all.

SLOANE

CHAPTER 37

"How much longer do we have to keep it a secret? It's killing me on the inside," Ethan complains.

"I know. Me too. It's just, they're getting along. I don't want to ruin it."

Ethan's brows furrow as he leans his hip against the counter. I'm currently making Bram soup.

He's not taking it well that he needs lots of rest this week, but it was doctor's orders. He needs to rest for the next few weeks and do a few routine physicals. His bruising from getting hit on his left side is severe, but nothing was broken. As for his head injury, it was minor, but they did give us some anti-seizure medication, just in case. In all honesty, I'm slightly terrified that he will push himself too far to try and get back on the ice. Max is not lacing up, but he is going to practice, which is where he's at now.

"Why would this ruin it? It's the best news," Ethan says, rubbing my flat stomach.

My heart does a little flutter, and I wonder if I'm not giving my Alphas enough credit.

"They just started getting along. I worry they might argue."

"Over what?" Ethan says, totally not getting where I'm coming from.

"Whose it is."

"Who gives a shit? It's our baby," Ethan says.

I stop stirring, and I hug him tightly. I'm not sure if it's hormones, all the emotional turmoil, or just knowing I'm pregnant, but I've been a complete emotional mess. I cry, and Ethan sighs, holding me tight.

"You're making us all dads. To be honest, Sloane, if they fight about this, I may just fucking lose it."

"Can we wait till Bram is back on his feet again?"

He sighs but nods.

"This is a big ask, sweetheart. I want to tell everyone."

"It doesn't feel right to tell anyone else before we tell the Alphas," I say, going back to my soup.

"No, you're right. I'll try to be patient."

"Do you want to take some soup to your dad?"

"I'd love that. Speaking of dads, are you talking to yours?" he asks.

I let out a frustrated noise. Of course, I saw all my parents when I was in the hospital, but all it led to was more resentment on my father's side. He was blaming Bram and Max for what happened when it was no one's fault. When I tried to explain that he was treating me like I was a child who needed coddling, I had to stand up for myself. We haven't spoken since. Well, my father and I haven't. I still text my moms and my Beta father every day.

I'm sure we'll get this all resolved sooner than later, but right now I have too much on my plate to deal with my dad trying to dictate my life. I'm a woman, I'm a grown ass Omega who can decide her pack. Hell, I'm about to be a parent myself.

With shaky hands, I ladle the soup into a to-go container for Ethan to take to his foster dad and send him off with a kiss. If I thought my dad was acting poorly about this all now, he's going to lose his mind when he finds out I got pregnant during my heat. Or before.

Max and I didn't use any protection in the locker room, and who knows how good we were with the diaphragm during my heat? It was a risk I knew I was taking during my heat. Ethan and Bram also knew my birth control methods well before my heat. Max did after signing my heat contract, and I worry he might feel trapped.

He's my scent match, which he had no control over. I was already with Bram, which he had no control over. And now we're all going to have a baby together while we're still in the midst of learning to be a pack.

Maybe there is some guilt lingering.

I should have sucked it up and went on the pill or the implant. But I don't like the way they make me feel. I don't feel like myself when I have other hormones running through me.

I glide my hand over my stomach. My baby wasn't planned, but I can't deny that I'm excited. Bram's house is large, and there's a perfect room for a nursery right next to the primary bedroom.

All of the guys can still have their own rooms. I don't really need my own space…

That's a lie—I totally do.

Thankfully, the men I chose aren't messy, especially Bram. But it is taking some training on my part to show them how I like things organized.

The soup tastes great, and I turn off all the burners and ladle up a bowl before bringing it upstairs to Bram.

He looks pissed off as he leans against the headboard of his bed with crossed arms and watches TV. If there's something I've learned about Bram, it's that he doesn't like to sit still. I honestly can't relate.

Watching TV and being doted on all day sounds like the dream.

I set up his tray on the nightstand. His water cup is still full.

"I'm fine," he says.

"Okay, Mr. Grumpy," I say, glancing at the TV. "No wonder you're cranky. You need to put something good on TV."

"This is fine."

"You're watching a baby seal get eaten by a killer whale. No, you need something juicy."

"Juicy?" he says with an arch of a brow.

I try not to look at the bruised side of him because it makes me so upset.

"Yeah, like trashy shows. They're the best."

"I just want to go back to work," he grumbles.

"I know you do, but hey, you get me all to yourself for a few weeks. That's not so bad?"

"Come here. Put a stupid fucking show on. Thank you for the soup."

"You're welcome. And don't get any on the sheets, or we'll have to wash everything," I say, snuggling up into the bed until I find a good show. "Oh yeah, you're going to love this."

"What is it?" he asks.

"So each season, there's three Omegas, and they can only scent the Alphas and talk to them through a wall. They never see what they look like."

"How is that entertaining?"

"Oh, just you wait."

Three hours later

"No, she can't pick Zach. He's an asshole."

"I know, right?"

"And why is Daniella literally leading every single Alpha on when she only likes Craig and Marcus?" he asks.

"And she keeps lying to the other girls about who she's interested in," I add in.

"This is a cluster fuck. Adrianna is the only one taking this seriously."

"I know, right? Plus, she's so pretty. I think she's going to choose Adon, Eric, and Heath."

"What about Raymond?" Bram asks, astonished, and I bite my lip.

"Raymond doesn't want kids. Adrianna does, in fact. She and Adon would make the prettiest babies."

"There's nothing wrong with not wanting kids, though," Bram says, and my heart sinks. I feel like I'm about to throw up.

I swallow thickly.

"Nothing's wrong with that, it's just they should be on the same page. You want kids, right?" I ask, my heart beating so fast it feels like it's going to beat out of my chest.

If he says no right now, I'm not sure what I'd do. Maybe lock myself in a closet and cry or something equally as dramatic.

I remember how Adrianna's face fell when Raymond told her through the wall it wasn't something he wanted. She really liked him. His scent was her favorite, but the moment he said that, she stopped booking pods with him.

"I want kids but probably not for a while," he says, and I nod my head.

"I have to go to the bathroom real quick," I say, and he furrows his brows at me as I skitter away off the bed like a scared animal.

As soon as I've shut the door, I splash some water on my face.

He didn't say no. He just said not right now.

Well, he has about eightish months to adjust to the idea. Because there's no turning back now.

It's probably a conversation we should have had before. We talked so much about my heat and creating a pack that we didn't get to the nitty gritty of how we saw our lives. I thought I had more time.

Story of my fucking life, right?

I thought I had more time, and now it's planning my life around circumstance, which is not how I saw my life going. Don't get me wrong, I'm not complaining. My pack is perfect, it's who I need. But everything has felt so out of my control. Nothing has gone to plan, and I just don't know how much more I can take.

I'm not a go with the flow Omega, as much as I may try to be.

When things are organized, life runs smoother, and as of late, it feels like everything is out of my control.

My fear of telling Bram gets even deeper. Fuck, I love him so much. But why am I so scared to tell him?

I splash some water on my face and flush the empty toilet so I don't seem like a complete fraud before crawling back into bed and Bram presses play.

"Everything okay?" Bram asks.

I'm saved from having to answer as Ethan comes into the bedroom, taking off all his clothes and stripping down into his underwear.

I've trained him well.

Outside clothes and inside clothes are a real fucking thing, and apparently none of these men got that memo until now. It's not even just about dirt, it's also about all the smells that come along with being out and about all day.

"Oh God, she's not going to pick Raymond, is she?"

"What's wrong with Raymond?" Bram asks again.

"He doesn't want kids," he repeats my earlier sentiment.

"He's twenty-four. Of course he doesn't want kids. I didn't want kids at twenty-four either. Hell, I'm twenty-seven and just now warming up to the idea of having a needy little demon running my life."

Ethan glances at me, and the ever observant Bram notices.

"What is up with you two? It's just a reality TV show."

No, it's just our entire life that you just admitted you're not sure that you want. It has me wanting to wait longer to break the news. Will he be upset? Or angry? I hate lying to Bram, but I'll hate his disappointment even more.

"Yeah, a show you've watched three episodes of already," Ethan says.

I hear the security alarm beep that Max has come home, and just like Ethan, he comes upstairs and undresses and lies in the bed, he and Bram on opposite sides.

"What's this?" Max asks.

"*Scent Your Match*," I say.

"I've heard about this show. Is it any good?"

"No," Bram says, and I poke his chest. "Fine. It's not horrible," he says.

I'm trying to let this disappointed feeling dissipate, but it's hard. Ethan's hand is firmly on my thigh for comfort as we all watch the show. I look around at all of them. Never did I think we would all be lying on Bram's bed watching a stupid reality TV show.

If we've overcome everything else, we'll get through this too.

But maybe I will keep it a secret for just a little longer…

❄ ❄ ❄ ❄

I wake up in the middle of the night with my heart beating out of my chest.

It's just a dream, Sloane, I remind myself.

Bram is in the other room. You're between Max and Ethan.

You're okay. They're okay.

But I can't curb my panic. Instead, I'm crawling out of the bed and making my way into Max's closet. It's a mess, and on a normal day I'd be disturbed, but right now, I sit in a pile of his clothes and clutch my phone against my chest.

I should tell them I'm having trouble sleeping. I should tell them about the baby.

My phone vibrates in my hands, and I take a deep breath as I pull back and look at the notification. It's a stream of comments talking about how I'm stringing Bram and Max along and I'm the reason Bram isn't back on the ice yet.

She's nothing but a typical Omega tease.

She doesn't deserve them. Leave some for the rest of us.

I'm so over the hockey news being about this stupid redhead and this subpar team.

They'll break up eventually.

No bond, no pack contract, no dice.

All the stupid comments from people who don't know me have tears running down my eyes. Part of me wants to put them all in their place. But both Bram and Max's PR firm have told them to keep their mouth shut until we sign a pack contract.

A pack contract that could take months from now because I can't get a clear answer on if bonding while pregnant is safe or not. Not to mention, I don't want them to feel what I'm going through right now. There's no way I could burden someone with all of these feelings.

I could ask Piper, but what if she slips up and tells Owen before I get a chance to tell Max? Not that I think she'd do that, but it could happen. All the things I search online are conflicting, some saying it's safe to bond, others saying they miscarried after bonding, though none of those are on medical sites. It's just too much information, and I don't know what to do.

My hands shake as I put the phone down. I'm crippled by fear, and I don't know what to do.

I'm scared I'm going to lose my pack because of some crazy accident. I'm afraid of losing them because the media is tearing us apart. I miss my family, and I don't know how to make it better.

I'm fucking scared of everything.

So I do what I do best. I disassociate and crawl back into bed and act like I wasn't crying in a closet.

It will be okay. I'll be okay… I think.

BRAM

CHAPTER 38

inally, after weeks of recovery, weeks I didn't even fucking need, I'm about to be back on the ice.

Minus some headaches and the time it took my bruises to heal, I've been more than ready to get back to work. I know I'm about to wake before my alarm, but when I turn over, Sloane is nowhere to be found.

I pull back the covers and hear her retching before I push the bathroom door open. I pull back her wild hair and hold it as she pukes while I rub her back with my other hand.

"What's wrong? Did you eat something bad?"

She doesn't answer as she just throws up more.

"Should I postpone practice? I can wait to go back."

Sloane shakes her head, and I realize I'm being annoying by asking her questions while she's sick.

It probably shouldn't be while she's throwing her guts up that I wish I were bonded to her, but it is.

We agreed to wait till I was cleared and healthy; I was shocked Sloane was okay with waiting. If I'm being honest, she hasn't been the same since the accident. She seems a lot more cautious about everything and hasn't left the house much.

She grabs a bundle of toilet paper and cleans her face and flushes, and I let her hair go free.

"No, go to work. I must have eaten something that didn't agree with me. I'll be okay. Plus, Ethan will be home."

"I don't like it," I say, and she gives me a watery smile.

"Seriously, go do what you love. I'll be here waiting."

"I love you more than hockey. You know this?"

"Yes, I know this," she says, tapping my thigh. "Your bruises are completely gone, you've been medically cleared, and the team needs you. I'll be fine, I promise. Go to work."

"Are you just tired of watching TV with me all day?"

"No, and I promise I won't watch any *Pack Island* without you."

"You better not. I need to know if Lyrik is going to stay and make things work with Remy and Cass or if she's going to fly back home."

"I promise I won't watch any of the good stuff without you."

"You aren't bored here, are you? I can get you whatever you want, whatever would make you happy," I promise her.

Her forehead rests on my chest, and she nods. "I'm happy, Bram. I'm just tired and don't feel so good. Send Ethan up before you leave?"

"Okay, *liefje*," I say, kissing the top of her head.

She brushes her teeth, and I help her back into bed.

"Text me if you want me and Max to pick up anything on our way home."

"You're driving together?" she asks happily, even though the dark circles under her eyes tell me a different story.

I wish she would tell me what's going on or talk to someone about it. I've spent most of my days and nights with the Omega since I've been recovering, but she's very good at putting up a facade.

Something's going on in her head, and I wish she would just talk to me.

"Of course, we're going to and from the same place. Why wouldn't we?" I say, not wanting to upset her.

"It makes me happy," she says, snuggling up against the pillow.

I kiss the top of her head again. "Get some sleep. I'll send Ethan up."

"Thank you."

I grab my clothes and head downstairs where Ethan and Max are both eating breakfast.

"Sloane woke up throwing up. She said she's fine, but she'd like for you to go be with her," I direct toward Ethan.

"You sure she's okay?" Max asks, getting up from his stool and glancing upstairs.

Ethan has a different look on his face. "I'm sure she's fine. I'll go check on her. I'll text you if anything is wrong."

"Thanks," Max and I say at the same time.

We take our breakfasts to go, and as soon as we're in the car, Max says exactly what I was thinking.

"Something is up with those two," he says.

"Right?" I agree.

"Ever since the accident, they've both been different," Max says.

While Max and I probably took the brunt of the medical issues during the accident—I was passed out, and he was so full of adrenaline trying to save my life—Ethan and Sloane were hopelessly waiting on shore. Apparently, she didn't know if I was dead or alive for some time.

"Do you think it's the trauma from the accident?"

"That was my best guess? I mean, they haven't been distant, but the fact she hasn't brought up bonding has been odd to me."

When did Max and I start being on the same exact page? It's honestly kind of crazy.

Well, no, it's really not. After the accident, I knew we would be starting over, but I guess I didn't expect to start having the same feelings I did my rookie year.

Max is fun and kind. Not to mention he's held a lot of shit down around the house while I've been out while still managing his place with the Foxes.

Against my better wishes, I may have a growing crush on the Alpha I used to hate. Not that I'll act on it, but if he did? I'm not quite sure how I would react, but I don't think I'd push him away.

Not that he's interested.

Sloane and Ethan are our priorities, even if it seems like they're pushing us away as of late.

But it's only been a month. It's been an adjustment living together and working past what happened on that bridge. None of us have been intimate since the accident, and it feels like Sloane is retreating in on herself. And Ethan, it almost seems like he's covering for her?

"She didn't even want to go out for her birthday," I say, and Max nods.

We did something small at the house, but it didn't feel the same. Sloane is so loved, and so many people wanted to be there for her, but she said she would just rather stay in.

"Maybe we should look for another therapist. There's no fucking way we're going back to that building."

"Agreed," I reply.

"Maybe the distance from her parents is making her depressed, or she misses her job with the Foxes. Should we talk to Coach?"

I grimace, hating the idea.

"You're right, it's not our place," Max says.

"If he asks, we can help, but I don't think that's going to earn us any points with the old man or with Sloane."

"We'll get through this. Together," Max says.

I glance over at him, his eyes fully glued to the road. Was he always this handsome? Or was I blinded by my grudge and forgot just how good looking he was?

❋ ❋ ❋ ❋

I'm suited up, but I doubt I'll get any playing time.

Sloane came to the game, and I couldn't be happier that she finally got out of the house. I know it wasn't easy for her, but Piper and Charlotte are in the box. It doesn't hurt that Anders is there either. Piper and Anders will look after her like she was their own.

Despite being ready to work and happy to have her here, I still feel somewhat uneasy.

With home games, all three of us have to work, and none of us can make sure she's okay. Maybe I have my own baggage after all.

"Nilsen, you're in," Coach barks, and I nod my head, waiting for the shift change as I jump over the barrier and head on the ice.

"You good?" Max asks, and I nod my head. We both look up at the box at the same time.

"She's fine. But are you fine?" he asks.

"Yeah, I feel good," I tell him, and I mean it.

The cold air and the feel of skates back on my feet means everything to me. But I meant what I told Sloane. I love her more.

If we were bonded, I'd be able to check in with her and know that she's feeling alright.

I shake my head and focus on the game. I need a win and to possibly get my groove back. Lately, life has been a little out of my hands, and I'm ready to take charge and get back to normal. Well, more than back to normal. I want to bond with my Omega and Beta, make a pack contract, and see my girl smile more.

There I go, getting distracted again.

I slap my stick against the ice and buckle the fuck down. The Jets are going down. I've got something to prove.

It's the third period. The score is two–two, and I'm hungry for a win.

As happy as I am to be back on the ice, my body clearly isn't completely back to the high-paced game, but I'm pushing through.

Luckily, the game hasn't been overly physical… until now.

We're foaming at the mouth for the win, and with only three minutes left, it's make or break.

No one wants overtime. I'm not even sure I have the fucking stamina for overtime. I just want to go the fuck to sleep. Sitting on my ass and waiting for my bruises to heal has set me back heavily, and I can feel it in how sluggish I'm moving.

I want to take the win and go the fuck home. But apparently, the Jets offense wants to make my first game a banger as they fly down the ice toward me and Martel.

He and the opposing player are pushed against the boards, and I skate over for backup, but it's all for naught as the puck dislodges and goes right to the stick of another Jets player.

He doesn't waste the opportunity as Martel and I scramble to get back into defensive positions.

Max is anticipating the lineman's move and is able to glove the puck, but as soon as he does, the opposing player's shoulder is hitting him and taking Connery down.

I've protected so many goalies in my career, but this feels personal.

All that sluggishness drifts away as adrenaline fills me, and I skate over and grip the prick by his jersey and take the first swing.

The crowd is extraordinarily loud, chanting for violence. I thrive on it, not caring when he hits me in the side that I'm still tender in.

Whistles are blown, and more players are joining the fray as I hold his jersey and continue hitting, even though I'm winded and each hit hurts.

Don't fuck with my goalie is the message I'm sending with every hit I give and take.

The tang of blood is fresh in my mouth as we're eventually pulled away from one another. Both of us get called for penalties, and the end of the game will be played four on four.

I smile, blood staining my teeth as they blare my face on all the screens in the stadium.

If there's one thing the Foxes can do, it's four on four.

Like they were born playing hockey together, Martel and Beckford show us why pack contracts are a real deal as Martel gets the puck, passing it to Beckford.

He doesn't even stop the puck, just rears back and slap shots it right into the goal. The horn blares, and the crowd goes wild as we wait for the final minute to tick down.

I skate out of the box and join my team in celebration, my arm around Max Connery of all people. I don't know what takes over me, but like so many years before, I pick the most ridiculous time to lean forward and kiss him.

But this time, he does the same.

It's a quick kiss, and when we pull back, we both seem surprised by our actions. But the smile that takes over his face has me feeling like I just won the lottery.

I don't deserve this life I have, but I'm going to hold on to it with every amount of strength I have.

SLOANE

CHAPTER 39

I didn't want to leave the house. In all honesty, I feel like shit. I can feel people taking pictures of me, and I can only guess what the next headline is going to be. Probably something about me ruining the team or how I'm still bondless. God, when they find out I'm pregnant, the headlines are going to be miserable.

I scrub a hand down my face as I try not to fall apart. Everything feels like too much. I feel like crap all the time, and I'm doing my best to hide it from two of the men who love me most, which in turn just makes me feel worse.

Part of me wants to tell them right now, but another part of me is just so scared that what we have is so fragile that this might just ruin everything we've built. It's like I've dug myself into this hole and I don't know how to get out of it. Deep down, I know Max and Bram would be able to handle my emotions if we bonded, but I'm not sure how they are going to handle us having a baby together. What if the headlines are right? What if I'm not worth all of this effort?

I shake all those annoying thoughts away as I watch Bram's first game back. Old habits die hard as I take pictures and videos of each of them—unfortunately, while people do the same of me.

Just because I don't work for the Foxes anymore doesn't mean I can't help them with their own social media.

"Have a second for your old man?" I hear behind me and sigh.

It's my dad Henderson. He must have heard I was coming to the game, or maybe he assumed because it's Bram's first game back.

"Hey, Dad," I say, not turning around.

Instead, he comes to stand next to me and watches the game with me.

"He's come back with the same tenacity he had before," he says.

"Bram is resilient," I say.

"We miss you, honey," he says.

My eyes well with tears because that's just what they do now, apparently.

"Hey," he says, grabbing my shoulder and pulling me to the corner of the room. "What's going on? I know you're mad at Kristoff. To be honest, I don't even blame you. But this isn't like you, not coming to dinners or replying with one-word sentences. I know the media has been brutal, especially after what happened. Are you doing okay?"

Well, yeah. I'm keeping a huge secret, and I knew if I got cornered like this, I'd likely cave in.

I nod my head, and he sighs.

"We love you so much, and we're worried about you. You tell me you're happy, and yet when I look at you right now, you don't look happy. This isn't you, Sloane. I don't know if it's these men or what happened. But I'm not going to let my daughter disappear before my eyes."

"I am happy," I say, and I mean it. I truly am.

I'm just keeping a secret that's making me sick. I've become addicted to reading terrible things about me and my pack, and it's making me even sicker.

"You can try to lie to someone else. What's going on?" he asks, staring down at me.

"Nothing's going on."

"Are you having some issues after the accident? You aren't listening to all these stupid motherfuckers online, are you?" he asks softly.

I wipe away a tear from my eye because yeah, almost losing your pack that isn't even officially your pack yet will fuck you up. But I need to be brave. I need to keep my cool because if I let myself feel it, I think I might just fall apart.

I liked it when Bram was home because I knew where he was, and I know that bonding with him would probably help some of this ache. But I just can't do that until I talk to a doctor, and even then, I wonder how inundated he'll be with my festering emotions.

"My life feels out of control," I whisper, not meaning to say it out loud.

My dad wraps his arms around me and squeezes me tightly.

"We're always here for you, Sloane. We miss you. I want to get to know your pack. It's been so boring since you moved out."

I let out a raspy laugh as he rubs my back.

"You'll always be our little girl. You can't blame us for making sure you're okay."

It's on the tip of my tongue to tell him that he's about to be a grandfather, but I hold back. Max and Bram need to hear that news first, and it's clear that I can't keep this to myself anymore. It's just making me worse.

I'm doing no one any good by holding in this secret. Bram is on the ice playing nearly up to par as he was before his injury, and Max has moved in. Getting this off my chest may be the thing that gives me some relief.

"I needed this. Maybe in a week or two we can come to your place for dinner. I can invite Lori and Ethan's foster dad, Dave. Though he doesn't get out much."

"We'd love to have you all over."

"Perfect," I say as he squeezes my shoulders and leaves the box.

I take a seat next to Piper who eyes me cautiously.

"What?" I ask.

"You're twenty-one now. You could have a drink at the game," she says.

"Oh, I haven't gotten my new ID yet," I say, and she clicks her tongue.

"They don't check IDs in the box," she replies.

"My stomach hasn't been right for a few days. I don't think drinking will make it any better."

"You haven't told anybody yet?" she asks, and my throat clogs as I blink at the overly perceptive Alpha.

She shrugs. "I see pregnant Omegas every day, not to mention Charlotte's two pregnancies. No drinking, tired, overly emotional, it ticks all the boxes."

"You can't tell anyone," I say quickly, panic filling every nerve ending.

She pats my thigh. "Hey, I'm not telling anyone. But you need to schedule an appointment at the clinic so we can make sure you stay healthy."

"I know."

"Your pack doesn't know?" she asks, her eyes sympathetic.

"Ethan does, the others don't."

"Sloane." She sighs my name.

"They're just now getting along, Piper. They finally don't hate each other, and I'm about to drop this piece of information that's going to change our lives, and I just don't want them fighting over who the father is. Bram mentioned he doesn't want kids for a while, and I feel like I trapped Max into this entire relationship and he's going to resent me for adding another thing he didn't ask for in the mix. Not to mention what fucked-up things they're going to say about me getting pregnant before we were bonded." I say it all like a run-on sentence.

"Sloane," she says my name sharply.

"What?" I say, wiping my face.

"I'm going to give you a piece of advice I gave to Charlotte so many years ago. If they aren't willing to make it work, then they aren't worthy of you."

"I can't lose them," I say, and Piper gives me a small smile.

"You're not going to. I've seen the way those two look at you. The news might be shocking to them at first, but they love you, and they're going to love this baby. You need to get this off your chest. Stress isn't good for you or the baby."

"You're right, I know you're right. I'm just scared."

She nods sympathetically, and I'm thankful she doesn't push me anymore.

"I'm here for whatever you need, and if I don't see you on the schedule within a week, you're going to be in deep shit."

I laugh and nod my head. I'll tell Bram and Max, schedule an appointment, and get all the answers we need to move forward. I just hope they aren't pissed at me for holding this in for so long. I focus back on the game where Max gets knocked over by a Jets player. I'm on my feet and watch as Bram gets into an altercation with the opposing team.

I'm not new to watching Bram fight. But I've never seen him fight so hard on a goalie's behalf, let alone Max's.

I wince as Bram gets hit on his left side and bite my nails. I'm holding my breath until they get pulled apart and sigh with relief. They show him grinning with his bloody teeth, and I have to laugh and shake my head.

That man is one of my child's fathers. I rub my stomach.

What the fuck am I doing? What am I so scared of? Hasn't Bram chosen me repeatedly? Hasn't Max stayed enthusiastically after finding out I'm his scent match?

It's clearer than ever that the incident on the bridge has given me more anxiety than I can handle on my own. I can't keep living in fear, and I surely can't keep this secret to myself for another moment. This weight that I've been carrying around, this pain, this fear, has to go.

Tonight, I'm going to tell them tonight.

I cheer as the team wins the game, Finnegan the Fox heading

out on the ice shooting T-shirts out of a cannon as the men hug and celebrate their win.

I almost can't believe what I'm seeing when Max and Bram embrace, kissing each other. I nearly have another emotional breakdown, but instead, I smile so hard my cheeks hurt. Camera flashes go wild, and I can only imagine how people are going to spin the narrative that they still hate each other.

When's the last time I felt this good?

The two men that I've fallen for are choosing each other, they're choosing our pack, and all I did was doubt how they would handle the news. Maybe it's because I'm doubting myself, doubting the pack. I need to have more faith in myself and the men I've chosen.

It's time to start actually living and not living in fear of what I can't control.

This time next year, I'll be holding a baby as we watch all three daddies on ice. I smile again. Maybe my life is clicking into place after all.

MAX

CHAPTER 40

He kissed me.

Bram-fucking-Nilsen just kissed me, and I kissed him back, and all I want to do is do it again?

He's grinning as we take in the stadium at full force after the victory. There's no time to talk as we skate off the ice and head to the locker room.

Coach is talking, but all I can think about is that fucking kiss, and I tune him out as I sit on the bench and take off my gear.

"Bright and early for game footage. Get some rest tonight," Coach says before leaving the locker room.

The team is rowdy, and I feel like I'm just running on autopilot trying to get my thoughts together. Bram and I have gotten along great, hell, I moved into his house. Despite that, I didn't think the door for anything beyond friendship was open.

I thought we were growing this friendship and solidifying a bond as the Alphas of the pack. I'm not even sure how to wrap my head around the idea that he's interested in me.

Everything between us has been resolved, and I actually like his company. I like his dry humor and how blunt he is about everything. I also love how fiercely protective and thoughtful he can be.

But I never thought those particular feelings were open to me.

I thought they were reserved for Sloane and Ethan. And I was more than okay with that. Honestly, I'm just happy to be here.

These last few months have been hard, but I've never felt more like me. Maybe I didn't even know who I was before, but I found it with these people.

I never really thought I was worth much, and maybe that's why I thought I deserved Bram's ire at the beginning of the season. When I look at the man I've become, I wonder if in some fucked-up way I needed this other Alpha to show me my potential.

I talk to my mom and brother more; I understand Sloane's Omega quirks. I'm even helping Ethan in my spare time fix up the diner so his father can sell it and live off of that money for retirement.

Who knew giving could feel so much better than receiving?

I feel fulfilled, and I know Sloane has taken the car accident hard, but I almost wonder if it's the best thing that ever happened to me.

The team is all dressed and leaving the locker room. I, thankfully, have no post-game interviews, and it seems like Bram doesn't either.

He's not even fully dressed, just in his underwear as he stands before me.

"Should we talk about it?" I ask, and he stares down at me.

He fists my shirt, and I stand to his height. Great, it was a fucking fluke.

But then he's shoving my back against the locker and kissing me even harder than before.

Maybe it's because I haven't had sex since the accident, or maybe because it's Bram kissing me, but my cock is so hard it's aching.

Bram grabs me from the outside of my underwear, and I groan, grabbing both sides of his head and kissing him harder.

It's rough, passionate, and fuck do I need more.

"Turn around," he says, and I pull away from the kiss.

"What?" I stutter, pulling back from the kiss.

"We can use Ahonen's coconut oil."

"Wait. You think you're going to fuck me? Uh. No. I could fuck you," I say, and Bram rears back like I slapped him.

"You're not fucking me."

"Well, you're not fucking me either."

There's a clearing of a throat, and we both turn to see Sloane covering her mouth, trying to contain her laughter.

"It looks like no one is getting fucked," she jokes and nearly doubles over in laughter.

"You think this is funny?" Bram says with a smile, both of us happy to see her laughing like this.

"It's kind of funny. I mean, you both hated each other, and now you like each other, and neither of you will bottom."

I think Bram and I both grimace.

"You know, anal is pretty great if everything is done right."

"It's not happening, Sloane," Bram says.

"I mean, one of you could try it just once. And let me watch."

"No," I say, and Sloane pouts.

"Ugh, fine. But you're missing out. You know, there's more to life than anal, right? Blow jobs and hand jobs are still on the table."

"Sloane, I'm about to spank your ass," Bram says, and I can tell my eyes go wide, but Sloane's fill with want.

"Please," she says softly, and Bram's brows furrow. "I think I need it."

Bram looks around like he's contemplating doing it right here. I mean, he was planning on fucking me in the locker room. But what if Coach walks in as he was smacking his daughter's ass? The man already hates us enough right now. That might be something we can't come back from.

Bram clears his throat. "At home," he tells her. "Also, why are you here alone?"

"Anders and Charlotte are right outside. Glad I didn't bring them in with me, huh?" Sloane says, and it's like her old spark is back.

Good, I fucking missed her smart mouth.

"Where's Ethan?" I ask.

"He's waiting out in the car. I'll meet you two at home. Try to keep your hands to yourself till then?" she jokes.

"Little Omega," Bram warns, but she just smiles and waves at him with her fingers under her chin.

But it doesn't sour the moment. If anything, Bram is shaking his head and smiling.

"Maybe she just needed to get out of the house."

"Or walk in on us nearly fucking, which apparently isn't going to happen," I mumble.

"She's not wrong, you do have a working mouth, though."

I shove his shoulder, and I try not to laugh, but I can't help it.

"You also have a mouth, you know?"

He puts his hand over his mouth and gasps. "Would you look at that? I sure do. Get fucking dressed, and let's go home and celebrate."

As soon as we walk through the door of the house, all I can scent is Sloane. Yet her scent smells just a little different.

I nudge Bram.

"Does she smell different?" I ask.

He deeply inhales and shakes his head like he doesn't know what I'm talking about.

We both head upstairs, and as soon as we open the main bedroom door, we're greeted by the image of Sloane on all fours… while Ethan fucks her in the ass.

His tattooed hands are pressed against her soft, creamy tits as he pushes in and out of her.

"Oh. We have an audience, sweetheart," Ethan says, pulling her up and holding her body against his chest while he continues to rock into her. "I'm not complaining about being a part of your evil little plan," he says, thrusting with each word, making her moan.

"Is this some sort of ploy to get me or Bram to agree to fuck each other?" I question, and Ethan stalls.

"Wait. Rewind, what?"

"Everyone just shut up. This is the best I've felt in weeks. Come here," Sloane whines.

Bram and I are undressing, and once we're fully naked, we stand by the bed. Everything feels far more real now. There's no heat driving us to be together, and this will be the first time since then that we've all been naked and in the same room.

Ethan pulls out of Sloane, and she grabs my hand, directing me to lie flat on the bed as she straddles my lap and slides her warm, wet cunt down my length.

"Fuck, baby. I missed this. God, you smell so good," I say, and she pauses before sliding down again.

Ethan realigns himself, straddling my legs and holding Sloane's hips before pushing inside.

I moan as my hold on Sloane tightens as Ethan fills her up. Each shift of his cock has me nearly ready to combust.

Apparently, Bram doesn't need to be told what to do as he lubes up his shaft and gets behind Ethan.

Holy fucking shit.

We should record this to watch later.

Sloane's front presses against mine, and I hold her, not even needing to move as Ethan fucks her for the both of us.

Her peachy scent has the slightest hint of something else to it, but I can't decipher it. All I know is she smells better than ever, even better than when she was in heat. I inhale her sweet scent, and it feels like I might come on the spot. But I can't embarrass myself, even if it has been a long time.

Sloane whimpers in my ear, and I pile her long red hair in a fist and bring her lips to mine.

"Missed feeling how wet you get on my cock, baby," I tell her.

She grabs my jaw and kisses me roughly as Ethan fucks her ass and Bram slides into him.

It's a cacophony of moans, slick, and lube.

I'm not sure what happened from the Sloane this morning to the Sloane from this afternoon, but it's a stark difference. Almost like she worked out on her own what was bothering her and she doesn't want to waste anymore time being in this weird limbo and actually start living.

It might be because my dick is being gripped so tightly with her pussy and the slide of Ethan's dick.

All I can think about is how perfect this is, how badly we should solidify this pack.

I need to be able to feel Sloane at all times. I need us to all get through this rough patch. Everything that we've ever wanted has been right at the tip of our fingers, we just needed to take it.

Her scent is suffocating me in the best way, and her neck is right there. God, her delicate, sweet-looking neck. I lick the flesh and kiss her warm skin, getting more greedy with each passing of my lips.

She's writhing on top of me, and Bram and Ethan are both grunting in pleasure, but the only thing I can focus on is the Omega on top of me and how much I need her.

"Fuck, baby," I tell her, knowing I'm close.

It's selfish, but as Ethan pulls out of her, I shift my knot inside of her. The Beta curses, but Bram just pushes him onto the mattress next to Sloane while he fucks him. It's hotter than it should be, but Sloane has all my attention as I fill her up.

She's moaning and shaking, and fuck, she smells so goddamn good.

I suck the skin that connects her collarbone to her throat into my mouth, only intending to suck, but as my knot swells and Sloane moans in my ear, I lose all self control.

I've waited so long for my purpose.

This pack is my reason for being here, and with all the pheromones and lust in the room, I can't control myself.

I sink my teeth into her neck, bonding us together.

There's a moment of pure bliss. I'd mark it as the happiest thirty seconds of my entire life as I feel the contentment and love down the bond from Sloane, and I know she feels it from me.

In those few short moments, everything is perfect—until it's not.

The amazing orgasm and feelings of complete happiness fade away as Sloane gasps and cups the side of her neck.

We're still knotted together, and there's nowhere for her to go. I blink up at her as all of her feelings of fear, guilt, and panic shoot down the bond.

"Fuck. Sloane, I'm sorry. I should have asked first. I'm so sorry, baby," I say in a panic.

Sloane's cries catch Bram's and Ethan's attention. Bram looks like he wants to kick my ass while Ethan looks more concerned for Sloane.

"I'm so sorry, baby," I tell her, my own emotion catching in my throat.

Was she not ready to bond me? Did she not want this?

"What did you do?" Bram says loudly, standing there completely naked, which somehow doesn't make him as imposing.

All of Sloane's feelings weigh me down with a tremendous amount of sadness. Has she been feeling this all the time? What the fuck is happening? I'm trying to push down my own panic so she doesn't feel it, but it's evident she does.

She catches her breath and breathes through her nose and shakes her head. "I want it. It's not you, Max. I promise. I love you, I wanted the bond… I just…"

"Just what?" Bram asks in my stead, and I'm happy for it because I'm about to have a mental breakdown all on my own.

"Tell them, Sloane," Ethan says, and we both glance over at the Beta.

"Tell us what?" Bram asks.

Sloane covers her face with her hands. I'm still holding on to her hips. I didn't think there was ever a time when knotting wouldn't work in my favor, but this moment proves otherwise.

"I'm sorry. I should have told you all sooner, but I was scared."

"Tell us what?" Bram asks again.

I don't even need to be bonded to him to feel and hear how scared he is right now.

"I'm pregnant, and I was going to go to the doctor to make sure bonding is safe for the baby, and I haven't had a chance, and now I just ruined our bonding moment, and I don't know what this means for the baby," Sloane says so incredibly fast we all blink at her for a moment trying to catch up with her words.

We're all silent as Ethan rubs her back, clearly proud of her for getting this all out.

"How long?" Bram asks. His tone is hard, a way I've never heard him speak to Sloane.

She can't even look at him when she speaks. "The night of the accident."

Bram lets out a puff of frustrated air, and I can sense how disappointed Sloane is of herself. I rub her legs, trying to reassure her as I collect my own thoughts.

Holy fuck.

We're going to have a baby, and I've never even held a child.

Sloane mistakes my trepidation over not knowing what kind of father I'd be to being angry with her as she tries to shuffle off my lap but can't.

"Stop squirming." Bram uses his Alpha voice on her, and she glares over at him. "You might hurt yourself or Max. Just sit still as soon as his knot goes down. We'll take you to the ER to get checked out." His tone is direct and no bullshit.

It's not the soft, tender Bram Sloane is used to, and it's evident she notices as she retreats into herself. She nods her head and looks away from all of us.

"Sloane," I whisper her name, wanting to comfort her and hating all these feelings that are transferring over to me.

"I can't right now," she sniffles.

Ethan sighs and rubs his hair as he and Bram get dressed. I can hear them arguing in the bathroom. I'm sure he's getting a lashing for having kept her secret for so long. Part of me feels sorry for Ethan. But I'm also frustrated. Why would she keep this a secret?

Also, what the fuck am I going to do? My stepdad was a good guy, quiet but not as involved. I don't know the first thing about really being a dad; kids weren't even on my radar.

Sloane's body shakes against mine, and I all but force her to lie down on my chest so I can stroke her back. For the first time in my life, a purr rumbles through my chest as I comfort her. She sighs against me, and I can feel how much it comforts her through the bond.

"Please don't hate me."

"Baby, I could never hate you. It's just a lot to take in all at once. I'm not mad, just scared."

She sniffles and shifts against my chest, letting the motion of my chest soothe her.

"Me too," she whispers.

"We'll figure everything out," I tell her, even though I don't even know what that means.

"What if something bad happens?" she asks, and I cup her face, forcing her to look at me.

"Nothing bad is going to happen," I say because what else do I say?

"You don't know that. I can't lose you, Max."

"You're not losing me."

"I can feel everything down the bond. You're terrified." I take a deep breath and nod my head, not knowing what to say because she's not wrong. "What if being so scared and worried has hurt the baby? What if me not telling you has hurt them? I'm already a bad mom."

"Hey. No," I tell her and stroke her cheekbones.

"I'm so scared all the time Max, and now you have to feel it too. I'm sorry," she says, putting her head back on my chest, clearly not wanting to talk anymore.

"It's going to be okay," I tell her because I'm not sure what else I could say to comfort her. I'm just trying to curb my own panic.

We're bonded and having a baby, and I have no fucking clue what I'm doing.

CHAPTER 41

Max and Bram are basically stalking the front counter, trying to get Sloane in quicker as I sit in the waiting area and hold her hand.

"What was the plan there, sweetheart? Hoping to get them in post-nut bliss and tell them about the baby?" I ask.

She smacks my chest but laughs a little, which is a relief.

"Maybe. I thought it would work."

"I mean, it worked, but I don't think how you wanted it to."

She rubs her neck with Max's bond mark and sighs. "I feel like I just ruined my and Max's bonding experience all because I was scared to tell them the truth."

"I'm just glad it's all out in the open now. I got you something," I tell her.

Sloane acts like she doesn't love getting gifts as much as she does, but I know my girl. I don't have to be bonded to her to know these things, but I'm hoping I'll be bonded to her both by Max and Bram, so it will almost be like a complete bond.

Just because I'm not an Alpha doesn't mean I shouldn't get to experience that part of pack life.

"It's nothing big," I tell her to not get her hopes up. But when I give her the gold engraved keychain, she smiles brightly.

Future Baby Mama is engraved in script, and she starts really laughing.

"I love you, Ethan Heart," she says.

"I love you too. So do those two big dumbasses. Everything with the baby is going to be fine. We're going to be fine."

"Bram seems so upset," she says as she adds the keychain to her house keys.

"Bram isn't good at change or not knowing shit. Especially when you've been sitting at home with him the last month. If anything, he's more upset that you didn't tell him and that Max bonded with you without knowing this information. You can't blame him for being shocked or a little upset."

"I know. But my stupid hormones don't seem to get the memo."

"It's been a month. It's not like you withheld until you're delivering him."

"Him, huh?" she asks.

"I think it's your misfortune to be surrounded by difficult men your entire life."

She laughs and leans against me.

"I was just really horny after seeing Bram and Max kiss. It wasn't my initial plan to get everyone riled up. I wanted to come home and talk about the baby, but well, that clearly isn't what happened."

"I can't really complain. This whole celibacy thing has not been my favorite."

She rolls her eyes at me.

Max walks over and holds out his hand. "They're taking you back now," he says, and she takes his hand.

Bram is still being standoffish, so I hold back and let Max and Sloane walk ahead of us.

"You've got to pull it together," I whisper to Bram.

"She's been keeping a massive fucking secret for a month. A secret that might not even matter considering we didn't know and

Max fucking bonded with her. She put her health at risk, all because she thought what? That we wouldn't handle it well?"

"I mean, you aren't handling it well."

"Of course I'm not. I'm fucking scared," he says plainly.

I grab his hand and interlace my fingers with his. "We're all scared, but you signed up to be pack Alpha, which means right now I need you to pull it together. The stress isn't good for Sloane or the baby, and right now she's consumed with guilt."

Bram sighs and scrubs his hand down his face. "No wonder she asked me to spank her."

I tilt my head.

"We can come back to that later. But she found out when she didn't know if you were alive or dead. She said she didn't want to upset the balance between you and Max, but I honestly think she is having a harder time with the accident than she's letting on. She needs you. We all need you."

He takes a deep breath and nods as we catch up our pace to Sloane and Max and enter the exam room.

Sloane takes the bed, Bram stands next to her, and Max and I take our seats as the doctor comes into the room.

She's flicking through a tablet and greets us with a smile. "I'm Dr. Mann. I'll be your provider today, so what seems to be going on?"

Sloane goes to open her mouth, but Bram speaks instead.

"She's pregnant, and he bonded with her not knowing about that, and we need to check on her and the baby," he says.

Dr. Mann glances at Bram, pushing her wide frames up her nose, making a humming noise.

"Do you know how far along you are?" she asks Sloane.

"No," Bram asks.

"I was asking the pregnant woman," the doctor says, and Bram huffs, crossing his arms.

"I think about ten or eleven weeks."

"How have you been feeling?"

"Some morning sickness and some fatigue, but other than that, not so bad. I think some of my stress has been self-induced."

"You think?" Bram asks, and Sloane sighs.

"You're allowed to request confidentiality with your medical professional if you would like to be seen alone," Dr. Mann says. Bram looks completely affronted.

Sloane sighs and shakes her head. "No, I want them here."

The doctor gives Bram a pointed look, and the large Alpha seems to shut his mouth and listen.

"We're going to do a blood panel to check your levels, and I'll send the tech in to do your ultrasound. As far as bonding during pregnancy, there have been no studies done that say it's harmful in any way. If anything, it can help bring the Omega mother comfort during her pregnancy. Being unbonded can cause a lot of unwanted stress, and it helps the expectant father, or fathers, help with the mother's emotions. But since you're here, we can check in and make sure everything is alright. Have you been taking a prenatal vitamin?"

"Yes," she responds, and Bram and Max both look at her, wondering where she's hiding them.

That would be in my nightstand. But they don't need to know that I'm her prenatal gummy dealer. We can keep that secret ours.

"Thank you," Sloane says.

"I'll be back, Nurse Sardea will get your blood sample, and I'll be back later to discuss the results."

She nods and leaves the room. The nurse takes Sloane's blood while Bram hovers over the poor woman like he's going to break her neck if she leaves a bruise. As soon as she leaves, Bram starts his inquisition.

"Why? Why did you keep this a secret for so long? Max and I have been worried sick wondering what we could do to make things better since that day. Don't you think we deserved to know?"

I stand up, and Sloane waves a hand at me.

"I can explain myself, Ethan. It's okay."

I sit back in my seat as Bram gives me a stern glare.

"I found out at the hospital when I didn't know if you were going to be okay or not. Ethan and I didn't know what was going on, and we were both so scared. Fuck, I'm still scared," Sloane says, wrapping her arms around herself. "Then you were recovering. You and Max were getting along, becoming friends. I didn't want to bring this up and have you two at each other's throats again."

"Why would we be at each other's throats?" Bram asks.

"Over who the biological father is," Sloane says plainly. Bram shakes his head, and she glares at him. "Don't give me that. You used to hate him, Bram. You two got in a physical fight during my heat. We were going to pack therapy to figure out how to make this all work when our life got flipped upside down. I've never been more scared in my life than I was that day. I thought I lost you. I thought I'd never get to bond with you. I wanted to make sure that you recovered and that the moment I told you we wouldn't be back to square one."

"You think I'm that petty?" Bram says.

We all give him a look, and he sighs and places his hand on the back of her bed.

"I thought about telling you when we were watching *Scent Your Match*," she whispers.

Bram furrows his brows like he's deep in thought as it dawns on him.

"Fuck, Sloane," he says, grabbing the seat and grabbing her hand. "In an ideal world, we would have had time to be a pack before having kids. But I'm happy. I mean, I'm fucking terrified, but I'm happy."

"You are?"

"We all are," I add in because I'm the helpful Beta of the pack.

"Oh, don't think you're off the hook, you sneaky fucking secret keeper." Bram points at me.

"Omega trumps Alpha. I don't know what you want from me," I say, and Sloane points at me like I have a point.

Max rubs his jaw.

"What about me?" he asks softly, and Sloane swallows.

"I didn't want you to feel trapped," she whispers.

Max looks like she just slapped him across the face.

"Trapped? This pack is the best thing to happen to me, and now we're having a baby. You never trapped me, Sloane. You gave me purpose."

"I'm not even pregnant, and I feel like I'm going to cry," I say as the ultrasound tech comes in.

"Can I have you push your shirt up?" she asks Sloane who nods her head.

I think she's more than happy that this time it won't be the wand inside of her.

Max and I go to stand next to Bram as the tech slathers some cold lube-looking gunk on Sloane's flat stomach. Well, maybe there's the littlest pouch on her lower abdomen, but that could easily be from eating too many snacks.

The tech slathers the sticky goo all over her lower stomach as she rolls the machine over her skin. We all watch the screen in awe as she finds the baby, and a much stronger thudding noise fills the room than last time.

Sloane lets out a breath of relief.

Max and Bram look at the monitor in complete fascination as they see our baby for the first time.

"I'd put you right between eleven or twelve weeks," she says. "But it's still too early to determine the sex. The heartbeat is in perfect range. Everything is looking great."

The amount of tension that leaves the room is palpable.

The tech prints off multiple copies of the ultrasound and hands them to Sloane.

"Dr. Mann will be back in, and we can get your discharge papers ready."

She hands the scans to Bram and Max who look over them like they've never seen anything so magnificent.

"Holy shit," Max whispers.

"We're having a baby," Bram says.

"Does this mean I'm forgiven?"

"Forgiven, yes. But now your health is in my hands," Bram says easily.

"I agree," Max says.

Sloane slumps into the mattress and mouths to me. "What the fuck?" Then her phone vibrates, and I already know what it is.

"And she's getting notifications for anytime we're brought up online," I blurt out.

I just shrug at her, and she looks at me like I'm a traitor.

"Oh God, Sloane. All those articles are fucking horrible. I blocked all that stuff on my phone, but you've been reading all of it?" Max asks, and her cheeks turn red.

"Give me the phone," Bram says, holding out his hand. She gives it to him, glaring at me the whole time.

Bram reads the article and looks back at Sloane.

"You've been reading all of these?" he asks, and tears fill her eyes. "No more reading this shit. It's not good for you, and it's all fake. This one says you're also fucking Ahonen. What the fuck?" Bram complains.

"I've been in the press enough to know that looking at this bullshit can put you in a bad headspace. Why are you doing this to yourself?" Max asks Sloane.

"I don't know. It was just right there. It all started with that stupid thread about where Finnegan the Fox was. I was proud that I had gotten Ethan enough attention that people were interested, and then it spiraled out of control. Maybe they got to me a little," she says softly.

"Yeah, of course they did. I've been dodging this for years, it will tear you apart on the inside."

The whole time, Bram has been messing with her phone, likely blocking all mentions of us in the media so she can't see it anymore.

"No more secrets. No more suffering in silence anymore. You

need to be having regular appointments, and we're going to get you eating better," Bram says.

Sloane glances back at me for help, and I grimace.

"Listen, sweetheart. I'm ride or die, but the baby can't survive off Cape Cod chips and Heluva Good French dip," I say, and the Alphas nod in agreement.

"I can't control what the baby wants."

"I can," Bram says. "Just like I'm going to control what notifications you get on your laptop too. No more of this shit, it's disgusting." Bram hands her back her phone, and he gives me a shitty look.

So I need to be better about what secrets Sloane and I share because I'm not a huge fan of getting in trouble.

"This is my penance for keeping this secret," she whispers more to herself.

"It is," Bram agrees, and Sloane sighs as Dr. Mann comes back into the room.

"Everything looks great, minus your sodium. I'd love to see that go down a bit," she says, and Bram gives Sloane a hard stare. "You'll need to get set up with a primary OBGYN for your care throughout your pregnancy. But beyond that, I have no concerns."

"So bonding, it's safe?" Bram confirms again.

"Yes, it's completely safe," she replies.

"Knotting?" Max whispers, and the doctor smiles and nods her head.

"Knotting is safe, and may be something that she actively seeks out, especially after the first trimester is through."

"Is there anything sexually that is off the table?" Bram asks.

"Something in particular you wanted to ask about?" she asks, looking at everyone in the pack.

"Spanking in particular," Bram says easily like he's talking about the fucking weather.

Sloane's eyes go wide, and she looks mortified.

"As long as it's not too hard and she isn't put in a compromising position where it's hard to breathe or too much pressure is put on her stomach, I don't see why not," Dr. Mann says with the utmost professionalism. "Do you need a list of clinics with openings?"

"No, I already have one, thank you," Sloane says, her cheeks red with embarrassment.

The doctor hands her a few pamphlets. "These are all reliable, medically-backed sites you can use as resources. You're all doing a good job. Just keep taking care of yourself, and I imagine it will be a happy and healthy pregnancy."

"Thank you again," Sloane says.

"Of course, I think you've all got this covered. Here are some resources for new dads," she says, handing us a bunch more information.

"Thank you," Max says as she heads out the room, and we prepare to take Sloane home.

"Did you have to ask about the spanking?" Sloane asks, her cheeks heating all over again.

"Oh, I definitely had to ask," he says.

Poor Sloane, but also I think I might want to watch.

"Can we please go home and get some sleep now?" I ask.

God, tonight's been long for everyone.

"First thing in the morning, we're setting up your appointments," Bram says.

"Okay."

"Can I tell my dad now?" I ask, hating that I've been holding this all in for a whole month. It's felt like the secret has been wanting to explode out of me this whole time.

"I guess we're going to have to tell my parents too," Sloane says with a wince.

Both of the Alphas look like that wasn't even on their radar and they'd rather stay at the hospital, but they both give Sloane a curt nod as we head home and try to go back to normal.

SLOANE

CHAPTER 42

I stare down at the oatmeal with complete disgust.

Bram sprinkles cinnamon on top, but it doesn't do shit for me.

"This looks like prison food."

"It's not prison food, it's healthy food," Bram says.

I glance over at Max and Ethan, the two who are more likely to give into what I want, especially if my eyes well up just a little.

"Don't even, Sloane," Max says, looking away.

Dammit.

"Maybe I shouldn't have told you till the baby was born so I could eat whatever I want."

All the men blink at me.

"Okay, too soon for concealed pregnancy jokes. You know, a lot of people don't even find out they're pregnant until now?" I say.

"Eat your oatmeal, *liefje.*"

I smell the slop. Nope, absolutely fucking not.

My stomach whirls, and I'm jumping off the stool and running to the trash can where I throw up the water I drank that morning and what little was in my stomach last night.

Max rubs my back, and I hear him complaining to Bram.

Ethan comes over with a warm washcloth and wipes my face. Poor guy has been on morning sickness duty for too long.

"Maybe just let her eat what she wants in the morning. It's when she usually gets sick."

"Or all the time," I say, closing the trash and going back to my stool and pushing away the affronting *breakfast*.

"Fine, for now until this passes," Bram agrees.

Max and Bram share a look, and I wonder what they could possibly be conspiring in what little time they've had alone since last night.

"What?" I ask, happily eating my chips and dip first thing in the morning.

The baby has great taste.

"We have a few minutes before we leave for practice, but we wanted to discuss something with you, both of you," Max says.

"Is this about how you two want to fuck each other but won't?" I ask, scooping a hefty amount of dip on my chip.

"Wait, what?" Ethan asks.

Both of the Alphas look at the ceiling, like I'll ever forget what I witnessed. Plus, I definitely will continue to push this button until they start kissing more.

"No, we can talk about that later," Bram waves off, and I smile.

"We want to formally become a pack before we tell your family," Max says. "My mom and Ethan's dad will immediately be excited and over the moon. But your dad, I just feel like coming to him as a more united front may soften the blow a little," Max says.

"Formally, as in submitting with the state or as in bonding?"

"Both," Bram says. "All of us," he says, glancing at Ethan. "Especially now that we know it's safe," he says, looking at my bond mark.

It's a silvery sheen against my skin. I can tell that Bram is jealous but nowhere near the jealousy I used to see from him with Max.

"You leave for some away games in two days," I say, glancing at Max.

I cuddled so hard with him last night, and I might be having an internal fit about him having to go to work today. My rational mind understands he has an important job and he doesn't want to leave me, but my newly bonded, outwardly pregnant mind needs him here to hold me and tell me he loves me repeatedly.

He must realize all my feelings as he comes behind me on the stool and wraps his arms around me, kissing the top of my head.

"I know you need more from me right now. That's why Bram wants to wait till we get back."

Bram is clutching the countertop like he wants to break it but nods his head.

"I wish it were the offseason."

"Me too. I hate that we have to be away from you right now," Max says on the top of my head.

"Max and I should bond before you leave," Ethan says confidently.

He's been so patient, so understanding of my wants and needs, I'm proud of him for expressing his. Ethan's cheeks heat as he rubs the back of his neck.

"I just think that I'm here with Sloane more, and if we're connected in that way, it would help everyone feel more at ease. Plus, it's inevitable anyway, isn't it?" Ethan asks, glancing over at Max.

"I think that's a great idea," Max answers, and I nod my agreement.

When I glance back at Bram, he looks like he's pouting. I sigh and round the island and wrap my arms around my sweet, needy Alpha.

"Such a patient Alpha," I say, and he swats my ass hard.

"Don't push me, Sloane. The only reason I'm waiting is because I know you need more nesting time with your Alpha after bonding."

"So thoughtful," I say, and he swats again.

Now all I want for breakfast is a heaping size of Alpha dick, but Bram is pulling away from me and grabs my face to give me a kiss.

"Speaking of nests," Ethan says.

"Right," Bram says, shaking his head. "The contractor is coming next week to discuss what you want. We'll be home in time. I think we'll need to make more adjustments to accommodate our new life," Bram says.

I can't help myself as I wrap my arms around him and squeeze even tighter.

Bram kisses the top of my head, even though I know my scent is going haywire and all I'm doing is tempting him. I kiss Max next as they leave for practice.

"It's just you and me, kid," Ethan jokes as the Alphas leave.

"How do you feel about being an absolute menace?" I ask him. If I don't stay busy today, I'll contemplate looking up the news about us online. Maybe I need to find a hobby because I know my pack is right, I can't keep putting myself through reading those articles.

I feel freer now that everything is out on the table, and I'm not going to do anything to mess this up.

Ethan grins, and God, he's beautiful.

"I was born to make their lives exceedingly difficult."

"Perfect," I say, grabbing his hand and dragging him to the basement.

❋ ❋ ❋ ❋

Ethan is sweating and panting, considering he won't let me help with much as he puts the mattress on the floor.

I'm not allowed to even use the ladder to string up the lights. He does let me make the bed and cover it with every single pillow in our house—which is an exceedingly large amount. Maybe I have a pillow problem, but right now it seems to be working to our benefit.

"Sweetheart, what's the plan here?" he says, wiping sweat off of his brow.

It's cool in the basement, and fortunately, the walls are mostly finished. The floor is still concrete, but I had Ethan steal rugs from the living room and the bathroom to make it more cozy in here.

Ethan hasn't questioned anything from me until this moment. I suppose I did have him move a lot of shit. I shrug my shoulders, and Ethan comes into my space, grabbing my hips.

"What is it?"

"Your bonding should be special," I say, trying not to cry.

The crying is out of fucking control.

"I don't need anything special. I just want to be connected to all of you."

"This is what I would have wanted for my first bonding… well, kinda," I say. It is definitely a hodgepodge nest, but it is cozy and sweet.

Ethan searches my face. My connection with Max and Bram may be a basic instinctual need—one rooted in feral desire. But Ethan? Ethan's my best friend and knows me better than my Alphas do. Even without a directly linked bond, Ethan knows what's going on with me.

"It's perfect," he says, not judging me or questioning me.

I get to control this; I get to enjoy this. I may not have had my dream bonding with Max, but I can ensure that he and Ethan do.

Maybe it's also a need to do something sweet for my Alphas too.

I do think I have some serious spankings in my future, and maybe a lifetime of dealing with "remember when you hid your pregnancy from us" lectures. But this, creating a soft, sweet space for Ethan and Max, I can control that.

"You know I want you here, right?" he says, kissing my face and holding me close.

"I know. I want to be here when it snaps into place."

"I never in a million years thought I'd have this," he says, his hand rubbing over my stomach.

We haven't talked much about how we feel about the pregnancy, just the anxiety of hiding the secret.

"You're going to be a great dad," I tell him, and I mean it.

His hand snakes over my belly, and he looks down at where his hand is like he can see our future child.

"You really think so?"

"I wouldn't have chosen you otherwise. You're soft, gentle, and kind, Ethan. You love me in a way that I dreamed of, and I know you'll do the same for our baby."

He rests his head against the top of mine and just holds me. I feel guilty that I've been so wrapped up in being pregnant and when I would tell the Alphas that I didn't consider some of Ethan's inner turmoil.

"Dave was the best dad I could have asked for. I'll do everything I can to be half of the father he was to me."

"Is that why you never cared about the biology?" I ask.

"I mean, the chances of me, the Beta, being the father are slim to none anyway. It doesn't matter who the baby gets their DNA from. This is my kid too, and I'll love them so fucking hard."

I laugh and put my hands up the back of his sweaty shirt. His skin is sticky with sweat.

"We need more blankets," I tell him, making him laugh.

"Your wish is my command."

I swat his ass as he leaves the basement, and I look at all the work I made him do.

This is going to be perfect.

ETHAN

CHAPTER 43

Sloane prepares what she calls the essential snack plate and brings it downstairs to the little nest we've made.

I think it's a mixture of wanting tonight to be special and her wanting somewhere to nest for her pregnancy. I've nearly read *What to Expect When Your Omega is Expecting* three times.

"Thanks for doing all the heavy lifting," she says, eating some cheese and nestling up against one of the millions of pillows we brought down here.

"Whatever you need, I'm your guy," I tell her, scooting up and putting my head on her lap.

She continues eating but pets my hair.

"We need a TV down here."

"You know we're going to have to move this all back upstairs when the contractors start working."

"Hopefully they don't take long," she sighs, and I make a note to mention it to Bram.

Maybe there are some modifications we can make upstairs while we get someone in here to finish the basement.

I turn around and kiss her stomach.

"Do you think it's a girl or a boy?" I ask her.

She smiles down at me, her soft fingers still playing with my hair.

"Hmm. I don't have a feeling one way or another yet. But you better believe as soon as we can find out, we're going to. No way could I wait till they're born."

"Me either, I'd want to know. We should probably pick a pack name," I tell her, and she hums.

"The guys will probably keep their last name, at least while they're playing hockey," she says.

"I don't want it to be my last name," I say plainly.

She doesn't make me explain; she just nods her head. "To be honest, I'm a little too mad at my dad right now to consider Applegate." I laugh in her lap, and she shrugs. "Bram is the pack Alpha, would make sense to take Nilsen."

"I think he would come in his pants if you told him you wanted to take his last name."

"That powerful, huh?"

"So tiny but so powerful," I tell her, kissing her stomach and rolling off of her.

"We're waiting for Max to get home," she points at me, and I give her a smile.

"I never thought I'd bond with someone. I'm kind of nervous," I admit as we both lie on our sides and look at one another.

"It hurts for a second, but then that goes away, and it feels amazing. You'll be able to sense Max's emotions the strongest. From what I've read, an Alpha to Beta bond might not be as intense as it is to an Omega, but it's still powerful. I'm not sure how much of me you'll be able to feel through the bond, but once Bram bonds with the both of us, it should be stronger."

"You're really okay with me bonding with them?"

"More than okay, I grew up in a house where everyone loved everyone. This has been my dream," she tells me easily.

"You know that you're the Omega. You're our priority."

"Ethan?"

"Yeah?"

"Shut up, and take a nap with me," she says as I gently tug her against my chest.

Never was a fan of naps before, but becoming somewhat of a kept Beta has made me soft. I'm not even mad about it.

※ ※ ※ ※

"Jesus fucking Christ. We've been looking everywhere for you two," Max says, startling us both awake.

The Alphas take in our very amateur nest, and all the irritation slips away.

"What's this?" Bram asks.

Sloane looks shy. Maybe she doesn't even realize how badly she needs her own cozy place to decompress, but Bram must understand as he doesn't even allow her to answer.

"It looks great," he says.

It doesn't look great, but they're kind enough to not bring that up.

"Have you two been down here all day?" Max asks.

"Mostly. We need a TV down here," Sloane says.

I'm surprised the man doesn't pull one out of the wall right away. He goes to sit on the mattress, and Sloane *tsk*s at him.

He removes all his clothes, putting them in a neat pile, before sitting on the bed in his underwear.

Bram follows suit, and then we're all just sitting on this mattress in the middle of the floor, wondering how this is going to go.

"I think you and Bram should both bond with Ethan," Sloane says.

All our heads whip over to Sloane who looks like a queen in her throne of pillows.

"What?" I ask.

"Bram is uneasy leaving without being bonded. I know it helps that Max will be bonded to both of us. But I think him having one bond will help with some of his anxiety."

"I don't have anxiety," Bram says back.

She holds out her hand and tugs at him so that he's basically spooning her.

"Whatever you say, Alpha. Plus, I think it would be nice. I get to feel what it's like when Max bonds with him, and he'll get to feel what it's like when we bond," she says to Bram.

"You're a romantic little thing, aren't you," I say, tapping her nose.

"Yes, and a needy one," she says, grinding against Bram's crotch.

The massive Alpha wraps a hand around her waist, and he slides his hand down the waistband of her shorts.

"Dripping wet," he purrs against the back of her head, and she sighs, tugging at my shirt and instructing me to get undressed.

Bram kisses down the side of her throat as he toys with her pussy at the same time Max's hand wraps around my hip and squeezes my cock. I groan as he rubs his hard length against my ass.

"Is that what you want, Ethan? Both bonds?" he whispers in my ear. A low rumble of approval slips out of him as he grinds harder against me. "Who knew you'd be such a greedy fucking Beta?"

"Why don't we help your Beta and Alpha out, hmm?" Bram asks.

Sloane moans as Bram slides his fingers out of her and reaches over to cover Max's dick in slick.

Both of the Alphas groan in satisfaction as Sloane's perfume chokes us in the small space.

She likes watching her Alphas touch each other, and I can't say I mind either.

"Now he's going to fuck our Beta covered in your slick," Bram says.

My dick has never been harder as Max tugs down my underwear and starts rubbing my hole with his slick-covered cock.

Sloane and I face each other, leaning in for a messy kiss as both Alphas push inside of us.

I swallow her moans as she does mine.

She moves Bram's hand from her clit to collect some slick before stroking my cock.

I'm not going to last.

Not with Max slowly pushing into me, hitting that deep fucking spot that feels so good, while my Omega strokes me.

"One day I'm going to knot this tight little hole," Max says, making me whimper.

Sloane crashes my mouth back to hers.

She pants against my mouth as Bram fucks her, and her movements on my cock become less structured. It makes me feel like I'm even closer to coming all over her hand.

Max is kissing the nape of my neck, his teeth dragging against my skin, a promise of what's to come. Bram watches us from where he lies behind Sloane.

What would have been a look of jealousy months ago is now a look of complete hunger.

Fuck.

It feels like my entire pack is fucking me in some way right now, and I'm not sure how to handle the attention.

That's a lie.

I devour it.

Max's grip on me tightens as I feel his knot press against my entrance.

"Fuck," he pants behind me, his hips hitting my ass cheeks with each rough thrust.

"Are you going to take my knot while I bond our Beta?" Bram asks Sloane

She answers in a moan as we get pressed closer to one another. Her hand doesn't have much room to move, so she just squeezes me instead.

It all happens so fast.

Bram grabs my arm, yanking my wrist to his lips, while Max

cups my jaw, and they both sink their teeth into me at the same time.

Sloane jerks my cock as I cover her hand in cum and let all the feelings move through me.

My orgasm seems to go on forever as Max fucks me, filling me with his release as he bonds with me.

It's a jumble of emotions hitting me at once, all of them positive: lust, love, contentment.

Then there's this speck of emotion that seems shinier than all the others. Pure happiness.

I know it's Sloane.

Part of me feels guilty about getting Bram's bond first.

"No," the Alpha rumbles, kissing the bond mark that is plain as day on my wrist. "This is what you wanted, wasn't it, *liefje*?"

She moans. I was so lost in my own pleasure I didn't realize Bram is knotted to her.

Sloane licks her lips and nods. I lean forward and kiss her, and she grabs my wrist and kisses the spot where Bram just bonded with me.

"This is exactly what I wanted," she says dreamily as Bram tucks her tighter into his arms.

Max pulls out of me, and I wince.

"I'll be right back," he says.

He has to run upstairs completely butt ass naked but comes back with multiple warm washcloths, handing a few to Bram before coming over to me. He doesn't even ask. He just cleans me and himself up before plopping down on the mattress next to me.

I turn in the bed so we're facing each other.

He's always been handsome, always been fun. But when I look at him right now, I see the real Max. The Max he always wanted to be but just didn't realize.

"Did you think this is where we'd end up when I asked you to move my dad's couch?" I ask.

"No, but I wanted it to."

My brows furrow. "What do you mean?"

"I had a crush on you and Sloane since that first night at the diner. I just knew I didn't deserve either of you then."

"And now?" I ask, rubbing the bond mark.

Fuck, it feels weird. It's definitely going to take some getting used to.

"Sometimes this all doesn't feel real to me. Like one day you and Sloane will realize I'm a fraud," he whispers it so Sloane and Bram can't hear.

Though they may be asleep and knotted, I'm not going to risk turning around and finding out.

I grab the back of his neck, rubbing my thumb against the muscle there.

"Secret?"

"Hmm?"

"I had a crush on you then too. You're not a fraud, and none of us are going anywhere. I'm pretty sure my and Sloane's matching bond marks more than prove that. You're a good man, Max. Sloane loves you. I love you. This is forever."

His pretty blue eyes get glossy for a moment as he searches my face.

"I'm going to try really hard to be a good partner to you," he says.

"You already do," I promise him, leaning forward and kissing him tenderly.

When I pull back, he's smiling, and it's contagious as I smile back. Sloane may be the center of this pack, and the one we all give a little more to, but at the end of the day, we're a pack who all have affections and feelings for one another. How it looks between each of us is different but treasured.

When I look at Max now, he's well beyond the cocky asshole I gave advice to at the diner. He's someone I trust, respect, and I've tied my life to.

I never thought about what it would look like to create my own family or forge my own bonds. But if I told twelve-year-old me where I would end up, I never would have believed it.

"Can you feel her?" he asks in a whisper, glancing over my shoulder. Sloane must be passed out. Pregnancy has made her tired.

"Yeah," I say with a slight blush.

"As soon as we get back from our away games, it will be official."

"And then we'll have to tell Coach," I say, and Max winces.

"Yeah, there is that."

"We've survived worse," I say, and he nods, wrapping his arms around me.

"We have," he replies, and before long, we're all passed out in the makeshift nest that Sloane and I made, and I don't think I've had a better sleep in my life.

CHAPTER 44

"Are you sure this is a good idea?" Ethan asks as he rolls my carry-on through the airport and we hail a ride share.

"Positive," I say.

"What if they lose and he's in a shitty mood?"

"Then I'll make his mood better."

"Fair," he replies as he clutches my thigh.

The driver is driving like he's a character from *Grand Theft Auto* through the streets of Tampa. Ethan looks like he's about to ask him to pull over, but it's the afternoon, and I don't feel as sick with the patch on the back of my ear and the medicine I took before the plane ride.

"He's coming home tomorrow," Ethan reminds me, like I don't know that.

"It's a grand gesture."

"I'm staying in the hotel room with you until he gets back."

"I expected you to. I'm not unreasonable."

He sighs like I am, in fact, unreasonable for deciding this morning that I couldn't wait to bond with Bram for another second. So here we are, in Florida where I plan to not only surprise him, but bond with him.

This string of away games has been too much, and I try to hide how sad I am, but both Max and Ethan can feel it. A girl can't even get mopey without someone being on high alert these days.

Something deep down in my gut tells me that bonding with Bram is the solution.

So here we are.

Ethan called Max as soon as we booked the tickets, so the front desk has a new room key where Max and Ethan will be staying the night and the room key for Bram and Max's current room.

We head up the elevator and tuck in, watching the game and waiting for him to get back.

Thankfully the Foxes win, and I know tonight is going to be an excellent celebration.

It takes a lot of effort, but Ethan finally leaves me in the hotel room alone. It smells like both of my Alphas, which has me feeling some sort of way.

A very horny sort of way.

I need to get knotted. *Bad.*

While I wait for Bram, I snoop through his room, finding a T-shirt of his that smells like me, which gives me more pleasure than it should. I'm smelling my scent on the shirt when he opens the door.

His jaw nearly drops as he sees me, and I give him a grin.

"Have you been using this to jerk off while you're gone?" I ask, and his brows furrow.

"Are you here alone?" he asks in a dangerous tone, and I roll my eyes.

"Ethan just left to go to his and Max's room tonight. It's just me and you."

He tosses his bag to the side, loosening his tie.

I know he hates wearing suits post game, but damn, does he fill one out nicely. Maybe one day I'll have him act like my boss and spank me over his lap like I'm a bad little assistant, but I know that I won't be for a while. The whole pregnancy thing has a few restrictions I'm not the biggest fan of.

"Did Max know about this?" he asks.

"Mostly," I reply, and he arches a brow at me, tossing his suit jacket off and unclicking his belt, making my mouth water.

"So you flew here and told him after the fact?" he asks, already knowing me so well.

"Well…"

"Panties down and hands on the bed, *liefje*."

Fuck yes.

I do as he says. Removing my jeans and panties, I turn around and place my hands on the bed, my ass completely exposed.

Bram comes to stand behind me, completely clothed, as his hand gently cups the cheek of my ass.

"What was so important that my *pregnant* Omega needed to see me tonight when I'll be home tomorrow?" he asks.

"I couldn't wait any longer," I say.

He presses his hard, covered length against my ass. "You were feeling needy for my cock and knot?"

"Yes. But also… I need your bond," I say softly.

He stills behind me and leans forward to kiss my shoulder.

"You flew here to bond me?" he asks, his tone sweet.

"I can't wait anymore. Haven't we waited long enough?"

"Don't you want to be comfortable at home? In the basement? Or in our bedroom?" he asks, and my heart flutters. Bram is always thinking about my comfort above all else.

"Please, Alpha," I say, knowing I'll get what I want.

Plus, I didn't fly all the way to Tampa just to get knotted. I'm leaving here with Bram's bond come hell or high water.

"I need to spank this sweet ass for plotting against your Alphas," he says, not bringing up the bonding.

"I can handle that," I say.

Slick is dripping down my thighs, and I know that Bram sees

it. He just wants me to be patient, but I think becoming pregnant has made me the least patient person ever.

"Please, Bram."

His hands are off of me, and my heart beats fast in anticipation. The first spank is barely even a tap, and I turn around and furrow my brows at him.

He laughs. "Harder?" he questions.

"Yes, what was that?"

"You're pregnant," he says like I'm the one being unreasonable.

"Yes, I'm your pregnant, horny Omega who wants to be spanked and then bond the shit out of you. I'm not made of glass. The doctor said it was fine, remember?"

He nods his head, and I face the bed again.

"You know I can deny you nothing," Bram says.

"You deny me my favorite foods all the time," I say, which is punctuated with a hard spank.

It's enough to give me that high I've been searching for.

"Is that what my little Omega needed?" he asks, teasing me.

"More," I tell him, and he thankfully obliges.

The next few are harder, and I'm so fucking wet I swear I can hear myself dripping on the floor. If he doesn't rut me from behind soon and give me what I want, I might just cry. I'm not opposed to doing what I need to to get what I want.

I moan with the next smack, and it sends Bram over the edge as he cups my pussy, his fingers playing in the mess I've made of myself.

"I missed you," he whispers in my hair as he slides his fingers in and out of me. "Did you know how badly I fucking needed you? Is that why you're surprising me with this wet cunt?"

His words have me grinding my hips harder into his hand.

"Lie down, I need to taste you. Fuck," he hisses.

I turn around and tug off my shirt, leaving my bra on as I watch Bram undress. His body is so big and masculine and so mine. His skin is unblemished and smooth, and it almost makes me want to mark him up.

Nearly as soon as I lie against the hotel sheets, which are not as soft as they could be—don't think about the sanitization of the sheets—Bram starts kissing up my leg. All thoughts of where we are slowly evaporate as he kisses his way up my thigh until his mouth is on my pussy.

His brown eyes don't leave mine as he spreads my legs and licks me lavishly. The sounds of pleasure he makes while he goes down on me have my thighs shaking and my need skyrocketing.

Bram needs me just as much as I need him, and it's a heady feeling. I love him so much, and I could have—no. Not going there, especially when he has his mouth on me like this.

He slides two fingers inside of me, fingering me while he sucks on my clit.

"Oh, fuck," I rasp, running my fingers through his dark hair.

I throw my head back as he hits just the right spot, making my breath hitch and a pleasurable tingle race through my nerve endings. My thighs shake against his face as my release spills out of me.

He moans, licking up my slick before sliding up my body.

The kiss is messy as I taste myself on his lips. He's careful with his body on top of mine, and as much as I'd like to press him closer, I don't. He's holding most of his weight on his elbows as he cradles my face.

"This is really what you want? Here?" he asks.

"Please, I've wanted this for so long," I tell him. I mean every word of it.

His fingers glide along my cheekbones as he looks at me like I'm his entire world.

"I want this to be perfect for you."

My cheeks heat as I grab his wrists. "All I need is you for it to be perfect."

"You deserve more than a hotel room bonding, Sloane."

"You. All I need is you, Bram."

If we were on a normal timeline without life throwing so many wrenches into our plans, we would have been bonded ages ago.

He hitches my thigh up as he slides slowly into me. We don't break eye contact as I take every inch of his thick cock. I'll never get tired of the way he makes me feel.

"You're so pretty when you take my cock."

He seems almost nervous, which is so unlike the larger-than-life Alpha.

"You're beautiful too, Bram."

Bram leans forward and kisses me softly. His hips move at a languid pace. He's savoring this moment, and it has me choking up with emotion. I let my fingers explore his skin, hair, and muscles as he pushes in and out of me.

"Where do you want my mark?" he whispers in my ear.

I tilt my head to the opposite side of Max's mark, and he moans, kissing the side of my neck before licking and sucking the tender flesh. Knowing my selection has pleased him only makes me want him even more.

I dig my heel into his ass, and his pace increases slightly before he's pushing his knot deep inside of me.

When I throw my head back into a moan, Bram fists my hair and tilts my head for easier access.

"I've never wanted something as badly as I wanted this," he whispers, his hips pressing against mine like he can get any deeper. "My Omega, my girl. The mother of my child. Fuck, I love you."

I can't even get a word out before his knot is swelling to its largest size, ripping an even fiercer orgasm out of me as his teeth sink gently into my neck. This time there's no surprise, no fear, only complete bliss.

Bram's love for me and the pack is vast, and only right now do I truly understand how deep his well of emotion is.

I clutch him tightly to me, never wanting this feeling to end.

It's like his soul is tethered to mine. Nothing separates us anymore. We're complete and so is our pack.

Everything we've been through has built up to this moment, and I can't help the cathartic cry that falls out of me. Thankfully, now that we're bonded, Bram knows they aren't sad tears.

Instead, he just holds me and kisses his bond mark repeatedly.

"You did so good. My perfect little Omega," he praises.

I hold him so tight against myself that he's actively pushing against me so he doesn't put much weight on me.

"Sloane."

"What?" I muffle against his collarbone.

He sighs and instead of explaining himself, shifts us so he's on the bottom and I'm on top. He's rubbing my back soothingly before grabbing a blanket that sucks and puts it on my back.

I'm being really brave about how terrible this blanket is, but it's slightly easier to do with how happy I feel at this moment.

"Good surprise?" I joke.

"The best surprise," he says, kissing the side of my head. "You can tell me, and we don't have to tell the others. Were you saving the best for last?"

I laugh, and he groans as I shift against his knot and sit up, his hands on my hips. He's grinning from ear to ear, and it's infectious.

"Thank you for being patient with me."

His thumbs rub along my stomach. "The best things are worth waiting for."

I wipe my face. "Stop, or I'll start crying all over again."

"Lie down, come here," he says, and I rest back down on his chest.

When I lie back down on his chest, I just get emotional all over again. What if he had died in the car accident and I never would have had this? What if my baby never got to meet one of their fathers?

"Hey. I'm right here. I'm not going anywhere," he soothes, easily able to track my thoughts.

"I wished I was bonded to you so bad that night," I tell him honestly. "I wished I hadn't waited, that we bonded right after my heat."

"I felt the same way. But we're here now. We're safe."

"You're going to be a good dad, Bram," I tell him honestly.

"You think so?"

"I know so. I wouldn't have pursued you the way I did otherwise."

"You were kind of obsessed with me," he jokes, and I pull back to cup his face, his smile radiant.

Me. I put that smile there. I make Bram happy.

"You don't regret how anything's turned out?" I ask.

"Not even for a second," he replies.

It's like my world stops feeling out of control, and for the first time in a long time, I'm not filled with fear of the unknown but excitement about what life has in store for us.

BRAM

CHAPTER 45

I hold Sloane securely against my chest all night, not even being able to handle the idea of her not being near me right now.

It's only now I realize how upsetting her bonding with Max must have been. Not only was she scared for her health, but she didn't get the nesting she needed either.

But it's checkout time, and I have to tell Coach that I'm not riding home with the team.

It's not my ideal way to spend the morning, but I'd rather deal with him than have Sloane fly home without me.

I'm washing Sloane's hair out. She packed all her own supplies, thank God. I could tell that she wasn't impressed with the blankets or sheets at the hotel.

My Omega needs the best. I make a note for the next time we travel to bring our own bedding.

Not that I'm sure when we will travel, she's pregnant after all.

"Maybe we could come back here during the off season," she suggests.

"You'll be very pregnant then. Are you sure you'd enjoy the heat?" I ask over the shower spray.

She scrunches her nose and nods. "Maybe not."

"We should stay closer to home," I tell her, my hand unable to stop itself from gliding down the front of her body.

It's still crazy to me that she's growing a human inside of her. I kiss her shoulder and hold her tightly as the water sprays against us.

"That's probably a good idea," she agrees, and I'm thankful.

"We should be near your doctors, just in case."

"Maybe Bar Harbor or a cabin in Maine."

"We can probably borrow Beckford's cabin in Vermont," I tell her, and she hums in approval.

"Like a little babymoon."

"What the fuck is a babymoon?"

"Like a honeymoon but this time with a baby. I'll need some more time with you guys before the baby comes or the new season starts."

I nod, guilt hitting me hard. She spins in my arms and cups my face.

"Hey, I grew up with my dad playing hockey. I know what I'm getting into. There has never been a moment I don't feel loved enough, okay?"

"I just... don't like the idea of missing anything. My father wasn't a terrible man, but he wasn't always present."

She grabs my hand and holds it against her face.

"I'll believe in you enough for the both of us. Okay?"

"Okay," I tell her because that's all I have for now.

My whole team, including Max and Ethan, are waiting in the lobby as I approach Coach with my arm tossed over Sloane's shoulder.

He looks down at his daughter with affection and immediately clocks her two bond marks.

"Sloane? What are you doing here?"

Her cheeks heat, and she shrugs her shoulders and looks away.

"I can't fly back with the team. I need to fly back with Sloane."

"Okay," he says easily, and Coach glances down at her. "Can I talk to you for a minute?"

She nods and walks off with her dad. I try not to eavesdrop, but I keep tabs on her emotions throughout the conversation. They don't appear to be arguing, so that's something.

Max and Ethan both approach me, and we try to act natural as Sloane speaks with her father.

"Good or bad?" Ethan says, nudging his thumb in their direction.

"I'm going good for them, bad for us," Max says.

"What does that even mean?" the Beta asks.

"That means it's time to really meet the parents."

This should definitely be interesting.

The Applegates' home is clean, large, and opulent in a New England waspy kind of way.

"Well, fuck. I knew Sloane was out of your league, but I didn't know you were marrying into a whole new tax bracket," Dave, Ethan's foster dad, says in panted breaths.

My Beta mate helps his ailing father through the house.

"Jesus, Dad, be normal."

"Right, let me just go home and put my fancy house pants on," the old man says, and Sloane grins, coming to his side and walking next to him.

"You don't have to change a thing about yourself, Dave," she tells him.

"See, she gets it. I bet you have all three of these bastards wrapped around your finger. If you need a fourth, let me know," he breathes through his mouth heavily as Sloane leads us to the dining room.

I pull the old man's chair out, and he sits down.

"I don't know, Dave. Do you think you could keep up?"

"I would sure as fuck try," he says with a laugh, and Ethan groans.

"Please, Dad. Coach is already pissed. Please don't give him another reason."

He swats his son's hand off his shoulder. "I wouldn't be scared of your daddy. I'm just saying," he whispers to Sloane, making her laugh.

Her mothers walk into the room and hug their daughter and shake Dave's hand.

"Well, I see where Sloane gets her looks," he says.

Ethan groans, but Sloane's Omega mother just grins at the old man and winks.

"Thank you, and you're Dave, Ethan's father?" she asks.

"That's me. You're Willow, and you're Rosemary," he confirms.

"Bram, do you have any family that will be joining us?" Rosemary asks. She's intimidating, possibly even more so than Coach. She doesn't wear her emotions on her sleeve like the male Alpha of her pack does.

"No, my mother passed away some time ago. My father is back in the Netherlands. We aren't particularly close."

"I'm sorry to hear that," she says.

The doorbell rings, and Sloane jumps out of her seat. "That must be Max, Lori, George, and Owen."

Of course, the moment she leaves, her fathers both come into the room, giving their introductions. Henderson is much more easygoing, but Coach glares at me. He quickly stops when his Omega elbows him in the stomach.

I would honestly rather be anywhere except here at this very moment. There's no way to know how they're going to react to the news. But I know if there's a moment of Sloane feeling hurt, we'll be the fuck out of here.

Max walks in with his family, and I can feel his worry. His mom is even more lively than Dave.

The introductions are friendly and thankfully cure some of the silence as we all sit down. I'm thankful Sloane sits next to me, and I wonder if it's because I'm the only one with no family joining us at the table.

She places her hand on my thigh under the table as the caterers bring out the food for the evening.

Dave is filled with joy as Lori leans into my side.

"Fucking fancy, huh?" she says, and I can't help but to snort.

"I'm so glad we could all finally get together. We've been wanting to get to know Sloane's pack and extended family better," Willow says cheerfully.

"Not to mention, so this one can stop sulking," Henderson says, squeezing Coach's shoulders like the man doesn't torture us on a daily basis. "Plus, we missed having our girl at home."

"Ya know, I'd torture them too if I was in your position," Dave chimes in, earning a rare smile from Coach.

"Dad, you're not helping," Ethan whispers.

"I mean, I'm sure he gave you all the 'don't touch my daughter' speech. Not that I don't blame you for not listening—look at Sloane. Despite that, you were all too hardheaded to listen."

"We're past that now, right, Kristoff?" Willow says to her mate with a glare that says he better not fuck this night up.

"Right. They're mated now, so it's all about getting to know each other better," Coach agrees, even though it is under duress.

"Well, we appreciate the invite. It's been such a blessing for both of my sons to have played for the Foxes and found their packs that way. So I'm forever grateful, so is George," Lori says to her husband who is just eating a mound of shrimp.

"I'd like it to be on the record. I didn't know they were together," Owen says, and Sloane gives him a disbelieving look as he grins at her. "Though I'm very happy to have a sister-in-law. I guess this also makes me your brother too, Nilsen," he says with a grin.

I always liked the other Connery, but right now, I could choke him a bit.

"Everything is water under the bridge. Right, Dad?" Sloane asks, and he looks at his daughter and nods. She takes a deep breath, and I squeeze her hand under the table.

Holy shit. This is it.

"I'm glad you're accepting my pack because as you know, we're bonded now," she says, really drawing this out.

"Of course, honey. You chose great. We're proud of you," her mother Rosemary says, speaking up for the first time since introductions.

"Thanks, Mom." Sloane takes a deep breath. "I'm glad you think so because there's no one else I could imagine myself with. I'm genuinely happy beyond anything I could imagine."

Coach tilts his head at his daughter. "And?" he asks, knowing there's something else she wants to say.

"And I'm glad that we can all get to know each other because you're all about to be grandparents come September."

There's a hushed moment of silence where no one speaks.

Max's mom, Lori, is the first to speak, hugging her son and letting out an exploit of happiness.

"I'm going to be a fucking grandma?" she says, getting up and hugging Sloane next, as well as myself.

It doesn't feel as uncomfortable as I thought it would, and I embrace her completely.

"Way to go, son," Dave says to Ethan, clapping his back.

Sloane's mother Willow is crying but is quickly on her feet, walking over to her daughter and wrapping her arms around her.

"My baby is having a baby, and hopefully it will be a Virgo," she says, holding her endearingly. "I'll be here for whatever you need."

"Sloane never was one to do anything by halves," Henderson says, getting up and joining the hug.

The two Alpha parents seem a little stoic.

Rosemary seems contemplative while Coach seems pissed.

"Pregnant?" Coach questions.

"That's what I said," Sloane replies, and I sigh.

He's going to make my life hell on the ice.

"We have a pack contract ready to go, sir," I interrupt, and he arches a brow at me. "I know things have been tense lately on and off the ice. But when I tell you the three of us are completely dedicated to Sloane and this baby, I mean it."

"It's not easy having kids in this profession," he says, rubbing his chin. "I have a lot of regrets," he says.

Willow comes to stand behind her mate and hugs his shoulders.

It all clicks to me now why he didn't want his daughter with his players. It has nothing to do with us being good enough; it has everything to do with how he viewed himself as a parent.

"You were the best dad," Sloane says. "I grew up loving hockey, being inspired by you and all my parents. I had the best life. I can only hope we can give our child half of what you gave me."

The stern take-no-bullshit Alpha, Coach gets up and hugs my Omega.

"So I'm going to be a pop pop?"

"I think I'll take pop pop," Dave interrupts as we all break out in laughter.

It might not be conventional, but I think I finally found my family.

"You should probably get ahead of this before the media finds out," Coach says, going from excited to concerned. "I know there's been a lot of speculation and the Foxes haven't commented on any of it. But if you all want to control the narrative, you should probably share the news on your own terms."

"That's a good idea," I agree, but I'd probably agree with whatever he said as long as it wasn't hurtful. I need this man to not hate me.

"Pussy whipped," I hear Dave mumble, and I glare at the old man who just gives me a feral smile.

I see exactly why Ethan is such a fucking menace now.

"We'll get ahead of it, but I think we want to keep this between friends and family for now."

"Understandable, sweetie, we're so happy for you," Willow says again. "Oh, let me go get out your baby albums."

"Oh yes, please. You know, Max has a ginger great-grandfather. Maybe the gene will pass on," Lori says, and everyone is quiet for a minute.

Sloane and Ethan look at me, and I smile. "No matter what, the baby will be beautiful."

Sloane's eyes well up with tears, and for the first time this season, I seem to get a look of approval from Coach.

The rest of the evening is lighter conversation now that the big secret is off the table. As the night progresses, I swear Coach smiles more than I've seen in my life. Having Sloane in your life will do that.

"You did good," I whisper to Sloane as her head rests on my shoulder.

"We did good. I'm tired. Can we go home now?"

I smile and nod. This isn't her home anymore.

Her home is with me.

CHAPTER 46

"Alrighty, so are we finding out what we're having?" the tech asks as she slides the device over Sloane's stomach.

"Absolutely," she says quicker than she can finish the sentence.

"Let's see," the tech replies, moving it around and hitting buttons to take images. The tech smiles and looks at Sloane. "It's a boy," she says, pointing to something that I guess is supposed to be a penis.

I swallow thickly.

I'm about to have a son.

A defenseless little baby is about to depend on me, and I have no fucking clue what I'm doing.

Sloane grabs my hand. I have no clue how she's able to decipher each of us through the bond, but she's incredible at it.

"A boy," she says with tears in her eyes.

"I'm just going to come out and say that I called it," Ethan says.

The tech prints off multiple copies of the ultrasound and hands them to us to take home.

"Just make your next appointment with the girls in reception," she tells Sloane who nods her head.

She hands me a copy of the ultrasound, and I think for the first time, it really feels real.

Of course Sloane is starting to slowly show, and I've seen her have an ultrasound before, but the image in front of me looks like a real baby.

This is fucking real. And completely terrifying.

What if I'm a shitty dad and don't have patience? What if I don't have enough time to give them? What if they grow up resenting that I travel for work and can't always show up?

"Max, can we get ice cream?" Sloane asks.

Bram sighs because forcing this woman to eat healthy has been near impossible.

"We'll meet you back at the house," Bram says.

I help Sloane clean up her stomach and get off the bench. "Do you really want ice cream?" I ask her.

"Hell yeah, I want ice cream."

I laugh and hold her hand as we leave and make our way to our favorite mom and pop shop.

There's a new girl working behind the counter, and she seems a little nervous as we order.

"What do you want, little guy?" Sloane asks her stomach before looking through the selection. "Can I get a scoop of strawberry and caramel crunch on a waffle cone?" she asks.

"I'll just have a lemon sorbet in a cup, please."

"Come on, Maxy, live a little," she says, and I shake my head at her.

The girl at the counter gets our orders together and rings us up, and Sloane and I sit at one of the small circular tables. She hums as she eats her ice cream and gasps, almost dropping her ice cream as she grabs my hand.

"He's moving," she says, putting my hand on her stomach as I feel the baby kick for the first time.

If I thought I was having a crisis earlier, my panic intensifies by tenfold.

"Hey, talk to me," she says, still holding my hand on her stomach.

"What if I'm shit at this?"

She smiles at me and takes my hand off her stomach and holds my hand.

"You know, you're too good at doubting yourself and over-thinking things. Everything you've shown me as a scent match, my bonded Alpha, has been amazing. You're a good man, and you're going to be a great father."

"You can't know that."

"I can. Plus, I signed us up for parenting classes anyway during the off season," she says easily.

I sigh. "I've never held a baby," I admit.

"Then we'll go to Charlotte's house. You can hold one of hers."

"I've never changed a diaper or know anything about keeping a baby alive."

"You also never considered pack life or had been with an Omega before me, and look at you now. These things can all be learned, Max. Not to mention, you have three other people who are here to help with the workload. You're not alone, and you never will be again."

I lean forward and place a tender kiss against her lips before taking a bite of her ice cream, which makes her laugh and retaliate by taking a bite of mine.

"Oh, that's disgusting," she says, scrunching her nose.

"You really think we can do this?"

"I know we can, as long as we have each other," she says with a smile.

Some of my panic disappears, even if there's still some fear of the unknown. This isn't all on my shoulders, and together, we can do anything.

❄ ❄ ❄ ❄

I'm exhausted and ready to go home to Sloane. She didn't come to the game tonight—the pregnancy is starting to wear her out. It makes me yearn for the off-season. I know I should be focused on making the playoffs and extending our season. Don't get me wrong, I want to take the Foxes as far as we can go, but I don't think we're built for it this season.

It's a harsh reality. Even if we do make the playoffs, I'm not sure how far we would advance.

What I do know is that Sloane needs time with us, time to enjoy being pregnant and bonded.

I scrub a hand down my face. I just want to get this press conference over with. I don't like the thought of Sloane home alone, and I feel on edge. At least with away games, we know she's safe and at home with Ethan.

I smile to myself when I think about the pair of them. They might be more trouble together than anything, but Ethan would do whatever it takes to keep her safe. It's a wild sensation, being able to trust someone as completely as I do Ethan.

Bram and I take our seats for the post-game press. We were on it tonight in defense, not letting a single puck through the net. Bram claps my shoulder, and I look out into the field of reporters —something feels off.

Maybe it's the years of backlash I've gotten in the media or just how long I've been dealing with the press, but I can tell tonight isn't going to go smoothly. I sit straighter in my seat and lean my hands against the wood of the table, preparing myself for the questions about tonight's game.

The cameras are rolling as the first reporter stands up. It's Serenity Jade, a reporter from *Pack Weekly*. Why in the fuck is she here, and who gave her a press pass?

"Max, is there anything you wanted to add to address the rumors?" she asks. Her voice is posh and demeaning.

My brows furrow, and I glance over at Bram. Our pack contract isn't official until next season, and only our close friends know about the pregnancy. I don't want to give her information if she's goading me.

I lean forward into the mic. "I'm not sure what rumors you're talking about."

"You haven't seen the article that published today in *Pack Weekly*?" she asks, and it's almost like she's getting enjoyment over having information I don't have. She probably is. That magazine has been a constant sore in my side since I joined the NHL.

"I tend to not read about myself in the press since they are mostly rumors."

She pulls out the magazine, and my heart sinks when I see the cover. It's me and Sloane at the ice cream shop.

"This article claims not only that you're bonded to Sloane Applegate but that she's pregnant. Can you confirm that?" she asks.

I look over to Bram who leans forward into his mic.

"I thought the purpose of a post-game wrap up was to discuss the game and hockey, not trivial rumors reported by gossip rags?"

Moments like this are when I know I love Bram Nilsen. Our love might be a little confusing and unconventional. But I know he has my back, no matter fucking what.

"Maybe you would like to comment, Mr. Nilsen, considering the rest of the article goes into detail about how you're also bonded to Ms. Applegate. Though you aren't her scent match, are you?" the reporter asks.

Bram's knuckles are white from grabbing onto the table. He stares at the woman like he wants to make her disappear with just his mental fortitude.

Coach is quickly on the press stage, grabbing a mic.

"Unless you have educated questions that actually pertain to the sport of hockey, I suggest you get the hell out of my stadium," he says, staring the woman down.

"Or maybe you would like to comment on your daughter sleeping with your players and getting pregnant before bonding. Sources place her earning her bond marks only recently, but—"

"I'd like to comment on how inappropriate this conversation is. How disgusting it is to comment on what an Omega is or isn't doing with her body. I'm extraordinarily proud of my daughter and these men before me who are excellent athletes and men. They say there's no such thing as stupid questions, but you've just proved them wrong. Please see your way out, and hand over your press badge. Now, if there are actual questions about tonight's game, we'd be happy to answer them," Coach says confidently as Serenity is dragged off by security.

Bram and I glance at each other.

It's one thing for Coach to accept that we're bonded and be excited for the baby. But that man just stood up for us in a way I didn't expect.

The rest of the questions are about the game. All the reporters are shaking in their boots as Coach Applegate stares them all down with crossed arms.

As soon as the press conference is wrapped up, Coach pulls us to the side.

"Go home, and make sure Sloane's alright. I pulled up the article," he says with a wince. "It's not a shining light on your relationship or Connery's past dalliances."

"I'm not that guy anymore," I say, feeling shame.

"I know that. Sloane definitely knows that. The only reason you're still here is all the work she put in this season to make you look better," Coach says.

"How bad is it?" Bram asks, and Coach hands him his phone.

We both glance down at the image of me and Sloane at the ice cream shop, my hand on her stomach.

"Rosemary is going to be on that ice cream shop like a hot rash figuring out what little shit sold the picture," Coach says, and I nod as we read through.

It's poorly written, speculative, and ridiculous.

Shotgun Pack

By *Serenity Jade*

We've been speculating for months about what is going on with the New Haven Foxes this season. Are Bram Nilsen, Max Connery, the coach's daughter, and the mascot in a relationship?

Well, this reporter has the scoop.

Spotted enjoying a casual ice cream on a brisk winter evening are none other than Max Connery and Sloane Applegate.

Most of you probably know Max Connery from his many instances in Pack Weekly. He would typically be featured with his flavor of the month. But it seems his new favorite flavor is the forbidden fruit.

(Collage of images of Max with other women)

But could the former playboy be settling down? My reliable source says yes, but only because the coach's daughter is not only pregnant, but the goalie's scent match.

What is in the water at that facility?

If you remember last season, Connery's brother, Owen Connery, hid his designation in order to play goaltender for the Foxes. He is now part-time staff for the team and in a formal pack with former captain, Alexi Bandnin, and his scent match, Piper Blake.

That leads us to question, can a zebra change its stripes? Is Max Connery capable of staying true to this Omega? Or is this a loophole in securing a long-term contract with the Foxes?

All this long-time reporter knows is that it all seems suspicious. The missing games, the speculative car accident, and now a secret pregnancy?

My best guess is Max got in a sticky situation, and now there's no getting himself out. Especially since there have been no rumors of pack contracts. My guess is the two Alphas are duking it out to figure out who's the daddy.

Join my poll to guess who you think the father is and how much time until we see Connery spotted with a new sweet treat.

"What the fuck?" Bram hisses as he hands Coach back the phone.

"How the hell did this get published?"

Coach is typing away on his phone. "Rosemary is already requesting a full redaction and apology from the paper."

I guess it helps to have in-laws in high places.

"Have you heard from Sloane yet?" Coach asks, and we both shake our heads. "Go handle that. I've got this covered."

Bram and I grab our shit to meet Ethan in the garage. He's leaning against the car, waiting for us, and whistles.

"I'm winning by ten percent in who people think the daddy is. It does say the mascot and not my name, but I'll take it."

Bram rolls his eyes.

"Oh, come on. First off, you have all that shit blocked on her phone, and she wouldn't believe in trash like this," Ethan says.

"Yeah, we had to take it off her phone because she was looking at it all. I don't think she's going to be too happy seeing a collage of me and all the women I fucked before her."

Ethan grimaces.

"Shit," he hisses.

"Yeah, shit," Bram agrees as we drive home, and I wonder what state I'm going to find my Omega in.

SLOANE

CHAPTER 47

Whoever invented pregnancy hormones deserves all the worst things.

As soon as the press conference was over, I grabbed Ethan's iPad and looked up the article in *Pack Weekly*.

Serenity Jade needs to take a journalism class because the article is shit. It's absolutely not how I wanted to announce my pregnancy. And I may be crying over all the pictures of Max with other girls.

I know it was before me; I know that he would never cheat on me.

But still.

Seeing his hands on other women has me ready to commit crimes. But since I'm pregnant and not capable of violence, I'm in my makeshift nest eating banana pudding and crying.

No one should cry while eating banana pudding.

I just wanted some time where I was in control. Where I could enjoy my newly formed pack and the human I'm growing who is currently making me weep over this stupid fucking article.

I sniffle as I look at the pictures again. When did I become such a masochist?

My dad was right. We should have gotten ahead on everything and made our own statement. I'm trying to push the guy's feelings away for now, even though they're hammering at me through the bond.

Most of it is anger and worry.

I wipe my tears, hating that they're inundated with my sadness.

God, I'm so tired of crying. I'm so tired of reporters and gossip. They've latched on to the potential of another pack contract and have lost their minds. What happened to human decency?

I switch to a show I've watched a million times as I wait for my pack to get home. My goal is to not be a complete mess when they find me down here looking pathetic.

Unfortunately, I fail.

As soon as they come downstairs, they find me sobbing.

Max is the first by my side, and he attempts to climb into the nest.

"Take your clothes off," I tell him.

"Sorry," he whispers, undressing quickly and crawling next to me.

"You ate that whole tray of banana pudding?" Ethan asks, and so I just sob more. I should have saved him some. His eyes go wide, and he pets down my hair. "It's okay. It's a normal amount of banana pudding to eat," he says, which is a lie. It was a fucking party tray.

"You know that whole article was bullshit," Max says.

"I know," I sniffle. "Doesn't mean it was easy to read."

"You shouldn't have read it at all," Bram says, which just makes me lose it again.

"Way to fucking go," Ethan chastises him.

"I blocked all her devices. She has your iPad," Bram tells him.

"So this is my fault?" Ethan says back.

"You are winning the poll," I add in as Max wipes off my tears.

Ethan laughs, which makes me smile.

"Don't let that trash get to you. I'm devoted to you, to this pack. This is my whole life," he says, rubbing my stomach.

"It's more banana pudding than it is baby right now," I tell him, and he smiles and kisses me on the lips.

"Did you see your dad shut her ass down?" Max says, and the sadness really starts to disappear.

"He really did."

"Your mom is also already suing the pants off of everyone, it seems," Ethan adds, which has me grinning.

"My mom is going to destroy them," I say with a grin.

Bram looks confused by the range of emotion I've had over the last five minutes but puts his hands on his hips.

"You need something more substantial to eat. What can I get for you?"

I hold out my hand, and he sighs. Undressing and coming to the nest, he lies behind me while Max has my front.

"Purrs," I tell him, and he sighs. But his chest starts up like an old engine as the sound and movement of his chest soothe me.

Max's fingers gently caress my face, and I let their scents soothe me. I can still sense his guilt as I grab his wrists and kiss his hand.

"I'm not upset because I believe it. I know the Alpha you are, Max. I'm just tired of everything being taken out of my control. And the past images may have upset me," I tell him.

"I'm sorry they had so many images to pull from and that it hurt you," Max says, and I can feel his sadness and guilt.

I cup his face in my hands, Bram's purrs still rumbling my back. "We're going to fight back."

His eyes are wide as Ethan bounces onto the bed, making all our bodies slightly shift.

"What evil plan did you have in mind, sweetheart?" Ethan asks.

"Devious ones. But right now, I need to feel better," I say with a slight pout.

As quickly as tears have left me, the need to be claimed by my pack is even stronger.

"What would make you feel better, little Omega?" Bram asks, his hard cock pressing against my ass as he wraps a hand around my hip to cup my pussy.

"You and Max could have sex. That would make me feel better," I say.

Max smiles at me and shakes his head. "You want to see your two Alphas together?"

"Yes," Ethan and I reply at the same time.

Ethan helps me get to my knees as both Alphas glance at me and then at each other. Their relationship is complicated.

They're clearly attracted to each other, but their relationship is based on friendship and making sure the pack stays whole. I'm not sure why it makes me feel so giddy inside seeing them express themselves physically, but it brings me joy.

So when Bram cups the side of Max's face and swipes his tongue into his mouth, I'm immediately wet.

Ethan sits behind me, fondling my breasts.

"Fuck, these are getting bigger. God, I love you like this," he whispers in my ear as he kisses my throat and slides one hand down my body while kneading my breast.

I moan and rest my weight against him as I watch Bram and Max. They're both kissing more desperately now.

Bram makes the first move, sliding his hand down Max's boxers and fisting his cock.

Christ.

"You're so wet. It's because you know you fucking own us, Sloane. They can write or say whatever they want. But we know who we belong to."

His words cause an obscene amount of slick to coat Ethan's fingers.

"That's it. You know I love it when you come on my hand," he says, which makes me do just that.

My thighs shake as I use his body for support. His fingers

don't stop, and I don't stop staring at the way Bram and Max are touching each other.

They're mine, and I'll be damned if anyone says otherwise.

Ethan kisses my shoulder, his fingertips just grazing over my clit, sending a chill through me with each touch.

"Please let me fuck you," he says, and I whimper as he helps tug my panties down.

Both of the Alphas are touching each other, and as much as I like it, I need them to touch me too.

I get on to all fours, placing my hand on top of Bram's before sliding Max's hard, weeping cock into my mouth.

"Fuck, baby," he hisses as I take him down my throat.

He doesn't stop jerking Bram off as Ethan fucks me from behind.

I'm not in heat, and yet here we all are, together like this. It's all I had ever wanted.

Ethan's hips thrust against my ass as he fucks me, not taking it slow, and it's just what I needed.

A claiming.

Max's one hand is wrapped in my hair, and the other is jerking Bram off. I shift ever so slightly so I can lick the tip of Bram's cock before going back to Max.

"Such a good little Omega. Do you like the way your Alpha's cock tastes?" Bram asks.

It seems like a challenge as I pull off of Max's length and give Bram enough space to taste for himself, which he does.

"Oh shit," Max says, cupping the back of Bram's head as the other Alpha sucks him down. "Fuck. I'm going to come," he says.

Bram doesn't stop, and Max's thighs clench as he moans out his orgasm. As soon as he's done, Bram's mouth is on mine. He tastes like a mixture of himself and Max's release, a taste I thought I'd never get.

I moan into his mouth as Ethan fucks me from behind, his pace increasing, and I have to go down on my elbows.

I'm not sure whose hand slides between my thighs to play

with my clit as I gasp into the mattress as my second orgasm takes me for the evening. I'm wrapped around Ethan, my pussy fluttering around him as I cry my release into the bedding.

When I pull back up, I see Max returning the favor as Bram comes into his mouth.

I lick my lips as I lie on my side, and Ethan cuddles me from behind.

"That is not how I saw tonight going," Ethan says.

Bram is catching his breath as the two Alphas collapse on the bed.

"I told you there was more to life than anal," I say, and they both laugh as they catch their breath.

Bram breathes through his nose, his massive forearm covering the top of his face. "You still need to eat something real for dinner."

"You're ruining the moment," I say, snuggling harder into Ethan.

"You're going to wake up in a few hours and be starving," Bram tries to argue, and I just shake my head and feign sleep.

I do, in fact, wake up starving a few hours later.

The camera shutter clicks rapidly as my pack and I pose for different photos.

"I think we've got our shot," the photographer says.

I nod, and Max takes my hand as we take a seat on the couch across from Cassie Escobar. She's the head reporter for the lifestyle section of the *New Haven Times*.

She's no bullshit and likes real hard facts, not sensationalized media.

"So," she says with a smile. "Let's hear your story."

We tell her the truth.

Puck Around and Find Out

By Cassie Escobar

I was fortunate enough to get an exclusive interview with none other than Pack Nilsen. That's right, you heard it here first. The alleged pack that has taken the media by storm has an official pack name, not to mention they are registered with the state and Bram Nilsen and Max Connery will be signing on with the Foxes next year under a pack contract.

I'm not here to discuss pack contracts or what the consensus is for a decision. What I wanted to do when meeting this pack is find out what's real and what's sensationalized in the media.

When did your relationship start?

Sloane: They each started at separate times. I had a crush on Bram far longer than I'd like to admit, but we became serious at the beginning of the season. Ethan is one of those people you immediately fall for, and I did. As for Max, that's a combination of friends to lovers and a case of being scent matches.

How does your father feel about the relationship?

Sloane: He is incredibly supportive.

Bram: Unless he's giving us extra drills.

Are the rumors about the pregnancy true?

Max: They are very much true, and we are extremely excited to welcome our son this coming fall.

Ethan: Unbelievably excited.

Bram: We're very blessed to have Sloane as the mother of our child.

Will you be getting a paternity test?

Sloane: Absolutely not.

There have been a lot of rumors circulating after your car accident. Is there anything you would like to set straight?

Bram: I was driving the vehicle, and it was indeed a complete freak accident. I'm so thankful that Ethan was able to get Sloane out so swiftly, and I owe my life to Max.

You two have had a tumultuous relationship in the past. Is that all resolved?

Max: More than resolved. We're different men; we're better men.

Speaking of which, prior to these rumors, your image was less than stellar. What do you say to people who think you haven't changed?

Max: I owe a lot of that to Ethan and Sloane. When I was traded to the Foxes, I knew I needed to stop filling that void with fleeting relationships. I found my people, and I'm never looking back.

Is it true you are suing *Pack Weekly* for their distasteful article about you and your pack?

Sloane: They (expletive) around and found out.

After sitting down with Pack Nilsen, one thing has become abundantly clear. Don't always believe what you read. And facts are always more important than fiction.

EPILOGUE

"It's fucking Vermont. It shouldn't be this hot," Sloane says as she all but waddles to the couch.

Pack Hodges let us use their cabin for the week, and while the idea had merit, Sloane is a bit too far in her pregnancy to enjoy much of anything.

I sit at her feet and rub her ankles.

"You're an angel, thank you."

"I have news," I tell her, unable to keep it in any longer.

"Good news?" she says, pushing a stray hair off of her face.

"Very good news. I, well, Finnegan the Fox is up for the mascot of the year through the NHL."

She sits up as quick as she can eight months pregnant and blinks at me before crying and wrapping her arms around me. Tears are about a daily appearance with Sloane, so we've all gotten used to it.

"I'm so proud of you."

"I wouldn't have been able to do it without you."

"So true," she says, and I laugh and pull back and cup her face.

"I mean it. No one else cared about how the mascot looked or was represented online. You helped give him a new look and helped me create the right personality for him. I wouldn't have gotten here on my own."

"You would have. I just made it go a lot faster," she says.

I rub her round stomach and kiss her belly over her shirt. The little guy gives me a swift kick to the face, which makes Sloane wince.

"He's fucking ginormous. I don't think he's going to be able to get out," she complains. "I had to fornicate with massive men, and this is what I get."

"I think he's normal sized; you're just small."

"Shut up," she whispers, lying back down on the couch.

"What do you need, baby?" Max says, putting groceries away.

"To give birth," Sloane complains.

"Do you want to work on the birth manual slash vision board?" I ask her. She arches an eyebrow at me and sighs. "Damn, not even up for that?"

"I just want to feel comfortable again."

"Whatever you need, sweetheart," I tell her.

"Minus activities vetoed by your doctor or Alpha," Bram yells from down the hall.

Sloane rolls her eyes and shifts on her elbows and smirks at me. "Does Ethan Heart, award-winning mascot, want to go down on his Omega?" she asks.

I laugh. "I thought you'd never ask."

I devour her like she's my last meal, and she passes out immediately after. I'm a lucky man.

※ ※ ※ ※

"I can't do it," Sloane says as she's covered in sweat.

Max and Bram look fucking panicked. Bram always knows what to do, how to calm her down. But she's in so much pain. She's been in labor for too long.

"I'm scared. I can try again. I can," she tries to plead with the doctor.

"I'm sorry, that's not an option anymore," he tells her, and Sloane shuts down, tears streaking her face as she shakes her head.

Bram and Max are both stroking her hair and holding her hands, but neither of them knows what to say.

I stand next to Max, and I cup her reddened cheeks.

"Hey, sweetheart. We're going to meet our baby boy soon. You did so fucking good. So good. He's too big and isn't coming out on his own, so they need to take you back for a C-section."

She shakes her head back and forth in my palms, and I stroke her cheekbones.

"I know it's been a long day. I know you're tired. You're so fucking strong, Sloane. One of the strongest people I know. Sweetheart, I know this wasn't your plan. I know you wanted to give birth this way, but they have to take you back," I tell her.

"He's right," Bram says. My words must have slapped him out of his own fear. He kisses the side of her head. "You can do this, *liefje*. We'll be with you the whole time."

"This is all your fault," she says, and both Bram and Max's eyes go wide. "If you weren't so fucking big, the baby wouldn't be so big," she says, sniffling.

"I'm sorry, baby. You're right," Max says, just agreeing with her worn-out anger.

"Okay," she says on a sniffle. "Okay."

The doctor looks relieved as they get the medical personnel needed, and they take us to get sanitized and ready. My heart is beating a million beats per minute as we're about to be taken into the surgical room.

A nurse who is as short as Sloane but with more curves wearing a pink scrub set stops us with a hand.

"Whatever scary emotions you're feeling right now, you need to cool them down. She needs the most serene happy feelings while she's in there. She's still panicking, and we need her to be as calm as possible."

"We can do that," Bram agrees in his light blue scrub dress and booties.

She gives us a nod as she opens the door, and we all crowd by Sloane's head. Dried tears streak her face as I rub her hair.

Max kisses her cheek, and Bram's hand is nearly on top of mine.

"I know this wasn't in Sloane's pregnancy manual. But you're doing amazing."

She seems like she's shivering slightly, but she nods her head.

"How much longer?" she asks.

"Not much longer," the doctor confirms.

Part of me wants to look over the paper curtain, but I don't need that trauma. Instead, I sit here with Sloane as each scary moment passes by.

"You're doing so great, baby," Max tells her.

Sloane is blinking rapidly, and I think she's trying to stay calm. Fuck, she's being so strong. I didn't think it was possible to love her more than I already do, but as she holds her composure to bring our son into this world, all I feel is full.

There's a sharp cry as the doctor holds up our son, and Sloane lets out a loud breath before crying again.

"Oh, he's a big healthy boy," the nurse says as they clear his airway and clamps the umbilical cord.

We all are touching Sloane in some way as she brings our wrapped son next to Sloane's face.

"Hi," she says softly to him.

He calms quickly to her voice as he pinches his small little face and looks around.

"He's beautiful," I tell her.

"Perfect," Max says.

And out of all of us, Bram is the one who can't compose himself as he lets a few tears slip and he touches our soft newborn's cheek.

"I'm so proud of you," he tells Sloane with a kiss to her head.

"He's really here," she says in amazement.

The doctors are working away, but it feels like we're having our small intimate moment here.

"He's really here," I confirm, and she presses her face closer to the baby.

"Alright, dads, two of you come with me and our little guy, and one of you can stay behind with mom while we get her prepared to go back to the room."

"I'll stay," Max says, petting Sloane's hair.

Bram and I both give him a nod as the nurse puts the baby in a clear little bassinet and pushes him back to the room. She does a few more things there.

I take pictures of everything while Bram calls Sloane's family, and I shoot off a text to my dad.

We already know all the protocol about what Sloane wanted for her birth, and she wanted her close family here at the hospital after. Friends would be once we get home.

Bram tosses an arm around my shoulder and squeezes me as we look at the tiny human we're now responsible for.

"Holy shit. We're dads," he says, and I bump his hip with mine.

Not so long ago, Bram didn't even know who the fuck I was, but now he's one of the people I trust most in this world. Now we have a child together. It's crazy how life brings you to the people you need at the right time.

Sloane and Max get brought back into the room, and I carefully pick the baby up. It's probably the most terrifying moment of my life. I grew up around kids smaller than me, but a baby is a whole different thing.

I put him in Sloane's arms, and she just stares down at him for a long moment before looking up at the three of us.

"Nothing ever goes to plan with us, does it?" she says before taking off the baby's hat and stroking his soft blond hair. He doesn't have a lot of it, but it's definitely there.

"What do you think about Arie?" she says, looking at Bram.

"He's ten pounds, *liefje*. You can't name him Arie," he says.

She snorts and looks back at the small little guy when in actuality, I suppose he isn't so small as far as newborns are concerned.

"He needs a strong name," Bram says.

"What do you think about a combination of all of your names?" I furrow my brow and look at the other men, and Sloane bites her lip. "Braxton," she whispers. "Bram, Max, and Ethan. I know the end is on and not an, but it's pretty close."

The three of us look at each other. She wants to name her son after all of us.

"I think that's a strong name, baby," Max says, looking down at our son. "Can I hold him?" She nods, and Max swallows. "Can I sit down and someone hand him to me?"

Bram clears his throat and picks Braxton up. "Brax for short?" he says, glancing at Sloane who nods. "Brax Nilsen, a third generation hockey player. Son of Bram Nilsen, Max Connery, and Ethan Heart, and grandson of the legendary Kristoff Applegate. You're going to go far," he coos at the baby.

Sloane smiles wildly as Bram hands the baby to Max.

Max looks a little panicked. "Am I doing this right?"

"Yes, just support his head. There you go." Sloane cheers him on as she nestles into the bed more, and I come over to her bedside.

"What do you need?"

"An entire sushi boat to myself and a Dr. Pepper," she says.

"I can do that. Are you okay if I pick up my dad and bring him over too?"

"Of course," she says, squeezing my hand tightly.

When I come back to the hospital with a massive bag of sushi, a six-pack of Dr. Pepper, and my ailing father, the room is full of family.

Sloane's mothers are checking on her while Henderson and Kristoff are holding Braxton.

Max gets up so my father can sit, and I help him with his walker as he looks up at me.

"You're the best thing that ever happened to me, son. Now this is the second best," he says, making me wipe under my eyes as I put Sloane's food down and transfer the bundle from Kristoff to my dad.

"Aw hell," he says as he gets choked up. "He's fucking beautiful, Sloane."

Sloane grins with a salmon roll in her mouth and swallows before replying.

"Thanks, Dave."

"No, seriously. This kid is all you, none of these assholes. No paternity test needed. Immaculate conception."

She laughs as my dad looks down at his grandson.

"What's his name?" he asks.

"Braxton," I reply.

My dad arches a brow and whispers to the baby. "Well, you can't be handsome and have a good name. We all have our strengths."

Thankfully, no one else can hear him, and I'm not going to call him out on it.

I sit down next to my dad and move the baby's blanket a little.

"I'm proud of you, son. I know I probably don't tell you enough. I know I was hard on your ass as a kid, but it's because I knew how incredible you could be. You're nothing like him, and I want you to remember that. If you don't remember anything from me, I want you to remember that. You're more of a man than he wishes he could ever be. You have a beautiful family, and you've made something of yourself. I love you, Ethan," he says.

I lean into him delicately and look down at my son.

"It's because I was raised by you," I tell him, and I mean it completely. Without him, I wouldn't be where I am today, and I owe him everything.

"I know that's right," he says, jostling the baby with a laugh.

"Alright, Dave, stop being a baby hog," Willow says, coming over to pick Brax up.

"I was only trying to get your attention, Willow," my dad flirts.

Some things will never change, and I dread the day my dad isn't here to make an inappropriate joke.

Willow holds her grandson and goes to Sloane's side.

"Don't let these moments go, cherish them all," my father says.

I hold on to that advice for the rest of my life.

SLOANE

EPILOGUE
TWO YEARS LATER

Ethan has Braxton on his hip as he swings him around in the pool.

"Not so fast, he just ate so much watermelon," Bram says to Ethan who rolls his eyes.

"Need anything?" Bram asks, rubbing my growing stomach in my bathing suit.

"Eli is making the hot dogs and hamburgers right now," Charlotte says from the seat next to me.

"My daddy makes the best hot dogs," her oldest daughter, Katie, says with a grin. She has purple flower sunglasses with a matching purple bathing suit. I can't deny how much I adore her. Maybe it's because we're both red heads, or I'm excited about the thought of having my own baby girl in a few months.

We figured we wanted our kids to be similar in age, and with me completely home and Ethan home most of the time, it just made sense.

"Well then, I'll just have to have a hot dog," I tell Katie.

"Fantastic choice," the little girl replies as she takes out three Barbies and sets them along the pool to play with.

Mikael has one twin, and Anders has the other as they splash around with Braxton in the pool.

Piper walks over with two margaritas in hand along with an iced tea for me.

"One of these days we're going to get you drunk, Sloane," Piper says, handing me my drink.

Bram arches an eyebrow at Piper, and she waves him off.

"God, they're all getting so big. I'm happy you're giving us a fresh new one," Piper says, pointing to my stomach.

"I'm just hoping everything goes smoothly," I say, running a hand down my belly.

"I'm sure it will," Piper assures me.

I nod my head and take a deep calming breath. If there's anything I've learned in the last few years, it's that life never goes to plan, but chances are it will all work out in the end.

"Would the children like to see the grand power of their Uncle Alexi?" the large Alpha says, showing off his muscles.

Max and Owen are behind him and shake their heads while the kids laugh.

"You sure you don't want to give that man a baby?" Charlotte says to Piper.

"Hell no, not when you two keep popping them out. We'll just rent them and return them," Piper says, and I snort.

Alexi takes a massive leap into the pool, grabbing his legs against his chest as he splashes into the crystalline water. He creates a massive wave, making the kids laugh.

When he breaks the surface, he comes over to Ethan.

"Give me my nephew," he says.

Ethan shakes his head but hands over my baby—toddler—to his uncle. The minute Brax is in his arms, he starts playing with his beard.

"See, *malyshka*, he likes my beard," Alexi says to Piper.

"Him and this fucking beard. I'm going to trim it in his sleep," Piper says while waving at her mate.

Max and Owen go over to the grill to help Anders with the food, and I really look around at the life I have and smile. It's everything I could have ever imagined.

Bram drags my chair closer to him so he can have his hand on my stomach.

"We did good," he says, looking out at the pool.

"No regrets?" I ask him.

"Not a single one, *liefje*." I smile at him, loving that I'm still as obsessed with him as I was when I first met him.

Alexi pulls Braxton out of the water, sending him running over to me with his swimmies on.

"Mommy, swim," he says, putting his cold hands on me.

"Okay, go to Pa, and we'll get in the water together," I tell him.

He immediately runs into Bram's arms, who picks him up and kisses him all over his face, making him giggle.

"Why don't you ever kiss me that way?" Max complains as he brings over a tray of food.

"You're not as cute," Bram says, and Max glares.

"Do you want to come to Dad instead?" he says, holding out his arms.

"Swim," Braxton says, not caring which one of his fathers has him, just that he gets what he wants.

He is my child after all. Though he looks like a splitting image of Max, there's no denying it. His bright blue eyes and bright blond hair don't seem to be making any shifts. To be honest, I was always under the assumption that he was biologically Max's from our first time in the locker room. We might have played it fast and loose with birth control during my heat, but I'm pretty sure that's the moment Braxton was made.

"Come help me up," I tell Max who places a quick kiss on Braxton's cheek before Bram walks into the pool with him.

I hold my hands out, and he grabs them, gently pulling me to my feet.

"Feeling okay, baby?" he asks, picking a piece of hair that was sticking to my face.

"Never better," I tell him.

He steps into the pool first, gripping my hips like I'm going to fall to my death if he doesn't hold on to me.

But I love it.

I was worried how our relationship would change after kids, and don't get me wrong, there are moments that have been difficult. But maybe because there's four of us to share the workload or because we have such a great village to help us, we've been able to stay more connected than ever.

As I wade into the pool feeling weightless, which is amazing, I join all the dads and the kids in the shallow end.

"Can you say grumpy?" Mikael says to Braxton as Bram holds him. "Pa is grumpy," Mikael repeats.

"If you don't shut the fuck up," Bram hisses.

"Fuck is a bad word. I'll bring out my swear jar later," Katie says, and Bram curses under his breath again.

Braxton splashes the water, and I hold out my arms to him. He grins as Bram holds his little body, shooting him through the water toward me.

I have him on my hip as Ethan goes underwater and then pops up, making Braxton splash and wiggle in my hold.

As much as I would like to say that Braxton is a mama's boy, it would be a lie. Ethan is his person, and I can't even blame him.

Ethan adjusts his hat, and Braxton smacks his hand away.

"Particular, just like mommy," Ethan jokes.

"Hey," I splash him lightly, and he smiles and leans down and gives me a kiss.

"It's something I love about you."

"Uh huh," I grumble back.

Braxton holds his hands out for Ethan, hating that I got a kiss and he didn't. So I begrudgingly hand him over.

"Foods ready," Eli shouts as everyone gets out of the pool and dries off. But I stay inside with my little family for a moment longer.

Tears well in my eyes, and I groan. This is the one thing I won't miss after this pregnancy.

"Aw, baby, what's wrong?" Max asks.

"I'm just really happy," I tell him.

"Group hug," Ethan announces, putting Braxton in the middle, making him laugh as we all hug.

Every tear, moment of doubt, and unknowing moment was worth it for this.

I thought I knew what I wanted in a pack, but what I got in reality is a million times better.

This. This is the life I always wanted.

ACKNOWLEDGMENTS

First and foremost, thank you dear reader for waiting for this book. I hope that you enjoyed this series as much as I have writing it.

Leisha - You keep me going.

Jess - You're so kind and helpful.

Marielli - You catch the small details, and your feedback has been great.

Jade - I hope your Nana likes that your namesake is an asshole in this, even though you're the sweetest.

Stephanie - AKA the hyphen queen.

Cj Lucci - Thank you for reading for Bram's Dutchness.

Kassie - For letting me bitch in your dm's.

Sandra - For slaying every cover you do for me.

Fallon & Leslie - For reading prior to ARCs and calming my impostor syndrome.

My ARC team for helping me find last minute errors, and continuing to pump me up for each release. I appreciate you so much.

Lastly, to 20 year old me, we're okay, we did it.

ALSO BY SARAH BLUE

High Roller Omegas

Queen of Hearts

Dead Palms MC

Nobody's Darlin'

Pucked Up Omegaverse

One Pucked Up Pack

Don't Puck With My Heart

Puck Around & Find Out

Heat Haven Omegaverse

Heat Haven

Omega's Obsession

Protector's Promise

Too Tempting

Heat Haven Holidays

Lavender Moon

Lavender Moon

Lavender Moon Meets Las Vegas

Want to take a walk on the paranormal side?

The Marriage Hex

Charming Series

Charming Your Dad

Charming the Devil

<u>Charming as Hell</u>

Love in the Veil

Petty Cupid

Lucky Cupid

Daddy Cupid

The Carlson Brothers - Contemporary Romance

Swallow Your Pride

Forget Your Morals

ABOUT THE AUTHOR

Sarah Blue writes contemporary sweet omegaverse, erotic, why choose romances. She loves romance in nearly any genre. When she isn't writing you can find her nose buried in a book or lit up from her kindle. She loves the sweeter side of romance and creating interesting characters while adding adventure and spice. Writing strong female characters and male characters willing to show weakness is something that makes her gooey on the inside.

Sarah lives in Maryland with her husband, two sons, and two annoying cats. If she isn't reading or writing she is probably working on a craft project or scrolling on Tik Tok.

www.authorsarahblue.com
@sarahblueauthor on Instagram and TikTok
Sarah Blue's Reader Group on Facebook